Imperfectly Perfect

K.G. Milewski

Copyright © 2024 K.G. Milewski

All rights reserved. No part of this book may be reproduced or transmitted in any form or by any means, electronic or mechanical, including photocopying, recording or by any information storage and retrieval system without permission in writing from the publisher.

Pretty Mama Cares Publishing—Merrimac, MA
ISBN: 979-8-9900887-0-2
Library of Congress Control Number: 2024913752
Title: *Imperfectly Perfect*
Author: K.G. Milewski
Digital distribution | 2024
Paperback | 2024

This is a work of fiction. The characters, names, incidents, places, and dialogue are products of the author's imagination, and are not to be construed as real.

Dedication

This is for every person who questions their worth. Know that you are enough!

Chapter One
The Start

Steam fog. That's not really what it was, but it looked like it. The vapor hovered eerily above the warm asphalt. The rain had recently subsided, leaving puddles in uneven portions of the pavement. The streetlights illuminated the puddles causing them to glisten like thousands of diamonds. The narrow street was void of activity— no cars, no people; just quiet. The night sky was completely clear of clouds now, displaying Orion's Belt, the Big Dipper, and a host of unnamed stars.

We walked hand in hand down the deserted street; just us, the stars, and the streetlights. We needed to get out of his parent's house. We needed to be alone, even if alone meant taking a walk down the middle of the street. It was an ideal evening for a stroll. The kind of evening you may only experience once in a lifetime. The kind of evening you never forget.

We had just come from dinner. He didn't know it, but it was his last chance to win me over. That sounds so bitchy, but it was my truth. We may have known each other for years, but admittedly, I'm fairly sure I was the only one having trouble moving past the whole friend thing. Even though I'd been so attracted to him from the start, I just kept thinking we were friends, and I didn't want to lose that, but I also let it block me from totally giving myself to him. Such a cliché to not want to ruin a friendship. Was our friendship worth not taking the chance? I mean, so what if it doesn't work out; we go our separate ways, end of story.

He'd found a piano bar just over the border in New Hampshire where we talked, or should I say, I talked, he asked questions and listened. He wore the faded blue striped button-down shirt that I loved. I don't know what the pianist was playing, but it seemed like every note he played was just for us. It was dreamlike. Were there other people there; it didn't seem like it. Just us; it felt like just us. He asked me questions like he was hungry for my answers, like he couldn't get close enough mentally and emotionally to me. I was cautious, keeping him at a distance, uncertain of where I wanted this relationship to go. I didn't want to hurt him.

As we sat there, he surprised me with his interest in my opinions, my future hopes, even my previous relationships. As I recall, he wanted to know how I felt about them, the good and the bad. It's strange talking to a new 'boyfriend' about your past loves. Kind of weird but I gave into it. He wasn't just fishing for information or trying to make me feel awkward in any way. I think he genuinely wanted to let me be emotional if I needed to be. He wanted to know me at that moment. He wanted to uncover things about me he needed to know. He showed how much he cared for me, how much he respected me, just by listening. Such a simple thing, and that one simple thing won me over. It was a departure for both of us; he was usually the talker, I was the listener, but not tonight. We connected, as if some alternate universe existed just for us. It was then I knew, at that unassuming piano bar, that he was the one I wanted to spend the rest of my life with, and I think he did too. Now it was on me. He had unlocked the door, I just needed to walk through it.

I was wearing my favorite mint green dress with the purple Hibiscus flowers. It hugged my body just enough for him to imagine my curves under it. Once we returned to his parents' house, he asked me if I'd like to go for a walk; how could I say no. He smiled at me and grabbed my hand. His hand was warm, and our fingers threaded effortlessly together. I remember looking up at him; so handsome, so tall, so broad. The air was warm, but somehow, I had chills.

As we strolled down the street where he grew up, he shared childhood memories. "That's where we played ice hockey on Sunday afternoons," he said, pointing to one of the last vacant lots left on the street. "You remember Joe, right?" he asked, looking down at me. I nodded. Joe was his best friend growing up. Of course, I remembered Joe; he had a crush on me in eighth grade, but so did Jack. Jack wouldn't ask me out because of Joe; now that's a loyal friend. Of course, I didn't see it that way then.

"Joe and I were so much smaller than the older kids and boy did they take advantage of it. They took every opportunity to throw a check our way, sending us flying onto the ice. I'm surprised we never broke any bones after the beating we'd take," he said laughing. "But believe me, they got theirs eventually. When we got older, we'd all gather on Thanksgiving morning to play football in that same lot. It didn't take long for them to realize payback was a bitch."

I looked up at him as he laughed; his laughter was contagious. I smiled; he was so happy. He was on a roll now, retelling childhood stories, mostly spurned on by the houses we'd pass. I watched him intently as he spoke; even his hazel eyes lit up as he told story after story. I loved seeing him laugh. When we were in high school, I can't say I recall him being a happy go lucky kind of guy. He seemed angry and troubled a lot of the time. I could only assume it was because of his home life. But tonight, I was seeing him in an entirely new light.

We'd been dating sporadically for about five months, so it hadn't been that long, but because of my insecurities, it was long enough for me to question whether we would last. Our physical relationship progressed slowly; I think we'd only kissed a few times. I'm sure he wanted more; he's a guy for God's sake, but it was like he was taking it extremely slow on purpose, probably the vibe I gave off. To be honest, I had no idea where his head was at, and I had no idea where mine was at, until after dinner that is. But what I did know was that we were attending colleges that were two hours apart. I always said I wouldn't date anyone who wasn't at my school, because the last thing I needed was a boyfriend who was hours away. I'd already been through that, and it hurt like hell to know he'd been cheating on me for months. I can remember being so heartbroken. I didn't put out for him and figured that's why he strayed. I want to say that was my fault, but was it? Being too far apart was not a formula for relationship success, in my book anyway, but for some reason this was different. Something was telling me to go forward, even if my forward was slow and questioning.

We'd come home on the weekends to see each other; my parents were not supportive of me spending weekends at his apartment. Too religious; my parents were too religious, not just spiritual, religious. They were the kind of parents that thought if there was privacy and a bed in the room, sex was inevitable. For some reason, they didn't think that if I really wanted to have sex I could do it in the backseat of a car, in the woods, in a hotel room, or God forbid, under a blanket in their living room, right under their noses, so to speak. Funny how I let them control me then. Little did they know, I wasn't jumping in the sack with this guy. Little did they know I was on the fence and that was the least of their concerns. Their assumptions and worries were misguided; closed minded people afraid that God would smite us all if Julia had sex before marriage. Old school to say the least. Little did they know, I'd already given myself away a year ago. I certainly wasn't easy, but if I wanted to have sex, I was going to do it with or without their blessing. Control—I was tired of them controlling me.

Coming back home was much tougher for him though; he didn't always feel welcome in his childhood home, and I didn't know why. Like I said, I attributed his anger issues in high school to his parents, but I'm not sure if I heard him talk negatively about them or if I got that information from his girlfriend at the time. Either way, I knew he wasn't happy there, not then, not now. He toughed it out on the weekends though, just to see me.

As we walked down the street that night, I'm not sure if he noticed, but my attention to him had totally flipped. I was clingier, wanting to hold his hand. I wanted our bodies to touch, his hand to graze my side. I wanted to be close to him. I gave my heart to him at that restaurant, whether he knew it or not. As we walked our conversation moved to the upcoming month, our plans, and how we would navigate seeing one another. Again, he had no idea I was on the fence prior to dinner, or at least that's what I thought. Of course, I was much more into planning our time together now, and I guess he could sense that.

"I remember always wanting to date you in high school," he said, looking down at me and giving my hand a squeeze, "but you were dating Nick and I just had to step aside."

"I had no idea," I said, looking up at him. I thought for a moment; if I had known, would I have dumped Nick for him? How different would our lives have been if we had dated back then?

"Well," I said shyly, looking down the street again, "I must admit, I always thought you were cute… I wish I'd known how you felt. You were always that guy to me… a stand-up kind of guy, and what Denise and John did to you was awful."

"That was one of the worst times in my life," he said, looking to his right, his gaze no longer on me.

All I could think was, "Great, I just ruined the night with that comment. Why in the hell did I just say that?" We walked in silence down the street. I could feel my heart pounding with each step I took. What was he thinking? Nothing had changed on the street—the lights, the lack of movement, the wet asphalt, the quiet. Everything looked the same, but I had just caused a cataclysmic shift. A rush of warmth came over me; I suddenly felt so incredibly uncomfortable.

"I'm sorry," I finally blurted out, squeezing his hand, and looking down at my feet. "I shouldn't have mentioned that. That was stupid."

Suddenly, he stopped, forcing me to face him. His six-foot-two frame towered over me. I didn't want to look at him, but he made the first move, forcing me to. He took my face gently in his hands and kissed my lips tenderly, taking a moment to pull back and stare into my eyes. He wasn't mad. I reached up placing my palm on his cheek, losing myself in his dreamy hazel eyes. We smiled at one another without saying a word, and then in one sweeping motion his hands lowered to my waist, and he pulled me closer. I closed my eyes as his lips met mine. The kiss was soft at first, but the longer it went on the more intense it became. I raised my hands, letting my fingers run aimlessly through his wavy ash colored hair. I envisioned us, standing there under that single streetlight, locked in that tight embrace, and I imagined the neighbors randomly glancing out their windows at us; it had to be quite the scene. I felt the heat of the light, or was it just us? Suddenly, we were desperate for one another. The kiss was the most passionate we'd shared so far. I didn't want it to end, but eventually all good things do. He gently pulled me to his chest, his arms wrapped tightly around me; he kissed the top of my head. I could feel his heart beating. Thank God there wasn't a bed on the street, or all my parent's fears would have come true. He pulled away from me, his hand gently stroking my hair. We just stared into one another's eyes for what seemed like an eternity, and then he kissed my forehead tenderly. We were on the same page; enough said.

Chapter Two
Julia

"Yes, I'm heading down today," I said, as I wandered around my tiny rental house picking up stray clothes that I'd left around the living room.

I wasn't really a slob, but over the past few days I'd just let things pile up, not wanting to care. I would say I was in an unhealthy slump, not that any slump would feel healthy. I felt like I'd spent the past two years mindlessly going through the motions. I hated my rental house, and even though I tried to make it a home, it just wasn't. My home was gone. Everything I'd worked for, every memory—good or bad, I'd left behind in the home where we raised our children. I needed a reboot. I needed an escape from myself. Can a person do that? Getting away seemed like my only option.

I walked to the sink with a stack of dirty dishes; unfortunately, it was full. "Julia, what's happened to you?" I thought. I put the phone on speaker and grabbed the sponge.

"Alone?" is all she said back, like I was a child. And then I heard the familiar complaint. "Mom, are you doing dishes? Are you even listening to me?"

I rolled my eyes. "Just because I'm doing dishes doesn't mean I'm not paying attention," I said, aggravated, but I knew she had a point. Getting sidetracked by my thoughts was an issue, and everyone in the family knew that my mind was always running, always planning, always thinking ahead. It was annoying even to me.

I tried to lighten the mood. "Your grandmother always said, leave a clean home and a lean fridge before a trip. And for God's sake, pee before you leave the house," I said, entertained by my own wit, but Jess wasn't laughing. She was waiting for me to answer.

"Yes alone," I snipped back. "Jess, I'm old enough to go on a vacation by myself you know. I'd love to go with someone, but you, of all people know, 'that someone' has not presented himself yet." I rolled my eyes again.

Who was I kidding, 'that someone' was illusive. I had no intention of meeting 'that someone' ever. Why would I remotely think someone, anyone, would be interested in me? I'm forty-five, the mother of three grown children, and divorced; no sane guy wants any part of that.

It was quiet on Jess' end for a few seconds. I could almost hear her sighing, and then she gave in.

"I know Mom, I just worry about you. Maybe I could come down with you. I could ask for the time off," she said, concern dripping from every word.

Now I was sighing. I glanced over at a card she'd recently sent me, "One day at a time is a pretty good pace, keep going." Solid advice. Jess was always looking out for others. She was always so attentive, always calling, always wanting me to be happy. But I just wanted to be by myself, at least on this trip anyway. Sometimes kids just don't get it.

"Honey, I love you, but I'm going alone. It's okay, I need to go alone."

Again, I heard a sigh. "Mom…" she said, her tone anxious and unyielding. She was going to keep pressing me on this.

"Jess, let me be a grown-up, okay. Put your worries away. I'm a big girl. I just really need this mini vacay by myself," I said, hoping to displace her concern. "I feel like I have writer's block. The change of scenery will do me good. You know… get my creative juices flowing again. I'm looking forward to waking up to those seagulls squawking at me," I said laughing, hoping she'd do the same.

"Well, at least text me when you get there," she said, no doubt hoping diplomacy was the way to reach me.

"I promise. Don't worry honey, I'll be fine. I love you."

"I love you too."

"Oh, by the way, let me know if you check out the inn, the one in Maine."

"I'm not sure we'll get there this weekend, but I'll keep you in the loop. Plus, it'd be nice if you could go too. I want Craig there, but a girl needs her mother when she's planning her wedding."

I smiled. It felt nice to be wanted. "I understand completely… you know I'd love to go with you. I promise I'll text you when I get to the cottage."

She seemed to understand and respect my wishes. I was lucky to have her. I knew it would be different down there, being by myself. I don't think I'd ever been to the cottage alone. I've never been one to complain about being alone. I'm the type that revels in being able to do what I want when I want. I guess that's one good thing about being divorced. Now, if I want to read or write or garden, I don't have to look over my shoulder to see if I'm pissing anyone off, pissing Jack off. I think he wanted us to be connected at the hip at times. I admit, I needed him then, and I'm not just talking about the money; he was my sounding board as well. We'd been together for a long time, and I can't lie, I was used to him paying the bills and making the big decisions. When we split, I panicked. How in the hell was I going to do this by myself? I remember hearing the Kelly Clarkson song, "What doesn't kill you makes you stronger," and thinking, you're not dead yet Julia, get your shit together and have some faith.

As much as this might not make sense to anyone, I have always considered my daughter a close friend. When I was raising my kids, 'people,' whoever they are, advised against making your kids your friend. I felt like I was going against the grain and doing something wrong by allowing that to happen. But really, I knew our age difference and what I needed to do as a mother for all my kids, plus Jess was different. She was my middle baby, my only girl, and we'd always been close, even through the tumultuous teenage years, we managed to dodge typical mother/daughter arguments about too much makeup and tight clothes. We both adjusted, making the necessary changes for each other so our relationship wouldn't suffer. It only works if there is give and take, and a shitload of honesty. I felt like we'd achieved significant levels of respect between us. Jack and I always treated our kids like people, not adults necessarily, but like people who have feelings and emotions that are just as important as any adult. I think because we respected them, they in turn respected us then, and hopefully, even more now.

Any parent worth their salt would tell you every kid is different. Our kids were, without a doubt, different from each other. Early on we learned who we could chat with in the morning and who was off limits. Jess was definitely off limits, but the two boys, well I wouldn't say they were chatty, but they were much more open to conversation than she was. Jack would tell me the car rides to school were more about listening to radio chatter than talking, which was difficult for him since silence was his natural enemy. He always wanted to know how they were doing, whether it was about school, sports, or friendships. But kids don't always want to share; you have to be sensitive to what they want and don't want to talk about. It's probably one of the hardest parts about being a parent.

It's funny, Jack was, without a doubt, the talker in the family, but I was the one who handled the sex talks, even with the boys. I really should have dumped that on him, but honestly, I didn't mind doing it. Jacob and I read a comically illustrated book about sex when he was ten years old; it was an ideal introduction. Justin could have been a bit younger since he was inquisitive. I remember one day; he and I were sitting on the front porch swing and out of nowhere he asked me what menopause was. I think he was around eight years old. That kid; full of surprises. Can't say I wasn't taken aback, but I came up with an answer, even though I didn't understand it fully myself. I gave him my best explanation, simple and to the point because I knew he could handle it. If any of our kids were going to test us, push the envelope, even figure out we got pregnant with Jacob before we got married, it was Justin, our little mathematician.

Jess was a different story. I remember devising my plan to talk to her about sex when she was ten years old. She, again, was not the type of kid to ask questions or bear her soul to her parents. Basically, I decided to trap her in the car when we were on our way to the mall. It was a foolproof plan; she couldn't get away from me while I enlightened her, my horrified daughter, as to the mystery of the birds and the bees. She withstood the onslaught of information, and I'm sure we never talked about it again. I bought her a lot of new things that day; it was a fair deal in my book. Now, thirteen years later, my baby girl is planning her wedding—I guess she figured it all out.

Jess always knew how to make me feel needed. When we hung up, I couldn't help but think how quickly the tables had turned. For a solid eighteen years I worried about my kids, especially my daughter, wondering who was she spending time with, and was she safe? I don't think that ever ends when you're a parent, and I mean never. But it is funny when your kids start playing parent to you; it's almost like you've lost some ground. Maybe the kids know something I don't. I love the three of them, but since the divorce, sometimes I feel like they're ganging up on me, and it makes me wonder if they do that to their father.

Chapter Three
Julia

With a two-hour drive ahead of me, I needed to finish packing and get on the road, or I'd be in rush hour hell. Just getting to the bridge would be a challenge, but I couldn't leave the place a mess, according to my mother, and I still needed to clean the bathroom and water the plants. The house I rented was small, a thousand square feet at best, but the right size for me. One bedroom, one bathroom, a gally kitchen, and living room. The one thing I loved about it was the exposed red brick wall. I always dreamed of having my own place when I was in college; a small apartment covered in red brick walls and filled with every nuance that said, this is Julia's place, just hers, but that never happened. Having a baby at twenty-one will squash that type of dream.

So, now I finally have my own place, and I have always enjoyed my alone time, but now all I feel is lonely. It's so quiet, even for me. No kids, no husband, no animals; nothing but me and my plants. I stopped for a minute and looked around the house. The things I'd acquired over the years had always meant so much to me. They were things I deemed important, things I wanted around me to bring me comfort. But as of late, I was feeling disconnected from them. Knick knacks, paintings, furniture from my grandmother. Whatever I was going through writing wise seemed to be affecting me as a whole. I breathed deeply, wondering where I went. Where did Julia disappear to? And just like that, the thoughts vanished and all I could think about was how much I didn't want to clean. I walked to the bathroom and cringed at the thought of cleaning it. It was only me here, but I still hated it. At least I didn't have to clean pee off the floor anymore, that was one perk of divorce. "Stop procrastinating Julia," I thought. I grabbed my supplies from under the sink and just went at it, my mind drifting back in time as I cleaned.

The farmhouse I grew up in didn't have exposed brick, and it wasn't fancy, but it had charm. The idea of generations living their lives in that house comforted me, touching me somewhere deep in my soul. Most people would feel haunted in some way, possible spirits afoot and all, but not me. The slanted floors, drafty windows, even the mice in the cellar—none of it bothered me. The only thing it had that I didn't have now was acres of open land. I missed having land.

When I finished cleaning the bathroom, I walked outside to water the plants, what was left of them anyway. The coleus and begonias were still going strong in the large terra cotta pots I had on the patio, but the hanging petunias were done; those damn bugs eat them alive every year. I closed the umbrella and put the couch cushions on end. I was thankful to have this space; it was secluded enough to allow me to be introspective. I could easily lose myself in a juicy novel or lose myself in my own writing, that is, as long as the neighbors weren't fighting. It was a tiny refuge for me.

I looked at the yard; a square patch of grass that I didn't have to mow. I missed mowing the lawn, can't believe I'm saying that. As funny as this sounds, there is a right way and a wrong way to mow a lawn. Jack taught me to mow at a different angle every time so the grass would grow healthier. He was right. I mowed my small patch of grass near the pool, and he did the rest with the ride-on mower. We worked well together, splitting most of the jobs around the house, but the one thing that was mine alone was the landscaping. I just loved making new beds, planting shrubs and perennials—I even completed a few rock walls. I didn't even mind the spring and fall clean ups. I'd rather be outside, working my ass off than cooking dinner, which eventually became a problem in our marriage. I was selfish with my time, and in so many ways I didn't care. Landscaping was always one of my passions, and it was the one thing that killed me about selling the house. I'd put an exorbitant amount of blood, sweat, and tears into that land, literally. I wanted to uproot it all and take it with me when we sold, but some things just don't work out the way we want. What an understatement.

After the divorce, I walked away with plenty of money from the sale of the house, but I didn't want to just blow it by buying another place until I was ready. Owning a house is a big commitment; renting seemed like a safer choice. I'd never bought property on my own. In fact, I'd never had to buy a car, a computer, set up my own utilities, and on and on. I'd felt so inadequate through much of our marriage, but that was on me. I could have stepped up, taken charge more, but because Jack was the bread winner, and I chose to stay home with the kids, I let him handle things. Old school mentality, I guess. Admittedly, I wanted him to be the provider, to take care of the five of us. I depended on him, and he knew it. Dare I say, he thrived because of it.

Jack was always supportive of me being home with the kids, I knew that. The problem wasn't him; it was me. I'd listen to other mothers talk about their jobs at the bus stop, or at school functions, and I couldn't help but feel less than. Of course, it didn't help when they'd say right to my face that if they didn't work, like me, they'd have the time to exercise or landscape or even cook. Try living with that bullshit. They were jealous, end of story. Even my own father, as much as he supported my mother staying home with us, was disappointed I didn't have a career. He'd describe me to friends as his daughter from Boston, not his daughter who stayed home to raise her children, or his daughter who enjoyed landscaping, or his daughter who was trying to get published. It was gut wrenching; I couldn't win. It made me feel like crap. It's just what happened; it's just what I let happen. And now, I feel differently, or at least I'm trying to feel differently.

I've never regretted being a stay-at-home mom. The years I had with my babies were priceless, but after the divorce, I realized I needed to grow up and take care of myself. I mean, I really didn't have a choice. I had to find a place to live, I had to manage my money, I had to pay for insurance, buy a computer, take care of me. At least in a rental I didn't have to panic if rainwater flooded the cellar, or if the furnace decided to shut down. I was twenty-one when we had Jacob, and we didn't know what we were doing. We pretty much had no support from family; it was up to us to figure things out. Despite feeling like I didn't do enough to help out through our marriage, I know we did a fantastic job raising our kids because we did it together. At least we got that right.

I walked back inside and headed for the bedroom. It was time to pack. I stopped at the threshold for a minute, staring at my bed—the bed I'd spent every night in alone over the last two years. Jack took the king size sleigh bed, and I chose the queen, something we'd picked up at an antique shop. It's sad to say, a queen was big enough; I didn't need to feel lonelier than I already did. I walked to the closet, grabbed my suitcase, and threw it on the bed.

I never thought I'd get divorced; it just seemed inconceivable. I mean, you spend X number of years with your partner, sharing the most intimate moments, and in our case, vomiting every stupid thought, which many times included disgruntled discussions about extended family. You raise your children, make a house into a home, and stand by the promises you made on the day you got married. Imagining life without the other person was not an option for me, and yet, here I was, divorced, renting this small house I didn't want, with a tiny backyard, and it felt empty. I felt empty. I think sleeping alone is the worst part.

"Packing sucks," I said angrily, throwing clothes onto the bed. I always hated packing, just like I hated taking showers, fixing my hair, applying makeup, etc. I didn't enjoy any of it as it took time, and I didn't have the patience to do what I didn't want to do when I really wanted to be doing something more worthwhile. I had every drawer pulled out of my dresser. It was mid-September, and I was at a loss for how to pack. Skinny jeans, shorts, T-shirts, sweatshirts; it's like I needed to pack everything I owned because the weather is so unpredictable in New England, especially in the fall. I had no intention of straying too far from the cottage, except to take a run on the beach, so as much as I loved my fancier dresses, I didn't need them. A few sundresses would suffice. I shook my head, "It's just a few days Julia, it's not like you're going away for a week."

"Pajamas," I said scowling. I didn't even wear pajamas, but I kept some to hang out in. I opened the lingerie drawer. I laughed just thinking that I called it that, since I never wore any lingerie. When you've lived with a man who covets your body and can heat up a bed in more than one way, you gravitate toward wearing nothing but the sheets to bed. Sex was the one thing that was a constant in our marriage. We made love as passionately as we fought, which is probably why we stayed together for so long. You fight, you make up, you mend. Jack was always a hound for sex; he definitely wanted to have it more frequently than I did, but the chemistry was always there. Our love making was always effortless. That wasn't the problem. It was our marriage in general; it was like the proverbial hamster on the wheel, never really getting anywhere.

I was looking for my favorite black velvet pajamas when my fingers encountered something silky in the back of the drawer. What old nightie did I somehow keep? When I pulled it out, I was shocked. A dusty colored pink nightie was saying, "remember me?"

"Yes, I do remember you, and I kind of don't want to," I said, but I couldn't help but smile.

Jack bought it for me one Valentine's Day. I ran my fingers over the opaque sequins and beads so delicately outlining the bra. Good ole' Victoria's Secret. Now, why the hell did I keep it? I just stood there, immersing myself in the memory of that Valentine's Day night because it felt good.

Miraculously, the kids were staying at friends' houses for the night, and Jack and I had the house to ourselves. He wasn't one to celebrate fake holidays, as he called them; in fact, he abhorred commercialism. Mother's and Father's Day were about all he'd allow, so with that in mind, I didn't bother to waste money on a gift for him. I did, however, make a wonderful meal, his favorite: New York strip with roasted potatoes, and green beans with slivered almonds. Oh yes, and his favorite chocolate cake for dessert. We sat next to each other at the table. The candles were lit, and the lights were dim. A Tony Bennett vinyl played in the background. We always sat next to each other at the table, even when the kids were little, and I always, always lit candles.

Every time we went out to eat, we'd sit at the bar, just so we could sit next to one another. I loved being able to put my hand on his leg under the bar, or whisper in his ear to make him laugh. It was intimate, and even though we had many times when we'd engage in conversation with the bartenders or other patrons, it was our time to talk. There were a few times that we'd fight on the way home, after someone, probably me, inadvertently said something stupid, and someone, probably him, took it the wrong way. But for the most part, we were happy. It makes me wonder why we couldn't hold it together.

After dinner, I remember being so shocked when he placed a red bag with pink tissue billowing from the top, on the table in front of me. I remember being a bit embarrassed as I pulled the nightie out of the bag. I looked at him as he sat there giving me a devilish grin. Cheater!

~

"I was thinking, tonight's a good night to try it on, don't you think?" he said, winking at me.

Oh, those hazel eyes—they drew me in every time. We acted like teenagers that night. He got up from the table and offered me his hand, gesturing with a nod of his head to follow him upstairs, but when we got to the bottom of the stairs, he stepped aside, motioning for me to go up first. He wasn't just being a gentleman; I knew he liked to watch me from behind as I ascended. I had exercised my entire life, and he obviously approved. We left the dirty dishes, what was left of the steak, an empty bottle of Cabernet, and a full chocolate cake on the table. Nothing mattered more at that moment than what was about to happen.

I slipped into the bathroom and put the nightie on, knowing in a matter of seconds, it would end up on the bedroom floor. When I walked into the room, he was waiting for me on the edge of the bed. He looked up at me and smiled. It's as if our desire for each other and the pounding of our hearts were in sync. I walked over to him, a little self-conscious because this was so out of character for me to wear something so frivolously sexy. He spread his legs so I could stand in between them. He pulled me close, nestling his face between my breasts. He breathed in deeply, then exhaled. My fingers wandered through his hair while his hands slid under the nightie, gliding effortlessly along my back and eventually down over my ass where he squeezed, inhaled again, and groaned. It was the kind of night you look back on and think, "Why couldn't we have just stayed like that forever." Passion was never the problem.

~

"Snap out of it!" I said forcefully, seeing my reflection in the dresser mirror. I was smiling as I relived the moment.

I almost felt embarrassed by the memory. I carefully folded the nightie and placed it in the suitcase. Now why in the world would I bring it with me—nostalgia? Why would I want any reminders of a man I'd divorced two years ago on my peaceful, healing, restorative vacation? I never answered my own question. I just kept packing.

Over the last two years, Jack and I haven't really spoken. With the kids basically being adults by the time we divorced, there really wasn't much to talk about, except for college tuition I guess, but he handled all of that. When we were forced to be together, it was usually at a function, like the last time at Jess' college graduation. We spoke to one another enough to make the kids comfortable. In general, it was far easier to simply stay away from each other, for me at least; my heart ached every time I saw him. The first year of being divorced was painful; I regretted it much of the time, constantly questioning myself, asking what I could have done to save us. But when I would see him, it was like every fight, every tear, every remembrance of being misunderstood or accused of something surfaced, and I could barely take it. So, the last year has been a godsend. Seeing him is just too much, but the thought of him being with someone else would also be a tough pill to swallow.

It's a lot for me to consider, even for myself. I know we both need to move on, and I know he eventually will meet someone else—he's just too good looking and despite our issues, too good of a guy to be alone the rest of his life. Just because it didn't work out for us doesn't mean there's not someone out there for him, maybe even for me. I just hope whoever he finds will be ready for all the baggage he comes with because unless he gets some help, and by help, I mean therapy, they're in for a rough road. One thing I'm sure of though, I will never marry again. One and done. I can't take that much passion and that much pain again.

Chapter Four
Jack

"You're going to have to cover that meeting Justin," I said, as I pulled into the parking lot. "An old friend just contacted me about some properties on the Cape."

"Dad, you know I can't deal with Charlie, the guy is so belittling, he's such an asshole, plus the Cape is kind of out of our bubble."

"Can I have a medium decaf with almond milk?" I said into the intercom.

"Sorry son, he's just one of many assholes, as you know. You're just going to have to deal with lovely Mr. Shattuck on your own, and yes, I realize how far it is, but it's the least I can do for a friend, right? At least I can get the ball rolling… it's not like we haven't referred a listing before. I'll hook them up with Carlene at Blue Ocean Realty. She's got a good reputation, and we'll still get our percent of the commission."

A huge sigh resounded from the other end of the phone. I could almost see him running his hand down the side of his face and over his scrubby beard. What's with this generation; their beards run down onto their necks, scraggly, like they don't give a shit. It's a look, I know. I'm no metro-sexual, if anyone uses that term anymore, but I always keep my beard trimmed. Julia always loved my beard.

"Fine, this trip better be worth it," he said, like an insolent child.

I chuckled. "You know it will be. I'll talk to you soon son."

Just as I pulled forward to the drive-thru window my phone rang again. I glanced at the number, rolled my eyes, and sighed heavily. I've been ignoring this call for days. "Christ," I mumbled. I agonized over picking it up, but then I succumbed. I felt like I had no choice; I just needed to get it over with.

"Hey… Annngela," I said, lingering, as if me lengthening her name would buy me any time.

"Hey Jack. I haven't heard from you in a few weeks. I thought you fell down a well or something," she said, followed by a nervous laugh.

Now it was me running my hand down my beard. I really didn't need this right now. For Christ's sake, we'd only been on a handful of dates. This is the third call in the past few days, and yes, I'm being a dick by not telling her I don't think we're going to work out, but who wants to have that conversation. It's been two years since the divorce, and I've struggled to let someone into my life again. Joe and Pat think I should be out screwing everything that walks and not giving a shit, but that's their shtick certainly not mine. Letting my marriage go after twenty-two years was the toughest thing I'd ever done, especially when I didn't want it to end. I'm just not ready to jump in again.

"That would be a problem," I said, with an uncomfortable chuckle. "But no, just busy with work… lots to juggle this time of year. Sorry I haven't been in touch." What a liar I've become.

I whispered a thank you to the worker clad in his bright orange and dull brown shirt. I handed him five dollars. "Keep the change," I said. The kid gave me a half smile, looking at the five-dollar bill like it was no big deal. Jesus, everyone wants to get tipped these days for just doing their job. You'd think he'd be happy to have a few extra bucks in his pocket. This is what I get for being a nice guy; how typical.

"Well, what about this weekend?" she said excitedly. "There's a night game at Fenway on Saturday and I've got two great seats right behind home plate." The hope in her voice was killing me.

Shit! Well, at least I have a legitimate reason to say no. I pulled out of the parking lot and headed down the road to my apartment.

"That would be fun, but I'm out of town this weekend for work. Maybe we can make a date for a few weeks from now, when things calm down for me." God damn it! I rolled my eyes at my own stupidity. Why'd I say that?

"Oh, okay. That's too bad, I really wanted to see you," she said, sounding down. At first, I felt bad, wondering if I had just crushed her, but then suddenly she sounded more upbeat. "But no worries, I'll just ask a friend. I look forward to seeing you when you get back. Safe travels and I'll give you a call next week."

"Sounds good, I'll talk to you then."

I looked in the rearview mirror and cursed at myself. "You're a fucking idiot Jack Jones. A cowardly fucking idiot. You just put her in the driver's seat… and now she's calling next week."

Secretly, I'm hoping she'll forget about the tentative date, and I'm seriously hoping she just forgets about me altogether. It'd be helpful for both of us if I weren't such a coward; if I'd just be honest with her, but I just can't seem to pull the trigger. She's actually a nice person, attractive too. It's just been so hard to wrap my head around seeing anyone who isn't Julia. I wonder if Julia is seeing anyone. Just the thought of it makes my blood boil.

I really shouldn't agree to these blind dates anymore. I couldn't be less interested. It's funny, people, even my friends just don't get that I'm actually an introvert. I mean, I may have the gift of gab, but that doesn't mean I'm always up, always on, always confident. I get fucking nervous, that's why I talk. But regardless of why I do it, it has come in handy for the professions I've chosen.

Being in sales was a necessary evil for me. I was the provider financially, I had to make the money, and then find more money as our family grew. That wasn't Julia's fault; I supported her decision to stay home with the kids. I didn't want some stranger raising our kids. It was the right decision for us but being the soul provider put so much fucking pressure on me that I thought I'd explode at times, and I didn't think Julia understood.

She'd get so pissed when I'd say that to her, that the pressure was all on me. It would start a fight almost immediately. She tried to help over the years, but the small landscaping and painting jobs she did hardly made a dent. I knew she felt guilty because she knew I was burnt out. I know she did so much for all of us, providing in ways that couldn't be measured by a paycheck, but at the time I was blind to it. Now I see that.

I pulled into my apartment complex; I hated this place. It reminded me of when Julia and I first started out; we were poor, and I hated being poor. The only positive was we were happy, just the three of us. We had nothing but each other. I'd leave in the morning and come home to a woman who loved me, who supported me, and to a son who could brighten my mood with a simple smile. We were both so young, raising a child. Our families were not helpful in any way, but what did we expect; that's the way they operated.

I looked up at my window. No one was looking back at me, no one was happy to welcome me home. It was an empty feeling. Julia and I were happy back then; the days when she made our curtains from cheap sheets and picture frames out of poster board. Maybe not having money was the key to happiness. All we had was each other, but then life got more complicated. We had more kids, which meant we needed more things, which meant more money was going out than coming in. I needed to make up the delta, and it wasn't easy. When we divorced, I panicked: where would I live, how would the kids navigate this, and what about the normalcy of life? But who was I kidding, Julia and I had been fighting weekly for the last ten years of our marriage—something had to give, and it was us. No matter who was right or who was wrong, we just didn't see eye to eye. She would fight to be heard, to be understood, and I would push back telling her she just wanted to be right. Again, realizations that have come too late.

My parents fought in front of me daily when I was growing up, but Julia's parents never fought in front of her. It was the one cue we took from them, the one thing we did right; we didn't fight in front of the kids. But eventually, we got to a point when the kids weren't home, that we'd light the house up. The yelling was unbearable, for me anyway, but we both couldn't stop ourselves. I'd shut down eventually, but she would keep the fight going and I would eventually retreat, recoil, so I wouldn't have to relive my childhood.

My emotions rode the roller coaster, and every fight led me to feel extremely misunderstood. What the hell happened? Admittedly, not every moment was a fight. We had so much passion, and Julia would always say that love was not the problem. Maybe I didn't understand what she was saying. All I knew was I felt insecure, and when that feeling flooded in, I felt like a tidal wave was coming at me, and it was merciless. I was drowning in my own insecurity.

I put my head on the steering wheel and thought, "Why? Why did we fail Julia?" And then as quickly as the thought came, I tried to push it down, down to the place where I pushed all my sorrow. "Stop Jack, stop doing this to yourself," I said, banging my hands on the steering wheel. "You've ruined me Julia, you've ruined me for anyone else. I'm too damaged. The divorce killed me. I can't go through that again. I won't ever marry again; I know that for sure. One and done, that's it."

Chapter Five
Julia

It'd been years since I'd been to the cottage. Probably the last time I was there was two years before the divorce. We'd invited Rob and Steph for the weekend. The signs were there then; the silent looks of anger, the annoyed roll of the eyes, but for our guest's sake, we held our tongues until the drive home, which was a disaster of course. I knew then we didn't have long together, but somehow, maybe because of the kids, trying to get them through high school, we hung in there for two more years. I don't know how that was possible. I read a lot, wrote a lot, and we tried to keep our distance, but there was always something said or misinterpreted that led to the weekly fighting.

I sighed just thinking about it. It's funny how just a few random thoughts can change your entire mood. I grabbed my bags from the bedroom and headed to the car. The house was clean, the fridge was empty, and so was my bladder; I was ready to go.

I threw the bags in the back just as the rain started to fall. I loved my Explorer; it was the ideal car for me. Of course, some may say a bit big for my needs now; no kids to cart around, no plants to shove into the back, but I still loved it. I'm no Dale Earnhardt, but I love knowing I can step on the gas and in a matter of seconds free myself from traffic. I remember the day we checked the car out at the dealership; I test drove it first. Since they let us take it out on our own, when I hit the highway, I let her rip. It seemed like Jack's entire body flew back as I accelerated, getting it up to eighty in a matter of seconds.

~

"That was awesome!" I said, gripping the wheel tightly, still feeling the rush. I looked over at Jack, he was not as enthused.

"Jesus, Julia, take it easy," he said, laughing through his fear.

"Hey, we need to know how fast she can go, what if we're on the run from the cops?"

"How 'bout we don't plan on having this be our getaway car, okay," he said dryly.

~

Even then, when he wasn't totally thrilled with me, he was still able to muster a smile. I could appreciate the times when we could laugh; at least the good times outweighed the bad, that is, until the good succumbed to the bad on a weekly basis. It was honestly like we just couldn't stop it. I could never tell when the bomb was about to drop. I'm willing to admit that I triggered some of our fights by randomly bringing something up, but I know now that his reactions to me were fueled by something from his past. I wasn't fully to blame—how could I be? How could he be? It was like we unintentionally collided, and the explosion was eminent. It was just a matter of how big it would be. I always felt like I had to scream at him just to get him to hear me. It was so contrary to how I thought I'd behave in situations like that. I never once heard my parents raise their voices. I never once heard my mother lose her shit. And yet, I would hit a breaking point with Jack and want to throw anything within range at him. One time, I dumped an entire pizza on him while he lay on the couch, mocking me. What a waste of pizza.

The rage I felt when he was verbally pushing me, even for me, was beyond reason. Deep breath Julia, deep breath is all I could say to myself, and then I'd escape to some hidden corner of the house and cry. But I know better now, I know myself better. I put those times in their place years ago, back in the past where they needed to stay. I liken those times to chapters of a book and sometimes it's best to leave the book on the shelf. There's no need to continually take that book off the shelf and reread a chapter that is painful. All that does is set you up for failure. It's my time now. My time to thrive, to find me, to feel good about myself. I didn't need to let my mind wander over the past anymore. I needed to leave the book on the shelf.

I hated driving in the rain; I was praying it wouldn't get too heavy. Don't get me wrong, I love the rain, when I'm inside, under a cozy blanket reading a book or watching a movie. Or better yet, sitting on the front porch when a storm was coming in. God, I miss the farmers porch. There was always something exciting to me about thunderstorms; that unexpected flash of lightning and the much-anticipated clap of thunder. Jack would sit with me, enjoying the show, until a good crack of lightning scared us both inside. I think he secretly loved it when I would grab hold of him. He was probably waiting for it.

I took a sip of my water. I've never been the best at getting my daily allotment of H_2O. I switched the radio station to rock. I've been listening to a lot of country music lately, so the change is good. Pink is playing; I'd forgotten how much I love her voice. Her songs are so poignant, so transparent. I can relate to almost every song she sings, especially this one, "I'm all out of fight." I feel the tears coming with every verse. This song is about me and Jack, as if Pink wrote it just for us. How does she do it? It's too much though, and I just told myself to stop dipping into the past. "Change the station, Julia. Think about something else," I said, reprimanding myself.

I switched back to the country station. Thomas Rhett's "T-shirt" is playing. I know all the words. Much better choice for me right now. It was my fantasy as a child to be a singer, well that or a gym teacher, neither of which happened, thank God. Jen was always right there with me, rifling through mom's vinyl collection until we found the album we knew by heart. We'd sit on the floor in front of that old record player, singing Simon and Garfunkel lyrics into old wooden mallets from my mother's antique collection. Jen: God, I missed my sister! I wished she lived closer.

I still can remember being a kid and weathering many a storm with her. We'd sit huddled together on the couch, hands clasped, hearts racing, and our bodies simultaneously jolting every time the lightning cracked and the thunder roared. It was scary and thrilling all at the same time. My sister Jen; my best friend. She'd been through hell as well and when the waters muddied around me, I remembered what she'd been through.

She'd divorced four years before me because her husband was cheating on her; what an asshole he was. I'm sure she had an inkling that he was out with other women—he was a huge flirt. I didn't understand why she put up with it, with him. Maybe she thought he'd change. Maybe she thought she could win him back. Maybe she just couldn't conceive of life without him. Maybe she was just scared.

When the thunder and lightning hit my life, threatened my family, I understood why she closed her eyes to his behavior; she was afraid. She was afraid financially no doubt, but it was her emotional stability that really took the hit. She'd been married for fifteen years, and he was all she'd known since high school. I'll never forget the day she called me from her car when he'd finally come clean. She could barely get the words out. Trying to offer your sister a shoulder to lean on is tough from two thousand miles away. He left her almost immediately for his flirtation. He left her broken.

But after a month of him leaving, she found what she referred to as her true soul mate. I begged her to take the time to find herself again, but my advice was not well received. It was one of the few times we didn't see eye to eye. She married him as soon as the divorce was final. Is she happy now? God only knows. That's why, when the shit hit the fan for me, I needed to take my own advice and focus on me. I had to face myself. It wasn't about Jack anymore; it was about me and what I needed. As I learned in therapy, it's about self-stewardship.

So far, the rain has been light, and my mood has followed its cue. I switched the station again; country isn't doin' it for me right now. "Everywhere" by Fleetwood Mac is playing, another great song. I turned it up and sang along, feeling hopeful this trip would be the key to lifting my spirits. The traffic was getting heavier, but I was just thankful that I didn't have to drive through the city. I hadn't taken any trips over the past few years, so this was a departure for me to say the least. It was like I was starving for a change in my routine. It wasn't so much a fresh start that I needed, just something different, something familiar, yet new. Would I find that something at the cottage? I had no idea, but it was a cheap way for me to find out.

My mind began to wander. I recently learned that I am a 'pluviophile'—lover of rainy days. For some reason I find joy and peace of mind when it rains. Most people seem to be sun worshippers, remarking about the beauty of a sunny day. I certainly don't want it to rain all the time, but a sunny day doesn't make my heart skip a beat. The one good thing about a sunny day was being able to work outside in the gardens, but even when it rained, I was out there, sitting in the dirt, getting soaked and loving every minute.

I guess what I love about rain is that it's so thought provoking. In my youth, there was one spot in particular that brought me not only peace but hope; the family camp in New Hampshire. The Camp was a beast, meaning it was not like any home I'd ever lived in. It was ruggedly finished, meaning it was unfinished. No insulation, no sheet rock on the ceilings or the walls. In fact, the interior walls were basically non-existent, except for some make-shift half walls thrown together with leftover plywood and thin wall board.

I remember snuggling under the cover of my sleeping bag, listening to the rain hitting the roof. The sound it made was so soothing, so peaceful. I'd lay under those covers with a flashlight in one hand and a book in the other, my head covered with the sleeping bag just in case a parachuting spider made an unexpected visit. The upstairs of the camp was completely open, so my sister slept in the bed next to mine and so forth with my other siblings and parents. I'd read for as long as I could keep my eyes open. Books, books, books. I loved any book about horses, but one of my all-time favorite books was "Mandy" by Julie Andrews. A bit of fantasy wrapped in real life circumstances; it was magical. Books like that made me want to write children's books.

My parents were always so generous, allowing me to buy as many books from the book club at school as I wanted. I didn't know then, but I was lucky; most kids had to rely on the library alone. I can vividly remember the stack of books being placed on my desk in fourth grade; my excitement was palpable. I'm sure all that reading propelled my love of writing. Maybe that's my jumpstart; I need to read more.

With one hour of driving left, I decided to pull off the highway into the infamous rest area with the giant totem pole. Thankfully, there was a coffee shop located next to the fast-food joint. I could see an open parking spot ahead.

"Really buddy!" A metallic gray pickup truck just emerged out of nowhere to claim the spot. I hate these situations. I stop, he stops. Should I let him just take it? Miraculously, he waves me on, and I wave back appreciatively. I guess chivalry isn't dead, and regardless of the whole 'women's lib' thing, I will take the kind gesture as just that.

I hadn't been driving that long, but I felt like I needed my caffeine fix. I got out of the car and immediately stretched. Since I almost completely tore my ACL skiing with the boys a few years back, the backside of my knee would tighten up if I let it stay in a bent position for too long. About the only thing I was good for now was running; no side-to-side movements, which meant tennis was out too, and I loved to play tennis. Because my leg was strong, the doctors advised me not to have the surgery unless I started falling over, which is a funny thought. They knew me; if I couldn't exercise for months because of rehab, I'd go out of my mind. I was forced to compromise, giving up tennis and anything else that put my leg in jeopardy. So far, I'm still upright, and still surgery free.

I grabbed my bag and walked quickly toward the entrance. When I reached for the door, a hand swept under my arm to grab the handle first, which startled me.

"Let me get that for you," a man's voice said.

As I looked behind me, I recognized him right away; the chivalrous gentleman who gave me the parking space. I'm not gonna' lie, this six-foot-tall man with his wavy brown hair, and even darker brown eyes, made my heart race a bit. Did I mention he was incredibly good looking? I'm guessing he was in his mid-forties. Oh yes, and in that split second of realizing just how good looking he was, I also couldn't help but notice the tattoo on his forearm. Something about the right kind of tattoo on a man is so appealing, to me anyway. I wasn't into the colored ink, or when people just put them sporadically here and there. Just from the quick glimpse I got, I had a feeling this tattoo worked its way up his arm, telling a story. I pressed Jack to get one, and he did, for me. He had always thought about getting one, but he had trouble pulling the trigger. Finally, something hit him, and he came home one day with his shoulder tattooed. He put it where no one could see it; he wasn't about getting attention. I'd like to think most people get them because there's a special meaning behind them, many times a painful meaning which makes me feel kind of weird for finding them sexy. I wished Jack had put it where I could see it every day, but he was modest. Just getting the tattoo was a big deal.

It took me longer to get one, basically because the thought of being an eighty-year-old with a tattoo on my arm that once was a flower but had morphed over time into a tattoo of God knows what, scared the crap out of me. And that tells it all; I was already putting it out there that I'd be fat and wrinkly when I got old. I shuddered at the thought.

"Oh," I said, surprised by the gesture, "thank you so much." I walked in feeling a little strange, but quickly let it go and chalked it up to the fact that chivalry wasn't dead. I took my place in line, not really thinking he'd be standing right behind me.

"Are you local to the area or just passing through?" he asked with that sultry voice.

It took me a second to realize he was talking to me. My eyebrows raised questioningly, and I turned slightly, kind of giving him that 'are you talkin' to me look'. His eyes were penetrating, like he was boring his way into my soul. I cleared my throat to find my voice which I'd suddenly lost. "I'm just passing through," I squeaked out, turning back to the counter. Was my face flushing? Jesus.

"Me too," he said. I could almost hear him smiling.

It's impossible, I know, but I could feel the heat emanating from his body. I was starting to feel really uncomfortable. I don't think I'd ever struck up a conversation with a stranger in this way before, especially not a man. I wasn't looking for it, and yet there it was. I didn't know how to handle it. I just tried to ignore him as I moved forward in the line.

"Could I have a medium cappuccino with two extra shots of espresso please."

"Name," the clerk asked without emotion, obviously thrilled with his job. He must be having a difficult day.

"Rachel," I replied.

I've always loved the name Rachel. If we didn't go with the same first initial for all the kids, Jess would have been Rachel. I should have used that for her middle name, but we decided to carry on my middle name which came from my mom, and her mom before her—Ruth.

"Whoa," I heard him exclaim behind me.

I suddenly felt invaded and awkward, like I was doing something wrong. Is this guy commenting on my coffee order? I had to make a joke, or I might crumble right there from embarrassment.

I turned my head slightly and said with a laugh, "I guess I'm livin' on the edge today."

I paid for my coffee and moved quickly to the other end of the counter. This guy was way too close, and he was kind of creeping me out, but I couldn't help but glance back at him. He was incredibly good looking. I didn't want him to be that guy; that creepy guy who hits on women at rest stops. I let my eyes wander over him. Brown hair, brown eyes; that's been established. Athletic build; noted. My eyes wandered down to his left hand; I didn't see a ring. Of course, that doesn't mean anything in today's world. People get tattoos symbolizing a ring, or just don't wear one at all, especially men. He also could be in a relationship, maybe even engaged. I mean how would I know. Guys, according to Jack, are all pigs; they only want one thing.

"Jesus Julia, what are you doing," I thought, questioning my own motives. And then it happened—he caught me looking. I quickly looked away, focusing on the counter where my coffee should be. When the clerk called my name, I grabbed my drink and made a beeline for the door.

"Here, let me get that for you," he said, scurrying over to the door. It was like he came out of nowhere.

"You didn't have to do that, but thank you," I said, looking beyond him at the counter. "Now it looks like you lost your place in line."

"It's not a problem," he said, his brown eyes never moving from mine. "I got my order in."

"I'm headed to the Cape," he blurted out as I walked through the door, "and you?"

This guy is persistent. Maybe he is a creep, just an extremely good-looking creep.

"Yes," I said hesitantly, "to the Cape."

My God, this guy has me jumping through hoops. Next thing I know I'll be giving him my phone number, home address, social security number; that's the pull he had on me. At least I didn't spew out what town I was heading to. Jess' voice must have been humming in my ears. "Remember Mom, don't talk to strangers."

"I hope you have a nice trip," I said, as I walked toward my car, "and thanks again."

I needed to get out of there before I did something stupid, whatever that means.

"It was really nice meeting you Rachel," he yelled from the doorway.

I stopped, confused when he said Rachel, but then I remembered that according to me and my coffee cup, it was my name.

I turned around and gave him a wave.

"Maybe fate will bring us together again," he said. Was he being creepy or just hopeful?

I took a few steps backward. He was smiling. I must have been twenty feet from him, but it was like I could see his eyes so clearly. Again, his eyes never wavered, just a constant focus on me. "Just keep moving Julia, keep moving," I whispered.

I lowered my head like a schoolgirl with a crush to hide. "Maybe so," I said, then turned and headed straight for my car, trying to fight back the smile. It wasn't just his attention that was drawing me in; he seemed to trigger emotions in me I hadn't felt in a long time. That first meeting emotion. That flirtatious first meeting; nothing rivaled it.

He was still standing in the same spot as I slipped into the driver's seat. I waved again and he waved back. I can't lie, I hadn't had anyone take a second look like that in years. Of course, according to Jack, guys were checking me out all the time, which pissed him off royally, but I never really noticed. Was this guy a player? Damn his attention felt good, but on the other hand, he was a stranger, and I certainly didn't need some horny guy coming on to me at a rest stop coffee shop thinking I'd be into it. I'm not that kind of woman. When I pulled away, he was still standing outside the door, like a lovesick puppy, or maybe that's just what I wanted to think.

Chapter Six
Julia

As I drove, I couldn't help myself; Mr. Chivalrous was first and foremost on my mind. I replayed the events at the coffee shop over and over. Part of me wished I'd given him my phone number. I mean, what if I just let go of 'that someone.' 'That someone' who could make my life feel complete again. And then my thoughts drifted to Jack; it wasn't exactly our first meeting, but it sure felt like it. It was without a doubt exciting, heart stopping, hormones bursting, and then years later, all of that just started to vanish.

When I was a junior in college, I headed home for winter break. I can remember finals being arduous, and since I didn't have plans to work, and with no boyfriend to tie me down, I would just take the break for what it was—time off.

Usually, I'd get together with a handful of high school friends to reminisce when I did go home, and true to form, a friend who had his own apartment in town invited a group of us to hang out. I remember exactly what I was wearing: black stirrup pants, ankle boots, and a long multi-colored sweater. I had pulled my long hair back on each side, clasped by a single barrette in the back. I had my father's wavy auburn hair, probably my best attribute. At least I had the good sense to leave it long; short hair would have looked horrendous on me.

As I ascended the stairs to the loft, I had no idea who would be there. When I turned the corner, I immediately spotted him standing in the back. At six-foot-two, he was hard to miss, and the instant I saw him the fireworks went off uncontrollably in every part of my body. I noticed he'd filled out since high school. It's amazing how that works for guys; they can gain weight and continue to grow taller into their twenties, while girls who gain the 'freshman ten' are considered fat, never mind the fact that a girl's height is stunted as soon as she gets her period. My only hope for added inches was heels.

This guy: God he was better looking now than he was in high

school. His ash-colored straight hair was wavy now, and he had chest hair poking out of his faded light blue striped button-down shirt. How did that happen? I was trying my best to get to him, but I got sidelined by a couple of old girlfriends on the way. I was so frustrated. Did he even know what a catch he was? Finally, he looked my way, and when our eyes met it was like the first time we'd ever seen each other. I felt uncharacteristically shy. How could he be so tan in the winter? This tall, gorgeous guy, whom I'd known forever, stared back at me with his dreamy hazel eyes and his sexy mustache and I just melted on the spot. My feet felt like they were stuck in blocks of cement and my legs felt like soggy spaghetti noodles. He waved me over and I nearly lost it.

~

"Hey," he said, wrapping his arms around me, slowly at first then intensifying as the hug continued.

"Hi," I blurted out, while I breathed in the scent of sandalwood. Whatever cologne he used was doing the trick. God knows I didn't want that hug to end.

He pulled back, and said, "It's been a bit."

I melted into those dreamy eyes. "Yah," I said, "way too long."

~

Fate seemed to be against us the rest of the evening. Every time we tried to steal away from the others, someone came in to crash the party. I recall being so angry that we didn't get to talk much; my attraction to him was beyond anything I'd ever felt before. I had just ended a relationship a few months prior, or should I say, I got dumped. My heart was feeling a bit trampled, but I was young, and as a girl who liked having a boyfriend, I wasn't about to let my heartache be the boss of me and ruin a chance with this guy.

I was completely bummed after the party, but within two days he was calling my parents' home, asking me out. We spent as much time as we could together during the break, and even though he had to work, we made the most of the time we had. We both seemed satisfied to move forward slowly, like we didn't want to rush whatever this might become.

Jack may have been a struggling college student, but he was always very generous to pay for our dates. Overall, it was a rush. It was as if I'd never had a relationship before he came back into my life. Every painful break up, every piece of me that was broken seemed to be caught up in this gentle breeze of a relationship until all the negatives floated away. It was everything I could have dreamed of; he was everything I wanted.

That memory made me ache just a bit for what was. Memories: sometimes I hated them, but that one was a one of a kind awesome. I miss those days. I miss that feeling of attraction and new love. I miss the old Jack and Julia. Why did things have to change? Why did they disintegrate right before our eyes? Why didn't we fight harder? I think we both felt powerless to fix us.

I glanced in the rearview to see a car dodging traffic recklessly. Before I knew it, the car was behind me in the fast lane. I had nowhere to go, there were cars in front of me and to the right. What the hell did he want me to do? "It's a two-lane highway you moron," I screamed. He flashed his lights repeatedly; my blood pressure was on the rise.

"Where do you want me to go asshole," I said, flinging my hand in the air. He laid on the horn, and although I didn't want him in front of me, as soon as I could pull to the right, I did. He slowed as he passed, and I flipped him off. Him and his backwards baseball cap; what a fucking idiot. I'm sure my obscene gesture just fueled him to be more of an idiot. He sped ahead, still dodging the traffic. I'm not sure when I started swearing so much, I never really did when I was younger. Who am I kidding; swearing is just a side effect of my life.

"What a fucking asshole," I repeated. "Where's a cop when you really need one?" Suddenly, I heard myself. "Jesus, Julia, you sound just like Jack."

He'd get so mad at people like that when he was driving. I'm not saying his reactions were wrong, but I knew he had a short fuse. Feeling disrespected was one of his biggest obstacles. If I interjected, said the wrong thing, he would remind me that if I were driving, I'd do the same thing. He was right, but when someone else is driving and they lose their shit, it makes the passenger feel extremely uncomfortable, and with Jack, I never knew if he'd pull over and beat the shit out of someone. I just wanted the anger to subside so we could be on our way and just be happy. I just wanted to be happy. But doing that wasn't right either because I wasn't acknowledging his feelings.

Eventually, I couldn't hold my tongue and within minutes we'd be fighting. It wasn't all him, I had to admit my fair share of stepping in it.

I took some deep breaths, but my thoughts were now clouded with anger and soon a very unpleasant memory invaded my thoughts. Suddenly, I'd gone back in time to when Jack and I had been married for about five years. We were living in a small rental house. The three kids had to share a bedroom while we camped out on the pullout couch in the living room. Money was tight. Needless to say, raising three kids under the age of five in a crappy rental was not a dream come true for either of us.

The mattress on the pull-out couch was doing its best to break our backs, literally. The only saving grace of sleeping in the living room was being able to watch television when we went to bed. I don't even want to talk about our sex life; without a door to our so-called room, it was difficult to have any privacy.

Our routine was to put the kids to bed, then lay in bed, chatting about the day, the kids, his job, and how much we hated the rental. But this night was different. Our conversation took a turn for the worse, as in a fight was inevitable. It must have been the movie that sparked the conversation that would lead us to sleeping with our backs to one another. It was always something small that spread like wildfire, even then, way back in the beginning.

~

"So, you're telling me the initial spark you feel when you're first dating doesn't last… is that what you're telling me Julia?" he said, completely irritated with me.

"I guess that is what I'm saying." My response came quickly, probably way too fast for his liking. I could hear it in his voice, he was extremely aggravated with me and then my explanation came when it probably shouldn't have.

"I just think that love changes over time, not necessarily for the worse, it just changes as the years go by, morphing into a different type of love. I mean, when you first meet, you have that initial flirtation, and then you spend every waking moment you can together because you can't get enough of one another and that's simply because it's so new. No one can sustain that kind of infatuation; it just can't last."

"Love changes huh?" he retorted. I could almost feel the wall going up between us.

Again, sensing the irritation in his voice I felt the need to explain, something I'd learn later not to do. I would have been better off just shutting up. Just letting it go. Conversations like this never end well.

"It's not like it's worse or non-existent," I said, trying to make things better. "It's just that the intensity of the flirtation, that newness, it's just impossible to keep that up, and then throw some kids in the mix, things are most definitely going to shift." I didn't want to look at him. I just lay there with my hands across my chest, biting my lower lip, knowing I'd touched a nerve, waiting for the onslaught of anger to hit me.

"So, you don't love me the same way you did in the beginning... nice Julia," he said, his words dripping with sarcasm. "Dare I ask your opinion on soulmates?"

Oh boy, here we go. The wound had been opened and I knew there was no way I could repair this now. I was sinking deep, so I just decided to go in, all in.

"I've never really thought about it," I said, trying to formulate my response. "I mean, I love the idea of having a soul mate, but I don't really believe in the concept. We make our own decisions on this earth. I guess with all the people there are in this world, I can't imagine there is only one person for each of us. I mean, what about people who lose a spouse and then remarry later... which one is the true soulmate? I think it's just a something to say... it sounds good."

I lay there very still. I'd thrown the grenade, and I was just waiting for it to hit the ground.

"So... you don't think we're soulmates, that we weren't brought together like it was destiny?"

But before I could respond he angrily interjected.

"Well, I do. I guess I'm more invested in this relationship than you are Julia. I thought I knew you, but now... now I'm really questioning what the hell you're doing with me, especially if you don't feel that first love anymore."

And with that, he shut the television off and rolled over. No more words followed. I suddenly felt alone. I felt like my opinion didn't matter, like I was being mean just to be mean. It wasn't my intention. I wasn't trying to hurt him or us. Crap! He's beyond pissed now. I rolled over, just as pissed. I made the choice right then to say nothing more, it just wasn't worth the argument, and the kids were in the next room. "Jesus, he's so crazy," I thought. "Overdramatizing everything. This is one of the stupidest fights we've ever had."

~

I just stared ahead at the cars in front of me. I shook my head repeatedly. "So stupid," I muttered. I never forgot that one, and I'm sure he didn't either. I never said I didn't love him. Why was it that my opinion didn't matter?

Jack had a great memory, but he also had a selective memory. I didn't know then, but that kind of fight represented fuel to him. He'd tuck it away in a safe place so he could pull it out to use against me at some later date. He was always twisting my words too, which was so aggravating. Sometimes, I'd think he didn't want me to love him; it's like he was looking for an excuse to sabotage our relationship. But if I had to go back and pick out one fight that could have been the catalyst for why we broke up, it was that one. Honesty: look where it got me.

I couldn't really understand how crazy things would get, because sometimes we were so in sync. For a long time, I accepted our differences, but just like anything, when you're truly in the thick of a relationship, you have to ask the question: is what I'm doing hurting or helping us? For me, his attitude always stayed the same, and he could never see my point of view. It was like he was blocked by something. Eventually I would understand what that blockage was. As much as he infuriated me at times, I felt like I had to give him a pass. The way he grew up haunted him, making him feel like he didn't deserve love, and in the end, it ended us.

I'd been so lost in my thoughts the rest of the drive flew by. Suddenly, I was going over the Sagamore Bridge, on my way to Eastham. For a four-lane bridge, it was extremely high and narrow. If I weren't driving, I'd be taking in the stunning view of the water so far below. Jack and I used to stop in East Sandwich for lunch and have Bloody Mary's and fish tacos at The Harbor, a restaurant located minutes from the bridge. Those were good memories.

Once I was on route six, it was like I was in another world. It was always a contemplative ride for me; the roadway was lined with the infamous burly pines and plenty of oak trees. I loved the pines because they weren't ultra-tall like where I lived. They were short, and awkward, and full; so "Capey." It was like driving through a well-lit tunnel. It was comforting to me for some reason.

I hit the Orleans traffic circle in no time. The Water's Edge Inn was still there, off the first exit. I remembered one vacation, taking the kids on a mini pirate ship docked near the inn. They had costumes for the kids, including fake moustaches and hats, and they let them pull the buried treasure up from the depths of the pond. They loved it. The rainy days were the toughest when we were on vacation, but we were always surprisingly good at finding things to entertain them.

Thirteen miles later I was entering Eastham. I drove by the Lighthouse Market and the old windmill—more memories, both good and bad. We rented various homes in Eastham when the kids were little because no matter where you stayed you were close to both the ocean and bayside beaches. When I pulled into the cottage driveway, the tall beach grasses were swaying, still bejeweled from the recent rain. I felt a calm come over me. It was like coming home.

As soon as my feet hit the gravel driveway I breathed in deeply. There was nothing like the smell of the Cape after a rainstorm. I could feel the past slipping away, and I let it go without a fight. It was time; time to let go of everything that was dragging me down and find myself again. Where did I go? I was so quick to judge my sister for not taking care of herself. Even after two years of being divorced, and two years in therapy, I had to question: how well did I really know myself?

Chapter Seven
Jack

I've never been a fan of long drives. Those family trips to the Cape as a kid with my parents and brothers probably cured me of ever wanting to drive long distances. It was less about the typical annoying antics four young boys could create in the back of a car, and more about listening to my parents argue that was even more disruptive. Also, we would drive completely out of the way, adding unnecessary miles to the trip, just so my dad could save a few bucks on the tolls, or so I learned in later years. Granted, I knew we weren't wealthy, but I was also ten years old, so I really had no clue. I just wanted to get to the beach and run. Run as far away from my parents as I could get. Run hoping I could escape the constant arguing. Run so I wouldn't be the problem they fought over. I wanted to be happy, we were on vacation for God's sake. If there was ever a time for us to be happy as a family, it was then.

It was raining now. I hated the rain. I needed sunlight. Rain was dreary and sad and made me feel depressed. Julia loved the rain. I never understood that.

The ride was taking me back to a time I didn't want to remember, a time with my family. When I was growing up, I thought we were just like every other family, but sadly, I was wrong. I mean, probably most of the kids on my street were treated the same way as me; you got hit when you did something wrong, and you got accused when you didn't do anything wrong. I was always accused. The mantra back then was, do as you're told, be seen and not heard, and if something goes wrong be ready for a punishment, whether you're at fault or not. I'm not saying I was a perfect kid, but I didn't think I was out of the ordinary. It wasn't until high school that I figured out that some families didn't have a consistent torrent of quarrelling going on in the house. I just accepted it as a young kid because I didn't know any better. Once I knew better, resentment grew in me like cancer. I didn't know how to handle it. I was just so angry with them; angry because they made me feel like I was a burden, a screw up, a problem. Was I the reason they fought so much? I was just a kid, trying to live my kid life. I hated them at times.

Julia could never understand my home life. She couldn't wrap her head around it, but she always tried to be there for me. God knows I didn't know what to do with it, but we tried to work through our childhood shit together, because she had plenty on her side as well, just different from mine. At least we did that; we tried to help each other. My thoughts led me to a memory with Julia, a memory that was both good and bad depending on how you looked at it.

~

"Wanna' sit on the porch?" I asked, one brisk October evening.

"Yah, sure… you want a cup of coffee?" she asked. I nodded.

I sat in the dark on the porch swing, just listening. Any type of rocking motion always seemed to calm me. She was carrying two cups of coffee and a blanket when she returned. She sat next to me and covered us with the blanket. She cuddled into my side, placing her head on my shoulder as I pushed the swing back and forth. There was a slight breeze, but it was a perfectly quiet night otherwise until I heard it; a train whistle sounding off in the distance, over and over. I breathed in deeply.

"You okay," she asked, in response to the deep breath.

I decided I could share my thoughts. It's not like it really upset me—it was actually the opposite. The train whistling was soothing to me. It brought me comfort in a strange way not many people would understand.

I nodded then tried to explain. "When I was a kid, I'd hear the train whistling as it made its way through town and I'd fantasize that it was coming for me… just for me, to take me away to some wonderful place."

Julia lifted her head slightly. "What do you mean take you away? Where did you want to go?"

Now I'd put myself on the hotseat, I had to explain.

"When I was younger, I'd lay in bed at night just waiting to hear the train. I would pretend it was coming to take me away, away from my parents. You know how they are," I said candidly, looking down at her. She knew all too well. "Back then they fought religiously… poor choice of words considering my mother would never step foot in a church. I think she was afraid she'd go up in flames as soon as she crossed the threshold," I said, with a half laugh. "Anyway, I wanted to escape. I wanted to get out of that so-called home, and get away from the constant, relentless turmoil."

"That's not a good memory… that's terrible," she said, placing her hand on mine, and raising her head to look at me.

"You'd think it wouldn't be a good memory, but that whistling comforted me. Maybe it gave me hope or at the very least, a fantasy… a fantasy that I could escape."

"I guess I understand," she said, resting her head back on my shoulder. "I wish you didn't have to feel that way though. I'm glad we don't fight in front of the kids."

"Me too," I said, comforted by her words. But deep down, I still felt like a vulnerable little kid.

~

My parents should never have married, and over the years I've often wondered why they did. The funniest thought both Julia and I entertained was that they had to get married. Not that they were ever forthcoming with their young lives, but I remember my mother mentioning losing a child at one time. It had to be before my oldest brother was born. How ironic if they did have to get married, considering the crap they gave Julia and me for getting pregnant before we were married.

The fighting plagued their entire marriage, which in turn, made it extremely uncomfortable in the house for me and my brothers. Unfortunately, I found out one of the reasons why things may have been so tumultuous between them.

It still haunts me; that day I came home early from school. I was in seventh grade, and I was supposed to be at football practice, but it was raining so we did a mini practice in the gym. I walked in the kitchen and yelled, "Mom, I'm home!"

I don't remember where my brothers were; it was just me. I heard noises coming from my parent's bedroom, and as I peeked around the corner into the dining room, I encountered a man I'd never seen before exiting their room. He looked disheveled and so did my mother as she pushed by him. She explained her way out of the situation, running her hand along her hair to smooth it into place. She said he was the handyman there to look at the sticky bedroom window. My parents knew everyone in town, but this guy was not anyone I knew.

I immediately thought, "No Mom... no way in hell you're telling the truth." I didn't buy it. I may have been an idiot seventh grader, which I was frequently told by my father, but I knew exactly what was going on. I never looked at my mother the same again. It was puzzling to me; why didn't my parents just split up? I knew money was always an issue in their marriage, but I really couldn't say whether my dad knew about her daytime escapades; of course, that was me assuming that it happened more than the one time.

My parents were a bit of a mystery to me. My mother came from a broken home; her father left when she was a baby, and my father's family was poor; they came from upper Vermont. The one thing I did know about them was that neither of them had great childhoods. I never met my mother's father, probably because she hated him so much, plus she was a spiteful woman; all of it seemed to render her incapable of showing affection to any of her children. I'm sure having four boys didn't help either. My dad on the other hand had what I'd call a split personality, meaning he was emotional and loving at times, but then he'd turn on a dime, seething with anger when any of his boys embarrassed him. We were always getting into trouble, especially me. Whether I pissed my mother off by being late for dinner or my grades sucked, I was always on the shit list. My father never minced words with me; I was a jerk, idiot, moron—I could do nothing right. I was a disappointment to them both, but he's the one who verbalized it to me, while my mother would just stand back, arms crossed, and give me a look that said it all.

As the years went by, I came to understand that my dad's embarrassment was fueled by his constant worry about how he looked to others. That worry fostered every cruel word and physical punishment we boys were dealt. By age fifteen, I left the house, emotionally that is. They didn't see what they were doing to the family, to me. I've wondered over the years why they didn't have the wherewithal to make the necessary changes. I guess they were just incapable, but does that mean they get a pass? I don't think, when I was living my life back then, that I really understood how not normal my life was. I knew I was angry, but I thought all kids experienced what I did, and I just needed to get through it, like everybody else. I needed to get over it, move on; stop being a baby. As I look back now, I wish I knew it wasn't a normal childhood. I wish I didn't think witnessing your parents argue, being told what a problem you were, was normal. How can you have hope for something better when you think the way you're living is normal? Hopping a train to escape them seemed logical, but also seemed like a fantasy. Maybe that was my way of being hopeful.

I could see the Sagamore bridge ahead. It distracted me for a moment, but not for long. That's the funny thing about driving alone; no one to talk to but yourself. Nothing to do but let your mind wander, through the good and the bad.

I realized so much later in life, that no matter what I did, and no matter how hard I tried to include them in my life, which is weird that I'd even want them in my life, I couldn't fix my parents' marriage. I tried for years, and I don't know why I bothered. Instead, I concentrated on my own marriage. I swore once I married and had a family, my kids would know they were loved, and they'd never bear witness to a fight. I would make that happen, and I did, they never saw us fight, but that didn't mean everything was perfect; we still fought, we just did it in private. That would be the one thing I should have protected more: me and Julia. But it's a two-way street, and she wasn't always forthcoming, in fact, it was like she didn't want to share things with me. It wasn't just that she was quiet or had no issues because she had plenty, but she just seemed to push me away, write off my compliments as something I had to say because I was her husband. The problem wasn't just me; she couldn't accept herself and that added to our issues as well. I'm willing to admit I had my shit, but she certainly did too. We just couldn't figure our way out. We couldn't figure us out as a couple, so we just stopped trying.

Julia was always so quick to point out that our fights were my fault. I would ask myself repeatedly if that was true, after the fact that is, which doesn't really help anything. When you're in the heat of an argument, thinking clearly isn't at the top of the list, neither is saying you're sorry. My parents never apologized for anything; her parents never apologized for anything. God forbid you own up to being in the wrong as adult, especially to a kid. For us, in the end, it didn't matter who started the fight, who continued the fight, or who ended the fight, because Julia made the decision to leave, and it killed me.

The miles flew by as I was lost in thought. I'd listed on the Cape before, but it'd been years since I'd made the trip down. Justin wasn't wrong; it was out of our bubble to list there, but I was never one to turn a friend away. Whenever I was out with the guys, whether it was in college or for work, there's always those few who were going to drink too much and get into fights. That wasn't me unless I was defending one of those idiots. I'm the guy who sits at the end of the bar and chats with the bartender while keeping an eye on the crew. No one gets left behind on my watch. So, I was going to lend a hand, it's just the way I operated. It's the one good thing I could say about my father; he never turned a needy person away.

I must admit, helping my friends was one thing, but spending some time at the Cape for myself was something I needed. I felt tired, and as of late, my thoughts about the divorce, about my life, were all over the map. Although the Cape was full of memories, it was a wonderful place to relax. Getting away from the city, getting out of my apartment was what I needed. Maybe I felt like I was being challenged to return, to face the past so I could get over it. I needed to take some positive steps forward away from remorse, away from guilt. That fucking word—guilt. Fuck, I always felt guilty about something.

Before I knew it, I was pulling into my first appointment, just after noontime. It was a small Cape style home, but the yard was pretty big and private. I grabbed my bag and walked to the door. I wanted to smell the ocean, to feel that breeze, but I was too far from it. I knocked and a young guy, possibly in his early thirties, answered the door.

"Jackson," he said, extending his hand.

"Call me Jack, Kyle, great to meet you. Your dad explained your circumstances. Sounds like you're more than ready to move on."

"I guess you could say we have officially outgrown this place," he said with a chuckle, as we ventured through the front entry, an obstacle course of coats, shoes, and toys.

"Indeed," I laughed.

As we walked through the house, I could hear the kids playing in the backyard.

"How many do you have?" I asked.

"Three with another on the way."

I couldn't help but laugh. "Jesus, you guys do need a bigger space. Well, no worries, I've got some properties for you to consider and although I'll do the consult with you, I have a realtor close by who can handle the open houses."

Suddenly, a screeching voice bellowed from the yard. "Daaad, Trevor's hogging the swing."

Kyle looked at me with a, 'can't I get a break' look.

"I'm sorry Jack, can you excuse me for a minute, duty calls," he said, then slipped promptly out the back door.

I watched from the window as he took each child's hand in his own and knelt in front of them. He was on their level, smart move. I watched as he tried to reason with them, trying to teach them how to share. Man, that was a long time ago. This guy is young, too young to have so many kids. Funny I would think that. Julia and I had three by the time we were twenty-four. Sometimes I wonder how we did it, how I did it. I think we were fucking crazy. As I stood there watching Kyle, I felt myself slip into another memory.

~

We'd just put Jacob and Jess to bed, and I couldn't wait to get into bed with Julia. Those were the days when a queen-size bed was not only all we could afford, but all we wanted. She liked the size of the bed because it meant we could snuggle more, but I'm a big guy, so a king was in our future. I just needed to find another sales position that would bring more money in. With one income and two kids in tow, I put myself on the hotseat constantly, always trying to climb the proverbial ladder. It was tiring.

"You realize this could happen, right?" she said, looking at me sheepishly with those emerald, green eyes.

"I do," I said, smiling at her. "It's just your damn girl parts… they are very distracting… they leave me incapable of controlling my actions." She laughed giving me a slight shove.

Reality can kill a mood, and there's nothing like putting a damn condom on to suck the romance right out of the room. She'd tried to use a diaphragm in the past, but that was not a comfortable option for her. If I had to be honest, romance really wasn't the vibe I was going for anyway, especially when private moments between the two of us were so rare.

"Remind me again why you're not on the pill?" I joked, leaning on my elbow to face her. "Oh yes, milk production," I said, rolling my eyes. She was still breastfeeding Jess, and she was a stickler for following the rules when it came to the kid's health. I couldn't argue with that, plus her breasts were bigger and that was a plus.

"It's a real thing Jack," she said, with an undertone of 'why the hell can't you understand you idiot.' But then she rolled her eyes and smiled at me.

Jess was only five months old at the time and Julia wanted to breastfeed for as long as she could before Jess decided to take a bite out of her like Jacob did. I had to give her props.

"Baby," I said, placing my hand along her cheek and stroking it gently with my thumb, "I do know, but it's so damn hard to resist you… you and your girl parts."

She leaned into my hand. I watched her eyes close as she melted into my palm, then she gently placed her hand on mine, lifting it from her cheek, kissing my palm tenderly. I took the cue. She wrapped her leg over my hip, and I pulled her close to me, grabbing her ass. We were so close there was barely room for an inhale or an exhale. I ran my fingers through her auburn hair, the waves trickling effortlessly over the pillow. I always loved her hair. There was no turning back now. We wanted more children anyway, so what better time to just have some fun and take the chance.

I never wanted Julia to work; she wanted to be home with the kids, and she was, is, an awesome mother. I must admit I was jealous of her relationships with them when they were young; they always gravitated to mom. I think that's just the way it is. Admittedly, I was more jealous that they took her away from me. We barely had any time together before Jacob came along, and as it was, she was pregnant, so it wasn't the typical newlywed scenario. And when Jess was born, private time went right out the window. It became a much sought after commodity. Eventually I accepted it; I'd lost her to the kids. She could only be spread so thin, and the kids took precedent—I was the one to lose out.

When we found out she was pregnant with Justin, we were both a bit shocked by how easy it was, even though we'd been in a comparable situation with Jacob. Despite her troubles in college with anorexia and not having her period for two years, she didn't have any trouble getting pregnant; it was almost laughable. But it was our laughable life together, until it wasn't.

~

The screen door slammed, jolting me from the memory.

"Kids," Kyle exclaimed, the exhaustion evident in his voice.

"Yah, I remember it well. I have three of my own. But you'll get through it, and before you know it, you'll be walking your daughter down the aisle like I'm about to do. It goes faster than you think."

He smiled at me. "Seems a long way off to me."

I let it go; he'd eventually figure it out for himself. The older you get the faster time seems to pass. Nobody tells you that morsel of truth.

When I returned to my car, I sat for a moment, letting my mind wander over random memories with the kids. Random memories of Julia; good memories, the ones you want to keep close. But as quickly as they came, this intense feeling of regret pushed those memories out of the way. Regret sucks, guilt is even worse, and then there are those thoughts that creep in telling you you're nothing but a disappointment. I've never forgotten those words my father would say to me. Eventually it was Julia's voice I heard reiterating the same disappointment. I felt like I was stuck in a hole, with no way of getting out, and I believed I deserved to be there.

Chapter Eight
Julia

I walked to the back of the car and popped the trunk. As I grabbed my suitcase, I could hear the waves breaking along the shore. I closed the back, dragging the suitcase behind me. I was more than ready to start this vacation. I climbed the short set of stairs to the deck; the view hadn't changed. I just stood there for a few moments soaking in the smells, the sounds, the familiarity. I could see the seagulls flocking to one spot on the beach, most definitely finding some washed-up dead fish that had been picked over multiple times. No one was on the beach. School vacations were over and there was nothing human making a noise. If it were possible to have a perfect moment, this was it. I could allow this to be defined as perfect.

The late afternoon sun was hiding behind a large cauliflower shaped cumulus cloud, until suddenly, the breeze pushed the cloud to the side revealing the sun in all its glory. I felt the heat on my face. I let it take me over, subsequently filling me with nostalgic warmth. The ocean is a one-of-a-kind place, the only place where no matter how you're feeling, one look at the water, one deep inhale of the salty air, one crash of the waves hitting the shore—it seems to take all the concerns, the worries, the drudgery of life away. I took one more deep breath and pulled myself away from the view. I walked to the side door, grabbed the key from under the ceramic frog and opened the door to my past.

It wasn't mine anymore, but it felt like it still was. We didn't buy the cottage until the kids were teenagers, so most of my memories here were of Jack and me. Even the furniture and decorative accents in the cottage were things we'd bought together. I ran my hand along the blue chenille couch; a bit impractical for a beach house, but I had to have it. I also had to have shell lamps which I filled myself with hundreds of shells from various trips to the Gulf of Mexico. Jack was a minimalist, as most men are, he just wanted kayaks and a telescope.

It's odd to go back to a place you once owned and find nothing has changed. When we sold the cottage to Steph and Rob, I had a feeling she wouldn't change much; she's in no way a decorator. She always raved about my sense of style; it was homey and put together in such a way that you felt as comfortable lying on the floor as you were stretched out on the couch. It wasn't a house, it was home, and it still felt that way to me.

I glanced up at the watercolor sitting on the mantel. It's as if it were speaking to me, welcoming me back. I always loved that painting. It made me feel warm every time I looked at it, like an old friend, until the divorce that is. Jack must have given it to Steph. Unfortunately, it was hard to look at it now in the same way. I turned away; I didn't need to cry.

I left my bags by the door and walked into the kitchen. I opened the fridge; just like Steph promised, there were a few bottles of wine, a bottle of prosecco, and a carton of orange juice. In the freezer, three labeled meals ready for defrosting. Obsessive compulsive Steph—she's so good to me. There wasn't much to do now but unpack and relax.

I grabbed my suitcase and walked past the kitchen to the back of the cottage. To the left, there was a small hallway leading to the outdoor shower, and a staircase to the second floor, which was basically an attic space we'd never got around to making into a master suite. In the far back, there were two bedrooms, one to the left and the other to the right with a bathroom separating them. The guest room on the left looked the same except for the quilt. Good for Steph, she actually made a change on her own. I took a moment, imagining Jess snuggled under the covers reading a book before bed. She was a voracious reader, just like her mom. I felt my body warm with the memory, and I couldn't help but smile.

I looked to my right—the master bedroom. I hesitantly walked to the doorway. The duvet cover had also been replaced, but my driftwood art still hung over the bed, and the driftwood night stands I made flanked each side. I would never say I was an artist, but I was artsy, or maybe crafty is a better word. I stared at the bed. Suddenly, I froze in place. Were my eyes playing tricks on me? Well, of course they were, no one was here, but it seemed like there were two people in the bed, so closely knit together they appeared as one. The moans and whimpers sounded familiar. I took a deep breath. Although I tried to fight back the tears, my eyes filled. I quickly brushed them away and tried to let go of the memory as well. Suddenly, I felt like I couldn't move, but then, somehow, I turned myself around and headed back to the guest room. The memory had invaded me, and I needed to escape it. But, once again, I stopped abruptly in the hallway, and froze in place.

"What the hell am I doing here?" I said, standing there, feeling lost and unsure of my next step.

"Jesus Julia, get over yourself," I said, now angry for questioning myself. What I really needed was a good slap across the face to wake me up. I shook my head aggressively instead.

"Yes Julia, be a big girl and get over yourself. The past is the past, and you can't erase it. This is a great cottage for a retreat whether it's filled with memories or not. At least the last one was kind of a good memory."

I turned around and defiantly walked into the master bedroom, throwing my suitcase on the bed. I sat down next to it and looked around the room, taking in every element until I was secure in the idea that I could do this. That memory would not get the best of me.

"I'm staying in this room so help me God," I stated loudly, as if I were chasing some evil spirits away, which I guess I was doing. It was time to confront the past. My therapist thought this was an effective way to do it, so, "I'm doing it Suzanne!" I shouted. She's such a bitch.

I unpacked quickly, throwing my clothes in the drawers. And then, there it was, the pink nightie. I picked it up, lightly touching the sequins again, and then I tossed it onto the chair in the corner. I couldn't help but laugh; why did I bring that piece of my past with me? Wishful thoughts? Wishful thoughts for what? I don't know. Why do we do the things we do; I can't be the only one.

After unpacking, I grabbed a glass of Rosé and headed for the deck. The double lounger was engulfed by the sun, and it was calling my name. I really should be using the umbrella, but I wanted to feel the sun. I guess I wasn't a total pluviophile after all; the Cape was already changing me. I sat down on the lounger, my wine in one hand and a book in the other. I had to have a double lounger so Jack and I could sit there together; I always wanted him close to me. He was comforting and warm and I'd meld into his body with ease. I wish I could fight off some of these memories; were they really doing me any good?

I could hear the surf lapping on the sandy shore and the seagulls squawking as they flew overhead. The breeze was soft but constant. I felt at peace. I opened my book, just a few chapters to go.

An hour later I woke, the book was upside down on the deck, but strangely enough the wine glass was still upright in my left hand. I looked through blurry eyes at the glass, stunned that I hadn't spilled a drop. What can I say, I'm a veteran, I guess. That's probably not something to be proud of.

The sun was actively descending; the sky would soon be brushed in sunset colors. I sat up quickly, realizing I'd almost missed my favorite part of the cottage. I placed my glass on the deck floor and pulled my knees to my chest. The wind had picked up, New England at its best; you never know when things will change. I watched as the sun slowly sank into the ocean. The once blue sky was now a mix of orange and pink. How fast a day can just disappear. I'd let too many days disappear in my life without a second thought, at least that's how I felt. One day at a time; just enjoy a day, a moment at a time Julia. All you have is now.

I sat for as long as I could before the wind chased me inside. I thought about making a fire but decided against it considering how tired I felt. The last thing I needed to do was burn the place down. Instead, I listened to my stomach and headed to the kitchen to defrost some dinner. I opened the freezer, hoping for something delicious to reheat. "Meatloaf! Really Steph?" I was not excited. I grabbed another freezer bag. "Chicken Saltimbocca," now that was more like it.

I grabbed a white plate embellished with sand dollars, unwrapped the chicken and slid it onto the plate and into the microwave. I looked behind me, my empty wine glass stared back at me. The poor pitiful thing, how could I possibly leave it empty? I took pity on it and filled the glass a third of the way. It always pissed Jack off that I liked my wine. "Screw you," I exclaimed to the kitchen, like it was some kind of victory. It's not like he didn't drink, in fact, he drank quite a bit. Like I told Jess, I'm a big girl and a glass or two or three of wine isn't going to kill me, especially right now. Well, my liver might say otherwise, but I was on vacation, and I needed to relax. "A little more won't hurt," I said, pouring more into the glass. The glass seemed pleased.

Suddenly, the microwave bellowed, and I clutched my chest; the adrenaline was pulsing through me. "Get a grip Julia," I said, with an enormous exhale. Just as I went to grab the plate there was a loud knock at the door. I bobbled the plate but got it to the counter in one piece. I think I was sweating in all of a few seconds.

"Jesus Christ," I exclaimed, then quickly added, "sorry God." It was dark now and of course I wasn't expecting anyone. I really wasn't scared, but my heart was racing. I looked around the kitchen and grabbed a knife from the block, holding it by my side as I slowly made my way to the door. I stood at the end of the small foyer, peering through the sidelight. I could see a tall, sturdily built man standing at the door, illuminated by the single deck light. He saw me and waved. He was smiling, which I thought was weird, but when the knife blade caught the light, his friendly wave turned into a frantic 'holy shit' wave, and he quickly backed away from the door.

"Julia, no, no, it's okay. Steph told me to stop by and check on you. I live a few houses down. My name is Sean. Text her, she'll back me up, please!"

He knows my name. I lowered the knife, questioning how this man I'd never met knew my name. I placed the knife on the side table and grabbed my phone.

~

Julia: "I'm at the cottage and a guy's at the door. Sean?"

She texted back immediately.

Steph: "Oh crap, I am so sorry Julia, I thought I told you that Sean would be stopping by to make sure everything is perfect for you. He's offered to keep an eye on things for us when we're not there. He's a great guy, you have nothing to worry about."

I could almost hear the sing-song tone of her voice. She's so sweet but such a ditz.

Julia: "Jesus Steph, he scared the shit out of me. Ok, ok, I'll let him in."

Steph: "So sorry again! He's really nice, I promise, you're gonna' love him."

I ended the call. "Love him?" I repeated. "Who is this guy?" I walked to the door, feeling really weird about what just happened, and unlocked it.

"Hi there Sean," I said, feeling like a complete idiot. "Looks like I'm the crazy one here."

"Hey," he said. "So sorry to scare you. I was under the impression that Steph told you I'd be stopping by… but if you don't mind me saying, Steph operates a bit differently from the rest of us." Now he was making me laugh, he had her pegged. I was already warming up to him.

"So, is everything good here?" he asked.

"Yah, yah everything is fine. She stocked me with the necessities," I said, nodding toward the kitchen.

"I can see that," Sean said with a grin, eying the wine glass on the counter.

"Looks like you have a plan for the evening," he said, winking at me. "Well, I'm just two houses down. If you have any problems just give me a call, here's my card."

I took the card. Langdon Landscapes, Sean Morse, Landscape Architect.

"Thank you, Sean, I appreciate it. Hopefully, nothing unusual comes up. I'm sure I'll be fine, just looking for some quiet time to refocus, if you know what I mean."

"I hear ya," he said, as he walked down the stairs. "By the way, you're not an idiot," he said, turning back to look at me; his smile was infectious.

I smiled and watched him walk down the driveway. Sean must be in his mid-thirties. Nice looking guy with sandy colored hair and blue eyes. I couldn't help but notice, and he was tall too. Is every guy over six feet these days, not that I'm complaining. "Stop kidding yourself Julia, he's way too young for you."

"Hey," he said, turning to face me again, "I've been known to enjoy a refreshing glass of wine too. If you need a drinking buddy, you know where to find me." He flashed another smile at me then walked away.

Did he just hit on me or is that wishful thinking on my part? Two in one day. Either God is trying to tell me something or I am a conceited bitch. I sighed to myself. It's been a while, a long while. Seriously, no one has hit on me since before I got married, that I know of anyway. I smiled as I closed the door, but also felt a sense of panic as well. The thought of opening myself up to another man, or should I say, exposing myself physically to another man was daunting to say the least. I mean, I know I've stayed in shape over the years, but after having three kids—c'mon. Suzanne would not approve right now. I needed to give myself more credit. I've always made the time to exercise, even when the kids were little. I just figured it out, whether it meant loading them into a wagon with books and snacks so I could get a walk in or getting up early before them to go for a run. Staying in shape has always been really important to me.

Dare I say, I'm in better shape now than when I was a teenager. After so many years, it just becomes a habit, I guess. But I would say the combination of being an athlete and suffering from anorexia in college set me up for being a workout fanatic. Once I moved past not eating, I learned that food was not my enemy, and it was more important to keep my body strong than let it wither away just to be thin. Thank God I lived through my problems and came out the other side, stronger and more sensible, but the years it took, Jesus, it was rough. If I'm being honest, it still is.

Legitimately, I now understand I will battle this disease forever, but sometimes it just sneaks up on me and I judge myself harshly. I could look at myself one day and think, "you look awesome Julia," and then something could trigger me and within minutes I'd be tearing myself apart. I have dissected every part of me from every angle; it's exhausting, but I've learned through therapy that it's just something I fall back on when I question my worth. It really sucks because most of the time I don't see the train coming right at me; the train that wants me to destroy myself. Train, that's funny. The train was Jack's salvation, but it's my demise. It's a rough road, one I wish I wasn't on, but it's the road I've unfortunately chosen. I'd rather it was a trail, or an inconspicuous path through the woods that would be hard to find, but it's not, and I'm the one to blame. I pretty much did this to myself.

Besides the kids, writing has really saved me. With two children's books already published, now I'm working on a chapter book, but what I'd really love to write is a novel. Pipe dream? Maybe so. It's more about convincing myself I can do it. How do you go from writing kid's books to that though, not exactly the same genre. Seems absurd, but I'm trying really hard to not think so negatively. Thoughts like that put me in a very recognizable space, and just because it's recognizable doesn't mean it's good. I need to be in a space where I believe the truth instead of believing the lies. I was brought up to believe that Satan is the deliverer of negative thoughts; negative thoughts that would rather you waste away in self-pity or self-deprecation than flourish in possibility. Damn you Satan, I want to flourish.

At least I've got my foot in the publishing door now. I'm trying to think more positively. I can manage the switch, as long as I can just get out of this writing slump. Hopefully, I can relax here and let my mind wander; this trip has already made for some interesting text.

    I grabbed my computer and the wine and set them on the coffee table. I actually have been trying to curb my drinking, but being alone lends itself to drinking more, for me anyway. And then there's Jack. I pride myself on not being vengeful but every time I take a sip, I see Jack's disgusted face, so I take another bigger sip. Why am I letting him into my sanctuary? I need a distraction. I walked over to the bookshelf, running my hands along the range of categories; everything from Huck Finn to Bill Bryson. I've read all these books. But then I came across something different. Rob must have bought this one; Dave Grohl, Storyteller. I took it off the shelf and walked to the couch. I didn't know much about the Foo Fighters, but I loved a good biography.

    I grabbed a blanket and snuggled in. I've got my computer nearby for ideas, my book, my wine, and a cozy retreat; what more could a woman ask for? Shit, I forgot the chicken, and shit I forgot to text Jess. I reluctantly dragged myself off the couch and headed to the side table, retrieving my phone from my bag.

    "Made it safely, love you." She responded immediately, "Be safe Mom, have fun." This is why it's great to have at least one daughter.

    I feel like I got Jess in the divorce, and Jack got the boys. Except for working with Jacob on the books, I don't talk to him much, and Justin works with his dad, so again, I don't talk to him much either. I know they're still my boys, but it's just the way I feel, and it's okay. I completely understand the connection they have with their father. I know they love me, they're just boys who need their dad. Funny, when they were young, they needed me more.

Chapter Nine
Jack

I went straight from Kyle's to the next client, about thirty minutes down the road. By the time I was done, it was around 4 p.m. I was starving. Kind of odd how I ended up down here, the one place where memories were sure to surface. I decided to pull over and grab a lobster roll from one of our favorite restaurants, The Captain's Catch. It wasn't like I couldn't get one back home, but there was something about a Cape Cod lobster roll—I had to have it.

I hadn't been to the Cape in years, but everything appeared to be the same. The same gas stations, the same shops, the same eating establishments with maybe just a few new perks. Back when the kids were little, we'd rent my cousin's place, which was close to the bike path, and about a mile from the ocean. We'd go to the ocean beach on occasion, but the kids preferred the bayside beaches; flatter shoreline with more places to play and explore. When the tide receded, the sand seemed to stretch for miles, leaving treasures behind like horseshoe crabs and shells. Julia would always be shrieking as she gingerly stepped through the shallow waters, always fearful that she'd step on a crab or something sharp hidden beneath the sand. Just thinking of that makes me smile. We did have some really great times.

The restaurant wasn't packed, and it looked as though they'd added more pirates and boats to the mini-golf experience. The kids loved this place. It was an all-inclusive spot: chicken tenders, mini-golf, and ice cream—what more could a kid want?

There was a young family in line in front of me. The kids were small, not school aged yet. They reminded me of us, of the family that once was. We always took our vacation in September because we hated the summer crowds. Actually, that was my issue more than Julia's. Not much had changed inside; multiple registers, fake lobsters and lobster traps adorning the walls, the raw bar located just before the throngs of tables. I grabbed my lobster roll and spied an empty table in the back. Perfect, no one to bother me. I could see the kids sitting at a table now, coloring outlined drawings of sea creatures and again my mind travelled back in time.

It was now my kids sitting at the table. Jacob and Jess were intently coloring, but Justin was looking back at the mini-golf course; I knew he was getting bored. Jacob was an artist through and through; even at six years old he was drawing cartoon figures. Jess was also content coloring, an artist in her own right. But Justin, he was always on the go. Getting him to sit still long enough to eat was a chore. The kid loved to be busy, and playing mini golf was where he wanted to be. Probably why he is the perfect fit for the business—he doesn't stop.

Suddenly, my phone rang, and I glanced at the number hoping it wasn't Angela again. It wasn't, it was worse; it was my mother. Nope, I just shook my head. Nope. I didn't have time for an hour-long conversation. So, I actually did what I needed to do; I ignored the call, saving myself the aggravation of listening to her complain about grocery prices and medical appointments. I unconditionally love my mother, despite what she did and how she treated me as a kid, but it was my dad, that bastard, who I really missed. He died just after the divorce. I think his heart was actually broken. He always said if Julia and I didn't make it, he wanted her in the divorce. I'm sure he was kidding, at least I'd like to think he was, but who was I kidding; she was the daughter he never had.

He and I knocked heads consistently as I got older, arguing about politics, big shot businessmen, and anything else that was remotely contentious. Thankfully, I did realize after he was gone, that despite all the times his worry and frustration got the best of him, and despite our clashes, he was the glue that held our family together. Kind of a shocker for me to think that, considering I literally felt like I was a disappointment to him. It seemed like all he did was worry about what people in town thought of him, so as one of his sons, I didn't want to screw up and jeopardize his reputation, but we all did anyway. Whether we got caught drinking in the woods, smoking pot, or taking the car for a joyride, he was thoroughly disappointed, and he let us all know it, especially me. I felt like I was wearing a target.

If anyone would come home with a bun in the oven before marriage, well that would be me. Word for word, that's what he said. What a soothing supportive loving memory. I'll never forget telling my parents about the baby. Julia sat next to me on the couch when we told them they would be grandparents. I held her hand tightly, certain this would not go over well. It was a different time then, when getting pregnant before you were married was shameful, unlike today. Then you were shaming the entire family. I'll never forget that night and neither will Julia.

After we told them, my father despondently got up from his chair without saying a word and left the room while my mother just sat there muttering, "How could you Jack." I mean, really Mom, after everything you did; she was lucky to have me in her life, never mind a grandchild. Julia and I would retell that story for years, wishing we had been more confident in ourselves to not let them treat us like trash. I remember her saying she wanted to slide under the coffee table to hide.

Her parents weren't exactly jumping for joy either. As Julia reminded me, all their fears for her had come true. Her parents, especially her father, were deeply religious people. In my opinion, a little too religious, but they handled the news far better than my parents did. Time heals all wounds, I guess, or maybe it's just that the wounds turn to scars and are less visible; they hurt less. I thought I'd been moving forward all this time, since those days anyway, but then again, I'm not really sure.

I made the mistake of listening to my mother's voicemail. She hasn't heard from me. She's lonely. The house needs to be painted. The landscapers are doing a horrible job. I'm hoping she called my brothers as well. Why am I the one who has to save her? I couldn't fix their marriage, and I didn't want the pressure of having to fix her life when my dad died. She exhausted me.

I needed a beer. I walked over to the bar and ordered a Sam Adams. I needed to cleanse myself from the voicemail. As I stood at the counter contemplating my youthful indiscretions, I felt a hand on my shoulder.

"It can't be... Jack, Jackson Jones?"

I turned around a bit confused. It took me a minute to recognize this guy I'd gone to college with. What were the odds of us running into one another now?

"Coop," I said, looking him over to be sure I wasn't seeing things. I shook his hand.

"Man, it's been a long time?" he said smiling. "How the hell are you... the family?"

Crap; the family. One of the other guys must have told him I got married and had kids. I didn't want to get into how much life had changed, with the divorce and all, so I brushed it off.

"Good, good, and you?"

"I'm good Jack. Living on the Cape, enjoying life. And you... are you living here as well?"

"Oh, no... I'm still living on the South Shore, working with my youngest son in real estate. I'm just here on business.

"Man, real estate... tricky business these days."

"I guess, but I can't complain, business is surprisingly good. I mean the usual ups and downs with the market, but we seem to ride the wave and come out on top, most of the time," I said, chuckling a bit.

"Good to hear. I knew you had kids…Tom told me, but it's been years now since I last spoke to him. You had three kids, right?"

Tom: figures, the guy could never keep his mouth shut about anything. I'm surprised Coop didn't know I was divorced.

"Yah, all the kids are doing great!" I really didn't want to give this guy my kid's life story. I mean it'd been a long time and honestly, I'm not sure what I really thought of him.

"I envy you man," he said, shaking his head. "I never could pull the trigger. But you know, I'm always lookin'," he said, with a disturbing wink.

That wink said it all. "I bet you're looking," I thought, remembering the player I once knew. Same ole' Coop, a womanizer of extraordinary proportions. Same playboy as the college days no doubt, and not an ounce of guilt to be found.

But regardless of how this guy treated women, I couldn't help but like him back in the day. We spent two years together on the football field. The guys loved him as much as the girls. Nice guy despite his antics. The girls knew what he was all about though; it didn't seem to bother them. I think he even hooked up with one of the secretaries in the central office. Guys loved that he was such a hound. I was probably the only guy not patting him on the back for screwing around. I don't think he cared about anyone he dated; he just was in it for the sex. I mean, a lot of guys were like that, I just wasn't. But I also had a lot of other demons that I was chasing away.

We chatted a bit more, laughed about playing college ball and surviving the party days, and then he got a call. I didn't care what he did for a living, so I didn't ask. I didn't want to keep the conversation going. All I could think was thank God he didn't ask about Julia.

We parted, exchanging numbers, saying we'd stay in touch, which is usually an empty promise. I'm sure he's a decent guy now, but the fact that he never got married could be telltale that he's exactly the same Coop he was in college.

I had two appointments Friday: one at noon in Eastham and then one in Truro that was supposed to be at 2 p.m. but they had to push it out to four. That kind of sucks because it's in the wrong direction for me to exit the Cape easily; it was closer to the inn. I contemplated staying an extra night, but it was the weekend so I wasn't sure that would be possible. When I left the restaurant, the family I'd seen before was on the mini-golf course. It was nice to see.

I drove another thirty minutes further toward Provincetown. The landscape was calming. I spotted the inn from a distance, sitting majestically atop a hill looking out over the ocean. It was appropriately named, The Lookout Inn. It was in the perfect spot, making me wonder how the owners were lucky enough to get this piece of land. I turned onto an extremely narrow one-way street. The tight knit houses dotted the sides of the road on postage stamp size lots. Cramped would be my word for it, while Julia would describe it as quaint. We had some great times at the inn, and she loved Provincetown. We would leave the car at the inn and walk about a mile in total, to the center of town. We'd walk hand in hand until she'd pull her phone out to take photos. I loved that she loved it here.

I pulled into the lower parking lot, grabbed my bags, and walked up the spiraling brick walkway, flanked on each side by stone walls and an endless array of flowers and shrubs. The outside of the inn was meticulously landscaped; it seemed like no matter the time of year, there was always something in bloom. Julia would snap numerous photos of the stunning flower beds, and she was obsessed by the arbitrarily placed stone statues that dotted the landscape. But the photo ops didn't end there. Once inside, I was reminded of the eclectic nature of the inn. As I stood at the front desk waiting to check in, I took a quick look around. The inside of the inn was filled to the brim with antiques, just as I remembered. Old plates and mirrors, framed artwork and photographs, stained glass interior windows and lampshades, vases, stone statues, and wood carvings; they all seemed to have their place, their purpose in the inn. A magnificent field stone fireplace took residence at one end of the living room, while the other end of the room bled into a sitting area with an extraordinary picture window. That room is where we'd share a glass of wine in the afternoon, as we relaxed in the plushy upholstered chairs, each with a view of the ocean. It was quite a unique place.

After checking in, I went straight to my room; I was exhausted. I threw my bags in the corner and collapsed on the bed. I rolled over, lying there with my hands folded across my chest, staring up at the ceiling. It was mesmerizing. It was shaped like an octagon, fully clad in richly stained tongue and groove boards. The ceiling fan was spinning. I wanted to lose myself in it, be devoured by it, forget my life.

The bed was comfortable, actually more comfortable than my own bed, which is the way it should be when you go to an inn. This was Julia's favorite inn on the Cape. She always wanted to stay in a different room every time we visited, because each room had a different theme. This one, though, this one of her favorites; The Queen Victoria. It was a small room, but what it lacked in size, it made up for in charm. It had two girthy hand carved mahogany columns separating the bedroom space from the small bathroom, each displaying intricately carved grape bunches and their leaves, protruding from the vine. There were countless photos of extremely solemn looking women hung without rhyme or reason on every wall, and antiques spilled out of every nook and cranny. There had to be at least five antique lamps lighting every corner. The room was uniquely excessive but homey. I wondered for a moment why I chose to stay here, but who was I kidding—it was all about Julia.

I looked toward the small balcony, overlooking the gardens. By the looks of the sun streaming through the windows, I figured it was near 6 p.m. I turned back and just stared at that magnificent wooden ceiling. I let my thoughts roam. It was so strange to see Coop today. The guy looked good; I couldn't lie. Maybe not getting married and not having kids keeps you youthful. God knows the stress of life alone can swallow a person whole, never mind throwing a wife and kids into the scenario. I didn't really feel bad about not telling him I was divorced, but I felt like I was hiding. I skirted the truth about my failed marriage.

"You're a failure, Jack," I said vehemently, then turned to my side. The women in the photographs just stared back at me, with eerie emotionless expressions. What the fuck? I turned away from their probing eyes, focusing on the ceiling again. "Why do I have to keep going back, delving into my old life with Julia? Was it really all my fault? How could it be all my fault?" I was letting myself get sucked into the negative. "I screwed up... I screwed up my marriage, my family, and now I'm lying on this bed that we once shared, and I can't fucking think straight." I rolled back to my side, but I closed my eyes; I couldn't take their judgmental looks.

My mind wandered. Towards the end of our marriage, Julia and I spent most of our time quietly avoiding one another; fights do that. During the fight, we'd both yell, but she definitely yelled more, and yelled louder, and the louder she yelled the more I shut down. I had my way of dealing with her; my plan was to wear her down by not talking and I think her plan was to go over and over and over the same points until she was satisfied that I was a beaten dog. But her yelling at me, man that just took me back to the house I grew up in. She knew it too, but she just couldn't control her frustration with me, so she'd yell at me until, like a turtle, I'd retreat way back into my shell, which infuriated her even more. Eventually, we'd hit the point in the fight where she couldn't take it anymore, and she'd leave the room. We wouldn't talk for hours or even days. Sometimes an entire week would go by. The only thing good about that was there was no yelling during that week.

I think we were fairly even on the apology front; sometimes it was me, sometimes it was her breaking the icy barrier that kept us apart. When we were both willing to talk things out rationally, we came back together like nothing ever happened, and the same passion we felt when we were fighting was now evident in our love making. We were all or nothing. And so it went, on and on until the day came when she stopped. She stopped fighting, she stopped talking, she stopped waiting for an apology, she stopped giving an apology. She just stopped.

Now my mind was racing. How did I go from the ceiling, to Coop, to blaming myself, to fighting with Julia? My mind was engulfed with negative thoughts. I started muttering under my breath.

"You never respected me... you always had to be right, and you always gave everyone else the benefit of the doubt. Therapy, you always kept pushing therapy. If it's so fucking easy, you get therapy Julia." When I'd push back on her, she'd say she'd already let go of her demons, but it certainly didn't seem that way to me. She still had so much shit with her father, her whole family for that matter, there was no way she'd gotten over any of it.

"Push, push, push, that's all you did Julia. I have dealt with my upbringing too; I don't need therapy." I couldn't stop muttering. I didn't want to stop. It felt good to tell my truth with no one to tell me I was wrong. I quieted for a moment.

"Julia, you always needed attention from other men," I said, closing my eyes. I hated it when I caught guys checking her out. I wanted to put them through the wall. I wanted to blame her too, but I had to admit, she was a natural beauty, and that certainly wasn't her fault. I was the one who couldn't deal with the remotest glance from another guy. She probably wasn't even flirting, I just felt like she had to be. She had to be looking for attention. Maybe she was, I don't know. It wasn't fair, especially considering her issues with her body, but she'd brush me off so quickly when I'd make the remark, "guys are pigs," or if I gave her a compliment. It was like she really didn't care how I felt. I felt disrespected, put off. I always felt like she'd rather spend time with other people than with me.

I took a deep breath, still staring at the ceiling. "I tried Julia," I said, as if she were in the room with me. "I tried not to be jealous, but Jesus, I'm only human, and you were mine."

Chapter Ten
Julia

There was a faint knocking sound in my dream. It continued until I realized I wasn't dreaming. I opened my eyes and immediately covered them with my hands. The sun was on fire, streaming in through the sliding glass doors like a thousand knives in my eyes. "Jesus, why didn't I close the damn blinds!"

I didn't even realize I'd fallen asleep on the couch, something I was known to do when I was reading. I rubbed my eyes incessantly, then suddenly realized someone was actually outside knocking on the door. I threw the blanket off and sat up quickly. It took me a minute to process what was happening, then I stood, and clumsily made my way to the door. Peering through the sidelight, I saw it was Sean.

"Good morning," I said, my voice raspy and hoarse.

"Did I wake you?" Sean asked apologetically.

"What time is it?" I said, yawning and stretching.

"It's nine. I guess you found a way to relax last night," he said with a smirk.

"Oh my God… nine, really? I fell asleep reading on the couch. I can't believe I slept that long. Come in, please. How does a mimosa sound?" Look at me, offering up the liquor right away.

"Sounds delicious," he said, walking past me to the kitchen. He was carrying a brown bag and seemed to know exactly where he was going.

Suddenly, aware that I'd just woken up, I glanced in the hall mirror, but there was no fixing anything now. I looked like I just woke up, I mean, I literally looked like I just woke up. Jesus! I watched him grab the prosecco and orange juice from the fridge, and then he removed two glasses from the cabinet.

"You sure know your way around here don't you," I said teasingly. "You keep working on that and I'll be right back," I said, dashing to the bathroom.

"You look like shit Julia," I said, staring into the bathroom mirror, poking at my face, "and you let him in... what's wrong with you?" But as quickly as the words came out, I threw them in the trash. Why did I care? A guy like Sean would never be interested in someone my age and I didn't need the aggravation of whatever this was. I had to be at least ten years older than him. Still, I brushed my teeth, washed my face, then threw on just a touch of makeup. I stood back hoping I'd made some small improvement.

"Just go in there and enjoy you idiot," I grumbled into the mirror. Then, as if I needed more scolding, I shook my finger at myself and whispered, "Suzanne would be very unhappy with your negative self-talk." Then I stuck my tongue out like a child because not only is it fun to do, but it centers me.

"You clean up nice," Sean said, using that sexy wink on me again.

I probably blushed, unfortunately. I was so out of the game.

He grabbed two plates and some napkins and took two croissants from the paper bag.

"Well, that looks delicious," I blurted out, taking a seat at the counter.

I felt slightly awkward hosting this guy I barely knew in my vacation cottage, but I also felt like I'd known him for years.

"How long have you lived here?" I asked, trying to break the awkward silence that I felt.

"About five years," he said. "My parents actually own the cottage. I've just been watching over the place for them. It's hard for me to commit to buying something on my own. I mean I can, I have a great job, but why do that when you can live somewhere for free," he said, with a smile so mischievous it was contagious.

I couldn't help but smile back. "Sounds like you've got it figured out. I see from your card that you are a landscape architect. That sounds really cool."

"Yah, I mean I do love it. It pays well. But if I had to pick another job, it would be painting."

"Like house painting?" I questioned, raising my eyebrows.

"God no," he said laughing. "Painting as in art, watercolors being my favorite medium. I have always loved it, but architecture spoke to me saying, you need to support yourself Sean, and you can't do that by being an artist if you want to eat... but maybe I'm just channeling my parents right now."

"I might have to disagree with you," I said, considering what I knew about the art world. "My son is an artist, and he seems to be holding his own." Suddenly, I heard myself. God Julia, why did you say that; now he not only knows your old, talking about your adult son, but you just insulted him. You better talk your way out of this right now. Putting my foot in my mouth was always a problem with Jack.

"But I hear you… my son has to work a couple of jobs to make ends meet, but I just love that he's living his dream."

"You can't possibly have a grown son Julia," he said doubtfully, as he popped the prosecco.

"What can I say, I was young when I had him," I said, resting my chin on my hand.

"Well, you look amazing. No one would know you're a mom. So, tell me, what does he do specifically?"

"Actually, he works as a videographer, but he does side jobs as an illustrator."

"Wow… very cool. And you, what's your passion?" he asked, genuinely interested in my passions, not my work, and not my age.

"I write children's books, well, two so far. Actually, my son illustrated both of them. I guess it comes in handy knowing an artist."

"That's awesome, getting to work with your son. You both are obviously incredibly talented. You should come by the cottage while you're here and check out my work. Maybe we could work together on a book, I mean, if you like what you see. No pressure," he said, waving his hand.

"Sean… I would love to see your work," I said, genuinely interested.

He handed me a mimosa and said, "Cheers to the artists of the world, the ones who have made it and the ones who are still trying."

We clinked glasses; I couldn't help but feel comfortable.

I hadn't talked with a man about, quote unquote nothing in so long. Jack and I were always talking about the kids, extended family, our issues with one another. It was nice to sit across from a guy who didn't know anything about me, but genuinely wanted to know me. As he talked about his parents and siblings, spending entire summers on the Cape, he sounded happy, fortunate. He seemed to have a good relationship with his parents despite their lack of support with his artistic desires, which I guess isn't that farfetched considering I'd like to think Jack and I have great relationships with our kids, and Jack had trouble with Jacob pursing his dreams. But I know what that was all about; he was afraid he'd have to support Jacob down the road. Overall, I think he was worried he never be free of having to support all of us.

As Sean spoke, I tried to remember his family. His parents must be about fifteen years older than Jack and me. I faintly recalled speaking to them once or twice; they seemed like a nice couple. Since we were only here on the weekends, I guess it's not unusual that our paths didn't cross much.

"I think I remember your parents. Your mom was always tending the gardens and your dad was a carpenter, right?"

Sean laughed. "They're the best," he said proudly. "My mom is like a warrior when it comes to outdoor work. Maybe that's why I like landscaping so much. And my dad, well he actually had a lengthy career in tech, something I wasn't interested in at all, but you're right, he was a master craftsman as well. We all need something to take our minds of the mundane work world I guess."

I shook my head in agreement. We spent the next hour drinking, eating chocolate croissants, and laughing. I felt like we were really connecting. I wasn't even bothered by the fact that I was eating one of my forbidden foods.

"This has been so much fun Julia, I've really enjoyed our conversation," he said, with such authenticity it surprised me.

"I agree. It's been great getting to know you, Sean. I feel like I've known you forever."

Sean gave me an 'I agree' kind of look while he cleared the dishes.

"Well, as much fun as this has been Julia, I do have an appointment later this morning and some work this afternoon at my mundane day job," he said, air quoting mundane. "The truth is, I really enjoy my day job, thank God."

"Work isn't really worth our efforts if we don't find joy in it, you know what I mean?" I offered that tidbit of wisdom in such a motherly way I had to scold myself. "Stop acting like a mom," I thought.

"I agree," he said, then turned to face me. "I know I painted my parents out to not be supportive of my passion for painting, but that's not really true. They think a lot like you; they wanted me and my siblings to find careers that made us happy. I always loved landscaping and with my ability to draw they just thought it was a perfect fit, and they were right. I would love to have more time to paint though… that would be a dream come true. You know, being able to sell something like that watercolor over the mantel," he said, giving a nod to the painting, "give someone something special that can evoke emotion."

I was blown away by his honesty. It was so real, so spot on. I loved it.

"I agree, that's why I write," I said. "I just want to pull at the reader's heart strings. Sometimes, I think if I don't make my readers cry, I haven't done my job."

Sean looked at me, shaking his head in total agreement.

"Can I read your work sometime Julia? I mean, I haven't read a children's book since I was a kid, but I'd love to read what you've written," he said, with such sincerity, I just couldn't say no.

"I'd love that," I said appreciatively.

And from there the conversation took a turn I wasn't expecting. He placed his hands on the counter and looked me square in the eyes.

"Are you busy tonight? Maybe we could share more stories over dinner?"

A date: am I being asked out on a date? This is crazy. I haven't dated since, well, since I was in my twenties. Am I ready for this? I have to admit, I've really enjoyed talking with Sean, and I do like the possibility of the unknown for some strange reason, whether I'd already decided he's too young for me or not. I felt myself giving in, nodding in agreement.

"Glenn's in Wellfleet, around six?"

"Glenn's... I know the place well," I responded. Another reality check, another painful memory spot to help me move on. "Sounds like fun," I said casually, but knowing deep down I was feeling uncomfortable with being so nonchalant about a date.

"Do you mind meeting me there? I'll be coming from Truro... so logistics."

"Absolutely," I responded, a little too exuberant.

"Awesome," he said, then turned and placed the glasses and plates in the sink and the bag in the trash. Wow, I thought, a guy who cleans up after himself. For all the years I was married to Jack, there were always crumbs and dishes left for me to clean up. Is this guy a dream come true? Could he be 'that someone'? I was about to find out.

Chapter Eleven
Jack

Why does the bed feel so fucking good? It's like I've become one with the mattress. I don't want to move. I know what's ahead of me. The truth is no one wants to get out of a warm bed to exercise. "God this bed is so damn comfortable."

I rolled over and grabbed my phone from the nightstand—9 a.m. I looked over at the wall; the solemn women stared back at me. I sighed and rolled the other way; they were there as well. I couldn't escape the judgment. Why did Julia love this room so much? I rolled on my back and stared up at the ceiling. The beautiful ceiling. The fan lulled me back to sleep. I dipped in and out of sleep for another hour and a half.

I'm holding Julia in my arms; it feels good, it feels right. I relish the feeling, and then I open my eyes—it's the damn pillow. I threw it on the floor, disgusted that I couldn't even get away from her in my sleep. It's 10:30 a.m. now and I have to get up. I rubbed my hand over my face, already feeling guilty that I was too lazy to drag my ass out of bed to exercise. I felt for Julia in that moment; this must be how she feels every day. This is why she does what she does, so she doesn't have to feel guilty.

"I'd be late anyway," I mumbled, trying to convince myself that skipping one day wouldn't kill me.

It took me years to get back in shape. During our marriage, Julia was always the one to stay in shape. It seemed that with every pregnancy, we'd gain the same amount of weight, but she'd drop it all within a month of delivery, while mine just sat there, creating extra unneeded cushioning around my waist. I could never lose it, and the stress from work just pushed me over the edge. I hated the way I looked, the way I gave into the job; I let it all get away from me. It's probably the one thing that was good about the divorce—I got back in shape.

I threw the covers off and sat up quickly. "Now or never," I said, willing myself to get up. Just as I was on my way to the bathroom, I got a text from Justin.

~

Justin: "Some calls came in, a couple more properties down on the Cape; the names are Donovan and Nichols. Word must be out that you're down there. At least your friends are loyal to you. Figured you could add them to the list. One Saturday and one Sunday. Guess that means you get to extend your vacation… lucky you."

Jack: "Send me the specs, I'll take care of it. And by the way, I'm still working ya know."

Justin: "I know, jk. Take some time Dad. Not a bad place for an impromptu getaway."

Jack: "True. Catch up later."

~

Shit, I never inquired about extending my stay at the inn. With two appointments today, one Saturday and one Sunday, I'd obviously need to stay somewhere, and I only had the inn booked for one night.

I walked into the bathroom and placed my hands on the sink, leaning in to take a good look at the man in the mirror. My beard needed a trim, my chest hair was as prominent as ever and starting to gray. I flexed for old times' sake; my pectoral muscles flaring a bit. "I still got it," I said to the naked man staring back at me.

I always slept in the nude and finally convinced Julia to do the same. It was the best part of going to bed at night, whether we had sex, or she just cuddled into me. I struggled every night to keep my hands off her; her body was so soft and yet so firm. She worked out five days a week and when she'd lay on her side, her curves were evident. I loved running my hand along her side, gently caressing my way down until her ass was firmly in my grip. It was all I could do to shut myself down. I knew she loved it too. She'd tell me I made her feel so sexy, even though she had a tough time believing it herself. It boggled my mind—how couldn't she see what I saw?

I jumped into the shower. As the warm water washed over me, I had an epiphany, no more thoughts about Julia or the divorce. The only memories I'd let in were the ones of the kids. Entertaining any good thoughts about our marriage would just derail any of the work I'd done to get over her. It'd been two years for Christ's sake. "Get over her Jack," I said, "let her go."

I wandered down to the inn's dining room to see if there was anything left of the complimentary breakfast, but first I checked in with the desk clerk.

"Checking out today Mr. Jones," the clerk asked, before I could say a word.

"Hopefully not. I was wondering if you have any vacancies for the next couple of days, I need to extend my trip."

"Let me check," he said, focusing intently on the computer screen. "We are booked solid for the weekend, but we have a room that will be vacant come Monday."

"That's too bad, but thanks for checking. I'll just try to find another inn. So, I guess I will be checking out today, but would it be okay if I grab my things later, like around one? I have an appointment to get to and I don't have time to pack up."

"Yes, that's fine Mr. Jones. Again, so sorry for the inconvenience."

Sucks that didn't work out. Now I truly need to find a place to stay. I walked to the dining room; it was empty. I spied a few scones and some bananas on a tray in the corner. I grabbed one of each and a cup of decaf to go, plus a couple bottles of water. Julia was the coffee drinker, and as I recall, the stronger the better. Damn it! Can I not have her invade my thoughts just once. Even coffee triggers me to think about her.

I exited the inn, glancing at the wicker tables and chairs set up on the covered porch. Julia loved to eat breakfast there, looking out over the lush gardens, the ocean just steps away. This was our spot, which made me wonder, why the hell did I stay here now, and in the room she loved. Was I trying to derail myself? How could I forget her when she was everywhere?

I walked to my car, fumbling with my phone while trying to carry my bag, food, and drinks—not a smart move. I threw the bag into the passenger seat and managed to slide into the car without incident, or so I thought. The coffee had other ideas.

"Jesus Christ," I exclaimed, "that just figures." I put the cup down in the holder and hurriedly found a napkin in the center console, dampening it with water and patting the stain on my shirt. "You're an idiot Jack!" I blurted out. Just what I didn't need—to show up to an appointment looking like I couldn't afford a decent shirt. Julia always laughed when I'd spill things. "That's why my grandmother always had a napkin tucked into her shirt," she would laugh. I wasn't laughing though. Being compared to her overweight grandmother was too much for me.

I glanced quickly at the specs for my first stop; the address sounded familiar.

"Christ, that's near the cottage," I exclaimed, and then I swallowed, hard.

Chapter Twelve
Julia

"What the hell am I going to wear?" I said, rummaging through the dresser drawers. I'd packed very casual clothing. I pulled out a pair of tight jeans and a T-shirt. "God no," I said, throwing them on the bed. Three more tops and two sundresses later, the bed was starting to look like a war zone. I stood back and stared. My "typical clothing trauma" was on display. "Jesus, I can't wear any of this to dinner, especially a dinner at Glenn's, especially a dinner at Glenn's with a man ten years younger than me." I stared at the pitiful array of clothes and my mind traveled back in time.

Jack had to be annoyed with me during one of my clothing traumas, even though he didn't say much. I was always late, and we both knew it would happen every time we went out. Why did I have to feel so insecure choosing an outfit? I treated it like I was going to the Grammys—way too much pressure. When it was getting near time to leave, I could hear him walking up the stairs while I was still in the bathroom. I knew once he took one look at the bed littered with unsuitable clothing options, he probably mumbled something under his breath, and left shaking his head. At least he never said a word to me about it, even though I'd make him wait another twenty minutes. I knew I was being ridiculous, but if he only knew how brutal it was for me. Just the wrong top or the wrong bottom made me feel terrible. It was an all or nothing with me; either I felt good about myself, or I was picking myself apart. That part he knew.

"That's it... I've had enough. I'm outta' here," I said, looking at the bed with disgust. "Cope," I said calmly, "just breathe Julia." I took a few breaths, trying to let go of my insecurities. I knew what this was, and I knew what I needed to do. I needed to remove myself from the trauma.

I didn't hesitate; I changed into my running gear. The best thing for me to do was not only leave the cottage but release the toxins. I needed to go for a run and clear my head; I needed to sweat. I was determined to not let my clothing trauma take me over. "I'll just go shopping later and find something," I said positively. "Maybe the boutique Jess and I used to go to is still in business." I loved to go shopping, but I only loved it if I could buy something. I wasn't a window shopper; what's the fun in that? The only thing that could make a shopping trip better was if Jess were here to go with me. I missed her already and I'd only been gone for a day.

I sat down on the bench by the side door and slipped my running sneakers on. Both Jen and I ran track in high school and college. Our parents were in no way athletic, so the fact that two of their kids were competitive athletes was a shock. The only reason I gave it up after my sophomore year was because I wanted to punish my father; I learned that horrible truth in therapy. It was the one thing I could take from him, the one thing he took pride in that I did. It was the one thing he could tell others about me, but it was really all about him. 'His' daughter, the track star.

I thought for years that his constant pressure to achieve was the sole reason for me becoming anorexic. Of course, after going to therapy I knew blaming him entirely was not right; I made choices on my own as well. I realized it was just how I coped with being the first of four kids to do well in school, to go away to college, and the first to have my parents almost completely forget about me while I was at school. At least that's how I felt.

It was a lot. My low self-esteem reigned supreme despite my abilities or achievements. My father's constant pressure to do more, to reach higher, to be better, spoken of in the most positive of ways of course, was too much to bear. How does a young woman who has already experienced society's warped view of the perfect woman deal with her own self-esteem issues? Well, she tries to control something, and for me, it was my weight. I thought I was in control. I thought I was sending a clear message to my father; "You can't tell me to be more, anymore!" The problem with that mentality was that while I thought I was taking control, I was literally being eaten alive by the disease.

As I laced up my sneakers my thoughts wandered to high school days when it seemed I could do no wrong in my parents' eyes. Of course, they never knew about the fake sleepovers at friends' houses just so we could camp out in the woods, drink, smoke pot, and spend the night with our boyfriends. Parents always think they know everything, but even I had to admit, Jacob, Jess, and Justin all had secrets, they all got away with things that Jack and I never knew about, and honestly, I could care less to know now. We're all kids at some point, and for many of us, we engage in activities that might just land us in jail or worse.

Jack and I weren't extremely strict parents. We doled out a few groundings, but really, we just talked to the kids. He was always grounded growing up. As I recall, his buddy Joe was laughably grounded for life. I, on the other hand, never received a single punishment. I guess we met in the middle when it was our turn to be parents. It was hard for him to be patient, hard for him to wait for the whole story before making assumptions, which is funny because that's what his parents did to him, and he hated it. He really didn't want to be like them. Sometimes I think things get so ingrained in us that it's hard to see straight sometimes.

I personally don't think it does a kid any good to rake them over the coals for doing exactly what you did as a kid. You can still teach, guide, love without being a dick. I guess we are all doomed to repeat the past.

I stood up and looked in the mirror. "You're still there," I said, disgusted by my need to constantly check myself out. I stuck my tongue out then turned toward the door when something shiny caught my eye—it was the knife. The knife I'd grabbed in panic when Sean knocked on the door last night. What a crazy bitch; this wasn't Boston for God's sake. I had little to worry about on the Cape. "I'll take care of you when I get back," I said, as if the knife could hear me. I had to laugh at the insanity of my actions.

I walked out the door, locking it behind me. I did a few warm-up lunges and stretches in the driveway, then walked down the grass lined path to the beach. The bayside beach was the ideal place to run. At low tide it was flat and hard. I grabbed my phone to listen to my favorite podcast, took a deep breath and went to work. I never needed to go to a gym to be motivated to work out. I could listen to sports radio, a country ballad, or even watch a freakin' Hallmark movie while I ran on the treadmill and still get my workout done with intensity.

Running gave me just what I needed, a complete workout in a short amount of time. Plus, I loved the runners high. As I ran, I glanced at the homes and cottages lining the beach. I never thought I'd own a home here. Since I was a child, and Jack too, we camped with our families on the Cape. I have such great memories from those days. It was the one vacation my father was present. Most of the time work kept him out late, and when he was around, it was hard to garner his attention. But when we were on vacation, he was there for us. As I ran, I noticed a young family setting up on the beach. They had four kids, appearing to be five and under. At least we stopped at three. I'm not sure I could have handled more than that. I was exhausted after having Justin; between being induced and actually giving birth, I couldn't conceive of having any more children. Originally, we thought we'd have four, but in the end, three was exactly right for us.

Those days were great, but I was happy to not be the mother of infants and toddlers anymore. I figured I'd get to relive those days eventually, on the other side, meaning as a grandmother. I couldn't wait to indulge those babies, then hand them back at the end of the day, fully satiated with youth, at least that's what they say will happen. "No rush guys; I'm not quite ready yet," I said, through belabored breathing.

Running seemed to stimulate my thoughts rather than dissipate them. It probably would have been easier for Jack and me if we divorced earlier. Fighting is awful. These days it seems like a great plan to divorce when you have younger kids. It seems like you are rewarded with extra time for yourself to do what you want while the ex takes the kids. Funny system we live in. "Someone finally figured that out," I mumbled. In today's world, being selfish seems to be the norm.

But let's face it, that would never be what I wanted. I tried to shake the thought from my mind. I was happy to be a stay-at-home mom, thrilled actually. I wasn't like other mothers who couldn't wait for school to start; I enjoyed the time with my kids. I recalled a commercial that persuaded parents that the most wonderful time of the year was when the kids went back to school. It was the opposite for me. I loved being with the kids, any time of the year. I didn't have them to pawn them off; they were my responsibility, they were my job, they were my identity, they were my joy, and I didn't need anyone else to help me raise them.

With each stride, my thoughts swirled around my own childhood vacations. My mom was a pro-packer, and it was her job to load the pop-up-trailer with bedding, clothing, food etc. The five-seat orange Ford Bronco had just enough space in the far back for the dog, my three siblings in the back seat, and me sitting up front on a plastic stool with a pillow on top, situated between the front bucket seats. Best seat in the house. Seat belts were not enforced then, which is why my make-shift seat worked so well. With the bicycles tied down to the roof, we made the trek to what seemed like the end of the world—Provincetown, Cape Cod. Back then, I thought the Cape was for vacationers only; I had no idea people actually lived there year-round.

All our time was basically spent at the beach, but I remembered riding the bike trails as well. With no gears on my green Schwinn bicycle, I'd have to spin those pedals like an Olympian just to make it up the hills, but it was worth it. When we weren't riding bikes or wandering through the streets of Provincetown, we were on the beach. My father was an adrenaline junkie, which means the Bronco was ready for "duning." We'd drive right onto the beach and scope out the ideal spot to spend the day. We'd body surf, play frisbee, and lie in the sun until night fall, when we'd cook our dinner over the charcoal fire. Those were the days: no responsibilities, no fears, just the family together, having fun. Keeping my brother from teasing me was just about the only issue I had. I felt myself smiling as the memories flooded in.

It was around 11 a.m. by the time I returned to the cottage. I grabbed a towel and walked down the hall that led to the outdoor shower. I tugged on the door. It was demonic; it seemed like it was pulling against me, as much as I was pulling to open it. It was still a pain in the ass to open; that hadn't changed either. I needed to breathe after that battle. I lingered in the shower for about ten minutes, just looking up at the beautiful sky. I loved the outdoor shower, communing with nature and all, but time was flying by, and I needed to get on the road. I quickly dried off, threw on a pair of shorts and a black artsy T-shirt with a mermaid on the front, wound my wet hair into a loose bun and headed out.

"I think I'll treat myself to lunch today… I deserve it, and hopefully a new dress," I said, as I slipped into the Explorer. Once I hit the ignition, "Everything" was playing on the radio again. I turned the volume up. What are the odds of that?

I checked my mirrors, lingering in the rearview. I smiled, like I was testing my own reaction. This time I didn't reprimand myself for being conceited, but I unfortunately noticed the lines around my eyes; those fucking lines staring back at me. Defeated again. "Okay, enough of that," I said, hearing my grandmother's voice echoing in my head. She complained about her wrinkles 'til the day she died at ninety-nine-years young. I was turning into her, and I needed to stop. "Stop it Julia," I said, looking in the mirror.

It was like I was constantly fighting a demon that would pop up out of nowhere, and I knew I had to talk myself through every 'bout of self-doubt. "It's enough Julia, it's enough," I said, my voice low and contemplative, and then I wondered, "when will it truly be enough?"

Chapter Thirteen
Jack

I hadn't been to the cottage in years. Part of me was excited to see it but there was an even bigger part that wasn't. I remembered the name associated with the new listing; they lived a few houses down from our old cottage. I couldn't get out of this now; my hands were tied.

Once I was within a few miles of the appointment, I felt, what I deemed to be, a panic attack coming on. I needed a second. I pulled over and took a minute to compose myself.

"Come on man, get ahold of yourself," I said, staring at the road.

My hands gripped the steering wheel like I was holding on for dear life. I lowered my head to the wheel.

"You can do this Jack, it's just a building."

I took a few deep breaths, checked my mirrors, then pulled back onto the road. Three minutes later I turned off the main road onto Gull Street. Every turn was all too familiar. I passed the Lighthouse Market; the kids loved to stop there for penny candy, which was a penny when I was a kid, but with inflation it's more like quarter candy now. Jess loved the sweet tarts, Justin the gummies, and Jacob was all about the licorice, like his old man. Julia always wanted to get fudge, even though she barely ate any, which meant I ate most of it. No wonder I could never lose weight.

The old windmill still stood tall across the street from the market in the square. We spent many Saturday mornings in the square; Julia loved the art festivals they held there. As I drove by, I couldn't fight the onslaught of memories.

~

"I've always wanted to buy a painting from here," Julia remarked, as we strolled through the aisles of white vendor tents.

I remember glancing down at her; it wasn't the first time she'd said that. We'd never been extravagant gift givers, as most of our money went into the kids and the house. This was my chance to show her how much I loved her. It was time to end the wanting.

"Let's do it then," I said without hesitation. She looked up at me, questioning the comment.

"I don't know… they're so expensive," she said pensively, as we walked by tent after tent.

I stopped her, knowing she needed a push. "We can afford a painting Julia. We spend money on some ridiculous shit sometimes. Let's make a purchase, something just for us, something that will last."

Julia grabbed my hand and smiled. We didn't hold hands as often anymore—it was kind of hard when the kids were vying for the same hand I wanted to hold. It felt good, reminiscent of the days when we were young and kid less, when we were just us.

The kids ran ahead to the playground. "Stay where we can see you!" Julia yelled after them, then she looked at me and smiled. We walked hand in hand, glancing into each tent as we strolled down the grass path. Finally, Julia pulled me toward an artist's tent she'd always admired. This was the place we'd find our painting.

"What about this one," I said, pointing to a watercolor of the beach, a boat off in the distance.

"It's nice," she said, trying to be kind. In other words, not that one Jack.

"Okay," I said, taking the subtle hint. She needed to pick the one she absolutely loved.

We decided to divide and conquer at this point. I watched her from a distance, painstakingly looking at each painting. Julia had a crippling fear of making a mistake, which meant making any decision was problematic. I could see this was becoming more of an issue. As we reached the back of the tent, I spied a watercolor detailing tall wispy beach grasses and beach plum shrubs flanking either side of a wooden pathway, the ocean off in the distance.

"What do you think?" We both said at the same time, then looked at each other and laughed.

"It's beautiful," she said, "but don't you think it's a bit much for us? I mean, a thousand dollars is a lot of money."

"Julia, we never splurge, let's just do it. Do you love it?" I asked, gently pushing her hair over her shoulder.

Julia smiled at me then wrapped her arms around my waist. "I love you," she said, "and not because you're buying me a painting, but because you're so willing to do it just to make me happy." Without hesitation I pulled her to me and kissed the top of her head. When we bought the cottage, years later, we hung the painting over the mantel.

~

"It was for us Julia, for you and me," I whispered, as if she were sitting in the seat next to me.

I shook my head to clear the memory, but I couldn't help but wonder if the painting was still in the cottage, still hanging over the mantel.

I drove to the end of Gull Street taking the last right onto aptly named Beach Plum Road. And there it was, the first cottage on the left. Rob and Steph hadn't changed a thing on the outside; the graying cedar shakes and royal blue door were still there. It was eerie how nothing had changed. I pulled over and just stared at it.

They kept the same name as well, "Summer Breeze," Julia's favorite Seals and Crofts song.

It had been years since I'd been here. More memories flooded in. Most of the time it was just the two of us here, grabbing free weekends when we could. We bought the cottage when the kids were teenagers. It was fun when they still wanted to come, but as time went by, the boys were not up for spending time with mom and dad anymore. Jess, on the other hand, was always up for a trip to the Cape. She was no dummy; we spoiled her rotten.

I took a deep breath. "I can't believe how little it's changed and how much life has changed," I said, the sadness creeping in. My emotions were taking over, a mix of sorrow and regret.

The noon appointment was just a few cottages down on the left. I remembered the owners; they walked early every morning, and again just after dinner. I recalled they had at least two kids, but they were much older than ours. It's ironic that Kyle's father knew the owners, and just a few doors down from the old cottage. I pulled into the gravel driveway and standing outside on the deck was a man who looked to be in his mid-thirties, about six feet, with dirty blond hair. He reminded me of Jacob, minus the beard. How Jacob ended up with blond hair I'll never know. He was on the phone, but turned toward the driveway and waved when he saw me pull in. He quickly ended the call and approached my car.

"Hey there, nice view you've got here," I said, as I emerged from my car.

"I guess I need to enjoy it while I still can," the man said with a chuckle.

I grabbed my bag and walked toward him. "Great to meet you Sean," I said, extending my hand. "I remember your parents. I owned a cottage a few doors down at one time. Nice couple."

"Well, thanks. Good to meet you as well. Yah, they're awesome. I wish they weren't selling, but Florida beckons, and they'd like to buy down there so something's got to give, if you know what I mean."

"I do know," I laughed. "It's a seller's market, so it makes sense for them to look in Florida right now."

"Let's head inside, see what you think," Sean said.

It was like going back in time for me. Even though it wasn't our cottage, it had basically the same layout, just on a bigger scale. We walked through every room. The two bedrooms on the first floor were spacious and shared a bathroom, while the master on the second floor had its own bathroom. The kitchen had an island instead of a peninsula, which was great. The field stone fireplace in the living room was impressive, and shocker, a watercolor painting of the beach sat atop a substantial timber mantel.

"My dad did most of the trim work inside, and he made the flower boxes and benches on the deck as well," Sean said proudly.

"Handy guy," I responded, glancing out the span of sliding glass doors off the front that led to the deck. "I tried my hand at carpentry back in the day, tried being the appropriate term, but we didn't get along," I said laughing. Probably another disappointment for Julia, just like the fact that I wasn't mechanically inclined either. She never got the man she really wanted.

"Let's check out that view," I said, eager to get back outside.

The bayside was calm, low tide exposing the wet sand where the ocean once covered it. The salty ocean breezes whispered their way through the beach grasses that were gently swaying near the deck railing.

"Great view," I said again, breathing in the salty air.

"I'll miss it," Sean replied, lost in the view.

"I'm guessing this is home for you?" I asked, hearing the

disappointment in his voice.

"Yah, I live here year-round. I work for a local landscape company in town… I'm a landscape architect," he said.

"Impressive; sounds like a cool job," I said, shaking my head, "and a convenient commute… that's kind of a plus. So, what's your plan once this place sells, if you don't mind me asking?"

"My boss is also a good friend of mine… he's got a few rental properties on the ocean side. Whichever one is up for grabs I'll rent. I've been taking advantage of my parents for too long. It's time for me to cough up some money now. It'll be different, but sometimes change can be a good thing."

Sean walked to the railing, placing his hands on top, looking out over the water.

"Lotta memories here though. My siblings and I grew up coming here every summer for years. When we hit the teenage years, we found summer jobs. Even then, I gravitated toward landscaping. We probably should have just lived here full time," he said, with a slight snicker, "but I kind of feel like we did. I made a lot of friends during those years, most of whom I'm still in touch with today."

I shook my head in agreement thinking what a great life for a kid. Nothing I could lay claim to unfortunately, but everything I would want for my own kids. It would have been nice to own a cottage here when they were little. Julia could have spent all summer on the beach with the kids; she would have loved that. But money; money was always an issue for me. If I only could have foreseen everything going to shit, maybe I wouldn't have freaked out so much; maybe it would have made a difference. But who am I kidding; buying her the cottage then wouldn't have changed a thing that went down between us. I don't' want to admit it was inevitable, but maybe it was. The one thing I could admit was that it wasn't all my fault that things ended.

"Sounds like you've got a great life down here Sean," I said, extending my hand to him. "I'll get back to you within the week. I don't think your parents will have any trouble selling this place."

"Great, I look forward to hearing back from you Jack. It was great to meet you," he said, and I believed him. He seemed like a good guy.

I walked down the driveway and randomly thought about stopping by the cottage, just for a quick peek. I started the car and backed out. I drove slowly, noticing that there was a new driveway pad on the right of the old cottage. I didn't see a car in the main driveway.

"Hopefully no one is renting this," I said, pulling in.

When I got out of the car, all was quiet except the breeze. It kept swooping in, rustling through the grasses, tickling the chimes, and filling the air with salt. I walked up the steps and knocked on the door just to be safe; there was no answer.

"Hello," I said, raising my voice. There was no response. The cottage appeared to be empty. I raised my hand above my eyes and peered through the sidelight. I could see the fireplace clearly through the glass; the infamous watercolor stared back at me.

"Christ, I can't believe it's still here," I exclaimed. Here we go again.

~

"You should keep the painting," I said to Julia, "you're the one who really wanted it."

"You're the one who pushed me to get it. It's not like I twisted your arm," she said defending herself. "You paid for it with 'your' money, you keep it."

"I don't want it Julia, and don't start with the 'my money shit.' I never said that to you."

"Oh, but you consistently reminded me that you had all the pressure of providing for the family. Single income, remember," she said sharply.

"Fine Julia, I'll keep it. Just for spite of course," I retorted with a smirk.

Her eyes lit up. "I get to say this now that we're done… you're just like your mother."

I glared at her. My mom was no saint, and even though Julia was right, there was no way I wanted to be compared to my mother who was a vengeful bitch in her own right.

"Low blow Julia," I said, waving my hand at her in disgust as I walked away. "Low fucking blow."

~

Julia was right, I did want her to have the painting, but the way I said it made her feel like it was her fault we bought it in the first place. I could see that now. In the end, I just couldn't keep it, it would always remind me of her, of that day when she was so happy—happy because

I made her happy.

I walked to the front deck, and grabbed the railing, taking a deep breath then I lowered my forearms and leaned onto it. As I looked out over the ocean, I could see a boat in the distance. I glanced to my right and spied a couple walking down the beach, hand in hand. I just stared at them until I couldn't look anymore. I let my head fall forward; my eyes filled with tears. The memories were flooding in, the good ones, and I couldn't stop the deluge of emotions. I tried to fight them off, but my body shuddered, and I gave in.

"Get it together man," I snipped, wiping my face in disgust. Suddenly, I could hear the haunting voice of my father saying, "real men don't cry." You got that right dad. Real men don't. I took a deep breath.

This is probably one of the stupidest things I've done since the divorce.

I'd already been living in memory purgatory; thoughts of Julia circling like a murder of crows just waiting to eat me alive. Was this a good thing or a bad thing? But as quickly as I thought it, I was questioning it. Maybe all these memories—maybe being on the Cape wasn't hurting me like I'd feared. Maybe I was actually healing. Maybe I had to face all of this to find myself again. I didn't hesitate. I grabbed my phone and started texting.

Chapter Fourteen
Julia

I drove past the Lighthouse Market and glanced over at the windmill. My first thought was of the kids running around, having fun while Jack and I strolled through the festival tents. And then I went there. I came to a stop at the lights and just stared at the open field remembering the day we bought the painting. I loved that damn painting.

"I wish that never happened," I said groaning, forcing myself to look away.

It was so strange, being down here without Jack and the kids. It was like I jumped decades backward; time seemed to stand still. The light turned green, and I took a left onto route six, heading toward Wellfleet. I drove a few miles checking out the new businesses that had popped up since I'd been here last. Even some of the old restaurants seemed to have changed hands. Now I was starting to think I might just be screwed for tonight.

I was relieved to see that the bakery was still a staple right next to the Surf's Up Sandwich Shop. I pulled in, excited to get my food and relax. I ordered a salad with grilled chicken, dressing on the side of course, and proceeded to grab my signature coffee hopped up on espresso. I found an open table on the blue stone patio.

The hanging petunias were still going remarkably strong, as well as the coleus, begonias, and sweet potato vine planters, but the newly planted mums were speaking to me. Fall had always been my favorite time of year, even when I was kid. Although summers meant time by the pool and vacations at the beach, it never compared to fall, and I know Jack felt the same. If we had a choice, we would have been married in October, but Jacob had other ideas, so we married in May, just after college graduation. Thank God we were both able to finish school on time.

That whole scene of getting pregnant before we got married was a nightmare to say the least. I never felt such a lack of support in my life. Some parents have this uncanny ability to make sure you know how stupid you are, or should I say, how your stupidity screws up their lives. Still makes me burn when I think of telling them all, and that was more me being mad at myself for letting them make both of us feel so small. Jack and I had each other, that was it, that was clear. No one was going to help us. It was our problem. But when that bouncing baby made its appearance, they all miraculously forgot how embarrassed they were by our behavior, well until we asked for some babysitting help; that's when they went back to being selfish. We swore we'd never do that to our kids. Time will tell, but I plan on being the best damn grandmother ever.

I could see a new mini-golf course across the street where the driving range used to be. Jacob loved to golf when he was a kid. Jack would take both boys to hit balls at least a couple of times during our vacation, leaving mom and Jess to shop. Those were good times. Jack was always willing to take the boys on trips; skiing, snowshoeing, four wheeling. For all my issues with him, I couldn't deny he was a great dad.

When I finished my salad, I packed up my recycling and trash and headed out. As far as I can remember, the boutique was up the road about two miles; hopefully, it was still there. As I walked to the receptacles, I saw a man two tables away staring at me. "Oh God," I thought, maybe Jack was right, or am I just being conceited, because I don't want to be. I looked away and walked briskly to my car.

The car felt like a sauna. I really needed to get one of those sun visors. I grabbed my sunglasses to cut the glare. As I pulled out, I noticed the guy was still there, but his attention seemed to be on a woman who'd just sat down where I'd been sitting. "Player," I muttered as I turned onto the highway. I hated guys like that. Maybe Jack was right about men.

As I approached the plaza, I noticed the boutique was gone. "Shit, I can't believe it went out. Crap, now what am I going to do?" I continued down the road about a half mile looking for a spot to turn around and thankfully found the boutique. Once inside, I was reminded again of old times when Jess and I would shop together. The clothes here were a bit eclectic, but neither of us were the type to follow the trends. No UGG boots for my daughter; I had to agree. I liked finding my own style as well.

I walked through the door to find the place hadn't really changed much, despite the move. I spotted the sale rack, but nothing piqued my interest. I moved methodically through each rack, rifling quickly through the dresses until I stumbled upon a few that might just work.

"That would look fantastic on you," the salesperson said from behind me. I was holding a sleeveless, black knit dress up against me, as I looked in the full-length mirror.

"You think so?" I replied trying to be nice. I always hated it when salespeople wanted to give their two cents, but I decided to play along.

"With those arms, you almost have to try it on," she said grinning.

Well, maybe she wasn't so bad after all.

I laughed, "Well, I'll try it, and this one too," I said, handing her the dresses. "Do you have any heels to go with them?"

She nodded and I followed her to the dressing room.

I certainly wasn't trying to get attention, but as a divorced forty-five-year-old woman, I couldn't lie; any positive feedback about my body felt good, for the moment anyway. But who was I kidding, there's a deeper truth that I know only too well about me and compliments like that; they invade me. I know they're given with the best intentions, but for me, those compliments just feed the beast within, and I knew it wasn't good. If the beast was fed too many compliments, the beast not only wanted more, but it also wanted me to think I needed them to survive. My entire soul was now its bitch. The expectations I had of myself were all consuming; I knew they could eventually swallow me entirely if I let them.

As I slipped the black dress over my head, my mind wandered. I always wondered what would happen if I got fat. What would people think? I know what they'd think, they'd love every minute of it. They'd love it that I'd given in just like them, proving I'm not untouchable. They'd all secretly love it if I let myself go. But I knew I would never let that happen because I couldn't let them win, never mind the fact that it would probably kill me, and I'd disintegrate on the spot.

"I'll take them both," I said, handing the clerk the dresses and a pair of black shoes with a chunk heel.

"Special night planned," she said, eager to get a scoop on my plans.

"Glenn's tonight," I said smiling. "I guess I'll just have to wait and see how special it is."

As I hung the dresses in the car, I suddenly felt overwhelmed.

"You should have just bought the black one Julia," I said, rolling my eyes.

I knew I was creating a potential mini clothing trauma by bringing them both home, but I'd have to face that dilemma when it reared its ugly head. Besides, maybe there would be a second date. Look at me being optimistic. I prayed the whole way home I would be able to make a quick decision. As long as I did, it wouldn't take long to get ready. I laughed to myself as I thought about one of Jess' friends who made a ridiculous comment to me when they were getting ready for junior prom.

"This doesn't just happen overnight," she said, circling her face with her finger. I think she forgot who her audience was. I had to laugh; a teenage girl was telling me she needed time to put her makeup on to look presentable. We all laughed at the time, but all I could think now was, really Sammy… you were all of seventeen and you were already feeling like your looks weren't enough. I knew she was kidding, but was she?

I had a few hours once I got home to relax, but I knew myself too well. I was totally worked up. I did my best not to overthink things, so after many deep breaths and much time spent getting dressed, I was ready by 5:30 p.m. and on the road to the restaurant content with my choice.

Chapter Fifteen
Jack

After stopping at the cottage, I drove back to the inn and grabbed my things. Since I had time to kill before the last appointment, I decided to take a detour to Provincetown. I'd always loved Race Point Beach. I knew Julia used to go there when she was a kid, but I'd never been until we took the kids.

I pulled into a parking spot at Herring Cove Beach with a prime view of the ocean. It was roaring. The waves were crashing well before the shore. "Jacob would be in heaven," I said, lost in the waves. For thirty minutes I just sat in the car; I couldn't bring myself to get out. Everything here sparked a memory and I had to question why I made the trek. "Why is everything so God damn hard," I said loudly, smashing the steering wheel with my hand. It didn't stop them though, the memories flooded in anyway.

I pictured the kids running down the beach, dragging driftwood sticks behind them, making lines in the sand. As the oldest, Jacob was always the ringleader, and when he stopped to draw something in the sand, they all stopped. Then just as quickly, they were running again, chasing the seagulls, and screaming at the top of their lungs. Julia and I would just laugh, recalling the wonderful freedom of being a kid with no worries other than hoping your parents would take you for ice cream. We'd walk for what seemed like miles. "Stay off the dunes," we'd yell trying to keep them away from the bird nesting areas. We'd walk hand in hand and talk about the future, it was nice, most of the time.

~

"This is where I want my ashes spread. I don't want a funeral and I don't want to take up space in the ground. It's not like I'd really be in there anyway," she said laughing.

I couldn't let that comment go without saying something. I stopped abruptly. Sometimes Julia would say things at the most inopportune times, and this was one of them.

"Julia, do we really need to talk about this now," I said, disgruntled by her need to ruin the mood.

"Jack, we have to talk about it sometime… what better time than now, it's right in front of us. You should know what I want, and so should the kids."

"Ok, I get it," I said, now even more put off, "but I don't want to talk about dying when we have so much living to do. We have our whole lives in front of us."

"Well, you never know, do you?" she said nonchalantly.

She always had a way of ruining a peaceful moment with a weird comment.

"What's that supposed to mean?" I said sharply. "Never know what?"

"Nothing," she said flustered. "I just mean, none of us know the future."

"Wait… what? I'm sorry, but I'm not following. Are we talking about death or something else here, because the kids don't need to know this now, they're too young. If you're so worried about having the funeral you want, maybe you should put it in writing, because the vibe I'm getting is that you're leaving room for the possibility that we may not make it, and that's why you're saying you want the kids to know your wishes because I won't be around?" My frustration was evident.

"Stop it, Jack," she said angrily. "I just think no one knows the future. I'm not saying we won't make it, but plenty of people don't, so covering the bases is important. Plus, how do you know I'm not thinking you could die first, or I might not be able to tell you what I want if, God forbid, I had an accident. Any of that shit could happen. Stop taking a simple comment and making it be more than it really is. I'm not a fortune teller and neither are you. You're being dramatic and insecure."

"At least I'm not entertaining the thought," I said angrily, releasing her hand. I walked ahead alone. Her brutal honesty was exactly that; brutal. Did she not hear herself? How does she think I'd respond to the "we don't know the future," comment? She was leaving room for our demise, not just hers. Why the hell does she have to do that, why?

We didn't speak for the rest of the night or the following day as I recall. I guess that was on me. "Good times. Guess she was right in the end. Hope she wrote down her wishes because I won't be handling any of it, which is probably what she wanted anyway," I said bitterly, the hurt was still so fresh.

My last appointment was pretty straightforward. The house was significantly larger than all the others. It had a clear view of the ocean, but also offered a view of the marshland as well, which meant it was prime for bird watchers. When I took the view in from the deck, I saw a blue heron fly overhead, landing directly in the marsh. Quite a sight. Again, Julia would have loved it. I texted Justin that the meeting went well and there was no reason this place shouldn't sell quickly. On the way back, I stopped at a sandwich shop. The liquor store was conveniently located next door. Chips, a sandwich, and a six pack of Sam Adams would do for dinner. I'd keep it simple tonight, no need to make unnecessary messes.

It was 6:15 p.m. when I arrived, and the sunlight was fading fast. I parked and headed straight for the deck; I didn't want to miss the sunset. I threw my bag down and took a seat in one of the Adirondack rockers near the firepit. I needed to rock. I cracked a beer, focused on the sky, and let all my negative thoughts go. As the sun set, it cast mesmerizing reflections on the shallow waters. It was two hours past low tide and people were still out searching the tidal flats for treasures. I had to laugh; such a simple thing to do; going out for a walk on the beach where the sand, the surf, and the sea critters were the only entertainment you needed.

I ate the sandwich quickly; five beers went down like water. By 9 p.m. I was completely exhausted. I walked inside and headed straight for the bedroom.

Chapter Sixteen
Julia

"Damn it," I said, under my breath as I entered the restaurant. I was hoping to get there first, to acclimate myself, but I could see Sean sitting at a table near the windows, waving me over. The restaurant was just as I remembered it: old wooden beams, fisherman's paraphernalia, candlelit tables with white tablecloths, a killer view, and the black baby grand in the corner. The tables were full, not surprising; this place was always so popular. A bit upscale for a family on vacation, but extremely popular with the locals.

Sean stood as I walked toward the table. I felt like it'd been years since I'd worn heels. I hoped I didn't look awkward. The dress fit me to a tee, and I had to admit, I felt like a woman again. I opted to wear my hair down even though turtlenecks usually make me want to wear it up. I looked classy, which for a first date was exactly the vibe I wanted.

Sean looked great as well. A bit leaner than I'd usually go for, but so good looking it didn't matter. His short blond hair and light blue eyes were appealing, and that smile didn't hurt either. I smiled and waved as I walked toward him.

You'd think I'd walked a mile for all the memories that were flooding in. Was there nowhere I could go where they couldn't find me? Jack and I frequented Glenn's whenever we went to the cottage. It was our favorite spot, just outside the center of Wellfleet. We always ordered the infamous Wellfleet oysters. Jack liked the horseradish sauce while I preferred the mignonette.

Sean immediately pulled me in for a hug. "Great table," I said, pulling back. He moved quickly to pull my chair out; very thoughtful. He sat across from me, my back was to the entrance.

"I know right," he exclaimed. "These tables are hard to get, even during the off season… good thing I know the owner. The view is almost as stunning as you, Julia."

I couldn't help it; I could feel my face flushing. I knew the dress was form fitting, but obviously Sean liked the way it showed off my curves.

"Not too wintry," I said, touching the turtleneck.

"No way. You look beautiful. Plus, it's technically fall. Let me say though, those arms Julia... they're perfectly toned, I'm jealous."

I laughed and I probably blushed again. Who knew naked arms could be such a turn on. Guess all my hard work strength training was paying off.

"Cocktail Julia?" he asked. When I nodded, he didn't waste any time waving the waiter over.

"Can I get you something to drink miss?" the waiter asked.

Miss, wow, I was waiting for ma'am, but I'd take it without a fight.

I was just about to answer when Sean spoke up. "If I may," he said, looking at me for approval, "we will both have a glass of the California Cabernet." I nodded in agreement.

After the waiter left, I grinned at Sean and said, "How did you know Cabernet was my favorite?"

Sean quickly retorted, "I have my ways, but let's be honest, any type of wine is a winner in my book," he said grinning.

We both laughed. It was uncanny how comfortable I felt with Sean, like an old friend you hadn't seen in years but picked up right where you left off. That feeling alone was confusing though. I felt like I was back dating Jack again, who was my friend at first. I remembered how I fought us being a couple because of the friendship, but I didn't need to think about that now. This gorgeous young guy was sitting across from me, and I just needed to go with it for whatever it was. It seemed like I was always having to reason with myself.

The waiter returned with our drinks and after a few sips, the conversation flowed easily, so easily in fact, that after about twenty minutes of talking, my glass was almost empty. I started thinking we needed to order some food soon or I'd be off my ass. We were embroiled in a conversation about local artists when we were unexpectedly interrupted.

"Hold that thought Julia," Sean said, raising his arm to wave at someone behind me. But he wasn't just saying hello, he was waving the person over to the table. I hastily glanced behind me to see a tall gentleman approaching the table. At first glance, I didn't recognize him.

"You made it," Sean said, standing and pulling the man in for a shoulder bump.

Suddenly, I felt a bit out of place. I was confused; were Sean and I on a date or not? Who's this guy he seemed to be expecting? I looked down at the napkin covering my lap, my eyes widened, and I thought, what the hell is going on?

"Yah, I thought I'd get stuck over at the Mitchell's place, you know how she can keep a conversation going." His voice was pleasingly sultry and recognizable.

"Julia," Sean said, causing me to lift my head, "let me introduce you to my boss, this is Andrew Langdon, Andrew this is Julia."

As soon as the man turned toward me, I recognized him instantly. I was in shock, and I think he was as well. We were both silent for a few seconds, just staring at one another until his eyes lit up and he smiled.

"Well, well," he said with a smirk, "hello again, Julia." Then he leaned in toward me and whispered, "May I say you look more like a Rachel to me," then he stood up and winked at me.

I looked at him and then at Sean who seemed dumbfounded by Andrew's weird comment. Andrew reached his hand out to me, and I placed mine in his. His hand was warm and soft, for a landscaper that is.

"Rachel huh," I said teasingly, "what a funny thing to say," then I threw him a wink. I was playing it cool, but inside I was flipping. What the hell!

Sean stood back, his expression telling. Now he was clearly the one not sure of what was going on.

"It's good to see you again, Mr. Chivalrous," I said, shaking his hand firmly.

Andrew lingered; it was like he was looking right through me.

"Mr. Chivalrous, I like it," he said, then added, "you have breathtaking emerald, green eyes Julia… I hadn't noticed before how intense they were. Andrew held on to my hand like he would never let it go. We just stared at each other completely lost in the moment until Sean broke what he perceived to be an awkward silence.

"Wait, what… you two know each other?" he said incredulously, looking back and forth at us.

"You could say that, right Rachel?" Andrew said, smiling at me.

"Well, Rachel sure does remember you. You're a hard one to forget," I said, removing my hand from his. He was even better looking than I remembered. Of course, I kept trying to dodge his glances at the coffee shop; guess I was the one who missed out.

Sean sat down, leaning on the table, just looking at me. Andrew took a seat next to him but kept his eyes focused on me. Dare I say, I felt more than uncomfortable with these two men staring at me. I tried not to smile. I had to look away. I pretended to be distracted by a couple leaving.

"Give me the scoop," Sean said, perplexed and excited all at the same time. "How the heck did you two meet and who the hell is Rachel?"

Thankfully, Andrew stepped up to explain.

"It's not much of a story. Remember I was in Boston yesterday, and, well, I stopped for a coffee on the way home and ran into Rachel... I mean Julia," he said, still staring at me.

"Rachel is my coffee cup name," I offered in explanation. "I've always loved the name Rachel. My mother said it was her second choice."

My mouth was dry. I took a sip of water. Andrew's eyes were focused on me the entire time and I felt every bit of his attention.

Sean, still dumbfounded, sat back in his chair, and crossed his arms.

As we sat in silence, I suddenly remembered that I was supposed to be here on a date with Sean. Again, what the heck was going on? I actually felt conflicted. I didn't know what to think or feel at this point.

"I'm sorry Sean," I said, hoping to come off with gentle directness, "but did I misread tonight? I didn't realize we'd be sharing the evening. No offense Andrew." Andrew's eyebrows raised, he leaned back and threw a glance Sean's way.

Sean looked at me, my confusion evident. "Oh God, Julia, I am so sorry. I didn't mean for you to think this was a date, well not a date date."

I sat in stunned silence staring back at Sean. If this wasn't a date, then what the hell was it? My mind was reeling with the possibilities, and then it hit me like a ton of bricks. I raised my hand to cover my mouth, mortified. I needed to hide from the two men sitting across from me.

"Oh God," I said. I needed to get up and go somewhere quick, maybe the ladies room. "This just figures," I said, lowering my hand

and gazing back at the two straight faced men sitting across from me. It all made sense now. Two really nice guys. Two extremely good-looking nice guys who apparently are not on a date with me. Two extremely good-looking nice guys who are not on a date with me, but who are hugging and sitting next to each other. And then it all just came out. "It just figures that the only two men I've met over the last few days are not only really nice and really attractive, but gay as well, and I'm totally clueless. What the hell is wrong with me?"

Sean and Andrew looked stunned. Both raised their eyebrows at me. I felt like I was speaking in tongues or something. Then they looked at one another and spontaneously started laughing. I sat back even more mortified. Being laughed at was too much for me, I didn't care how I looked now. I pushed my chair back and stood up. "Excuse me fellas, but this is all a bit much." I grabbed my bag.

Sean could see I was in flight mode, and he immediately stopped laughing, stood up and grabbed my arm. "Julia, we're not laughing at you. Believe me. Please sit down." He released me, and I sat down, still feeling like a fool. Sean sat down and smiled. He placed his arm around Andrew's shoulder. "I know I'm a catch Julia, but this guy, he's just not that into me," he said, laughing once again.

Andrew pushed Sean away and returned his gaze to me. He leaned in and said, "I'm not gay Julia, and even if I was, this guy isn't my type."

"Hey," Sean said, giving Andrew a shove.

Just then the waiter returned. I grabbed my glass, swallowed the remaining wine, and motioned for another. Sean did the same and Andrew ordered a beer.

I still felt like an idiot, but now it all made sense. This was a blind date that I didn't know about, but Andrew did. Of course, there's no way he could have known I was the blind date. I felt the need to explain my confusion.

"I am so sorry," I said, "I just thought the way we talked yesterday, the conversation, the wine, I... I just assumed this was a date."

"No, I'm the one who's sorry. I should have seen the signs. I do love the ladies," Sean said smiling, "but not in that way. But look on the bright side Rachel, now you and Mr. Chivalrous have reconnected."

Without hesitation, we all burst out laughing. God, I needed to laugh.

Once the laughter subsided, I saw Sean glance at his watch. "Chad will be joining us in about fifteen minutes," he said, then he gave Andrew another shove. "Now go sit next to Julia, so my man can sit next to me."

"Gladly," Andrew responded. He seemed eager to sit next to me and I had to wonder was this fate? I didn't usually believe in that, but I'm getting older, changing my ways, maybe, just maybe the stars were aligning. It got me wondering if Andrew, the man I dubbed a creep at the coffee shop, could be 'that someone.' How quickly I'd gone from being attracted to Sean to being attracted to Andrew. I guess I was really looking for someone to fill the void in my life.

Once seated, Andrew leaned on the table, crossing his arms, and looked at me. "What are the odds we'd meet again?" he said smiling, brushing my arm with his. I smiled back, raising my eyebrows and biting my lip slightly. I really didn't know what to say. This man had me tongue-tied. Was I breathing?

Chad arrived moments later and of course we retold the confusing story.

"Well," he said, shaking his head and smiling, "next time I'll be sure not to be late. I can't have Andrew moving in on my guy," he said, amused by the story. We all laughed.

With the air cleared, the night was full of stories, food, and drink. Laughter filled the room, only to be outdone by the piano playing in the background. I had to laugh just a little at the irony. Here I was, sitting next to an extremely attractive man in a restaurant where a piano played in the background. Funny how life repeats itself.

I couldn't help but be enamored by Andrew. Sean being gay didn't even bother me now. He hadn't rejected me, he just preferred someone else. I looked at it as a bonus—a new friendship with a guy who had no ulterior motives. I guessed Andrew was closer to my age anyway, and besides, we sort of had a history—coffee shop history albeit, but still some history.

When Sean and Chad made their way over to the piano to make a few requests, Andrew jumped into teasing mode.

"Rachel, huh," he said, nudging my arm with his.

I shook my head, just a little embarrassed. "That's me, livin' on the edge," I said chuckling, my fingers tracing the rim of my wine glass.

"Well, as much as I love the name Rachel, I am doubly partial to the name Julia," he said, with a smile so infectious I thought I was having a hot flash.

Was I having a hot flash? God it was hot in here. Why did I wear a freakin' turtleneck? I looked at Andrew and smiled, trying not to let on that I was giving into his charm.

"You are stunning," he said softly.

The moment was heavy in flirtation and attraction. My head dropped and I looked away, feeling a crazy amount of uncomfortable.

"So, Sean said you're a writer," Andrew said, cutting the sexual tension instantly.

"I guess I am," I said, trying to agree, "that's if children's books count."

"I would say that counts," he said, taking a sip of his beer.

"And you, Sean said you're his boss. You own a landscape company?"

"Yes, it's been about fifteen years now. We do property management as well. It certainly wasn't my intention when I first went to college, but you know how it goes, sometimes things just fall into your lap and you either go with it or you fight it. I decided to go with it, and it's worked out so far."

"Are you originally from the Cape?" I asked, looking away to touch the rim of my glass again.

"I grew up in New Jersey, attended college in Boston for a couple of years and then finished back in New Jersey. I did an internship on the Cape and fell in love. Now it's home."

"I love it here too," I interjected. "There's nothing quite like it. We used to have a cottage here, but that was a long time ago."

"We?" Andrew asked, a bit confused.

My face flushed immediately. I just blew that. I cleared my throat, knowing I'd just said too much.

"I'm divorced," I said. "Sorry to drop that bomb so nonchalantly. Sometimes I still refer to things like I'm married. Hard to break the habit I guess."

I could feel his eyes on me, forcing me to look his way. "Lucky me," he said grinning. "I've never been married… bombs away."

"Bombs away indeed," I said smiling. "I've got one more bomb while we're being honest." I closed my eyes and offered it up. "I'm a mom of three grown children. Hope that doesn't scare you off?"

"You're not scaring me off Julia. It's hard to believe though," he said, with such a genuine tone to his voice that I had to believe him.

"What are you two laughing about now?" Sean asked, as he sat back down at the table."

"Oh, you know… marriage, divorce, kids… the usual," I said, with a laugh. Andrew was laughing as well. At least we seemed to be on the same page.

"All of me" by John Legend was playing in the background. The words swirled in and around us, and by us, I mean Andrew and me. Giving my all to someone new was a bit much to think about, no matter what the song was saying. Despite not wanting to believe the song, I couldn't help but sing a few lines.

"You seem to know this song," Andrew remarked.

"Sure, doesn't everyone," I retorted back. "What about you, have any favorites?"

"I'm more of a country guy, I guess, although I'll listen to just about anything. I'm a bit old school though… I prefer vinyl to Alexa, but sometimes she comes in handy."

"Me too," I said. "There's nothing like putting an old record on and hearing any small crackles it may offer. I love when that happens, especially with the crooners, like Sinatra or Bennett, it just makes it all seem more authentic."

Andrew shook his head in agreement.

I could hear Sean telling Chad he knew we'd hit it off, meaning me and Andrew. I watched as Chad wrapped his arm around Sean, whispering something in his ear. Sean smiled, like he was embarrassed by what Chad said. It was heartwarming watching the two of them. They seemed right for each other.

It was after ten by the time we decided to leave.

Andrew opened the door for me, and Sean and Chad followed me out. Before I knew it, Sean had sidled up next to me, slipping his arm through mine. "I want the scoop tomorrow," he said, leaning into me. I just kept walking, but I couldn't fight the smile, and the butterflies that seemed to be circling.

I stopped, and looked at him, the grinning fool, and said, "I'm not sure what more I could possibly report, you just saw everything that happened."

"The night is young Julia, have some fun," he said, then winked at me and turned to find Chad.

I stood there alone, not really knowing what to do. I turned around to see the three of them standing behind me, laughing about something. Awkward. I guess I'll just say goodbye and be on my way.

"Thanks for dinner Sean, it was a great date."

Sean could see I was leaving on my own, and quickly looked at Andrew. "Andrew, looks like Rachel needs someone to walk her to her car."

Andrew rolled his eyes at him; the two were obviously good friends. Sean raised his eyebrows at him, then looped his arm through Chad's and the two walked arm in arm to the parking lot across the street.

"He didn't give me a chance Julia. Of course I was planning on walking you to your car," he said, smiling at me. "Where are you parked?"

"Just up the street." I was silently loving that he was walking me to my car.

"Well, I'm hoping you're in town for a bit... I think I need a true first date with you, no offense to Sean and Chad," he said, smirking a bit.

"I'm here for a few days," I said coyly, twirling a strand of hair through my fingers like a schoolgirl. "What do you have in mind?" Did I just say that? What's happening to me?

"Well, I have to take care of some things tomorrow morning, but I could be persuaded to take the afternoon off," he said, imploring me to say yes.

I stopped walking and said, "Feel persuaded. Let me see your phone." I took his phone and proceeded to put my contact information in it. Brazen Julia. Again, who are you and what did you do with quiet little Julia? Maybe Rachel had taken me over.

When I handed it back to him, he looked down at the phone. "Rachel, huh?" he said with a chuckle. "Okay Rachel, how 'bout we do something outside... maybe go for a hike, then grab a bite somewhere casual later?"

"That sounds like a fun day," I said, trying not to blush for the umpteenth time.

Andrew and I continued toward my car.

"An ST huh?" he said, looking at the Explorer. "That's got some horsepower."

"Yes, it does," I said, raising my eyebrows. "What can I say, it's not a sports car, but I think it's as close as I'll ever get."

We both laughed. Andrew looked up at the sky and I followed his cue. We stood quietly for a few moments. "It's so clear tonight," I remarked, "so many stars. It's so beautiful."

"I agree," he said.

When I looked over at him, he wasn't looking at the stars. Was the dress cutting off my air supply? I felt like I was on center stage; it was uncomfortable and thrilling all at the same time.

"Would it be okay if I gave you a hug goodbye?" he asked, those brown eyes melting me on the spot.

It was exactly what I was hoping for. Who was I to deny him? I smiled and nodded. Andrew wasted no time taking me in his arms. Thank God I was wearing heels. It felt like he was just a few inches shorter than Jack. My face brushed against his shoulder. His cologne was intoxicating, and I felt oddly safe in his muscular arms. His hug was not fast or firm; it was slow, soft, and gentle, intensifying in delicate pressure the longer it went on. It was like he valued every bit of me, breathing me in. Did he know how desirable I felt in his arms? It felt like time had stopped and I never wanted it to start again, and then he pulled away, breaking the embrace.

"I'll pick you up tomorrow, around noon. Two cottages down from Sean's, right?" he asked.

"Yes, that's it, the one with the blue door. Looking forward to it," I said, turning to get into the car, but before I knew it, he was by my side, opening the door for me.

"You've got this door opening thing down," I said laughing.

"I think I've been practicing all my life for this," he said, smiling back at me.

Before he shut the door, he had one more thing to say, and I really appreciated his candor.

"Julia, I just want you to know that I don't make it a habit to hit on women in coffee shops. It's not my style, but I'm sure you can understand why I did it."

I blushed again; he just made my year. "It's fine Andrew. I'm glad you did."

I watched him in my rearview as I pulled out. He just stood there watching me leave, just like Thursday, except now he didn't look like a lovesick puppy, he looked like a man; a handsome man who wanted to take me on a date.

I couldn't help but smile as I drove back to the cottage. It'd been way too long. I could get used to feeling so desired.

Chapter Seventeen
Julia

It was 10:30 p.m. by the time I pulled into the driveway. The nearly full moon in conjunction with the multitude of stars lit the sky. I walked onto the deck, placing my hands on the railing. I closed my eyes and breathed in deeply. The grass was swaying in the mild breeze. I felt like I was swaying too. I was in heaven.

"Why did I agree to sell this place," I said quietly, shaking my head with regret. "We never had a bad trip here... so why did I let it go?"

I stood at the railing, asking myself the same questions over and over until I'd had enough regret to last me a lifetime. I took one last deep breath and headed for the door. In those few seconds, my demeanor changed entirely. I could feel the smile spreading across my face. I'd let thoughts of Jack back in, but just for a moment. I knew my smile wasn't because of Jack, it was because of Andrew. It was like I couldn't control it. Once inside, I put my bag on the bench and slipped my shoes off. I walked straight to the bedroom. I didn't care about washing up, I just wanted out of my clothes and to be in my bed where I could replay the night's events over and over, until I fell asleep, which is exactly what happened.

~

I didn't wake up until around two. I sat straight up in bed, wide-eyed. Did I just hear the side door open? I pushed my hands into the mattress, trying to hold myself as still as possible while I listened intently. The room was pitch black. I heard more sounds coming from the side entry.

"Shit," I said, then quickly covered my mouth. Someone was in the cottage. My mind raced and I immediately retraced my steps from the night before. I remembered kicking my shoes off by the door, but did I lock the door? My phone, shit, where was my phone? I moved my hands along the comforter, then the nightstand, coming up empty. "Maybe it's on the dresser," I thought, but then I remembered my phone was in my bag which I left by the door as well.

I was trapped in this room with no way to call for help. I frantically scanned the dark room, my eyes still adjusting to the darkness. I could see something in the corner behind the chair, leaning against the wall. It was a large piece of driftwood. What should I do; should I hide or fight? I'd watched too many shows where people don't fight hoping to not be found or to be released if they are, and then they get killed in the end anyway. I decided in that split second to take control of the situation, even if it was a stupid decision. I quietly climbed out of bed, and suddenly realized that I was naked. I needed to put my pajamas on before doing anything. I put my hands out in front of me, feeling my way down to the end of the bed, until I reached the footboard. I knew the chair was to the right in the corner. I quickly sifted through the clothes I'd thrown there earlier until I found the pajamas at the bottom of the pile. I put them on as quietly as possible then reached my hand out for the driftwood, lifting it carefully from behind the chair. I walked to the door and listened. I could still hear someone out there.

I slowly opened the door, and tiptoed down the hallway, my breathing labored and my heart beating rapidly. When I peered around the corner, I could see a tall figure standing by the side table near the door; from what I could see, he was rifling through my bag. I leaned back against the wall, trying not to panic. I wanted to scream or cry, but I thought, "Push it down Julia, you can't." I knew I only had one chance to handle the situation, and I didn't want to do it. "What about the door to the outside shower," I thought, "should I try to sneak out that way?" But then I remembered that fucking beast of a door was difficult to open, and whoever was out there would definitely hear me. I wanted to make a break for the sliding glass doors off the living room, but I knew there was no way I'd make it. I doubted myself repeatedly in the matter of a few seconds, but then I felt a surge of strength and confidence; I didn't have a choice. Never in my life had I been in a situation like this. This is the kind of thing that happens to other people, the kind of thing you watch in a movie or on an investigative news program.

I took a deep breath and slowly crept out of the hallway. The cottage was mostly dark, but the front room was partially lit by the moon. I could see his back was to me. When I was within range, I raised the driftwood and hit him squarely across the back. He called out, the force of the blow causing him to step forward awkwardly, but he didn't fall.

I stood back, the driftwood still in my hands, fear now engulfing my body. My worst nightmare was staring me in the face. He moved quickly, lunging for me. I pulled the wood back again, but he grabbed it, spinning me around while twisting my left arm behind my back. It happened so fast I didn't even have time to scream. He threw the wood to the side, then aggressively slapped his hand over my mouth. I could barely breathe. I felt my chest rising and falling rapidly. I felt his body pressed against mine. I could smell his scent.

"You're not going anywhere," he whispered crudely, his mouth next to my ear. "Looks like I need to teach you a lesson." I shuddered. I was in this man's grips, and I felt helpless, disgusted, and afraid. My heart felt like it was on the outside of my chest.

He started to push me forward toward the living room, but I knew I couldn't let him get me to the couch, and then he said, "I think you and me could have a little fun tonight." Panic surged through me; I didn't want to be a statistic.

I could feel myself giving up, giving in, but that's not me; I had to do more. I pushed back with everything I had. We both stumbled, and then I had a moment of clarity; I suddenly remembered exactly where I'd left the knife on the side table the day before. I lunged for it and did the only thing I could. With as much force as I could muster, I plunged the knife into his thigh.

He released me instantly as he screamed out in pain. I turned quickly; he'd lowered his head focusing on his leg as he stumbled backward. I couldn't see his face. He instinctually grabbed his leg, and I watched in horror as he pulled the knife out. "You fucking bitch!" he bellowed. I was in shock. I should have been running, but it seemed like everything was going in slow motion. When I finally decided to run, he was on me instantly, grabbing me viciously around the waist. I felt his head against mine. I could smell the liquor on his breath. My hands grasped his arms tightly, like they had a mind of their own. He was pushing me again, pushing me toward the couch.

"Please... please don't hurt me," I said desperately, as I tried to catch my breath. "Just take my purse and anything else you want... take whatever you want." All I could think about at that moment was what would happen in the next few minutes. No one was coming to help me. I was alone in this house with a deranged man.

"After what you just did, I think I will take what I want," he said grotesquely. "You're a bad girl who needs to be taught a lesson."

His words pierced me. Suddenly, I knew what it meant to lose control. Hours ago, I was standing on the deck, wishing I hadn't sold the cottage. Hours ago, I was letting my thoughts linger on Andrew and an evening I wouldn't soon forget. And now, I was here, fearing the worst—I was going to be raped. I knew I had to do something; I had to fight him off with all I had. I could see my daughter's beautiful face. God was she right to be concerned for me? How could this be happening?

Suddenly, there was a loud crash, and in an instant, I was free from his grip. As I fell forward, landing on my knees, I heard a loud thud behind me. I turned and saw his body, now prostrate on the floor. What the hell was happening? I stood up hurriedly, still trying to make sense of the scene when I noticed another figure moving toward the kitchen. In a matter of seconds, my newfound relief had turned into panic again. My heart was racing; I was breathing hard. I started to search for something to defend myself when the kitchen light flicked on. I was blinded. I stepped back awkwardly and saw the man lying face down on the floor, the shell lamp shattered by his side. I looked to the kitchen, squinting at the person who was now making his way toward me. I was scared and relieved all at the same time.

"Jack?" I squeaked out, in disbelief.

"Julia?" he said, just as shocked.

"What the hell are you doing here?" I asked breathlessly, my body shaking uncontrollably.

"I could ask you the same thing," he said, breathing heavily, "but now's not the time. Call 911, I'll get something to tie him up."

I stood there in shock, staring down at the man on the floor. Jack walked over to me and placed his hands firmly on my shoulders giving me a gentle shake. "Julia… Julia!" he said, increasing his grip on my shoulders, "listen to me, call 911."

I looked at him as if in a daze, and yet the adrenaline was pumping through my body like crazy. "Julia," he said again, giving me another shake. I shook my head, breaking the trance I was in.

"Okay!" I said, looking into Jack's eyes, "okay."

I rushed to the entry and found my bag on the floor. As I spoke to the 911 operator, I watched Jack grab what was left of the lamp, pulling the cord from the base. He tied the man's wrists behind his back.

When the police arrived, the blue lights replaced the moon's glow. The police entered the cottage with guns drawn. Jesus, I felt like I was the criminal. They stopped in the entry, eyeing the bloody knife on the floor. Jack put his hands in the air, and I followed suit.

"He's over there," Jack said, nodding to the living room.

The first officer rushed to the body, shouting, "stand down," to his partner.

"You both okay?" the second officer asked.

"We're both fine," Jack said, lowering his arms. Then he looked at me and gently grabbed my arms, pulling them down. The officer nodded and told us to wait in the kitchen. They cuffed the man and pulled him to his feet. His pant leg was bloody at the thigh where I stabbed him. He was conscious now. He stared at me, his eyes dark and penetrating. "Fucking bitch… I really wanted a taste of you," he said, his tongue licking his upper lip hideously. Jack moved in front of me; I knew it was everything he could do to restrain himself from attacking the guy.

I turned away and started to cry, wrapping myself in a protective embrace. Jack placed his hands on my shoulders. "Jack," I said, through the tears, "if you hadn't been here, I… I don't even want to think about what could have happened."

Jack turned me to face him. I could see how much he wanted to protect me. He pulled me in, wrapping his comforting arms around me. We stood completely still for a few moments. Jack kissed the top of my head. He released me and then placed his hands on each side of my face, forcing me to look at him. "You're good now Julia, you hear me? You're going to be okay."

After giving our accounts of what happened, the officer said, "We've been looking for this guy for a couple of weeks now. Thanks to you both, no one else will have to deal with him." He reached out to me placing his hand on my arm and said, "You were extremely brave, not everyone would fight like you did."

I shook my head, acknowledging his attempt to make me feel better.

While Jack finished up with the police, I took the moment to walk out to my refuge—the deck. If I had to guess, it was nearing four now. It was unusually warm, but I felt the need to wrap my arms around myself again, looking for consolation. I looked up at the moon, the same moon I had shared my excitement with just hours earlier. It was higher in the sky now. How could one thing mean so many things to me? In one instance it was a friend, then a beacon, and now a consoler. I let my head drop. I started to cry. I succumbed to the chaos of the night.

"Julia," Jack whispered as he approached me. "Julia," he said, placing his hand reassuringly on my back. "C'mon, come to the lounge chair with me."

I lifted my head and pulled my hands away from my face, then without hesitation, I fell into Jack's arms. I felt like all my strength had been sucked out of me. He quickly scooped me up and carried me to the lounge chair, lowering me gently, then he sat down next to me, his arms wrapping tightly around me. I instinctively nestled into him; my arms pulled into my chest. "Please don't leave me," I begged.

"I'm here Julia, I'm not going anywhere," he said calmly, rubbing his hand soothingly over my back. "I won't leave you."

Chapter Eighteen
Jack

Thankfully, the night was on the warmer side. As I lay there holding Julia, my thoughts couldn't help but travel back in time. This scene, despite being provoked by having to fight off an intruder, was not far from the times we'd spent together at the cottage over the years. It was familiar, warm, thought provoking—nice. The beach grass was swaying in the gentle breeze while the ocean quietly lapped the shore; it was the perfect sound machine. Julia fell asleep instantly, but I wanted to stay awake, to relish the moment of holding her again. Despite my efforts, my exhaustion overtook me, and I succumbed to my need for sleep.

When the sun finally made its appearance, she was still asleep on the lounge chair. Her leg was casually draped over mine just like when we were married. It felt reminiscent of days gone by. It felt like we'd gone back in time, back to the days when we were happy just lying in bed together, satisfied to just stay there; satisfied to just be. And here we were now, tightly knit together without a breath of space between us, just like the old days. I closed my eyes again, feeling her against me, enjoying the moment.

I slept for two more hours until the squawking gulls woke me. I looked down at Julia, sleeping peacefully, my arms still wrapped protectively around her. It felt like the divorce had never happened, like we were on vacation, just the two of us. Her body felt warm; it felt right to have her next to me. The only thing that was different, out of the ordinary, were the pajamas; she never wore pajamas to bed. As I lay there waiting for her to wake, I couldn't help but wonder why we let each other go. It was a moment like this, a moment I thought would never happen again that made me realize she was the key to making me feel whole again.

Within fifteen minutes of me never wanting it to end, Julia began to stir. She sat up, removing her leg from mine. She pulled her hair to one side, rubbed her eyes, and looked at me intently. Did she even remember what happened last night?

"I'm so sorry… what time is it?" she asked, looking around for her phone.

"I'm guessing after eight, according to the sun," I said.

Julia promptly swung her legs over the side of the lounger and stood up. She stretched and walked over to the railing. She looked out over the ocean. "So peaceful," she said, "like it's oblivious to what happened last night."

She remembered. I got up and joined her, putting my hands on the railing, looking out over the ocean. I felt happy in that moment, but little did I know, my happiness was fleeting. I was totally unprepared for what came next.

"Why are you here?" she blurted out, her gaze still on the water.

"Why are you here?" I said back sharply.

And just like that it began; the habitual, the wrong. Annoyed that I'd flipped the question back to her she decided to skip the typical fight and just answer the question.

"Steph told me the cottage was free, and I needed a getaway. And you?"

"Well… Rob told me the cottage was free. I stayed one night at The Lookout, but I needed to extend my stay for work, so I texted Rob to see if the cottage was empty." I looked down, then said with a chuckle, "Figures, it's like they never talk to one another. Nothing's changed there. Probably a good thing they never had kids."

Julia turned to look at me. "Well, that's a bit harsh," she said, irritated by my comment. "So, I'm wondering, where's your car? I didn't see it when I pulled in last night?"

"It's on the driveway pad on the other side of the cottage. I guess you didn't know they'd put that in about a year ago."

Julia shook her head, returning her gaze to the water, and then bit her lip before speaking. I knew something was coming.

"Okaaay…" she said, with an elongated tone. "Well, not that I'm not grateful for everything you've done for me… for taking care of me last night, but what happens now?"

I looked at her, astonished she was going there. "What do you mean?" I said innocently. I knew what she meant, but I didn't want to believe it. My feelings for her were so raw, so on the surface—was she going to crush me again?

She turned to look at me. "I mean, technically, I was here first, sooooo…"

I never took my eyes off her. "You kickin' me out?" I couldn't help but snarl back. How could she want that after last night, after the time we spent sleeping under the stars. Was I the only one on that lounge chair? It's as if she had no feelings for me at all. I felt alone and rejected.

"Well, I guess I can't force you to leave," she said annoyed, "but don't you agree this is a bit awkward?"

I turned around, leaning against the railing, my arms crossed. I took a deep breath. I didn't want to feel this way, especially since just hours ago I was holding her protectively, reliving old feelings and wanting so badly to return to happier days when we loved each other. How quickly my desire for her had been replaced with anger. Whether she was right or not, I felt like a volcano ready to erupt.

"Listen," I said, trying to speak calmly. "I'm sure you're not going to be comfortable staying here alone after last night. I also don't have a place to stay… so Julia, if you could find it in your heart to let me stay, I'd appreciate it," I said succinctly, sarcasm dripping from every word.

She pushed back from the railing and put her hands to the sides of her head, running them into her hair, then she took a deep breath and exhaled slowly. I knew she didn't want to admit that I was right. There's no way she was going to stay here alone.

"I hate to admit it, but you're right Jack. I don't want to be here alone. So, fine, you can stay," she said, clearly frustrated, her hands on her hips.

"Look," I said, hoping to offer some kind of compromise, "I've got appointments over the next few days. We'll probably see each other very minimally. I'll try to stay clear of you if you do the same for me."

It's not what I wanted. I wanted her. I wanted her to see we could be good again. Why was it so evident to me, and yet to her, it wasn't. Then I couldn't help but wonder where she was all day yesterday, and into the night. She wasn't at the cottage, so where was she?

"Okay," she said reluctantly, then turned and walked inside.

I watched her walk away. It felt reminiscent of the past. I wanted a different outcome, but she wasn't having it. "Stubborn Julia," I said, "stubborn as ever, but I still love you."

Chapter Nineteen
Julia

What I needed was to be alone. I went to the bedroom and fell backward onto the bed. "What the fuck!" I said, covering my eyes with my hands. Suddenly, after years, we're thrown back together, now? God this is awkward.

I felt confused, still trying to process what had happened the night before. And now trying to process having fallen asleep in Jack's arms. Lying there with him felt so familiar and good, but it also felt incredibly wrong. How was any of this possible? I'd just spent an evening with an incredible guy who made my heart skip a thousand beats, and yet here I was, confused as hell by my ex-husband.

I lay there for a few minutes, reiterating the same words, then suddenly I stopped. Jack was there for me when I needed him the most. Last night was a horror show and without his help I don't know where I'd be right now—in the hospital or dead on the side of some back road? I needed to not think about what could have been. This is my new now, not last night.

It was so easy for me to mourn my relationship with Jack. Over the past two years, I was consistently full of regret, wondering if I'd done the right thing. But it's easy to mourn a relationship that's gone, especially if you convince yourself there is nothing out there to replace it with. I needed to believe I had a second chance at love, whether it was with Andrew or someone else. I deserved a second chance.

"You can do this Julia," I whispered. "It's not a big deal, just go on with your vacation. You have a date with Andrew today, focus on that. Just because Jack saved you last night, doesn't mean you're getting back together. You don't owe him anything more than a thank you. Not all is lost."

I pulled myself up, walked to the bathroom and grabbed a towel. I peered out the door; Jack was still standing on the deck, his forearms resting on the railing, his head moving back and forth, no doubt trash-talking me. I walked to the door that led to the outside shower; it was stuck, just like I thought it would be last night. I grabbed the doorknob with both hands and tugged. When it finally opened, I lost my grip and the door smashed into the wall with a loud crash. So much for being discreet. Once the warm water hit me, I melted. The entire situation, from the break-in to Jack being there was crazy. In all the years we'd owned the cottage, I'd never once heard of any break-ins. What were the odds this would happen? What were the odds Jack would be here on the very night it did? What were the odds of me reconnecting with Andrew?

I looked up at the clear blue-bird sky, as they say in Utah. The sun was ascending quickly, and the warmth of its rays were intensifying. The forecast was perfect for the day; a balmy seventy-five. All of nature seemed so unaffected by everything we had just experienced. The sun still rose, the ocean still crashed against the shore, and the birds still sang the same songs they sang the day before without an ounce of drama. How nice to be so unincumbered, so clueless, so in the moment.

I just felt like I was in survival mode at this point. So many thoughts were running through my head about Jack, our life together, and the times when he was there to support me, like now. But then, the other memories flooded in; all the fights and the devasting hurt that followed. All the memories, the good and the bad were just that, distant, past, and I knew that. I also knew that letting go of it all was the only way out, but could I really do that?

I stood still, the warm water caressing my entire body. Jack and I had been through a lot together. It wasn't just about the disagreements; we shared one another's individual pain as well throughout our marriage. I had my demons, but so did he, which is why I encouraged him to consider getting therapy in the past. But the one thing you can't do is change other people, and you can't make someone see they need help, they have to do it on their own. I had to admit, it took me years to go back to therapy. It's not easy; it's scary, difficult, and oh so revealing. With Jack, I just couldn't wait any longer for him to see that what he was doing in our marriage was killing me, killing us. Being the one to leave was the hardest thing I've ever done. Am I blaming him? In a way, I am. I guess that means I still need to work on me.

I grew up in a home where quitting was not an option. It was ingrained in me to never give up, to find another way, to solve the problem. I felt guilty and ashamed for leaving my marriage. It was as if I were admitting I'd failed. Even before I left, I was haunted by my wedding vows: 'in sickness and in health, 'til death do us part.' I felt like my parents were disappointed in me, maybe a worse fate than if I gave God that coveted seat. But how many times are you supposed to forgive someone? I asked that question numerous times throughout our marriage, and I knew the answer: according to the Bible, seventy times seven—an infinite amount. More guilt. But then it hit me; at what point do you face the facts and say love is not enough? At what point do you say, I matter. At what point is any of that okay? Answering to Jack and the kids was one thing, answering to God was completely overwhelming. I've learned over the years to push my parents out of the equation, I had to, or I wouldn't survive. It was between me and God now. I know better than to think this, but I hope He can forgive me.

The good moments Jack and I shared were distant memories, and so were the bad. It was all in the past and to save myself I needed to let all of it go. Thankfully, my thoughts quieted. I moved on to other more pressing concerns, like the future, like a date with Andrew. But then the doubt came piling in.

"How in the hell is this going to work?" I muttered. "Should I tell Andrew about last night… about Jack?"

Why did I feel guilty when I'd done nothing wrong? It was like the part of me that felt guilty and the part of me that was trying to reason my way out of that guilt, were battling each other, vying for the number one spot. One would not yield to the other. I'd had enough. I shut the shower off and buried my face in the towel, but I didn't cry, I screamed in frustration.

I walked back into the cottage and spotted Jack standing at the peninsula. I was wrapped in the towel, my hair still dripping as it fell over my shoulders. I stopped at the sight of him. He turned to look at me. I watched his eyes roam from my feet to my face; I was frozen in place. And then suddenly, he looked down at the counter, stirring cream into his coffee.

"I cleaned up the shells… they're in a bag in the closet. I'm going out for a bit," he said, trying to break the uncomfortable silence, "you need anything?"

"No, no thank you. I'll be heading out as well," I said, then quickly retreated to my bedroom. I heard him leave moments later. I heard him lock the door. I walked out into the living room and just stared at the ocean. I wanted this vacation to inspire me, to give me the surge of energy I needed to go on with my life. Returning to the Cape was difficult enough without Jack actually being here. Could he really stay here with me while I was searching for myself? What good could come of this? So many questions. So many questions with no answers in sight.

I sighed. "You're in this now Julia," I whispered. "There's no turning back." I felt like a child again. I felt like I had no one to talk to about what I was feeling. I'd just met Sean and Andrew; why would I share any of this with them? It was way too much.

"Shit…" I exclaimed. "Andrew will be coming to pick me up. Jack will be back at some point. How am I going to explain this?" I sighed again. "It's just going to be what it's going to be," I said, defeated, and trying desperately to reason with myself. There really wasn't much I could do about it. "Why the hell do I have to do anything," I said angrily. "This is my life, God damn it!"

I was angry; angry with myself for letting any man make me feel like I had to make excuses. I wanted to go on the date with Andrew, but I barely knew him, so what did it matter if he and Jack met? I had to stop feeling guilty about any of it. Life is full of curve balls, and they were coming my way, fast and hard.

Chapter Twenty
Julia

I removed the towel and just stared at myself in the bathroom mirror, then I leaned in, contorting my face. I widened my eyes and opened my mouth, like I was in shock. I tipped my chin up, a sure-fire way to reduce lines and bags—too bad I couldn't walk around that way. I was always trying to find the younger version of me. I recalled the movie "Hook." One of the characters pulls at the corners of Robin William's eyes, searching for the younger Peter Pan. That's exactly how I felt; where did the younger version of me go? I wished I could get her back. And just like that, I could feel it coming on, like a force I couldn't fight. I felt the negative, the questioning, the insecure Julia trying to get out. I wasn't sure if I could fight her right now. Why was she making an appearance anyway; was last night not enough of a wake-up call to stop the insanity.

"You're under there somewhere," I said, pulling at the corners of my eyes. Then I stopped and turned sideways, giving myself the once over.

"You're not that bad," I said. "Actually, you look pretty damn good."

I placed my hands on my ass. "Could be worse," I said, with a laugh. As Jen always said, how can you be upset with your ass if you were never high and tight in the first place. How true. I was fit, but not perfect in any way, and that bothered me more than I could ever say. The idea that I needed to be perfect consumed me. I couldn't stop it. I always felt inadequate.

"Maybe someday I'll be able to look in the mirror and not be so harsh," I said, trying desperately to talk myself through the insane scrutiny. As I stood there, feeling pulled between the sane Julia and the insane Julia, I felt the anger surging.

"Why can't you just be content with who you are!" I snarled through clenched teeth. "Will this ever stop?" I closed my eyes, wishing I could be normal. But even as the thought crept out from the crevices of my brain, I had to admit I was wrong. "The trouble is, there is no normal Julia," I said, agitated with myself. "No matter what you feel right now, the truth is, no one is normal… no one is perfect."

It'd been a lifetime for me; a lifetime of dissecting every part of my body. A lifetime of self-loathing, of wanting more, wanting to be better, or maybe even thinking there was a 'best' to be attained. Depending on my mood, I was either full of confidence or full of self-hatred. It was no way to live life. I recall one time when Jack and I were sitting on the couch together. I was crying uncontrollably saying to him, "When will this stop… will I ever be free of this?" When I was at my worst, he was at his best. He always tried to listen, to console me, even if he couldn't quite understand me, the way I perceived myself. I had to give him that.

Growing up in a time when models were tall, stick thin, and miraculously still maintained cleavage, didn't help. I was at best five-five, and weighed around a hundred and fifteen pounds, the same weight I was in high school. At least I was consistent, but I hated that it was important to me. As I stood obsessively looking in the mirror, my past engulfed me, tempting me to relive childhood experiences, and without realizing what I was doing, I gave in. One of my first therapy sessions came to mind.

~

"Tell me Julia, tell me about yourself as a young girl."

"Well, I was one of four kids… middle girl. I guess we were a normal family," I said, air quoting normal. "I was a quiet, but happy kid. I didn't cause my parents any trouble. I was innocent, I guess. I was just living my life. I was interested in art and sports. I was a good student. Since I'm here to talk about my issues with my weight, I guess that started with my brother; he teased me relentlessly."

"Tell me about your brother."

The nicknames echoed repeatedly in my mind. I cleared my throat.

"My brother was a teaser, as most brothers with three sisters probably are. He gave me 'fat' nicknames. Even though it was so long ago, and deep down I knew my brother was just being a stupid kid, those names became the seed that started it all, at least that's my opinion on it." I sighed.

"Without a doubt, my brother was a pain in the ass. Maybe he teased us because he was the only boy in the family besides my father; for God's sake, even the animals were female. My sisters were given nicknames as well, but their names were just silly made-up names, where mine was directed at my weight."

"How did that make you feel?"

"I hated it, of course. But as I think back, I think I was more irritated with him for being a jerk than thinking what he was saying was true, but I'm not sure. Either way, I just didn't understand why… why me? It wasn't until I was well into my thirties that I held my mother somewhat responsible for not actively protecting me. I'm not sure if it's fair to hold her responsible, it's not like I can remember if she tried to make him stop or not. I'd like to think she yelled at him, but the name calling continued, so did she really try? In my mind she didn't, and even though I love her, I can't quite understand what she was thinking then. Did she not hear him saying those awful things to me? Did she not think there could be disastrous repercussions? I'm her child for God's sake," I said angrily.

"Take a breath Julia," Suzanne interjected, acknowledging I was upset. I took a deep breath and cleared my throat again, fighting back the tears. I was wringing my hands uncomfortably.

"The funny thing is, I wasn't fat at all. In fact, other than when I was pregnant, I've never been fat in my entire life. His teasing didn't make any sense to me, it still doesn't. As I got older, I didn't really think about it anymore because eventually he stopped doing it, but I never forgot it, and it never forgot me. The problem with being teased is that it sticks with you; not exactly the actual name calling, but the essence of it, the stuff that makes a person question their worth. It was as if my DNA had included the lie; it was part of me. The damage was done, and I couldn't repair it."

I grabbed a tissue; there was no stopping the tears now.

"The teasing, his names for me… I thought I got rid of them by hiding them in some remote part of my brain. Little did I know that by doing that, it meant they were always there, waiting to be unleashed when I felt bad about myself. That kind of teasing is like a tiny snowball, if it has the chance to gain any momentum, its power is unstoppable. Being a kid is rough; whether your siblings pick on you or you get bullied in school—it's all shit."

"Did you get bullied in school?"

"You know… I guess I did. It seems like I was a target, looking back now. I got teased for being the new girl at school, and I got teased for being a good student. It lasted for about five years, until I got into high school. I think my confidence grew as I got older, but I sacrificed some of myself along the way to get there."

"How so?"

"I wanted to be one of the 'cool kids,' so I started smoking cigarettes and pot. I had a lot of boyfriends… one in particular who was far too advanced for me. I wasn't myself for a few years. But somehow, I found myself again in high school. I re-centered. I was lucky… until college that is. I think having to leave the safety of high school crushed me.

~

Suddenly there was a knock at the door. I shook my head, attempting to leave the past behind. Just thinking back to that session set me off. Why—why did that all have to happen to me? I heard the knock again. "Who the hell is that?" I thought. I looked down, realizing that I was totally naked. I wrapped myself in the towel, peered out the door, and ran to the bedroom. I grabbed my pajamas from the chair and hastily put the top on. Just as I was about to slip my foot into my pant leg, I looked at the window in the bedroom. The fucking window. Why didn't I crawl out the fucking window last night? Jesus! I could have avoided that whole scene. And then, in typical Julia fashion, I got my foot stuck in the fabric of my pajama bottoms. I lost my footing and fell into the chair. "Jesus, calm down Julia, it's not the Pope for God's sake." Once I regained my footing, my second attempt at getting dressed proved more fruitful. I took a breath and made my way down the hall, but then stopped abruptly. I knew someone was at the door asking for permission to enter, but because of the previous night's events, I got spooked, and Jack was gone. My mind was racing. Who could be out there, and then I remembered Sean was ribbing me before we left last night about getting the scoop on Andrew. I took another deep breath, pulled my wet hair into a loose bun, and proceeded to the door.

"Hey you," Sean said, walking past me, headed straight for the kitchen.

"Hi back," I said, exhaling, grateful it was him. "I decided to leave the knife in the kitchen this time," I said, my poor attempt at humor.

Sean laughed. "Thank you, I truly appreciate you not trying to stab me, Julia."

Sean pulled two wine glasses from the cabinet. I followed him, waiting for him to ask about the police cars from last night.

"So, tell me everything… did you and Andrew hook up?" he asked, grabbing the orange juice and prosecco from the fridge.

"Sean, for God's sake… I just met the guy," I said, furrowing my brow.

"Well, technically Rachel, it was your second meeting," he said, grinning at me.

I rolled my eyes. "Well, I'm not that easy my friend. I told you I'm not that kind of woman," I said, taking a seat at the counter. "I actually have some morales, at least I'd like to think I do."

"What kind of woman would that be Julia… the sexy kind that is interested in a hot guy. The kind of woman that might just get swept off her feet. There's no shame in that," he said, raising his eyebrows at me.

I blushed, then sighed, placing my elbows on the counter, and resting my chin on my clasped hands. "I actually thought you'd be more interested in why the police were here last night."

Sean immediately put the prosecco down and just stared at me. "You're kidding, right?"

"I am not kidding," I said, wishing I was.

"The police were here… last night? What are you talking about? What happened last night?"

"This guy broke in here last night," I said, like it was no big deal.

"What, oh my God… are you okay?" he said, reaching his hand across the counter, placing it protectively on my shoulder. "I spent the night at Chad's… I had no idea. When did this happen?" His facial expression had gone from playful to full-on concern.

"I'm fine," I said, waving my hand as if it were nothing. "It was around two in the morning. If Jack wasn't here though," I started, then my voice quivered, and I quieted, trying to control my emotions that just came out of nowhere. My hands dropped to my lap and my eyes fell along with them. "I don't know what would have happened," I finally squeaked out. So much for making light of the situation.

"Jesus Julia, what do you mean… what could have happened? This doesn't sound like just a robbery." Sean looked confused and afraid all at the same time. I knew the feeling all too well.

"And who the hell is Jack?" he said. "Should I know who he is?"

I cleared my throat, trying to swallow down the emotion. "Long story," I said, with an uncomfortable grimace. "Jack is my ex-husband, and without me knowing, he was here last night."

"What... how... why was he here? I... I don't understand?" he said stammering.

"It was a mix-up, plain and simple," I said, taking a deep breath. "Steph told me I could stay here, and Rob told Jack he could stay here. I didn't even know he was here until the guy had me in his grips and then Jack came out of the other bedroom and smashed a lamp over his head just as he was forcing me to the couch." I stopped again; the tears were coming now, no matter how hard I tried to hold them back. "Let me just say this, he definitely was telling me what he planned to do to me." I looked up at Sean, the tears were streaming down my face. He was just staring at me. It was like we were both frozen in that decisive moment, that moment of horror.

"Oh my God Julia! Jesus," was all he could get out.

"I shudder to think what he would have done to me," I said, through the tears. "Thank God I left the knife I threatened you with on the side table, but he got really pissed when I stabbed him in the leg."

Sean placed his hand on his forehead in disbelief. "You stabbed the guy... you actually stabbed him?"

"It was intense. The way he was touching me and the words he was whispering in my ear while he had hold of me." I shook my head, trying to get rid of the memory, trying to fight back the tears.

If he could have, Sean would have climbed over the counter to get to me. Instead, he rushed behind me and enveloped me with his arms, hugging me tightly.

"You're okay Julia... it's over now," he said, desperately trying to reassure me.

"Jesus... of all nights for me not to be here. I am so sorry."

I leaned back into him, placing my hands on his. "Sean, you couldn't have known and even so, you couldn't have helped. You wouldn't have even known anything was happening until the police arrived. They said this guy has been breaking into places over the last few weeks."

"Jesus! How could I not have heard about that?" Then Sean grabbed me by the shoulders. "C'mon, let's sit on the couch. This conversation deserves a spot where I can sit next to you." I stood up, leaning into him, letting him guide me to the couch. I sat down. Sean adjusted the pillow behind me, then put his arm protectively around me pulling me to him. I wanted to be stronger, but I gave in. I'd been trying so hard to forget it all, but just the mention of it brought everything to the surface.

"I probably shouldn't have approached him," I said, as I wiped the tears from my face, "but I was taken over by the fear of what could happen if I did nothing. I felt like I had to fight back."

"Don't even question yourself now. I'm sure you did exactly what you needed to do," he said, squeezing me tighter.

Then I lost it, again. "If I wasn't such an idiot, I would have gone out the bedroom window and avoided the whole thing."

"Don't Julia. Don't do that to yourself. It was a pressurized situation. Thinking straight is not exactly at the top of anyone's list in a moment like that."

I shook my head, disagreeing with him as the tears flowed. He just let me cry while he did his best to console me. He rubbed his hand up and down my arm like he was trying to warm me up. Suddenly, I realized what a fucking mess I was. Here I am, sitting with yet another someone I'd just met, acting like a complete lunatic. What was happening to me? I would have never been so unguarded in the past. What happened to not telling him?

"Okay," I finally said, sitting forward, wiping the final tears away, "that's enough about that." Sean released me, sensing I needed to move. I stood up quickly and walked over to the end table. I grabbed some tissues then sat back down on the couch, facing him. "Let's talk about something else please," I said, patting his leg, hoping to leave the memories of the night's horrifying events in the past where they belonged.

Sean turned toward me, resting his arm on the top of the couch. "Are you sure," he said, "I'm worried about you."

"I'm sure Sean, I need the distraction."

"Okay," he said reluctantly, "then let's move on to the good stuff. Let's talk about last night's dinner," he said grinning. "What do you think of Andrew... hot right?"

Sean's timing couldn't have been better. I had to hand it to him; he's the only one that could be such a caring, honest, gossip. I couldn't help but laugh. "Hot indeed," I said, while I blew my nose. "Sorry, that was gross," I said, then I looked at him and smiled.

"Julia," he said, rolling his eyes, like I was being ridiculous. "Anyway, you two seemed to hit it off. Am I right?" he asked. He was practically beaming waiting for my answer.

"I would say you are right." I couldn't help but glance up at him, a huge smile spreading across my face.

"I knew it!" he said, slapping his leg, his excitement apparent. "Awesome… are you seeing him again?"

"Yes," I said, smiling at him. "In fact, he's going to pick me up around noon today. God that sounds so weird to say. I haven't been on a real date in years," I said, raising my eyebrows concerned that I wasn't ready for this.

"Well, I'd say it's about time then," Sean said, hoping to alleviate any concerns I might have. "So, Jack…" he started to question, then he suddenly stopped mid-thought. "You said Jack is your ex, right?" I could see him trying to formulate another question for me. "Is his name Jackson Jones?"

"Yes… you know Jack?" I asked, wondering how in the hell he knew him.

"Jackson Jones came by my cottage yesterday. My parents are selling and… yah, I guess you could say I know him."

"Jack's your realtor? That's crazy."

"He seemed nice," Sean said, treading lightly. "He said he used to own a place a few cottages down… guess I know what cottage that is now. I can't believe I don't remember you guys. Well, anyway, I'm thinking he had to find another place to stay, right… did he?"

"Well, that's an interesting one." Now I was the one stammering. "He's staying here… with me. I mean he's staying in the other bedroom. It's complicated," I said, wringing my hands uncomfortably. "He added more clients to his trip, and he has nowhere to stay considering it's the weekend and all. Looks like there are no vacancies around here."

"He could stay at my place," Sean offered, knowing the situation was uncomfortable for me.

"I appreciate that Sean, but considering everything that's gone on, and him coming to my rescue and all, I actually feel better with him here, so I said it was fine. It's strange, but we'll figure it out," I said, then sighed leaning back, letting my head hit the couch cushion. "So, yah… there's that story."

"Straight out of a book," Sean said, raising his eyebrows. "Think about it Julia, in the minimal amount of time you've been here you've gone out on a date with a guy you thought was into you only to find out he's gay, then you unknowingly get set-up with his hot friend you'd previously met at a coffee shop, and to top it all off, later that night, your ex-husband becomes your knight in shining armor, fending off an intruder. Julia, you should start writing this down right now."

I laughed. "You think? I've never written a novel but boy this reeks romance novel, or maybe even horror story." Then I shook my head slightly. The worry and panic about what the hell I was doing here set in. I instantly questioned my plans with Andrew.

I leaned forward, staring at the floor. "I don't know if I should pursue Andrew," I said, not wanting to look at Sean. "The whole thing is ridiculous."

"Hey, don't you dare call that date off," Sean said sharply, placing his hand on my back. "You deserve a second chance Julia. You and Jack aren't married anymore… don't let this strange set-up end something before it can even begin."

I looked up, then looked him in the eyes with an 'I don't know' expression. I stood up, sighed deeply, then walked toward the sliding glass doors, my arms wrapped around me. I just stared out at the ocean. It was calm, unlike the way I felt inside; nothing but turbulence.

"I hear you," I said, sighing again, my back to him. "It's just so complicated. I haven't been on a date since before I was married, and now my first chance comes along and it's going to happen right under my ex's nose."

I turned to face Sean still seated on the couch. He was quiet, letting me get it all out before he said anything. I appreciated that about him; he was sensitive, and extremely patient.

I shook my head, giving into my fear. "It's too much Sean… this is crazy," I said exasperated, throwing my arms in the air. "I should just text Andrew and call it off."

Sean stood defiantly. "Don't you dare," he said. "No way in hell will I let you cancel. Julia, you deserve this even if it doesn't go anywhere. Trust me, it's just a date. Take a chance to have some fun. You owe it to yourself. Hell, you owe it to me. If you call it off, what does that say about my matchmaking skills?" His hands were on his hips now. He looked at me, grimacing. I'd only known Sean for two days, but it was like he knew me. He knew exactly what I needed to lighten my fear-based, uncertain, confused mood. I inhaled deeply then let the breath out. Breathing deeply seemed to be the only way I could find my calm these days.

I put my hands on my hips, my head down, and watched as my foot tapped the floor rhythmically. I was thinking over the situation, but then, suddenly, a wave of clarity hit me. I lifted my head, looked him in the eyes and said, "You're right… you are right." I repeated it because I needed him to know I meant it. "Jack and I have been done for years. It's my time now. Screw it."

"That's my girl," Sean said, clapping his hands.

"Just one thing," I said, holding up my hand. "Please don't tell Andrew about any of this… not about Jack or the break-in, please."

"Julia," he said, the protest evident in his voice. Then he took a breath. "Okay, I won't, but how are you going to hide Jack being here?"

"I'll be careful. I just can't do this if I have to explain everything to Andrew. I just want to go on like none of this ever happened. Okay… yes?" I said assertively, imploring Sean to agree.

"Okay, I understand, but if this seems like a relationship you want to pursue, you can't keep Andrew in the dark. Okay… yes?" he said, pushing the ball just as assertively back in my court.

"Yes," I agreed, shaking my head, and smiling. It felt good to talk about all of it, get it out, reason my way back into the date. I suddenly was excited again. Everything I felt last night with Andrew was starting to replace my fears and worries.

I walked to the couch and said, "Now, tell me about Chad, give me the scoop on this romance."

Sean smiled at the mention of Chad's name. He held his hands out to me, and I grabbed them happily, joining him on the couch.

"Hold on," he said. "This calls for mimosas."

I wasn't going to object. When he returned, I listened intently as he told me their story. Meeting at a noisy bar in Provincetown, wanting desperately to get out of there so they could spend some time alone together. They discreetly slipped out of the bar, leaving their friends behind, and spent their first evening together walking along the boardwalk; talking, laughing, falling for each other. That was a year ago. I felt swept up by their love story. Just by sharing that story, Sean was giving me everything I needed. In simple terms, I just needed to feel that a new beginning was possible for me. I needed to drop the fear and let myself feel hopeful. I needed to give myself possibilities. I needed to live, and I guess, just maybe, I wanted to get swept off my feet, just like him.

Chapter Twenty-One
Jack

Julia's car was still in the driveway when I returned at eleven. I can't lie, I was happy for a split second. I glanced at the back deck, but she wasn't there. When I opened the door, I saw her sitting next to a man on the couch. My first reaction was to protect her, but then I could see she was laughing. And just like that, my urge to protect her was replaced with an emotion I was all too familiar with—jealousy. I walked in, slamming the door behind me, my emotions clearly flaring.

"Julia?" I said, looking for an introduction to the stranger sitting on the couch. After twenty-two years together, I was sure she could read my expression. The man turned toward me, and I recognized him immediately. Just like the police the night before, I stood down.

"Hey Jack," he said, standing and walking toward me extending his hand.

"Sean?" I said, with a questioning look. "Sorry, I didn't recognize you from the back."

"Small world," Sean said laughing. "Man, just so glad you were here last night. Julia filled me in on the night's events."

"Yah, it was a scary scene, but between the two of us, we took him down, and lived to tell the tale," I said, with a nervous chuckle.

What was Sean doing here? She could only have just met the guy, and suddenly their best friends sitting intimately on the couch, talking, having mimosas, and laughing about God knows what. I suddenly felt extremely uncomfortable. I cleared my throat.

"Well, I'll let you two get back to your conversation, and Sean, like I said, I'll be in touch about the cottage."

"Sure thing Jack, looking forward to it," he said, nodding his head and smiling.

I put my head down and retreated to my bedroom. If I ever needed to go out for a walk, it was right now. Just seeing Julia with another guy was gut wrenching. Being here, at the cottage, at the Cape, was like being on a roller coaster; the ups and downs were wreaking havoc with my emotions. I looked angrily in the dresser mirror. "Fucking guy is younger and in better shape than me," I muttered. Even though I knew there was nothing I could do about it, the thought of Julia with Sean made me feel like shit.

Since the divorce I'd been faithfully exercising. It just hit me that it was time for me to take my health more seriously. I didn't have any excuses anymore. No young kids, no wife; just me.

As I changed into my workout gear, I wondered if Julia had even noticed that I'd dropped weight. She'd always been on me to do it, which is probably why I didn't—way too much pressure. And now here she is, flirting with a guy at least ten years younger than her, and in shape just like she always wanted me to be. I needed to get out of this cottage. Walking on the bay beach was one of my favorite things to do, especially at low tide. When I returned to the kitchen, I could see Julia on the deck, with her computer. I wanted to go out, sit, talk with her, and more, but I didn't. She made it clear earlier; she was just putting up with me being here.

I had just enough time to get my walk in then get to my appointment at 1 p.m. I walked out the side door, and down the path to the beach, hoping to find some clarity in my life.

Chapter Twenty-Two
Julia

I saw Jack out of the corner of my eye heading to the beach path. It looked like he was going for a walk. "Good for him," I thought, "he looks like he's dropped some weight." Jack had always been a big guy, but he gained a lot of weight over the years, mostly due to stress. It was easier for me to find the time to exercise during our marriage, plus he struggled so much with how he grew up; I think he had a tough time putting himself first. I think he felt like he didn't deserve to feel good about himself. He lost part of himself somewhere along the way, and I tried, but I couldn't find it for him. I felt like I was part of his problem as well. I didn't want that.

As soon as he disappeared down the beach path, I grabbed my phone and computer and bolted to my bedroom to get ready. I knew I had a short window to exit the cottage before Jack returned. After seeing his face when he came through the door earlier, when Sean was here, I knew there was no way he could handle Andrew showing up at the cottage. Little did he know, Sean was gay, and not a threat.

I was back to staring in the mirror when a text came through.

~

Andrew: "We still on for today? I can be there in thirty minutes."

Julia: "Yes, definitely! I'm starving."

Andrew: "Me too. Can't wait to see you. Be there soon."

Wink emoji or thumbs up? "Jesus Julia, just respond without overthinking for once."

Julia: "Wink emoji"

I held the phone to my chest. Shit, I just lost some time. I took a deep breath and said, "Here we go."

~

It was supposed to be warm today, so I dressed for a summer day. Since I wasn't sure where we were going, I pulled on a pair of jean shorts, a sleeveless workout top, and pair of sneakers. That was all I had for hiking gear. I quickly grabbed a backpack and tossed sunblock, sandals, skinny jeans, an artsy T-shirt, and jacket inside. He was making the plans for the day, and I was grateful for it. I didn't really mind being in the dark, it was kind of exciting.

I walked to the bathroom and put some makeup on, then took the elastic out of my hair. I watched it cascade over my shoulders. "Hair up or hair down?" I said, questioning myself yet again. But one thing I could admit, I did love my hair; it was the one thing I never complained about. I fussed with it for a few seconds then thought I couldn't have styled it any better if I tried. You gotta' love when that happens.

Just then I heard a knock at the door; thirty minutes had flown by in what seemed like a matter of seconds. I checked myself out in the mirror one last time, then thought, there's no time to improve on what's there—I needed to be okay with it.

In a flurry I bolted to the living room, pulled on a black cap, and grabbed my bag. I just wanted to get out of there before Jack came back. After this morning, I was reminded of how jealous Jack could be, and that was nothing I wanted to stir up, not that it mattered anymore, but just me thinking that meant it did. Before answering the door, I stopped for a moment, thinking Jack at least deserved a note. I grabbed a pen: "Out for the day and into the evening, just letting you know." I stepped back knowing it was the right thing to do after what he'd done for me, but I also didn't want to say too much. It was enough; he didn't need to know more than that.

I opened the door to see Andrew standing there with his back to me. He quickly turned around and smiled. God that smile—did he know what that did to me?

"Hey you," I said, trying not to smile too much.

"Hey right back at you," Andrew said. "You look fantastic, as usual."

I looked down at myself. "I'm wearing jean shorts and a workout top. You're silly."

"Well, it suits you," he said with a grin.

Andrew was wearing dark grey shorts and a powder blue T-shirt. The design was very cool: a skeleton wearing a winter hat, scarf, and sandals, holding a surfboard with the caption, 'Surf's Up.' His tattoos were clearly visible on his right arm. It was like I was taking him in, all in a few seconds. I felt the intensity of his deep brown eyes, but what I really wanted was to run my hands through his thick hair and let my fingers roam over his tattoo. Again Julia, who are you?

"Shall we," he said, offering his hand.

"Let's do it," I replied, smiling back.

I closed the door, locking it securely, then grabbed his hand without hesitation. His hand was warm in mine, just like last night. Just the touch of him sent shivers down my spine. It was like my hand was meant to hold his; they fit perfectly together. Another perfect I'd allow.

"Did you bring some extra clothes for later?" he asked, as we approached his truck. I held up my backpack and winked at him. He opened the door for me; I could tell he was looking at me as I stepped onto the running board. I'm not sure what he was checking out, my legs or my ass, but either way, I liked it.

Once in the car, I glanced toward the path—Jack was nowhere in sight. I sighed deeply; thank you God. One bullet dodged. As soon as we drove away, the guilt started to stream in. I felt guilty for not being honest with Andrew about Jack. I felt guilty for not being honest with Jack about Andrew. I was silently fighting an internal battle while Andrew drove. He didn't know it, but I was forcing myself to listen to the truth, and the truth was, I didn't answer to anyone—not Jack, and not Andrew. I answered to me.

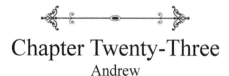

Chapter Twenty-Three
Andrew

Calm. The landscape on the Cape was calming to me. The colossal pines, the ebb and flow of the dunes, the Japanese silver grass, the salt and fresh water; it was predictable, familiar, quiet, and unmatched. Even the birds seemed at home here. The skyline wasn't blocked by unseemly buildings; even the trees were the right height. Living here was like living in another world.

Along the highway, the sand seemed like it had crawled from the beach to the roadside, begging to be seen and experienced by all who passed by. Post and rail fences, and cedar shake sided buildings dotted the landscape. It was almost like the air was cleaner here. It was like I could breathe easier here. I didn't feel bogged down by anything. My past took a backseat to the Cape.

I kept stealing glances at Julia; she looked right at home in the passenger's seat, like she'd always accompanied me. It was so strange how comfortable she seemed, like this was one of a thousand trips we'd made together. I know that's how I felt. I watched her roll the window down and take a deep breath. She looked so cute in that black cap, and man that hair, it spilled effortlessly over her shoulders like a warm blanket wrapping her up.

She didn't seem to mind the breeze sweeping over her. She didn't seem typical in that way, worrying about the wind ruining her look. The ocean may have been miles away, but I swore she could smell the salty air. She reached her hand out the window and let it ride over and through the stream of rushing air, as if it were riding a wave. She looked like a teenager, just living in the moment. I couldn't help myself, I had to comment.

"Didn't anyone ever tell you not to put your hand out the window," I said with a parental tone.

Julia looked over at me. "Oh yes, many times," she said. "You might get it cut off, right?"

"You got it," I responded. "But I'll allow it this one time." I winked at her, she smiled at me. Those eyes. Jesus!

I kept glancing over at her. I watched as she closed her eyes and let her head fall back against the seat. The sun washed its warmth over her face; how could it not be attracted to her; I know I was. I wished I wasn't driving so I could just watch her constantly—so I could sit right next to her, feel the warmth of the sun alongside her.

"I know you're looking at me," she said with a grin, breaking my silent adoration.

She was right, but how could I not; she was gorgeous, and although I wouldn't deny that her physical beauty was beyond words, it was the way she let herself go, how comfortable she was sitting there that really got to me. There was no pretense to her, she was just who she was, and I appreciated that. I knew we'd just met, but it was hard to imagine her not being in my life. "Slow your role," I thought to myself, "you'll scare her off."

"You're right," I said. "You caught me, but can you blame me?"

Julia smiled; her eyes still closed. "If I say no, would you think I'm conceited?"

I glanced over at her for what seemed like the millionth time. "You conceited… I have a hard time believing that."

Julia opened her eyes, rolled her head to the side, and smiled at me. Again, Jesus! Then she sat up in the seat. She looked like a little kid wanting to know when we'd be there.

"Where are we going anyway?" she asked, now less interested in the wind and the sun and more interested in my secrecy.

"It's a special spot… you'll see," I said grinning.

As we drove, Julia spotted my business sign. "Langdon Landscapes," she said, pointing to the sign. "Where nature and art intersect. Is that your business?"

"That's it," I said. "It's been a lot of work, but I'm finally at a point where the name is out there, which means steady business."

"That's an impressive building. I'm guessing you have some big crews to do the actual landscaping?"

"Yah, I've got some good people working for me, Sean being one of them. In the beginning, I was working outside daily, getting my hands dirty alongside the crew, but now I'm doing a lot more of the design work, along with Sean, which I love. I'd say we are an upscale shop, which is a good thing and a bad thing."

"Why is it a bad thing?" she asked, not understanding my comment. It was a good question.

"Upscale is good because of the money, but it can be tiresome dealing with people who have a lot of money because they're on board with the plan one day and change their minds the next, or even worse, they have the work done only to tear things out if they suddenly decide they don't like it. It's a slippery slope, but for the most part, the people are surprisingly good." Then I paused for a moment and decided to retract my statement. "I just heard myself… maybe I retract the bad thing comment. I just hate dealing with people who yank you around."

She glanced over at me nodding in agreement. "I understand. I hate that too." Then she added, "I love landscaping, getting my hands in the dirt, trying to make something beautiful out of an empty space. It's rewarding. It's kind of like writing, you get to see a finished product when you're done."

"You like landscaping?" I questioned, not seeing her as the type to be covered in dirt, plus her hands were so delicate, dare I say beautiful. I just couldn't imagine her working the land.

"Yah, I do… well I did. I rent now and the place is small, so I'm limited to planters on the patio, but back in the day I was making flower beds, planting trees and shrubs, and building stone walls. I even put our brick walkway in. It was so satisfying, and being outside was like heaven. The only problem was that I used it as a distraction… a distraction from writing."

"What do you mean, a distraction?" I asked, not making the connection.

"Writers don't always want to write Andrew. Sounds weird, doesn't it? I think the word is sabotage. I would sabotage myself by painting, landscaping, taking care of my kids… all good things in their own right, but all the things I could do to occupy my time when I fought writing."

Now I was shaking my head in agreement. "I get it. Even if it's something you really want to do, sometimes staying focused or even pushing yourself to be in the mood to do it can be a chore. Isn't it strange how we fight the things we love the most."

"I wish I wouldn't fight it so hard," she said. "Fighting something you really want doesn't make sense, but it still happens. Right now, although I'd say I'm in a bit of a writing slump, I have no excuses… no kids to take care of, no landscaping to do, no house to paint. I literally have no distractions... well, that is until now," she said, looking my way.

"Are you calling me a distraction?" I said teasing her.

"If the shoe fits," she said, teasing me right back.

I liked the way she teased me, which means I couldn't let her get away with it.

"Oh no," I said, giving her a quick shake of my head, "you can't rope me into this, plus it's the weekend, even I take time off on the weekend."

"Well, I'm glad to know you take some time for yourself. Everyone needs a reboot every now and then, don't you agree?"

I nodded and smiled at her. This was looking to be an awesome reboot day for me. I hoped it would be for her as well.

Julia took in the sites as we drove through Wellfleet Center. She pointed to the Harbor Inn and talked about eating lunch there on the outdoor patio with her mom and sister a few years back. It was nice to share common spots with her; we both had memories from here.

I watched her looking earnestly as we continued, trying to figure out where we were headed. We made numerous right turns through rural neighborhoods loaded with multitudes of pine and oak trees. Eventually the road led to a small bridge where a large salt marsh covered the low land. The cordgrasses were engulfed by the ocean tide and the surrounding islands looked like uninhabited guardians of the marsh. After another mile, I pulled into a drive to the left.

"Great Island," she remarked, reading the sign just before the parking lot. "How have I never heard of this?"

"It's an awesome spot for a hike. Lots of pines, lots of marshes, lots of ocean, lots of sand. Great Island trail is a beautiful place to kill three hours."

"Whoa, three hours... okay," she said, sounding a bit overwhelmed.

"Don't worry," I said, reaching for her hand, "it sounds more intimidating than it is. You're an athlete, I can tell. This will be no problem for you."

She looked at my hand, then covered it with hers and I gave into those emerald, green eyes. How does she do that to me?

"I'm excited," she said. "I've never been hiking on the Cape, which is weird considering how many times I've been here."

I loved the feeling of our hands together; I didn't want to let go. I could have stayed happily in the truck, just sitting in that parking lot with her. There were only a few cars in the lot, so I assumed we'd basically have the trail to ourselves. I parked and grabbed my backpack from the backseat.

"You ready for an adventure?" I asked, in sighting her to play along.

Julia took a deep breath. "I am. Just let me put this on and then I'll be ready to go," she said, grabbing the sunblock from her bag.

We walked side by side toward the trail. A plethora of tall pines littered the dirt with orange pine needles. I suddenly felt indecisive; should I grab her hand again or not? I just did it in the car, why wouldn't I do it now? I reached for her hand and grinned. "Just thinking about your safety."

"I'm not complaining," she said, threading her delicate fingers through mine.

Once through the pine grove, it was like the heavens opened. I could tell Julia was stunned by the open vista. We walked down a sandy path; the cordgrass was swaying gently in the breeze. There was something so soothing about ornamental grass, the way it moved, how hearty it was. I loved using it in landscapes.

"This is so beautiful," she said, mesmerized by the setting, "and the dunes are majestic, the way the ebb and flow through the landscape." Was she reading my mind from earlier?

"You sound like a writer," I said, squeezing her hand. She squeezed my hand back. I took that as a good sign.

"I'm guessing all your surfing is done on the ocean side?"

"How'd you know I surf," I remarked, totally forgetting about my T-shirt.

"Surf's Up… I love that store. We to used stop there every time we came down. My son Jacob loves to surf. Actually, he took his first surfing lesson from the owner, I think his name was Matt. Of course, we picked the worst or maybe the best day for it. I recall a storm was approaching and I remember thinking, what kind of mother am I sending my teenage son out into the wild surf."

"I'm sure it was an awesome time. Surfing can be dangerous… you just have to be smart. I love it because it's the one place you can go, by yourself, and just get lost. You a surfer?"

"I've made some attempts over the years," she said laughing, "but I'd hardly say I'm any good at it."

"Sounds like another possible date for us," I said, gripping her hand tightly. "I'd love to teach you." She nodded and smiled.

Soon the path we were on provided a detour to the ocean.

"Can we walk by the water?" she asked. I hated to say no, but I had my sights set on a specific spot just up the trail a bit.

"Not yet," I said, "this way."

Julia nodded and followed. The peaceful salt marshes occupied the land to the left, and in the distance, Wellfleet Harbor. We walked silently for another half mile. The sun was high in the sky, the ocean was softly lapping the shore, and the view was beyond compare.

"We'll take a right off the path just up ahead." I said, encouraging her on.

We stepped off the path and headed toward a secluded spot, where a few trees provided a refuge from other hikers. It was like the perfect hideaway; the beach was right there, but we could sit comfortably under those trees, undetected. Finally, I stopped and faced the water. I stared at the vastness of the ocean, then closed my eyes, and just listened. I peeked over at Julia; she had taken my cue. She looked so peaceful, her hair fluttering slightly in the breeze. I placed the backpack in the sand and removed the blanket. We sat down and just stared out at the water. Even though the trees offered a bit of shade, Julia seemed content sitting in the sun.

Within a few minutes, she removed her sneakers and socks, submerging her painted pink toes in the soft sand, wiggling them in and out, creating two small holes. She leaned back, placing her hands behind her for support and tilted her head back. She closed her eyes allowing the sun to warm her face. She looked so peaceful. It was exactly what I wanted her to feel.

"Pretty nice, right?' I asked. I just couldn't not talk to her. I wanted to know what was going on in that beautiful head.

"It's breathtaking," she said, "even with my eyes closed. This is officially my new favorite place on the Cape."

I laughed then removed the cooler from my pack. "Ham or bacon?" I asked, holding two large sandwiches in each hand.

"How 'bout we split... they both sound delicious."

"Sounds like a plan," I said, unwrapping them both. I handed Julia one half.

She took the sandwich and breathed in. "Oh my God... this smells like heaven. I'd almost forgotten I was hungry."

She took a bite and immediately closed her eyes. "Oh my God," she declared again, trying to cover her mouth which was now full of crispy bacon and Boursin cheese. "Did you get these from that French place on route six?"

"Yah… they've really expanded their menu over the years," I said, taking a bite of the ham and cornichon sandwich.

"Mmm, that one looks good too," she said, eyeing my sandwich.

"You wanna' bite," I offered, holding it out to her.

"Absolutely." I had to smile; she didn't even hesitate. I kind of enjoyed feeding her.

"Oh my God, that one is excellent as well," she said, holding her hand delicately to her mouth again.

She held her sandwich out for me to take a bite. There was something kind of intimate about being fed by someone. I loved that Julia wasn't afraid to eat. She seemed so unlike other women who were too self-conscious about their bodies to eat bread and cheese, or even bacon. After we ate, I stretched out on my side, propping my body up on one arm. I wanted an unobstructed view of her; I wanted to be able to look at her without her knowing. She pulled her knees to her chest, and just stared out at the ocean.

"What made you want to be a children's book author?" I asked.

"God, that makes it sound so legit," she said. I could sense she was uncomfortable with the label.

"Well, it is," I said, smiling at her supportively. She smiled back and told me the story.

"I didn't always know. I mean, I loved English in high school, but I don't think I took writing seriously until I went to college… that's when I started dreaming of being a writer. It just took me awhile, you know—kids came along." She glanced back at me. I gave her an understanding look.

"When the kids were young, I tried to get published, but it just didn't happen for me then. It became that thing… that thing, like if I talked to other people about what I was doing, I felt like I was just blowing smoke, like I was lying. I hated that feeling. I felt like a liar, a dreamer, a person who talked the talk but didn't walk the walk. You know what I mean?"

I shook my head again, knowing exactly what she meant.

"I have to give my sister the credit for helping me get connected to a publisher; she's always had my back. I had a slew of children's books I'd been working on, but that industry is so difficult to break into. I mean, if I were a celebrity there'd be no issue; even Trump could get a children's book published."

I couldn't help but laugh. She looked back at me and smiled.

"It was never about making money, it was about accomplishing a dream, my dream. Now, I'd really like to give adult fiction a try. I don't know if I can make the switch, but I'd love to write something meaningful. I don't want my legacy to be some stupid chocolate cake recipe I leave to my kids. I want to write something that really makes an impact on people… even if the cake is awesome."

I laughed, amused by her last comment. I couldn't help but ask the next question.

"So, tell me Julia… what's this cake you're talking about?"

She just looked at me, smirking. "You're funny," she said, then laughed and turned back to the water. "Actually, it's a damn good cake. The 'Ultimate Chocolate Cake.' Maybe, if you're lucky, I'll make it for you someday."

"Looking forward to it. I love chocolate cake."

We sat there quietly for a few more minutes, until she broke the silence.

"Can I ask you a question now?" she said, glancing down at me.

"Sure, anything," I replied.

"Your tattoos, I assume there is meaning behind them."

I looked down at my arm. When you put a tattoo in plain sight, you know someone will ask about it at some point. I drew in a deep breath and looked out at the ocean. It's not like I didn't want to tell her, it's just that it was a story, one I didn't think I'd be sharing on a second date. I knew she could tell I was stalling, so she sweetly offered me a way out.

"You don't have to answer that… it's personal, I understand."

I was quiet for a moment, then I offered an apology. "I'm sorry Julia," I said, my gaze now on the water. "It's definitely got a lot of meaning."

"Again, you don't have to explain it to me. Maybe I should have just said it's beautiful and left it at that."

The last thing I wanted was for her to feel bad about asking. My tattoos covered my forearm, and not that she could see, but they continued up my arm to my shoulder.

"It's okay Julia. It's right there in plain sight, plus, I'm really not trying to hide it. I'll tell you." I sat up and pulled at my sleeve revealing the whole tattoo. "It's in memory of my mother," I said, running my fingers over my arm. "She died when I was in college... breast cancer. I've been adding to the original over the years."

A single dove carrying a solitary orchid flew above the ocean waves, heading up my arm to where a set of stairs extended into the heavens, clouds surrounding it. Ecclesiastes 3: 1-4, was written on the stairs. Just at the top of the stairs, were two outstretched arms, presumably Jesus, reaching out from the heavens, with fields of wildflowers and more clouds surrounding them.

"I'm so sorry Andrew," she said apologetically, probably wishing she'd never asked.

"Thank you," I said, clearing my throat. "It was a long time ago. I guess I just needed something to remember her by, something I could see every day. It was a tough time in my life. She was an incredible woman. If it weren't for her, I wouldn't have my business. She was always setting money aside for me, but I never knew that until she passed." I took a deep breath. I didn't want my emotions to get the best of me, not yet. "She was quite a gardener as well, probably where my passion for nature comes from. She always went out of her way to support me, no matter what my crazy schemes were. I can't say as much for my dad, but we'll leave that thought for another time."

Julia's fingertips feathered my tattoo delicately. It felt like she was trying to be part of the story somehow.

"I'm sure she'd be very proud of what you've achieved."

The mood changed between us. We were both introspective for a moment, then Julia turned her back to me. I felt like I'd ruined the date at this point, but when I looked over at her, she was pulling at her shirt, exposing her right shoulder. She had a tattoo. It was on the inside of her shoulder blade; a dandelion puff, with some of the seed heads flowing off into the unseen breeze. I reached up and ran my fingers over it, wondering what this meant. And then she offered an explanation.

"After we had Jacob, our first, I got pregnant again, pretty quickly," she said, her voice suddenly distant. "I lost the baby after a month." She took a deep breath and turned to face me. "I needed to acknowledge that baby in some way. I didn't really want to see the tattoo every day, but I just needed to carry that baby with me. So, two years ago, I got this. I'm not sure why I waited so long. I feel more complete with it."

Her voice trembled, and I could see tears welling up in her eyes. I sat up instantly and pulled her to me; she rested her head on my shoulder. I breathed her in; her hair smelled of coconut and apricot. We sat quietly, huddled together, absorbing each other's pain. Past or not, pain is pain. Then Julia suddenly pulled away. "That's enough of that," she said, wiping her eyes. "Let's choose happiness now. I'd rather focus on being happy."

I rubbed her back, then lay back down, propping myself on my elbow again.

"Tell me about your kids," I said, hoping that would make her happy.

"My kids..." she said smiling, her focus back on the water again. "My kids are the best! My oldest Jacob is twenty-four. He lives in Utah. He's a videographer and an illustrator. He illustrated both of my books. He is beyond chill," she laughed. "I would be a better person if I just followed his lead. He's got that snowboarder slash skateboarder vibe. He's an outdoorsman for sure."

"Sounds like a cool guy," I interjected.

"He most definitely is. And he still loves to surf. Obviously, Utah doesn't provide much on the surfing front, but he trades the snow for the surf when he travels to California and Hawaii... he loves to travel as well."

"Jess is my middle child, my only girl. She's twenty-three. She's an apparel buyer for a small company near Boston. She's planning her wedding for next fall. She's confident, straight to the point, and yet so open-minded. Oh, and can I gloat for a second... she's gorgeous as well."

"I don't doubt that with a mom like you," I said, hoping to embarrass her just a little bit. She looked at me and smiled. It was the kind of smile that said, 'you're just saying that.' I let it go at that.

"Justin is my youngest. He's twenty-two and he's a realtor. He is full of it, to say the least. He's never afraid to speak his mind, and obsessive compulsive to boot. I'm told he's a lot like me," she said, sighing deeply, "but sometimes that angry side spills out and I won't lay claim to that side of him."

I brushed the last comment off, assuming she was referring to her ex.

"Sounds like they all have made their way in life," I said, then added, "Jesus, you must have been really young when you had kids, and they're really close in age too."

She paused for a moment. Did I overstep?

"Well," she said thoughtfully, "despite what the standards are today, yes, I was young. We were just finishing college and boom, we got pregnant. We never talked about abortion; it wasn't even a thought. We both wanted to have kids eventually, but it just happened earlier than we were prepared for, and having three in four years wasn't easy," she said laughing. "But I don't regret it, being so young and having them one after the other because it meant I'd still be young when they got older. I guess I feel like I have a leg up on other parents because even though I feel old sometimes, I also feel kind of young. At least I have the energy to live life on my own now," she said confidently.

"You are young Julia," I said, looking into her eyes, "cuz if you're old, then I'm old too, and I'm not ready for that."

Julia laughed. "I wouldn't trade them for anything. I was always happy to be a stay-at-home mom. I just loved being around them. I mean, they got into their fair share of trouble, but what kids don't. Then she paused. "They were… scratch that, they are everything to me."

"I can see how passionate you are about being a mom. I bet you were a great mom when they were little." I could tell I'd made her feel a little uncomfortable because she flipped the questions to me now.

"What about you, have you ever been married? Have any kids?"

I should have known that question was coming. I placed my focus back on the water. "Never found the one I guess, and to my knowledge, I have no children." I laughed, then apologized. "Sorry, I'm just joking."

"Do you want kids?" she asked. I was surprised by the question, but I knew why she was asking.

"I think that ship has sailed. I'm not sure I could handle it at my age anyway, plus, if I wanted kids now, I'd have to find a woman who's a lot younger than me, and I'm not looking to share the rest of my life with someone I can't even relate to, you know what I mean?"

"I do," she said in agreement. "With kids in their twenties, I could never seriously date someone younger. It's just too weird, never mind what you said about having nothing in common." Then she paused and said, "Of course, I did think Sean and I were on a date, soooo… not sure what the hell I'm talking about," she said laughing. "At my age, interest from a thirty something was just fun to think about, it's not something I'm looking for."

I felt like the two of us were on the same page, which was a good sign. After another twenty minutes of chatting, we packed up and walked along the shore. I didn't hesitate this time to take her hand in mine. The water was calm, and I felt a strange sense of calm with her by my side. Talking with her was easy; none of it was forced. She seemed to enjoy hiking as well. Again, all of it was effortless.

Hours later, we were back in the parking lot. I opened her door, taking in every part of her as she eased into the truck. Her physical appearance was perfect, that wavy auburn hair, those emerald, green eyes, and that body. But I knew there was more to my attraction to her than that, but God that didn't hurt. I wanted more moments like the one we had on the beach. I wanted to know everything about her all at once; her struggles, her dreams, her fears, her every day. Everything in me said, she's the total package. I desperately wanted to submerge myself in her. If I uncovered what I thought was there, the phrase, 'where have you been all my life,' would truly fit. I didn't know I was looking for someone until I met her; guess Sean was right.

"Phew," I said, feeling the hike as I climbed behind the wheel. "How you doin?"

"I'm good," she said. "Nothing like a great workout."

"Too tired to extend the day?"

"Depends, what do you have in mind? More hiking?"

I lowered my head and smiled. "If we hike any more, I'll be too sweaty to go anywhere else." She laughed.

"How does a trip to 'P-town' sound… there's a restaurant there I think you'll love. You up for it?"

She had that look in her eyes, like are you daring me. Then she smiled and said, "I am definitely up for it, even if we are sweaty."

Why did her response not surprise me? I couldn't help but smile.

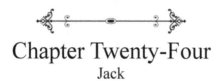

Chapter Twenty-Four
Jack

I walked up the path from the beach, drenched with sweat, but satisfied. Despite all that had transpired, I felt damn good about myself, which these days was rare. Julia's car was still parked in the driveway, so I expected to find her on the deck or inside.

"Julia," I called out as I entered the cottage. No answer. I knew she wasn't on the deck, and I knew she'd already taken a shower. Just thinking about her standing at the door in her towel sent me over the edge. That gorgeous hair, even wet, was a turn on. I glanced down at the entry table and read the note she'd left.

"She's probably out with Sean," I muttered, my jealousy rearing its ugly head again.

Couldn't she just put dating on the back burner while I'm here. Jesus! She obviously didn't even think how it would make me feel. I walked into the kitchen and opened the fridge. One beer stood next to the bottle of water; I grabbed the beer. I walked out onto the deck hoping more fresh air would stop the negative voices in my head, but I couldn't stop muttering about Julia and men and flirtation.

I chugged the beer and slammed the bottle down on the railing. "Fuck it," I shouted, then walked into the cottage and grabbed a towel. Maybe a shower would drown out the noise. I always loved the outdoor shower. It was the one place Julia, and I could escape and just take one another in. "Fucking hell... this fucking door is such a pain in the ass." After three tries, the door finally opened, and I was on my way to relaxation. As I stepped under the stream of water, I couldn't help but wish Julia was here with me. I loved standing behind her, rubbing my beard against her neck and shoulder, letting my hands roam over her breasts. She's all I knew. The warm water felt good running down my face. I rubbed my eyes repeatedly, then looked up at the sky.

"What the hell! What the fucking hell am I doing here? Why can't

I just let her go."

From there my thoughts moved with lightning speed to high school days. "Why does this happen to me? What is it about me that makes women want to leave?" I thought Julia and I had something unique, something lasting, but even that went to shit. "Is it them or is it me?" I sputtered. My emotions were getting the best of me. I tried to suppress them by taking numerous deep breaths, until finally the anger welled up and overcame my attempt to cope.

"This is bullshit," I shouted, infuriated by my thoughts. I shut the shower off, and placed my hands against the fencing, as if that would support me emotionally. I needed to do something. I needed to get the fuck out of here. I toweled off quickly then flew into the house to get dressed. I grabbed my keys and started for the door, but then I stopped abruptly, the note on the table caught my eye. I read it again then crumpled it into a ball.

"If you can go, so can I," I muttered spitefully.

I threw the note into the living room. The pain I felt was familiar, just like when she left two and a half years ago.

I walked to my car. Where could I go? I was leaving it up to the car to decide; I just drove. I pulled into a bar about five miles away. I was familiar with the place, well known for its party scene. Of course, it was early afternoon, so I didn't expect much to be going on, which was exactly what I wanted; time alone to get lost in the booze.

When I walked in, there were plenty of seats at the bar. I picked one and hoped to find some peace. "What can I get you?" the female bartender asked placing a napkin in front of me.

"I'll have an extra-dry dirty martini, grey goose, two olives and rocks on the side."

"Bleu cheese?"

"Nope, just regular, thanks."

The bar was pretty empty, but within thirty minutes the college football crowd was filing in. I looked around; mostly younger people, hoping to do what I was doing—letting the booze take us away. I remembered those days in college; out all hours, hitting the bars, meeting girls, hoping to get laid. But I had to admit, I really wasn't that kind of guy. Before Julia came along, I dated, slept with a few, but certainly wasn't a womanizer. I left that shit up to Coop and others like him. And after what my mother did, it wasn't easy to treat sex so casually, even if I wanted it. I had to at least feel something for the girl.

I took a sip of my martini, then turned my stool to get a better look around the room. There were certainly women here closer to my age. What if all this time I'd been wrong? Maybe playing the field was what I should have been doing. Maybe I should be looking right now to get to know someone, so to speak. After about an hour of sitting there, making minor chit chat with the bartender, the man sitting next to me left, and a woman sat down.

"Hey there," she said, with an Australian accent.

"Hey," I said, not sure if I wanted to engage. But then in a flash, after checking her out, I thought, what the hell?

Just then the bartender interrupted.

"What can I get you Dee?" she asked. "The usual?"

She nodded, then fidgeted with her napkin.

"Jack," I said, extending my hand to her.

"Denise," she said, shaking my hand.

I had to laugh. Denise, of all names. I couldn't help but notice how pretty she was: long wavy blond hair, deep blue eyes, and tall; the opposite of Julia. I'm guessing she was around forty. I can't lie, she was the distraction I was looking for.

"I've never seen you here before'," she said, "you on holiday?"

I laughed. It was certainly no holiday. "Holiday… no, no, just business," I said. "And you?"

"I own a health food store a couple of towns over."

"That's interesting," I said. "I'm assuming you weren't' born here."

"Ah, good ear," she said, with a chuckle, "actually, I was born in Melbourne, Australia."

"How the heck did you end up here?" I asked, interested in her story.

"Family," she said. "My brother moved here five years ago; he opened a surf shop and begged me to come, and it's by far the best decision I've ever made."

"That's a big move… impressive," I said, taking a sip of my martini. It wasn't hard to see there was more to her than good looks.

"And you Jack, what is the business that brought you here?" she asked, then delicately placed her lips on the straw in her water glass. I was mesmerized for a second. That feeling hadn't happened for a long time. I didn't realize it was possible unless Julia spurned it on.

"Real estate," I said, looking away quickly.

"So, I'm guessing you don't live here. Where do hail from?" she said, pushing her straw around the ice cubes.

"South Shore. A few friends needed my help with their listings, so I made the trip. I used to own down here, so I'm familiar with the area," I said, taking as many glances of her as I could without getting caught.

The bartender delivered a Cabernet to Denise, Julia's favorite wine.

"Let's toast," she said, raising her glass. "Here's to your success with your listings," she said, clanking my glass.

We both took a sip. As the afternoon slipped into the early evening, Denise and I swapped stories about traveling, family, and business. We ordered some appetizers and before long we were laughing about favorite comfort foods and things we would never do.

"You wouldn't bungee jump, huh. I figured you for a daredevil," she said laughing.

"God no, not me," I said, brushing her comment off. "Two feet firmly on the ground, that's about as daredevil as I get."

"I'm just kiddin'," she said, bumping my shoulder with hers. "There's no way I would do that either... too bloody scary." Her flirtatious blue eyes met mine in an unusually intimate moment. I didn't know what to do with it. It'd been a long time since I needed to impress anyone, but then again, I felt like she was just accepting me for who I was.

Before I knew it, I was six martinis in and feeling no pain. By 7:30 p.m., Denise checked her watch and did what I was hoping she wouldn't do.

"Jack, I have thoroughly enjoyed this spontaneous meeting, but I have a commitment in 'P-town' at eight, so I hate to say, I've got to go."

She got up and gathered her bag and jacket. I was taken aback by the abrupt halt to the conversation. I was actually enjoying myself. It'd been a long time since I talked to any woman like that. I didn't want her to go.

"Here's my information," she said, pulling a business card from her bag. "Give me a call when you're back in town... I really enjoyed our conversation." She placed her hand deliberately on my shoulder.

Women today are so unapologetically forward, but I can't lie; I was loving it. I took her card, then pulled a card from my wallet and handed it to her.

"You too," I said, "I mean give me a call if you ever venture off the Cape. I enjoyed it as well. Just what I needed." I winked at her, then watched her leave. She was incredibly attractive and fit as well, just like Julia. Damn it! Why the hell am I comparing her to Julia?

All the feelings I had successfully fought off over the last seven hours came rushing back in. Suddenly, I was inundated with them. Even the noise level in the bar couldn't drown out the noise in my head. I motioned for the bartender to make me another—I wasn't ready to leave yet.

By 8:30 p.m. I had the bartender call me an uber. At least I did that right. On the ride home my thoughts circled around Julia; was she home, where had she been, who was she with? I felt lost. When I got back, I walked around Julia's car, grabbing it for support. I clumsily made my way up the deck stairs, nearly falling as I retrieved the key from under the ceramic frog. As soon as I got inside, I staggered to the couch, and passed out.

Chapter Twenty-Five
Julia

By the time we reached 'P-town' it was 4 p.m. The ride was stunning; everything I remembered it to be. Between the rows of houses to the left, dotting the shoreline, and the sloping dunes to the right, flowing effortlessly in and out of the landscape, the scene was beyond beautiful. It was like coming home again.

Andrew pulled down a side street; he'd obviously been here countless times, knowing secret short cuts to get us to the pier. He parked in the main lot near Macmillan Wharf, which was almost full. As I remembered, parking in 'P-town' was always an issue, especially on the weekends when the crowds were abundant. The lot was basically located in the center of town, so it put us right in the middle of all the action.

I hopped out of the truck, stretched, and lifted my face to the sun.

"You're a sunworshipper," he said, glancing over at me. "Seems like you can't get enough."

"Believe it or not, I truly love my rainy days; guess that's the introspective writer in me, but I have to admit, there is something about the sun here. I just want to absorb every ounce of it even if I shouldn't… but that's a story for another day," I said, not wanting to ruin the moment. "I can't believe how warm it still is. God, what a gorgeous day!"

He must have understood because he let my comment slide.

"It's one of the reasons why I love the fall," he said. "It's truly the best of all the seasons. One day you could be outside, basking in the sun, and the next you're sidling up to a cozy fire for warmth."

"I agree," I said smiling, loving that we shared yet another thing in common. "Dare I say the air just feels crispier, more fragrant in the fall."

He put his sunglasses on and walked over to me. I missed seeing those gorgeous brown eyes, but Jesus, he looked like a model from

GQ.

"Grab your jacket, just in case it gets cool later," he said, grabbing my backpack. "I'm hoping the storm they've predicted holds off long enough for us to enjoy the evening."

I'd forgotten about the forecast. I recalled the storms on the Cape could be extremely intense. I grabbed my jacket from the bag but took my sandals out as well. My sneakers were a bit too casual for this part of the date; they certainly did not, in any way, make me feel sexy, and I wanted to feel sexy, look sexy for him.

We started walking down the boardwalk. Andrew instinctively grabbed my hand, like it was just what we did—we held hands, like a couple who'd been together for years, or at least for a few months. There didn't seem to be a lot of thought behind it; I didn't feel like either of us were overthinking it. It was just us being us, as if there were a real us. Was there?

I could see the infamous building at the end of Fisherman's Wharf where five enormous, larger-than-life, black and white portraits of women were on display.

"I love those photos," I said, pointing to the building as we walked. "They make such a statement."

"They Also Faced the Sea," Andrew said. "That's the title of the collection. Those five women represent all the Portuguese American women of Provincetown who were considered the backbone of the fishing village at one time. Pretty inspiring. The locals know that building as the old fish-packing plant at the end of Cabral's Pier."

I looked at him, wondering how he knew that.

"I never knew that's what it was called. I've always been fascinated by it. They just seem like real people; you know what I mean… like hardworking women who lived hard lives but embraced every bit of it. Inspiring to say the least."

I felt his grip tighten on my hand acknowledging the moment we'd just shared.

"Did you ever go on a whale watch with the kids?" he asked, as we strolled across the boardwalk.

"We did when they were a lot younger. We used to rent a place on the cheap in Eastham. We found some pretty cool things to do besides going to the beach. Climbing up Pilgrim Monument was fun for them, a workout for me," I said, with a chuckle.

"Well, I bet you did it with ease. We'll skip it this time," he said, leaning into me. "I think we've done enough exercise for one day. Maybe a sunset cruise would be a better choice for us sometime," he said, as we turned onto the narrow street.

Another date? I liked the way he was thinking.

"That sounds like fun," I said, echoing his interest. "I've always wanted to do that."

Commercial Street was a one-of-a-kind experience, and I was thrilled to be back. 'P-town' was just as I remembered it, bustling with activity. It was certainly one of the most unique places I'd ever visited. The one-way street was littered with a plethora of shops, from jewelry and clothing to candy and art galleries. And oh God, the Portuguese Bakery; I could smell the sweet bread as we passed by—even I would splurge on that. The town provided an eclectic array of visitors with the ideal place to just be themselves without judgment. Wear what you want, hold hands with whomever you want, love whomever you want. Freedom, I guess, that's the best way to describe it.

As we walked, I told Andrew my recollections of being a kid on vacation in Provincetown.

"I think, right over there is where my parents had us sit for portraits," I said, pointing toward a wide alleyway where the artist's cramped studio used to be.

"Wow, really," he said. "How old were you?"

"Probably around eight, I guess. It's funny we all did it without much complaint. I mean, being a kid, on vacation, and having to sit still for a portrait is kind of a lot to ask."

He laughed. I loosened my grip on his hand, allowing my fingers to feather his palm. He looked down at me and smiled. I smiled back.

Street performers were gathered in front of the town hall, some playing guitars and others playing steel drums. Andrew stopped and pulled a few bills from his wallet. It didn't surprise me to see how generous he was. We walked another hundred feet and then he stopped. "Here we are," he said, looking to the left; The Watering Hole."

I stopped in the middle of the street, taking a moment to take it all in, and there was a lot to take in. It was a small, old, white clapboard house turned into a restaurant. It was decorated outside with lobster traps, multi-colored buoys covering an upper deck railing, planters filled with mums and maiden grass, and inviting signs just begging potential customers to grab food-to-go or head to the Beach Bar in the back. I knew exactly where Andrew was headed.

It wasn't crowded yet, but I had a sense it would be soon. There were large picnic tables as well as round wooden tables with red umbrellas and blue chairs set up in the dining area outside. The floor was a combination of decking and sand, creating a free-flowing, casual atmosphere. The entire area was lit with outdoor string lights. I loved how they used pieces of tall driftwood as poles to float the lights high above the dining area. Over the years, I'd gotten overly attached to driftwood; the possibilities for this preserved wood were endless. The bar was located at the back of the building. It was small but accommodated at least ten red metal stools. Past the dining area, in between the dense beach grasses, I spotted a path leading out to the beach. I could see an old piece of weathered fencing decorated with more buoys and a few more planters flanking the path with enormous yellow and orange mums in them. My view of the ocean was unobstructed.

We found a table in the left corner, providing us with some privacy, but also a lot of people watching as well; one of my favorite activities. I could get a lot of writing ideas from this place. Andrew walked up to the bar to grab some drinks, while I just sat back, taking photos of this amazing spot.

"Here you go," he said, handing me a beer.

"This place is so quaint, so cozy, I love it."

"Me too. It's a go to spot for me whenever I'm down here, which isn't as much now as it used to be. For some reason, more work has been popping up near Chatham lately. This is definitely the spot to be though, especially if you love the nightlife. It gets pretty lively as the evening goes on."

The server interrupted just then. "Hey Andrew, how've you been? It's been a while."

Andrew smiled at her, they obviously knew each other, which didn't surprise me at all. He sat back and looked up at her. "It has been a bit. I'm good Sherry. You're lookin' good."

"Thank you, my friend, I'm doing well."

Then he turned his gaze to me. "Sherry, this is Julia."

We traded hellos. Andrew was a thoughtful guy; he didn't have to introduce me. It felt good to be the one here with him. I kind of felt like a shiny new toy; hopefully, that wasn't exactly the case. It was sweet though, and even that small gesture made an impact on me.

By the time the food came, the outdoor lights romantically engulfed the area in a warm glow. Every time Andrew looked away, I took the moment to take him in. He kept saying I was beautiful, but God, he was so handsome. He took my breath away.

"Lobster rolls and chowder," Andrew said between bites, "can't get any more Cape Cod than this."

I shook my head in agreement, taking a sip of my beer. I'd decided prior to ordering that I would just go with the flow and not freak out about food. But in the back of my mind, I'd just eaten a sandwich at lunch that was full of cheese, bacon, and bread. I had to even things out somewhere. So, I got a salad with grilled shrimp, but not chowder. He seemed fine with it, but I must admit, the chowder looked delicious. One bite wouldn't kill me.

"What's your stance on sharing soup," I blurted out, eyeing his chowder.

"I'm indifferent," he said, holding a spoonful out to me. I let him feed me, just like on the beach. He was being so sweet; not everyone will share soup, but he didn't seem to mind. I mean, it's not like I was being one of those women who don't order fries and then eat all their date's fries. I wasn't that crazy. But who am I kidding; I don't eat fries.

"Good?" he asked.

"Good," I said.

"You want some more?"

I held my hand up. "No, I'm good with just a taste."

Little did he know that just me eating the sandwich at lunch, and tasting the soup, I was well over my limit. I know it seemed like I was really into it, which I was, but no matter how much we had hiked, my guilt, my fears started piling in. I kept telling myself I'd be fine, I had to be. I wasn't ready to divulge my secret to him yet. Then my brain really took over; why couldn't I just be normal? My face must have been telling because the next thing I knew, he was asking me if I was okay. Guess I wasn't much of an actor.

"Yes, of course," I said, placing my hand on his. "I guess lunch just filled me up more than I thought."

"No pressure… lunch was pretty awesome," he said, smilingly at me reassuringly.

I immediately felt relieved, but the voices still haunted me. I wanted to enjoy the night. I hated myself for scrutinizing my food. The never-ending battle waged on. I knew the constant negative voices would forever haunt me, but I was begging them to stop, just for tonight.

We finished dinner and watched the sunset from our seats. If anything could deter me from agonizing over my ridiculous self, it was a sunset.

"Another beer?" he asked, standing to go to the bar.

"Sure, that'd be great." Somehow alcohol didn't work into my food paranoia equation.

I couldn't stop looking at him as he walked away. Everything about him was so appealing. Of course, he was very handsome, in shape, and I assumed financially sound. But it was the hidden from view qualities that made my heart skip a beat. Everything he shared on our hike, the way he prepared a meal for us, the way he watched over me while we hiked, the way his fingers traced the tattoo on my back; that in particular—his gentle touch, it still gave me shivers.

I watched him as he stood by the bar, leaning in to talk to the bartender. It looked like they knew one another. I couldn't stop watching him; the way he laughed, the way he ran his hand through his hair. "Stop staring, Julia," I thought, lost in him. But suddenly, I got caught off guard and my moment of indulging in him came to an abrupt halt.

"Who the hell is that?" I said, under my breath.

I watched as this pretty, young, blond woman walked up behind Andrew. She was about my height but thinner. She placed her hands over his eyes from behind. He stood upright and turned to her. She practically jumped into his arms. He held onto her for a second, but he seemed like he was trying to release her. I watched as he glanced my way. The woman wouldn't let him go. I knew I shouldn't feel what I was feeling; I barely knew him.

I watched them talk. She kept rubbing her hand up and down his arm. Was I jealous? Was I feeling jealous over a guy I just met? Yup, I most definitely was, but was I jumping to conclusions? Why can't I just think she's another acquaintance? I mean, I don't even know who this person is. But I wasn't in the mood to be rational; she was clearly flirting with him.

"Get a hold of yourself Julia," I whispered. I sat there frozen, caught up in their moment. I knew I was staring. "Stop staring, Julia." My elbows sturdied me against the table, while my clasped hands covered my mouth. I let my thumb nervously trace my lips.

I could see Andrew looking at me. I wanted to look away, but I couldn't. And then things got worse. She hugged him again. "What is this chicks deal?" I feel like he's just putting up with her, but before he can push her away, this guy walks up behind him, and taps him on the shoulder. The woman finally releases him and steps back. I almost think she's smiling. This scene is going to shit fast.

The guy is in Andrew's face. I can see his jawline tighten; he's poking his finger into Andrew's chest. I can only guess he's here with her. I watch the scene unfold like I'm watching a movie. Andrew backs away from him, his hand waving him off. I can hear their voices getting louder, but I can't make out what they're saying. Suddenly, the guy shoves Andrew and just as quickly I see his arm clock back. I stood up instantly, my chair hitting the floor, as I watched Andrew catch the guy's arm mid-punch and spin him around, arm behind his back and his face pressed firmly into the bar.

The bartender hurriedly walked over to them. Andrew leaned into the guy and said a few more words. The woman who started it all just stood there, calmly watching the scene unfold. She had a huge smile on her face. And then she did it; she looked my way. "You are such a bitch," I mumbled. The bartender leaned over, whispering something to the guy whose face had now become part of the bar. Andrew released him, grabbed our beers, and walked back over to me. The guy stood up, notably embarrassed. He was talking to the blond, his unhappiness with her evident. I could clearly see the frustration on his face, and then I watched him turn away from her, and leave the bar. Jesus, that was some scene. I turned to grab my chair and sat back down.

"What the hell was that?" I asked, "Are you okay?"

"The guy's drunk. I know him… he's drunk," Andrew offered looking back toward the scene. He didn't offer me an explanation about the woman.

I can't take not knowing who she is.

"What's her story?" I asked, probing a bit.

Andrew took a sip of his beer. He looked at me, then gently took my hand in his and told me the truth.

"I used to date her. Erica… I used to date Erica. She obviously just wanted to make the guy jealous," he said, taking another sip so he didn't have to look at me.

I didn't really know what to do with this. I looked over at her; she was still standing at the bar, chatting with some people, but she hadn't taken her eyes off Andrew. I felt so uncomfortable. I cleared my throat. I didn't want him to think I was jealous, but it was hard not to be. I decided to go for diplomatic and charming instead of accusatory.

"I think she still likes you… who could blame her." Andrew didn't look her way, he was focused on me, which is a good sign, for me anyway. He smiled, his thumb sweeping gently across my hand.

"You're making me blush," he said, then he gave me a 'thank you for understanding' smile. He looked down into the beer as if he could make what just happened disappear in it.

"Let's forget that just happened," I said, knowing we both needed to forget it. We sipped our beers and talked about our tattoo experiences and how we'd like to get more. We laughed, our eyes met over and over, our hands still touching. With the warmth of the sun now gone, the cool evening air was circling around us. He was right about the temperature, but I didn't grab my jacket because he was pulling my chair next to him. He put his arm around me, and I snuggled in. We talked about our dreams for the future. I talked again about writing a novel, and he told me he's always wanted to go to Europe, especially Italy. We opened up to one another without hesitation. It was magical, under the lights, under the moonlight, his arm around me. When the beer glasses were empty, he stood, offering me his hand, and led me to the beach.

We stood close to the water. The waves were calmly lapping the shore, but we could see the storm brewing in the distance. I could see what was left of some old wooden pilons standing like soldiers in the water. There must have been a pier there at one time.

Andrew stood behind me, wrapping his arms around me as if it were a normal gesture. The way he was holding me made me feel so safe. I raised my hands to his arms, my fingers roaming over his tattoo. The moon was almost full, casting a long sliver of light along the water; it was headed right for us. It was breathtaking and mesmerizing all at the same time.

"I feel like I've known you longer than a few days," he said, whispering in my ear. I could feel his warm breath on my cheek. I leaned into his whisper and reciprocated his feelings. "Me too."

If he could have read my mind at that moment, he wouldn't have been able to make any sense of my thoughts; there were just too many. It's funny how you can never truly know what the other person is thinking. I guess that's where trust comes into play, because once you start guessing, you've entered the danger zone.

"It's so calm now," he said, breathing in the salty air. "It's hard to believe in a few hours the storm will take over." I wasn't really listening. I was just in the moment. I didn't want to think about our night ending. Everything in that moment just felt so right with him.

We stood there for what seemed like hours, enjoying the scenery, enjoying being so close, swaying to the music. We took a walk along the beach, holding hands and laughing about our coffee shop meeting. But finally, we had to call it a night. The clouds were filling in now and it looked like the rain would fall at any second. The water was getting choppy, and I could see the moored boats in the distance, swaying and rocking as the waves rolled in.

We zigzagged our way through the tables and crowds of people that filled the tiny spot. The music was pumping, and I could see a small group dancing in the corner. People were just free, having fun, feeling the night. We walked out hand in hand, but then Erica appeared, stopping us dead in our tracks.

"Hey," she said, looking straight at Andrew. "It was great to see you. Give me a call or better yet stop by sometime, you know where to find me." And then she grabbed his shoulder and gave him a peck on the cheek. I was taken aback, shocked, out of my mind jealous. Did that just happen? I'm standing right her honey. I'm holding his hand. What the hell are you doing? It was everything I could do to hold myself back from dropping her on the spot. I'm not a fighter, but something in me suddenly became very possessive and aggressive.

I could see Andrew was clearly uncomfortable. He just looked at her, completely stunned, then smiled politely, and pulled me out of there. I couldn't help but look back. She was smiling at me, then she lifted her hand and waved, like she was in total control. My eyes narrowed and I wanted to stop, walk back over to her and slap that condescending smile off her face. Andrew could feel me looking, pulling, trying to turn back. He tugged on my hand; I followed. We didn't talk about it on the walk back to the truck.

By 9 p.m. we were heading back to the cottage. I had no reason to be mad at Andrew. Little Miss Erica though, I must admit, I was pissed at her for being such a bitch; a hot, younger than me bitch. I let the rage build up in me but then realized, I was wasting precious time. I didn't need to go on and on about this. "Be a big girl Julia," I thought, "let it go." And I did, just like that. I guess therapy is paying off.

I sat back and stared at this guy I'd just met sitting next to me. No matter what just happened, Andrew had been so open, so transparent, I couldn't falsely blame him for any of it. I felt content for a moment until I suddenly stiffened, forgetting that he was about to drop me off at the cottage where my ex-husband was staying. How was this going to play out? The last thing I wanted was another bar scene.

It felt so good to laugh today, to talk to someone who listened and didn't judge or jump to conclusions. It felt good to be a bit anonymous as well. Andrew had no idea who I really was. I could honestly play a part if I wanted to, and, in a way, I guess I was. I mean, it was only our second date; it's not like I was going to blurt out all my inadequacies, faults, and struggles to this man I hardly knew. I'd already shared enough of that with Jack. If I did that, he'd probably shut the whole thing down, and I couldn't risk it. For once, I was living in the moment, trying to fend off any expectations. I just wanted to enjoy it, and if Andrew was just a distraction, I'd gladly take it.

Suddenly, he reached over, placing his hand on top of mine, as if he were reading my thoughts and he knew I needed to be comforted. I let my head drift slowly backwards and then placed my hand over his. We shared a quick glance. I could hear the rain hitting the windshield, and I tried like hell to keep my eyes open, but eventually they shut, and I fell contentedly asleep.

Chapter Twenty-Six
Andrew

I drove in silence, still holding Julia's hand, rubbing my thumb over it. I'd glance at her every few seconds; she was peacefully sleeping. It was just me now and my thoughts, and there were plenty of them.

First, I couldn't believe what went down at the bar. Jesus, of all times for Erica to make a play, right in front of Julia. I'm quite sure if I'd let Julia's hand go, she would have gotten in her face. I shouldn't be smiling at the thought of it, but I can't help myself. I could actually see Julia slapping her, or worse. I really think she would have done it. She's no wallflower, that's for sure.

Second, I can't believe I've met this incredible woman. "I'm forty-six," I whispered, looking skyward, "and now you finally bring someone into my life that is perfect. What took so long?" Whom should I applaud, Mom or God for this unbelievable gift?

I still had so much to share with Julia, that is, if she wanted to pursue a relationship with me. I wasn't about keeping secrets; definitely a disastrous way to start a relationship, which is why I came clean at the restaurant about Erica. I guess I didn't have to tell her, but she's a smart woman, I'm sure she was figuring it all out anyway. Maybe, at some point I'll tell her that it wasn't exactly a relationship, and that Erica was the pursuer. Hell, Julia might not even believe that considering how she approached me at the bar. I could tell the whole thing made her as uncomfortable as it did me. But now, no, I don't need to go into my history on this one. I don't need to ruin whatever this is, whatever it could be. Hell, here I am thinking about the what ifs, and I don't even know if Julia's on the same page. Almost everything in me says she is, but even that look at the restaurant where she seemed distant, what was that about, and that was before the Erica debacle. "Don't overthink it man," I thought, "just keep going with the flow. There's no rush here, just enjoy the fact that you can spend time with this gorgeous woman right now."

As the oncoming headlights flashed in my eyes, and the rain hit the windshield, I wandered back in time. Back to high school and college days when I didn't want to be serious with anyone. Unfortunately, I took my cues from my older brother, and he was no role model. He played the field; he looked at women like trophies, or more like dominations, and he definitely didn't respect them. I shouldn't blame him though; I made my own decisions to distance myself; it seemed like a safe bet. But look where that's got me. I've been alone all my life. Just dating is a sad way to go through life, and as far as I know, my brother is quite possibly in the same boat. I've changed a lot since those days, mostly because of my mother. I glanced down at my tattoo; she was always with me.

My thoughts soon moved to my dad; another man who should never be a role model. The guy was never supportive of me and my "ridiculous dreams" as he put it. I always thought dad was screwing around during their marriage, but it wasn't until she was diagnosed the second time with cancer that I was certain.

I'll never forget the day I found out. I was home from college for the weekend and mom had just been told the cancer was back. I found her sitting in the solarium, staring out the window. The expression on her face was telling. The birds were flitting around the feeder; she was in a trance. My father had already broken the news to me rather abruptly when I walked into the house. It was always about him; he couldn't even let her tell me. I walked into the room and placed my hand on her shoulder. The tears were streaming down my face. I pulled a chair over and sat next to her. She turned to me and wiped my tears away.

"Andrew, my love," she said, "please, please don't cry." She knew I knew. Seeing me so upset was not what she needed right then, but it was so hard to stop. She looked out the window and said, "This life isn't fair… we all know that. I want you to know, I'm not afraid. I know there's more to life than what we see here. It's okay, my sweet boy, it's okay." She turned back to me, taking my face gently in her hands. She kissed me softly on the forehead. I was crumbling right there. I wanted to look at her, but all I could do was hide behind my tears.

I winced at her words. I knew she was right, but why did it have to be her? She was too young. Life wasn't fucking fair. She was the good one; why couldn't it be my father instead? He deserved this fate, not her. This saint of a woman deserved to be here. Even though getting married wasn't something I intended to do, I still could picture her as a grandmother. She deserved to be here when I got married, and she deserved to have her grandchildren gather round her as she taught them about the flowers and plants in the garden. She deserved to live a long full life. She just deserved better. Better than my father; better than enduring the pain that cancer would bring.

When she died, my eyes were opened. I realized how precious life was. But for some reason I still had a difficult time giving myself to anyone. It was like I was stuck in protection mode. Maybe, deep down I was looking for someone with substance and passion, dare I say a woman like my mother. Someone who is decent, kind, and honest wanting nothing in return, with no ulterior motives. No one could ever live up to my mother, well, not until now. Did you send her to me, Mom? Has it been long enough? Is it time for me to lower my guard and share my life with someone? Is that someone Julia? Could I trust her? Could I trust myself?

I glanced over at her again. She looked like an angel sleeping there, her hair laying gently over her chest. My gaze wandered from her hair to her soft pink lips. I wanted so badly to kiss her on the beach, but for some reason I held back. Maybe it's time I stopped holding back. What would I be protecting myself from now? I once heard, to avoid sadness is to avoid love. Is that what I've been doing all this time? Sadness sucks, but love, well I wouldn't even know what that is, because I've never been in love. But after spending the last twenty-four hours with Julia, maybe I could be persuaded to give love a chance.

Chapter Twenty-Seven
Julia

I had no idea until Andrew shut the ignition off that I'd fallen asleep. How embarrassing. Hopefully, I wasn't drooling. I remembered him taking my hand in his. It was warm and comforting. I felt at ease, relaxed, taken care of. No wonder I fell asleep.

"I'm so sorry," I sputtered, sitting up, releasing his hand. "I'm so sorry I fell asleep." When I looked over at him, he was smiling.

"It's fine," he said reassuringly, "you were exhausted… it's fine. You're a peaceful sleeper, and you don't snore," he said laughing.

I gave his arm a shove and rolled my eyes.

The house was dark except for a small light coming from the entry; the nightlight Jack plugged in. My mind was suddenly racing. His car wasn't in the main driveway, and I couldn't see to the other side of the cottage. Was he here, or was he out? If I knew for sure Jack wasn't in there, I would totally invite Andrew in, but then again, it'd be much worse if Jack walked in and found us on the couch, like with Sean. I wished I didn't lie to either of them. Now this whole hiding the truth thing was screwing me over.

"Walk you to the door?" Andrew asked. I set my fears aside right then; how could I say no? I just prayed Jack wasn't home.

"Yes," I said, "I'd like that." It didn't sound like he was thinking of coming in. Maybe my impromptu nap was a signal that I'm tired out, and what I really needed was more sleep. At least I didn't have to make up some lame excuse. I looked at him sitting next to me; how did I get so lucky to find this man? A man who doesn't seem to want to escalate things before we're both ready, at least that's what I was hoping for.

Andrew grabbed an umbrella from the backseat. He slipped out of the truck and walked around the front to open my door. I took his hand and stepped down from the truck until we were standing face to face. The rain was pouring down all around us, but neither of us seemed to care. He smiled at me, taking my hand, lacing his fingers through mine as he led me onto the deck. We stopped by the door, I turned to face him. "Guess we planned this day right," he said. The rain was coming down even harder now. I could hear the surf smashing the sandy shore. The moon had vanished behind a deluge of thick cloud cover.

We just stood there for a few moments, looking into one another's eyes. The sound of the rain hitting the umbrella was melodically mesmerizing. I knew what I wanted and was hoping he felt the same. He removed his hand from mine and gently placed it on my cheek, his thumb caressing my skin while he just stared at me. My heart was racing with anticipation. It's like his deep brown eyes were penetrating me, in all the best ways. I felt naked, like he could read my mind, then he leaned in. His lips were soft against mine. His movements were gentle and caring. When our lips parted I just stood there with my eyes closed for a moment, savoring his touch. If he didn't know my knees were buckling, that he had sucked all the strength out of me with a simple peck on the lips, well, he would be totally missing the boat.

I didn't want to open my eyes because the moment would be over, but when I finally did, I found out I was wrong; it wasn't over. He swiftly dropped the umbrella, placing one hand firmly around my waist and the other gently behind my head. I could feel his fingers nestling into my hair. He just stared into my eyes as he slowly walked me backward until my body was flush against the shingled siding. Our eyes were locked as the rain washed over us. I melted in his grip. His lips lowered to mine again, softly at first, and then he parted my lips with his tongue. He felt warm and sweet in my mouth. He wasn't aggressive, he was passionate. I let my tongue wander aimlessly over his. The intensity between us grew and I couldn't help myself. I let my hands do what they'd been wanting to do since last night; his hair was practically begging to be touched. Both his hands were on my back now, roaming, caressing, pulling. I could barely breathe. I hadn't felt that much passion for a man in years. I didn't want it to stop.

He pulled back abruptly, softly kissing my lips one more time, then my cheek, then my forehead. Both our faces were wet. I stood completely still. I lowered my hands pressing them firmly against the building; I needed something to hold me upright. He looked at me; it was as if he wanted to ask permission to kiss me again, but then he lowered his head, placing one hand on the siding by my head to brace himself, while holding me around the waist with the other. He was breathing hard. I lowered my head, resting it against his chest. I knew the waves were pounding the shore, but I couldn't hear anything at that moment, I couldn't feel anything other than our racing hearts. We stood there for a quiet moment, both out of breath, both fighting ourselves. It was moving fast.

"I… I think I should go," he said, his eyes still closed. I looked up and he placed his wet lips against my forehead. We were both trying to catch our breath.

"I hate goodbye," I whispered, but I knew we were both going to explode if he didn't leave, plus the storm was moving in. My words to Sean were dancing through my brain, 'I'm not that kind of woman' but I wanted to be that kind of woman right then. Suddenly, my fantasies took a backseat because reality was staring me in the face. Jack might be inside, and if he was, I needed this to end, right now, even if I wanted it to go on forever.

I placed my hands on his chest and looked up at him as the rain continued to fall. "What are you doing tomorrow?" I asked, knowing the grin on my face was in no way camouflaged.

"Surprisingly, I'm free," he said, with a laugh. "I always take Sundays off."

"How 'bout I plan the day. Let's start early. Breakfast?"

"Breakfast with you sounds perfect, just like you," he said.

That comment ran through me like a knife. I had to correct him before that word became a habit. "I'm not perfect Andrew," I whispered, "better you know that now."

He didn't hesitate to set things right. "You are to me," he responded.

He took a few minutes to walk away. First, I felt his arm release me, and I felt sad. Then he touched my face, running his thumb over my cheek, and I felt desirable. Then he stepped back and just stared at me; I felt lost; lost in his eyes. Then he grabbed the umbrella, turned, and walked away, and I felt alone. He left me there, practically glued to the wall, illuminated by that one deck light. How odd, we were under a light, for anyone to see. Once he was back in his truck, he took a long look at me. I refused to go in until he was out of my sight. I was soaking wet, but I didn't care. I smiled and gave him a small wave. He waved back then turned to back out.

I walked into the cottage as if in a daze. I made sure to lock the door this time, and then turned around, standing with my back against it. I needed to breathe—I needed to breathe a lot. I needed the door to hold me upright. "Deep breaths, Julia, deep breaths," I whispered. I needed to calm down. I had a date to plan before bed. I put my bag on the side table and left my backpack on the floor. I slipped my shoes off and walked gingerly to the kitchen. There was no sign of Jack. I felt relieved; I'd dodged a bullet on both ends.

I opened the fridge and I started to sing quietly, "I'm never gonna' not dance again," by Pink, but just as I pulled a bottle of water from the fridge a hand swiftly reached over my shoulder and slammed the door shut. I was startled, to say the least. My blood pressure spiked. My first thought was another intruder, but then I heard Jack's voice. Where the hell did he come from? Did he see me with Andrew?

"Where have you been all day, Julia?" he asked, his voice deep and edgy.

I turned quickly to face him. I suddenly felt the anger welling up inside. It was like venom rising from my gut until it spilled uncontrollably from my mouth.

"What the fuck are you doing Jack?" I said hotly. "After last night, are you trying to fucking scare me?"

He paused, and just stared at me.

"No Julia," he said, with a calm that unnerved me. "I just want to know where you've been all day. Is that too much for your husband to know?"

"Ex-husband," I reminded him vehemently. "We've been divorced for two years Jack, or have you forgotten that little detail?"

He took an annoyed, deep breath.

"Who were you with Julia?" he asked again, annunciating every syllable. "Was it Sean?"

I just stared into Jack's eyes. They were as sharp as my emotions. The words flew from my mouth without much thought. It was all so reminiscent of our past fights.

"It's none of your business, Jack, who I spend my time with. It hasn't been your business for years."

Jack slammed his hand on the refrigerator door behind me. I jumped startled by the frustration and anger he'd just unleashed. He leaned into my space, exhaling. I could smell the vodka on his breath. I turned away.

"Jack, you're drunk." Then I turned back and looked him in the eyes. "Maybe I should ask you where you've been?"

"Don't turn the tables Julia, just answer the question... who were you with?" He was slurring his words at this point.

I could see his rage building. I didn't want a repeat of the many fights we'd had before. The only time in our marriage when Jack literally put his hands on me was when we were fighting one night after attending a holiday party. He was jealous and he questioned my actions at the party. He grabbed my shoulders, then released me in frustration, sending me flying backward into the bedroom door. His eyes were full of rage. When he saw the tears forming in my eyes, he backed off and left the room. That night I curled up in a ball in the guest bedroom. He left me feeling worthless. The fights were always the same, but this one was intense. How many fights would it take for me to finally be brave enough to leave.

"No," I said defiantly, "no, I will not tell you!"

Jack just stared at me, his rage building. He grabbed my face forcefully with both hands, then moved in quickly; his lips met mine in a hard kiss. No, I thought and pushed back, trying to get his mouth off mine. When he finally released me, he stepped back unsteadily. I'd had enough. I raised my hand to slap him, but he miraculously caught it midway. He came at me again, trying to grab my other arm but I pushed him hard and followed with a swift slap across the face. He was so shocked by my actions that he just stopped, placing his hand on his cheek. I ran to my bedroom and locked the door.

I could hear him gathering himself in the kitchen. I could hear him walking down the hallway, bumping against the walls, then he paused at my door. I could hear him breathing heavily. He struck the door over and over with his fist.

"Julia, Julia! I'm sorry Julia," he said, his words disintegrating as they came out. "I'm sorry... I can't stop... I can't stop loving you," he said. "It's killing me to think of you with someone else!"

My breath was short and quick. I went to the door and turned to lean against it but crumpled to the floor. I wanted to scream. I wanted to yell and tell him I'm over this, over fighting with him, over him being jealous, just over it all. This is why I wanted a divorce, to leave all of this behind. Why was this happening again?

I could hear him sobbing on the other side of the door. It was everything I'd known for the last ten years of our marriage, and everything I wanted to forget. I'd forgiven him over and over. I'd admitted my own faults in the relationship. I'd accepted his jealous side. I tried to understand his childhood and the marks it left on his soul. And despite how I felt then, despite trying to move forward, despite allowing love to work in and through us, we still couldn't stay together. And now, over two years later, I'm sitting on the floor, locked in my bedroom, caught in the same circumstance. He was still capable of igniting my rage while making me feel worthless in the process. And then there's guilt, compassion, and sorrow. I felt guilty for not staying with Jack. I felt compassion for his struggles. I felt sorry for him, even amidst the anger. The tears were coming, coming on, wave after wave; I couldn't stop them.

"You're drunk Jack, go to bed!" I screamed through the tears. "Please, just leave and go to bed." I sat on the floor, my head in my hands. If I could have pulled all my hair out, I would have. "I just want this to stop," I sobbed, "please God, make it stop!"

He was breathing heavily on the other side of the door. He pounded on the door one final time and then I heard him walk back down the hallway. I sat there for a moment, trying to collect myself. Then I got up, walked to the bed, turned, and fell aimlessly backward. I covered my face with my hands, as if they could soak up the tears. How much more could I endure?

Every fight we'd ever had filled my thoughts. Every ounce of me that had ever felt less than, crept back in through any open crack until I was full of them. Those fucking cracks. I'm a terrible person. He can't help himself. I'm wrong. This all is my fault.

After about fifteen minutes of crying, I sat up as if possessed. I put some shoes on, grabbed a jacket and wiped the tears away. I wanted to run. This was so reminiscent of our past fights; there was no steady, no certain. With Jack, the arguments would happen in a flash. I was never prepared. I knew at any moment things could explode. I couldn't live like that then, I refused to live like that now.

The cottage was quiet. I slowly opened the door; Jack wasn't in his room. I tiptoed down the hallway and could see him standing on the front deck in the rain. I felt conflicted for a moment. Should I go and try to mend this now? No Julia, no; he's drunk. I realized in that split second that this was my chance to get the hell out of here. I carefully opened the side door and slipped out undetected. In past years, I would be calling Jen. I'd be leaning on my sister for support. But not this time. I couldn't burden her, especially when I felt so unhinged.

Sean: I would go to Sean's place. I couldn't stay in the cottage with

Jack another second. I glanced behind me then started to run; the tears were blinding me. I felt out of control. We'd been apart for over two years, and now, I was living it all over again. My thoughts were all over the place. I'd opened the floodgates for negativity to fill the empty crevices in me. Could I possibly outlive all this crap? I felt like I'd never be free of any of it. It was about Jack, but it wasn't. This entire trip was not what I expected; the good and the bad. It was overwhelming and I felt myself unraveling at the seams. I was losing touch with reality. I thought therapy was the answer, a way for me to cope, but I feel more lost now than ever. The rain relentlessly attacked my face; it hurt. Did I deserve it? Did I deserve to be crushed, broken, spit out, left for dead? Maybe the intruder was my way out of this life. Maybe it was supposed to be the end of me, the end of all the turmoil. I didn't care anymore. I was walking toward the edge, the edge of my sanity, and I just didn't care what happened to me.

Chapter Twenty-Eight
Andrew

I couldn't get the grin off my face the entire ride home. If I hadn't left when I did, I don't think I could have resisted her. I hadn't felt that way about a woman in a long time. Actually, I don't think I've ever felt that way about anyone. For all the women I've dated, Julia is by far the most real. I turned into my driveway and put the truck in Park. I just sat for a minute, reliving the day, the night, that kiss. The rain washed incessantly over the windshield. It's all I could hear; the rain hitting the roof of the truck as I lost myself in thoughts of Julia. I wanted her to ask me in. I wanted to sweep her off her feet and carry her to the bedroom. I wanted to feel her bare skin next to mine. Just then, a huge gust of wind knocked the trash barrels over, breaking me from the sweet trance I was in. I shook my head and looked in the rearview mirror. "Dude, get ahold of yourself. It was one date." But I had to admit, it was a date like no other. It was the kind of date that makes you feel like you've not only known the other person forever, but makes you feel so understood and completely accepted.

"Okay, man, enough." I reached into the back seat to grab my backpack, ready to get inside to change out of my wet clothes, but out of the corner of my eye, I noticed something on the floor near the passenger seat. I reached down and grabbed it; it was Julia's phone.

"Shit." We never talked about what time I'd pick her up tomorrow, plus she's probably going crazy right now looking for it. I didn't have a choice but to drive back. Leaving her tonight killed me, so the idea of seeing her again, maybe even kiss her again; decision made. I glanced at her phone; it was only 9:50 p.m. It wasn't that late, I'm sure she's still up. I started the truck and backed down the driveway. My heart was pumping faster already. The anticipation was insane. I was starting to wonder how I'd gotten attached so fast, but then again, I didn't care. I just wanted to be with her.

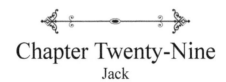

Chapter Twenty-Nine
Jack

The deck has become a refuge for me, but I'm sick of standing here, plus it's like a fucking monsoon out here. I can't even see straight, and my head is fucking pounding. I needed to lie down. I walked back into the living room; my hair was wet, my shirt as well, but I didn't care. There were two things I knew for sure: Julia was pissed, and she was locked in her room. At least I know she's not out with anyone. I sat down on the couch, my head in my hands. I grabbed the blanket, wiping my face with it. My brain was scrambled. I knew I drank too much, but what I said to Julia was the truth; I still loved her and the thought of her in someone else's arms was excruciating. How am I going to fix this now?

I leaned back, melding into the couch. I could feel myself dozing off despite my thoughts. Then suddenly there was a knock at the door.

"Jesus Christ! Who the hell could that be?" I said angrily. I ignored it, letting my head hit the cushion again. I closed my eyes. But then the knocking started again, louder, and even more persistent.

"Fuck!" I pushed myself off the couch and went to the door. "Sean coming back for her?" I grumbled. My blood was starting to boil at the thought of them being together. I opened the door, and I looked at him; the confusion had to be written all over my face.

"Coop?" I said, shocked and surprised to see him standing there.

"Jack?" he said, seeming just as surprised.

Coop was standing outside the door. The rain was coming down hard. I didn't understand. I watched as he looked behind him, like he was making sure he was at the right house. Then he looked back at me, his face mimicked mine.

"What are you doing here Coop?" I said, still confused. "How the heck did you find me?"

Coop ran his hand through his wet hair. Fucking guy still had a great head of hair, even in the rain.

"I uh.... I... I'm not here for you, I'm looking for Julia," he said, completely baffled.

I stepped back, not understanding how he could be looking for Julia.

"You're looking for Julia?" I said, beyond confused. "Why are you looking for Julia? How do you know Julia? What are you talking about?"

"How do you know Julia, and why are you at her cottage?" His eyes were penetrating and relentlessly pushing me for answers.

Suddenly, he was putting me on the hotseat. I was shocked by the questions coming my way. I just saw Coop a few days ago, and he never mentioned Julia by name. Then like a light bulb going off, I put two and two together.

"She wasn't out with Sean today was she... she was out with you. She was out with you, Coop."

Coop stepped back. I could tell his mind was reeling. I kind of felt for the guy; he seemed to be in the dark.

"How do you know Sean," he said, questioning me, I could see the confusion plainly on his face. Then before I could say anything he said, "Sean is a friend Jack... Sean is gay, but you're right, Julia was with me today." And then he paused, running his hand through his fucking hair again. He looked at me intently. "Again, how do you know Julia?"

"Well, well," I said, laughing uncontrollably, "looks like you're the one in the dark Coop. Julia's my ex-wife." I couldn't help myself; I leaned over, placing my hands on my thighs to steady myself while I laughed. This was priceless. I seemed to stop the guy dead in his tracks. He looked like a lost puppy. Must be quite a shock to find this little tidbit out. Sounds like Julia hadn't been completely honest with him. I couldn't stop laughing, which only seemed to aggravate him more, but I didn't care. He just stared at me. I could see his anger building, but again, I really didn't care.

"Look Jack, I don't know what's going on here, I just want to talk to Julia. Where is she?"

"Oh, you need to talk to my wife?" I said, standing upright, trying to stand taller than him.

"You mean your ex-wife," Coop said, now staring me down. "Where is she?" he said, pushing his finger into my chest angrily.

"By all means old friend," then I stepped to the side and nodded toward the hallway behind me. "Have at it," I said, still laughing.

Coop pushed by me. I could hear him knocking on Julia's door. I could hear him whispering her name.

"Julia, Julia," he said, "Julia, open the door, it's Andrew." There was a slight pause and then I heard him say, "If you're in there Julia, stand away from the door, I'm coming in." I heard the door smash open. "She's not here Jack," he yelled from the bedroom. Within seconds he was standing at the end of the hallway.

"She's not in there, Jack. Where is she?" he shouted at me.

I turned toward the noise flowing out of his mouth. "Hell, if I know," I said, touching my face, the slap still fresh. And then I couldn't help myself but say, "She was pretty upset after I kissed her."

Coop rushed at me, grabbing me by the collar, pushing me against the wall. "What did you do to her?" he said vehemently.

"Nothing," I said laughing, my arms raised in the air. I was surprised how quick he was. "I just kissed my wife... guess she wasn't in the mood."

His grasp on my collar was volatile. I tried to pull away, but he had a firm grip; he was in my face.

"You're drunk Jack, I can smell the vodka on your breath," he said. He tightened his grip, pulling me forward, then he released me, sending me backward into the wall. At this point I didn't care if I was drunk or not; Julia made her bed, this wasn't on me.

"I'm going to look for her. Do yourself a favor and stay here, sleep it off. I'll let you know if... I mean when I find her," he said, like I cared what he was doing.

"Gee thanks Coop... you're a real friend," I said sarcastically.

Just as he was walking out the door, I couldn't help but say, "Another notch in the old belt Coop?"

He turned without hesitation; I knew I'd pushed him too far, but I wanted him to hit me, to give me a reason to hit him back. I really wanted this guy to give me a reason to beat the shit out of him for being with Julia. Instead, he just stared me down.

"I'm not that guy anymore Jack," he said, glaring at me, "not that I need to prove that to you. I'm not that guy."

Then he slammed the door and left.

Chapter Thirty
Andrew

Jack and Julia? How is this possible? Why was he staying with Julia? Why didn't Julia tell me about him? Why didn't Julia tell him about me? Is Julia lying about anything else? My head was about to explode. How could I be so wrong about her?

It's like the rain was demonic now; the storm they predicted was going to pummel the coast, and at high tide to boot. I ran to Sean's cottage. Hopefully, Julia was there. Hopefully, she was just leaning on him for support after what happened with Jack. He was drunk, and I had a feeling that whatever happened wasn't good. I didn't believe that after our day, our night, that kiss, she would just go into the cottage and make out with Jack. I had to make sure she was okay.

My mind was reeling as I ran through the rain. I assumed Julia needed to get things off her chest, and Sean was the only one she had close by to help her. I would be okay with that; they were friends. I pictured myself knocking on Sean's door and seeing Julia sitting on his couch. I expected to see her face red from tears. I expected her to run to me and explain it all to me, and I would accept her explanation and hold her tightly, reassuring her that everything would be fine. That's what I wanted, but all I could think now was that whatever went down in that cottage made her run, and that scared me.

"Andrew, what are you doing here?" Sean asked perplexed.

"Is Julia here with you… is she here Sean?" I said, forcefully pushing past him to scan the room.

"No, no she's not here. I haven't seen her today. What's wrong dude… I thought you two were together today. What's going on?"

"We were," I said, rubbing my head and letting a panicked breath out. "We were together all day and then I dropped her off around nine-thirty. I uh, I…," I stopped. I couldn't even finish my thoughts. It's like my mouth couldn't keep up with all the shit running through my head.

"C'mon, take a seat, catch your breath," Sean said, placing his hand on my back.

Once I sat down, he ran to the kitchen to get me a glass of water. I felt a sense of panic suddenly. A glass of water wasn't going to calm me. I stood back up and started pacing, repeatedly running my hand over my head. I took a deep breath, then found the words.

"Her phone," I blurted out. "I found her phone in my truck when I got home. I drove back to give it to her and when I knocked on the door Jack answered. He didn't even realize she wasn't there. Then he said she was upset after he kissed her. According to him, she locked herself in her room. But she's not there. She's not there Sean," I said, frantically pacing, the panic truly setting in now. "Where the hell is she?"

"Jesus... Jack kissed her?" Sean said, realizing my worry was justified.

It took a few seconds for his comment to register. I stopped pacing and just stared at him. "What do you know about Jack? Did you know he was staying there?" I said, feeling doubly deceived.

Sean put his head down. He did know. Suddenly, I felt like an idiot. Was I the only one who didn't know about Jack?

"I'm sorry man," Sean said, looking down at his feet. "I did know... she didn't want to tell you. She made me promise not to. She wanted to explain things herself."

Bombshell after bombshell. Jesus, this night was turning into some crazy plot from a movie. I felt betrayed by Julia and Sean. The only one who was being truthful was Jack.

"Okay, okay," I stammered, pacing again, trying to formulate a plan, and then I walked over to Sean and grabbed him by the shoulders.

"You gotta' help me find her, okay!" I said, gripping him hard. "The storm is comin' in hot, and I know her car is still in the driveway so she either went for a walk on the road or she's on the beach."

I had so many questions I wanted to fire at Sean, but all of that was insignificant right now. Julia's safety had to be my focus.

"You're right. I'm with you man, let's go," Sean said, without hesitation.

He grabbed his jacket, phone, and two flashlights. I knew the beach was probably the best place to start, because it was the most dangerous place to be in a storm. We walked unsteadily down the path; the wind and the rain ferociously whipping through the grass, trying its best to set us off course. The moment was surreal. Is this really happening right now?

When we reached the bottom of the stairs, I yelled to Sean to go right, and I'd go to the left. "Text me if you find her," I shouted through the bellowing of the wind.

"I will," Sean yelled. "You the same." Then he walked down the beach, calling her name.

As I walked, my eyes darted from the possessed ocean water, across the sand, to the cliffs. All I could think about was the day we had just spent together. The perfect day. How in a matter of an hour could everything get so crazy. "Julia, Julia!" I yelled, placing my hand by the side of my mouth. The rain was piercing; like little knives cutting into my flesh. The beach was being beaten, swallowed by the surge of waves. Where was she?

I looked to my left, shining the light on the stairway leading to Julia's cottage. It was empty. From all the times that I'd been to Sean's place, I knew the portion of beach I was entering could be tricky. There were multiple areas where rock formations protruded from the cliffs, and during extremely high tides, those rocks created a barrier, cutting one side of beach off from the other. So, if she had walked beyond those rocks, she'd be cut off from this side by the ocean. There were no more homes after her set of stairs, not for at least a mile, which meant there were no other access or exit points off the beach.

My focus was on Julia, but I couldn't help feeling betrayed. As I walked my mind raced, pulling me in opposite directions. I was so concerned for her, and yet I was trying not to give into my feelings of betrayal. I had so many questions, but I had to fight them off and make her my priority.

"Julia, Julia!" I shouted, over and over, only to be outdone by the brutal roaring of the ocean. The surf was high, and relentlessly abusing the shore. The waves pounded one after the other, smashing against the rocks sending surf flying high into the air. I pulled my phone out as the rain battered my face. No text from Sean.

Claps of thunder roared like an angry god and jagged lightning strikes lit up the sky. The wind was pushing me to the cliffs; I was at the point of feeling helpless. "Mom… if you're there, please help me find her," I pleaded.

I was at least a quarter mile down from the beach stairs when a second flash of lightning lit a large group of rocks ahead. The surf was flying. I wiped the water from my face, trying to focus. A second lightning strike lit the sky, and I could see something just beyond the rocks. Refocus Andrew, is that her? I shined the light, staring into the distance.

"Julia!" I yelled, frantically running toward the rocks. The closer I got the clearer I could see; it was her. She was trying to walk along what little beach was left; what little beach hadn't been swallowed by the tide. She was trying to shield herself from the storm. She was moving away from the water, being pushed toward the cliffs; she was trapped. She didn't look up when I called out. I wasn't even sure she could hear me. I watched as the waves crashed against the rocks. I saw her fall to her knees.

Without hesitation, I trudged through the water. I must have been about two hundred yards from her. The storm surge had pushed the water in so that it was over two feet deep. The waves relentlessly washed over me, pushing me, trying to prevent me from getting to her.

"Julia, Julia!" I screamed. She didn't acknowledge me. It was like she was in a storm of her own, completely oblivious to what was happening around her. She was huddled in a corner, against the cliff. Whatever happened between Jack and her had to be bad, bad enough to make her want to be alone—alone in a dangerous storm that could ultimately drown her. She had to know the danger she was in.

I pulled myself through the water and onto the small amount of sand still visible. The wind was howling, whipping, and I lost my footing, falling to the ground. It was a moment like no other; a moment where I could have just stayed there, on the sand, losing myself in the storm, but then I pulled myself up and ran to where she was. I knelt down in front of her, taking her face in my hands.

"Julia, I'm here, Julia!"

She looked at me blankly. Her face was covered with water; she was completely drenched. What the hell was wrong with her? It was as if she wanted to be stuck here. I couldn't wait for her to answer, for her to wake the fuck up. The water was rising, the waves were blasting, I had to get her out of here. I grabbed her and swept her up into my arms. She resisted, as if she suddenly realized the danger she was in. I'm not gonna' lie, I didn't want to go back into the water either, but sometimes you only have one way out of a situation, and this one required us to go back into the water. I whispered into her ear,

"It's okay Julia, I've got you," and then I walked back into the water. The waves were bludgeoning us, and I slipped, sending both of us into the water. I watched as the tide brutally pulled her away.

"Julia, Julia!" I yelled hysterically. I'd lost her; how could I lose her! But then I caught sight of her, the surf flipping her viciously as it continued to drag her out. I pushed through the waves to get to her. I reached out, grabbing her arm and pulled her to me. This time, I put my arm around her waist, dragging her through the relentless onslaught of waves, until we were on the sand.

The sand, thank God, we were on the sand. I collapsed to my knees, releasing her, then I fell beside her. I looked up at the sky; it was dark and angry. I was losing myself in it. The rain was still pounding, I was trying to catch my breath. The sky lit up again; I knew we needed to move. I leaned over her, placing my hand on her face.

"You're okay Julia, we're okay," I said, trying to comfort her. "We're going now, get up."

I stood up and pulled her to a wobbly stand.

A crack of thunder pounded the beach. It was as if it penetrated the sand beneath us, and Julia jumped, clutching my jacket. "Grab my waist," I ordered, "you're going to have to help me, Julia."

Thank God the stairs to the cottage weren't far. We hobbled up, the wind blowing us back and forth as we ascended. The path, thank God we were on the path to the cottage. We were unstable, our feet sinking into the wet sand. Julia slipped and collapsed to her knees. I pulled her to her feet.

"The grasses," she said, as if she were in a trance, "the grasses are swaying." That's when I knew she wasn't all there. She was somewhere else completely. It was as if she didn't have a clue as to what was happening; the danger she'd been in. Once we reached the truck, I opened the passenger door, and scooped her up, placing her on the seat. I belted her in, then grabbed the blanket from the backpack and tucked it around her. "I'll be right back," I said, kissing her forehead. As I turned, she latched onto my arm. She wasn't looking at me; her eyes were vacant. I touched her hand, "I promise Julia, I'll be right back." I ran to the cottage and banged on the door. No matter what happened between Jack and her, he needed to know she was safe.

"I found her... on the beach," I said breathlessly. "She's okay if you care. I'm taking her to my place."

Jack nodded. I was surprised he was giving in so easily. Just as I turned to leave, he reached for my arm. "Coop," I could see he was struggling, "thank you for finding her," he said, then he released me and closed the door.

I heard what Jack said, but I was in no way feeling sorry for him. I hopped in the truck and texted Sean immediately.

~

Andrew: "She's safe. I'm taking her to my place. Talk tomorrow."

I waited a minute; I couldn't leave until I knew Sean was okay.

Andrew: "Text me you got this. I don't want to have to come save you too."

Sean: "Thank God! I'm heading up the stairs. Go home. We'll talk tomorrow."

~

I started the truck. I could see Julia shivering; why wouldn't she be, we were both soaked to the core. Her hood was covering her face, and her knees were pulled tightly into her chest. I backed out, my tires spinning, forcefully ejecting the gravel from the driveway. I threw the truck into Drive. I couldn't get home fast enough. I wanted this entire night to be over. I wanted to go back to the hours before all this, to when Julia and I were enjoying a day of hiking, laughing, eating, kissing. Again, in a matter of an hour from me leaving her, the day went from one of a kind in the best way, to one of a kind in the worst way.

"Stay focused man," I said with determination, wiping the rain from my eyes. "Just get her home; just get us home."

Chapter Thirty-One
Andrew

Her body was shaking. I wanted to pull her to me, but all I could do was find her hand under the blanket to let her know I was there. I just kept looking at her. She was passed out, curled into a ball, leaning toward me. I could tell she'd been crying, a lot. What the fuck did he do to her? The storm was at full force now. When I pulled into the driveway, the divots I'd put off fixing were full of water, so I needed to get as close to the house as I could. Once I parked, I ran to unlock the door, and then returned to the truck to get Julia. She felt lifeless in my arms, but she knew enough to put her arms around my neck.

I carried her to the bedroom and sat her in the chair. She was awake but still not there; it was like she was comatose. I bolted to the bathroom and started the shower, then quickly removed all my clothes, except my underwear. She hadn't moved. I removed all her clothes except her bra and panties and carried her to the shower. I stepped under the warm water with her in my arms. Her eyes were closed. I placed her feet on the shower floor and stood behind her for support. She felt heavy in my arms. Suddenly she turned toward me nestling her arms and head against my chest; she was still shivering. I wrapped my arms protectively around her. My hands rubbed up and down her back; I was desperately trying to warm her up. Then I held her tightly to me, tight enough that I could feel her body flinch with every tear she cried. The water washed over us and everything in that moment felt right. For any other couple, this would have ignited a sexual encounter, but not tonight.

After standing there for a good fifteen minutes, after she stopped shaking, I shut the shower off. I grabbed a towel and wrapped it around her, then I grabbed another towel and carefully dried her face and hair. I turned her around, so her back was to me and with a great deal of difficulty, removed her wet bra and panties. I dried her body off, grabbed another towel, wrapping her tightly, then I picked her up and carried her to the bed. She clung to me, her arms wrapped tightly around my neck, her head buried into my shoulder. I placed her gently on the bed. I was trying so hard to hide her body from my view, but the towel fell away, and she was all I could see; it was perfection. It was just as I imagined, I almost felt guilty.

I pulled the covers over her then gently brushed her hair back onto the pillow. She looked so peaceful. I kissed her on the forehead and shut the light off. She'd been through enough; she didn't need me in bed with her, it wouldn't be right.

I pulled on a pair of sweats and a T-shirt and walked to the kitchen. After seeing Jack tonight, a beer was not even a remote thought. A simple glass of water would do the trick. I couldn't believe how exhausted I felt, both physically and emotionally. The water felt good going down. It was like I'd been stuck in the desert for days, but I didn't know I was dying of thirst, which is an ironic thought after being out in that storm. My head hit the back of the couch, the ceiling was closing in on me, at least that's what it felt like.

"What the fuck!" I whispered. "What the fuck just happened?"

How the hell was I going to manage all this? What do I say to Julia? How hard should I press her knowing she'd just been through hell? The same questions from earlier kept resurfacing. Why didn't she tell me Jack was staying at the cottage? Why did she feel the need to lie? Is she lying about anything else? She could have more secrets. I mean, I barely know her, and yet I feel like I've known her forever; how is that possible? I'm not a love at first sight kind of guy. Is that what this is?

I couldn't stop the onslaught of questions; my mind was racing. I was starting to question myself, my feelings for her. And then, just as fast as the negativity reared its ugly head, I suppressed it, because in the end I couldn't deny my feelings, my truth. Yes, I was falling hard for this woman I barely knew. Yes, I was falling hard for this woman who'd kept secrets from me, this woman who is the ex-wife of a college buddy. It was a lot to process.

I felt paralyzed, thinking but not wanting to think. I needed to check on Julia. Get up Andrew and check on Julia. I willed myself off the couch and walked to the bedroom door, pushing it open slightly. She was sleeping, her back to me; she was curled up in a ball. Seeing her like that was killing me. I needed to be with her. I grabbed our wet clothes and the towels and walked to the laundry room, then I walked back to the living room, grabbed a blanket from the couch and shut the lights off. When I got to the bedroom door, I stopped and just stared at her for a moment, the night light in the bathroom illuminating her slightly. Her hair, still wet from the shower, lay gracefully on the pillow. I couldn't believe she was here, in my bed, and the only thing I could think about was making sure she felt safe. I climbed on top of the bed covers, pulling myself against her back. I pulled the blanket over me and pressed my body next to hers. I could still smell her perfume. I reached my arm over her until I could find her hand. She whimpered slightly and placed her other hand on my arm; she knew I was there. I couldn't deny my feelings—I felt at home. Julia was my new home. I fell asleep wrapped around her.

Dawn seemed to arrive earlier than usual. The sunlight trickled through the opening of the curtain panels covering the French doors, casting just enough light for me to see Julia clearly. We were in the exact same position as when I'd climbed into bed with her. I rolled onto my back and stared at the ceiling. The negative thoughts started again, so I rolled back toward her. The blanket had pulled away exposing her right shoulder. I couldn't help but run my fingers over her tattoo. It was gentle and delicate, just like her. I couldn't imagine losing a child. She was a child when she got pregnant the first time. There's no way I could have done what she and Jack did, having a kid right out of college. I was still a mess then. I stopped touching her when she stirred. I wanted her to sleep. I quietly rolled off the bed and went to use the bathroom near the laundry; I didn't want to wake her. This may have been the one and only time I'd slept with a woman and not "slept with her." It was strange to say the least, but I'd be lying if I didn't admit that I was happy not to have 'Coop's' mindset anymore.

As I looked in the bathroom mirror, I whispered, "Mom, I want you to be proud of me and I hope you can guide me because I don't know what the hell happens from here."

I placed my hands on the sink and hung my head, not wanting to acknowledge the tears that were forming. It took me a minute, but in what seemed like a split second, I realized that I had willingly not told Julia about myself, my younger self. She had no idea what I was like back then, she was taking me in the moment. I raised my head and stared into the mirror again.

"What do you want?" I asked, the man in the mirror. "Do you want honesty from her, because if you do, you better be willing to give her the same."

Revelations suck. I needed to be less judgmental. I didn't have Julia's perspective yet. I needed to give her the chance to explain. I needed to fight the idea that she and Jack were still in love, still in a physical relationship. I needed to give her the break I was going to need. I brushed my teeth and headed to the kitchen. Coffee.

Chapter Thirty-Two
Andrew

I stood like a statue, gazing out at the lake. I could barely see it, some clouds still lingered from the storm. I took a sip of coffee. My thoughts weren't as groggy as my body felt; they took me over without a fight.

~

"Sean, I'm not looking to date anyone. You know that," I said emphatically.

"Uh, yah, I know what you think you don't need, but I'm telling you what I think you do need. I trump what you think... just come."

I really didn't need to go on a blind date. I'm forty-six, and I've managed quite well in life without getting tied down. Sean is just being his matchmaker self, trying to force me to change.

"How old is she, because I'm not into dating someone half my age... Erica was a catastrophe."

"Don't worry, she's around your age. Believe me, I learned from the last time. Listen, I'll admit, I just met her, but in the few hours I've spent with her, she seems really nice. She's definitely not a diva. She's normal. I swear. Just come and give it a chance. I'll even buy dinner."

I didn't need him to buy me dinner, but he's never going to stop badgering me, so I finally gave in.

"Fine... where and when," I said, tired of fighting with him.

"Yessss!"

I could see him high fiving himself on the win.

"Meet us at Glenn's, around 6:30. I told her to meet me at six. Gives us time to get comfortable before you show up."

"Okay, but this is the last blind date you set me up on, you hear me?"

"Oh, it will be because I have a feeling about this one, trust me."

Sean always had a feeling. What about the other three blind dates he set me up on? I'm over this, but, since we're friends, I'll just keep playing his game. Free dinner, that's what I'll focus on.

~

It was hard to believe that conversation was just two days ago. I took another sip of coffee. Coffee: it's hard to believe that I met Julia three days ago at a coffee shop. I've never approached a woman like that, it's not my style, but I really couldn't say what my style is. Lately it's been to not get involved with anyone. I just haven't wanted it, no matter how many blind dates Sean sets up. Maybe it's safer that way. But when I saw her, shit, I couldn't help myself.

She may have been in a car the first time I saw her, but the first thing I noticed was her hair, that gorgeous auburn hair sweeping down over her shoulders. That alone made me want to give her the parking spot. I remember trying to park quickly so I could catch up to her. I was immediately drawn to her. But when I saw those emerald, green eyes, man, I was blown away. I could tell she was skittish, like she probably thought I was some creep trying to hit on her for a quickie. It's so hard to not come off like that these days. She didn't seem interested in me at all, but I did catch her glancing my way once, so not all hope was lost. But then she was completely elusive about where she was staying on the Cape. Rightly so I guess, I was a stranger to her, so when the time came to say goodbye, I just felt it would be too forward to ask for her number, so, I let her go.

I wrote her off completely, until Friday night. When I saw her sitting at the restaurant, I couldn't believe it. There she was, Rachel. So funny she uses that name on her coffee cups. She's funny. I couldn't wait to sit next to her, to breathe her in, to feel our arms touch, to feel my leg graze hers under the table. The conversation with her flowed so easily. It was so clear to me; she's what'd been missing in my life all this time.

That night was awesome. I must admit, Sean and his matchmaking skills; the guy finally got it right. God, I wanted to kiss her right there, by her car, but I settled for a hug, which in retrospect was probably even better because I could feel her whole body against mine. By the time Saturday came, I was falling hard.

Just the way she was, so casual on our drive, floating her hand out the window. The fact that she loved being outside. The honesty in her voice when she asked about my tattoo and then revealed her own. The dinner in 'P-town', embracing on the beach, even the way she didn't press me about Erica, it was like nothing I'd experienced before. And then, the way she looked, sleeping so peacefully on the way home. There was nothing inauthentic about her. She seemed so open and honest; it was refreshing. I'd never met anyone like her.

And now, that same woman is lying in my bed, trying to recover from a horrific night, and I really don't know what the hell is going on with her. I truly don't know. I don't know her at all really, which means I don't know what I've gotten myself into. But what I do know is I can't help the way I feel about her. That's it. I'm falling for her so that means I'm going to help her, and I'm going to give her the chance to explain things to me.

This was going somewhere, where I wasn't sure, but I was in it now. I wanted to be in it. I wanted to know everything about her, even her past with Jack. I felt like she trusted me. I had to trust her.

I took another sip of coffee and felt my phone vibrate in my pocket. It was Sean.

~

"Hey, is everything okay there? It's been killing me all night not knowing how she is… how you both are." I could hear the concern in his voice.

"She's still sleeping. She went through hell last night… we both did."

"Where did you find her?"

"She was just past the first grouping of rocks. She was trapped against the cliff. It was fucking insane out there. I almost lost her in the surf. I never want to be out in a storm like that again."

"Jesus… I agree, it was brutal out there. So, did she say anything? Give you any explanation?"

"She was so out of it last night, I just put her in the shower and then put her to bed. Sean, whatever happened between them… it wasn't good. We'll see what she remembers today, but I'm not going to press her… this has to be on her terms."

"I hear you. I just wanted to check in. Dude, you're a good guy… don't forget it."

"Thanks man. I'll let you know how she's doin."

~

I knew how Sean felt. It was killing me not to know if she was all right. I couldn't wait for her to get up, and yet, I knew she was probably exhausted. I had so many questions, but I couldn't push her. I just needed to be there for her, like last night.

I glanced down at my tattoo. I ran my fingers over the dove. We all need something, someone to pick us up at times. I was there for my mother, and now I'm here for Julia. It's funny how life circles around, placing you in situations you never thought possible. One day you're just going along, feeling immortal, conquering the day, and the next you're in fucking hell, trying to figure out your next move. I didn't want to look at this situation like that. I didn't want to be negative, thinking Julia was hiding things from me. I wanted life to be perfect. I wanted to be happy. But life isn't perfect, and I know that. It's fraught with unexpected shit, but it's also full of wonderful moments as well. I needed to stay positive. I'd already decided to wait for Julia to tell me her truth. I needed to be patient. I needed to not go to the dark side. How could she be evil in any way? She wasn't. I couldn't let my mind go there. She wasn't. She was Julia. I needed to let her be Julia.

Chapter Thirty-Three
Julia

I woke up alone. I had no idea what time it was. It was like I had no memory at all. I didn't know where I was or how I got here. I didn't know if I was alone. I felt alone though. I lay there for a moment, then sat up trying to adjust my eyes to the room. Where the hell was I?

I could see slivers of light seeping through the separation of the curtain panels. I got up from the bed and walked toward the light. I pulled the panels apart and much to my surprise, an unbelievable view of a lake stared back at me. Any normal person would have felt panic, but I actually felt calm. I just stared at the water. I felt like I was ten years old again. I had no idea where I was, but somehow it made me feel peaceful.

I just stood there, frozen, until I felt a blanket being draped around me. I didn't even realize I was naked. I could smell his cologne; he was behind me. Then I remembered he was with me all night. He wrapped his arms around me in a protective embrace. I felt safe, he made me feel safe.

"Hi," he said, softly pressing his cheek to my ear. His breath was warm.

"Hi," I responded, leaning into him.

"Where are we?" I asked. "It's so beautiful."

"We're at my place Julia… I brought you here last night," he whispered.

I grabbed his arms and held on tight. Last night was a blur. Life felt like a giant blur. I leaned my head back against his chest. He kissed my cheek.

"I feel like I just woke up after a nightmare, but I can't remember it. But I also feel remarkably calm and peaceful. Does that make sense?"

"It makes perfect sense," he said, holding me tighter, rubbing my arms, trying to console me. But console me why?

"I've been waiting for you to get up. I put some clothes on the bed and a new toothbrush in the bathroom. Get dressed and come out to the living room," he said, kissing the side of my head. And then he slowly released me and walked away. I remembered that feeling; the feeling of him leaving me. I didn't like it.

I stood there for a few more minutes. The sun was rising above the lake, shooting shimmering diamonds across the water right toward me. It was as if the lake was speaking to me, telling me it's a new day. A day full of hope and unknown possibilities. Dare I say, I felt happy.

As I changed into Andrew's T-shirt and a pair of sweats the thought crossed my mind; did we do more than sleep together? My memory was shit. Could that have happened? I let the thought go, but for some reason, I felt like it couldn't have been a romantic evening for either of us. I brushed my teeth and splashed cold water on my face. I stood looking in the mirror waiting for the negative thoughts to flow, but they didn't. I didn't pick on myself for looking plain without makeup, or for wearing clothes that were too big for me. I didn't make a fuss about my hair. I just looked and thought, that's me.

I peeked out the door. Down the hall I could see a kitchen. I could smell a fire burning. I walked to the end of the hallway and looked to the left; Andrew was sitting on the couch. The view was even more stunning in the living room. A wall of windows extended from the floor to the top of the A-frame. There wasn't a bad view anywhere. The lake was looking back at me again. He looked up, sensing I was in the room, and patted the cushion next to him. I smiled and walked toward him; I needed him to hold me. I sat down and he wrapped his arm around me and asked, "How are you doing... you okay?"

Just the sound of his voice brought me peace, but it also triggered me to get closer to him. I turned immediately, climbing on top of him, straddling his legs, and placing my arms and head on his chest like an infant cuddling into its mother. He wrapped his arms around me and just held me, like he didn't want to let go. I felt safe; his hug was the best place to hide, to lose myself, to avoid reality. But as much as I wanted to stay there, to hide, I felt myself coming back. I felt myself returning to my life.

"You smell like a candle," I whispered, letting my fingers roam over his chest.

"A candle?" he questioned. I felt him laugh a little.

"Yes," I said, breathing in deeply. "You smell like coffee, and bacon, and cologne."

"Is that a good thing?" he asked, with another slight chuckle.

"Yes," I said. I felt his chest rise and fall. He was breathing me in.

"Well, you smell like a candle as well. Like a mixture of rainwater, laundry detergent, toothpaste, and just a hint of perfume."

I couldn't help but smile. "Is that a good thing?" I asked, with a slight chuckle.

"Yes," he said, tightening his grip around me.

"Julia," he said quietly, resting his chin against my head, "we need to talk… about last night, but when you're ready, okay?"

I nodded. And then he said something I wasn't expecting.

"I want you to know something… we weren't intimate last night. I slept on top of the blankets. I wouldn't do that to you… I would never take advantage of you."

I nodded again, relieved that he was who I thought he was.

We sat there quietly for a bit, the fire crackling in the background until he heard my stomach growl.

I felt him pull back a bit.

"You hungry?" he asked.

"I guess I am," I said, slightly embarrassed. I didn't want to be, hungry, that is. I didn't want us to move from that spot. I wanted to freeze the moment; keep it forever.

I reluctantly slid off him. He stood, looking down at me and said, "I'll get you some breakfast. You wanted a breakfast date, right?" He winked at me, and my heart melted.

I nodded and smiled.

I watched him walk to the kitchen; so domestic. He was taking care of me like I was his sick child. I pulled my knees to my chest and thought, I could do this every day. I looked around the room. I spied a bookshelf in the corner, a few paintings on the walls and one over the fireplace. I stood up and saw a large dining table behind me and a few plants near the windows. I walked over to the large grouping of windows. The sun had moved, extending above the tree line now, but the same stream of glistening light that reached out to me through the French doors in the bedroom was still there, shooting across the lake, reaching for me. Suddenly, the previous night's events were flooding in. I wrapped my arms around me as the memories downloaded; I hung my head. I started to shudder from the tears. The kiss with

Andrew, the fight with Jack, the walk to Sean's, the beach, the storm, the rocks, the waves, and Andrew calling my name. After that, my memory faded. All I could think was that I'd become a woman who needed rescuing. First Jack, then Andrew. What kind of mess had I become?

I was lost in the memories, trying to piece them together, when I felt his arms wrapped tightly around me. He knew. I was like a child unable to process them all. I felt embarrassed. He turned me around slowly, and took my face in his hands, gently brushing my hair back. He kissed my forehead, my cheek, my other cheek, and finally my lips. He was tender and gentle; everything I needed right then. Suddenly, I remembered him pulling me through the water, then up the stairs. I remembered him covering me with a blanket in the truck. He had no idea why I was on the beach in that storm, but I had to guess he'd come back to the cottage for some reason. Unfortunately, he must have found Jack instead of me. He probably had no idea what happened between Jack and me. But the biggest realization I had at that moment, was that he had no idea I was a woman who would fight every day, battling the negative thoughts in my head. I hadn't been honest with him; it wasn't fair.

"Let's eat," he said, pulling me toward the kitchen island. I sat on a stool while he served me coffee and a plate full of eggs, bacon, and toast. He was serving me a candle for breakfast.

"Almond butter… blackberry jelly?" he offered.

I nodded. How did he know my favorites?

It took all of five minutes for me to devour my meal. I was starving. I didn't even question eating the bacon.

I took a sip of coffee then put my hands on my lap. I looked at him and said, "I'm ready now."

He nodded, pushing his plate away. He placed his elbows on the island, folding his hands, resting his chin on them.

"First of all, I can't thank you enough… for finding me… for saving me," I said, trying not to break down. "I didn't remember it all 'til now, but I know what you did for me."

His eyes were pleading with me to not thank him. I put my hand up.

"If not for you, I shudder to think what would have happened. I'm a better runner than I am a swimmer," I said, trying to be funny. Second," I took a deep breath, "I'm guessing you met Jack."

He nodded. I took another deep breath. God, I didn't want to talk about Jack.

"I am so, so sorry I didn't tell you he was there," I said, my eyes casting downward. I couldn't look at him. I just kept talking to the island.

"It all was a fluke, and you and I had just met, and I didn't want to lay that all on you. I… I didn't want to ruin things between us by bringing my ex-husband into the mix. Jack came down on business, I was there for my own getaway and our friends who own the place gave each of us the invitation to stay without checking with the other. I wasn't happy about it, but if it wasn't for Jack," I faltered, "if he hadn't been there, I think something much worse would have happened." I looked up at him then; he looked confused. "During the robbery," I finally said. "Jack saved me Friday night."

Andrew's hands fell to the counter as he stood up quickly, knocking the stool to the floor. "What robbery Julia, you never told me about a robbery."

"Please sit down," I pleaded. He looked at me questioningly then reluctantly turned and grabbed the stool, his facial expression a mixture of concern and betrayal.

"It happened after I got home from Glenn's. I didn't even realize Jack was in the house, sleeping in the other bedroom. His car was parked on the other side of the cottage, and he didn't see my car; neither of us knew the other was there. This guy broke in around two in the morning." I paused, trying to gather myself. "When I got home, I was so happy, so not wanting to do anything but get into bed and relive the night, the night with you." He smiled at me, acknowledging he felt the same. "I've never felt so scared in my life. When I realized someone was in the cottage, I immediately started looking for my phone, but then I remembered I'd left it by the side door. I panicked. I had no way out. I grabbed a piece of driftwood from the bedroom and walked out thinking I could hit whoever was out there and make a run for it, but that only slowed him down for a second. He grabbed me and he was trying to get me to the couch when I remembered I'd left a knife on the side table by the door. I stabbed him in the leg, but even that didn't slow him down."

"Jesus Christ Julia!" Andrew was wide-eyed now, incredulous as to what I was telling him. He was shaking his head in disbelief. If it hadn't happened to me, I wouldn't believe it either. He placed his hand on mine.

I took a breath. "He pulled the knife from his leg and grabbed me, pushing me forward to the couch. I don't want to tell you what he said he was going to do to me." I stopped talking, turning my head away from him until I could regain my composure. I felt his hand on my back, trying to steady me, trying to support me. My fingers mindlessly roamed over my lips. It was like I could feel the man's breath on my neck all over again. "Jack appeared literally out of nowhere and hit him over the head with a lamp."

"Julia," he said, sitting back and running his hand through his hair. "Jesus! Does Sean know about this? I mean he must right, he lives right there."

"He knew after the fact; he wasn't home that night." I looked into his eyes, "Don't be mad at him. I told him not to tell you about any of it; the break-in or Jack staying at the cottage. I wanted to do it myself, I just didn't think I'd be telling you like… telling you like this."

Andrew took a few deep breaths. He stood up and walked toward the entry, I'm guessing the download of information was a bit too much. I didn't blame him. I watched as he ran his hand through his hair, and down over his beard.

He walked back toward me, placing his hands on the counter.

"What happened last night? What happened between you and Jack?" he asked, his eyes dark. I needed to remember that to him, all of this looked like I was shacking up with Jack; why wouldn't he think that? I'd had my thoughts about him and Erica, plus, he didn't know anything about my history with Jack. He didn't know why we divorced, what happened in our lives that led us to that point of giving up. He didn't know me; he didn't know my triggers or my demons. At that moment, I wondered what he thought about me; people get divorced all the time, but what did he think of me specifically. Did he wonder why I would give up like that? Did he wonder if I was faithful, trustworthy; did he think I was incomplete? I just needed to stop with the voices and tell the truth. Whatever he thought of me, whatever he would think of me wasn't up to me. He'd have to sort all of this out for himself.

I took a deep breath, blowing it out slowly, then came clean. "Last night, after you dropped me off, the house was dark, so I assumed Jack was either out or in his room. I went to grab a drink from the fridge, and he reached from behind me and slammed the door shut. At first, I didn't know it was him, so of course I got scared, then I heard his voice questioning me about where I was, and who I was with, and then I got angry. I told him it was none of his business. Then I could smell the vodka on his breath. I knew he was drunk. He grabbed my face and forcibly kissed me, but I shoved him, and slapped him across the face, then I ran to the bedroom and locked myself inside. He followed, professing his love for me but I wasn't listening. I didn't want to listen. He finally left me alone and that's when I lost it. I felt like I was living the past ten years over again; the fighting, the jealousy, the accusations. I couldn't bear it. After about fifteen minutes, I peeked out the bedroom door and saw him standing on the deck. It was my chance to get out of there. I bolted, intending to go to Sean's. I just needed someone to talk to; I didn't want that someone to be you. I'm sorry."

I could see the hurt in his eyes. I knew what he was thinking. I continued. "I was on my way to Sean's but then decided that I couldn't put all of it on him, so regardless of the rain, I decided to go to the beach instead. The beach had always been my safe haven in the past, a place for me to sort out my life when Jack and I would fight. At first, I knew I was being stupid, going there during a storm that was intensifying with every step I took, but I just kept walking, walking down the stairway, looking out into the vast ocean, and that's when things blurred. I fell into old habits; negative thoughts flooded in as fast as the water was flowing in. My thoughts crippled me. I had successfully shoved out anything good in my brain about the time you and I had spent together and replaced it with old memories of fighting with Jack, old flashes of feeling bad about myself. It was like I was freefalling, and I didn't care." I paused for a moment, then continued. "I did have one thought of you though," I said, looking directly into his eyes, "you didn't deserve to get caught up in a relationship with a woman like me. You should be running."

Andrew shook his head in protest. "Julia, that's not at all what I think."

I shook my head. "Please Andrew, let me finish, let me explain." Tears trickled down my cheeks with such ease, it was as if they knew that path to take; it was habitual. "There's something else I want you to know about me," I said reluctantly. Now the secret would be out. A secret I knew I'd tell him eventually, but I never wanted that day to come. I swallowed hard and just said it.

"I suffered from anorexia in college. I went over two years without having a period. I wasn't even sure I'd ever have children, which is probably why I got pregnant so young; we were used to being careless. I went to therapy back then, but it was short lived. I've been in therapy for two years now, some because of the divorce and some because I'm going to suffer from this fucking disease for the rest of my life," the anger was seeping out now. "I just slip sometimes and give in to bad thoughts, thoughts that tell me I'm not good enough. The thoughts attack my physique first and then my character. They tell me I'm not doing enough; I'm not enough." I wiped the tears from my face, shaking my head, disgusted with myself. "It may seem like, considering last night, that I'm really not making any progress, but I am... I know I am. I just get triggered sometimes. What went down with Jack triggered me, and I couldn't fight it.

I was wringing my hands at this point.

"I'm so sorry, Andrew... I'm sorry for hiding this from you. I'm sorry for hiding it all from you. That's not the kind of woman I am, not the kind of woman I want you to think I am." This was all too much. Too much after just two dates. Way too much to dump on someone I'd just started seeing. I couldn't help but ask the next question.

"Are you regretting me now?" I said, looking into his questioning eyes. "Regretting getting involved with me, regretting saving me," I said, turning away from him, "because I wouldn't blame you," I said, through tearful sobs, and then I totally came clean. "I know we just met, but... I'd be crushed if you didn't want me." I could barely contain the onslaught of negativity and my need for him right then.

Andrew leaned in and grabbed my hand forcefully. "Look at me," he said strongly. "You are struggling Julia, and it's okay. We're all struggling with something. I'm struggling too." He wiped the tears from my face. I looked up at him, trying to give him the chance to be human. I'd made him into this superhero, this guy who didn't have any issues or anything to hide, and then I realized, that's what I wanted him to think of me; a woman with no issues, dare I say, a 'normal' woman. I had to let him speak now without labeling him. I just wanted him to accept me for the mess I was, I am, even though I didn't. It might be easier to deal with it all if he just let me go.

"My turn," he said, releasing my hand and pushing his hands against the counter.

What was happening? I expected him to cut me loose after all that, but instead he was offering some kind of olive branch. Some form of solidarity. I wasn't ready for this.

"First of all, I'll never regret you," he said, his eyes reaching deep into my soul. I knew he was telling me his truth.

"That being clear, I need to come clean with you," he said, pausing before he opened himself up to me.

"I told you the story of my mom dying of cancer, but I didn't tell you the whole truth." He cleared his throat. "I've known Jack since college," he said, "he knows me as Coop, my middle name is Cooper." I looked at Andrew in disbelief; how could that be true?

"The funny thing is, I met Jack on Thursday at The Captain's Catch. We chatted for about ten minutes. I had no idea he was your ex-husband. I didn't ask about his wife. I didn't even remember your name. He didn't tell me he was divorced."

He could see I was struggling. That is so random, what are the odds? But then I realized it was no crazier than Andrew and I ending up on a blind date after meeting at the coffee shop.

"College... you went to college together," I said, more like a statement than a question.

"Jack and I lived on the same floor the first two years in college. I had a reputation with the ladies, if you know what I mean, and just so you know, I'm not proud of it." I nodded, he continued. "When I was in high school, I had a steady girlfriend. She cheated on me, at least twice. I was young and I couldn't handle it. When it was over, I spent a lot of time with my older brother. I took note of how he handled relationships; he just didn't have them. He would date, would sleep with girls, but never allowed a relationship to develop. To me, it seemed like a safer way to live than to be hurt again. I guess that watching my brother, the way he treated women, influenced me, but I can't blame it all on him. I made my own decisions. I just didn't value relationships. I didn't value women. I grew indifferent, maybe in the end, I didn't value myself. When my mother got sick, I left school to be with her, that's when I found out about my father's indiscretions."

Andrew's eyes cast downward. He swallowed hard, fighting back the tears. I placed my hand on his.

"He'd been cheating on her for a while. I don't know if she even knew. I wanted her to know, but it wouldn't have been right to tell her, she'd be heartbroken. She was already going through hell. It was like my eyes were opened and I couldn't keep living the way I was. I hated my father for what he was doing, and I hated myself for what I'd become. I didn't want to be like him. My mother was a saint 'til the day she died. And as for my dad… I can't talk to him; I'll probably never forgive him."

Andrew's tears fell easily now. It was like a burden had been lifted from both of us. I stood up and walked behind him, wrapping my arms around his waist, and resting my head on his shoulder.

"You're not your brother, and you're not your dad," I whispered in his ear. "You're you, you're the best version of you right now. Do you know how wonderful you are?"

He pushed the remaining scrambled eggs around on his plate, while taking some deep breaths.

"Jack will tell you different Julia, he knew what I was like in college. He's not going to hold back. He's going to try to poison the way you see me. When he opened the door at the cottage, I can't even explain how taken aback I was. From there things escalated and I grabbed him and threw him against the wall. He was spewing shit at me about him kissing you that night, about you being a notch in my belt; he was treating me like I was the guy he knew from school. I'm not that guy Julia, I'm not."

I walked to his side and took his face in my hands, wiping the tears from his cheeks. "I may only have met you a few days ago, but I know what you're like, and you're not like that. I believe you. If I've learned anything worthwhile in therapy, it's that you can't erase the past, the good or the bad—it's a part of us. All we have is now."

He melted into me. Suddenly I was the one trying to console him. I felt at peace. It felt right to tell him my story. It felt right to listen to his story. We wanted to comfort each other through the pain. I felt like a bridge had been built between us, and we were standing together in the middle, high above our problems, high above the past. It all felt right. It felt like that bridge was leading us somewhere and it was time to follow it. I desperately needed to believe that we were meant to be on this path together.

Chapter Thirty-Four
Jack

Fuck! My head was pounding. I forgot to close the curtains, and the light was pouring in through the bedroom window. I didn't want to get up. I looked up at the ceiling, blinking repeatedly, trying to focus, trying to remember what happened last night. One thing I knew for sure, I was drunk. I recalled something happening with Julia, but I wasn't sure what I did, what she did. My phone started ringing and the pounding intensified. Where the fuck was it? Finally, I reached for it at the foot of the bed. Christ, my fucking head. I looked at the phone; it was Justin.

~

"Dad, I've been texting you. Where you been?"

Jesus, I didn't even realize he was trying to reach me. "I uh, I went out yesterday, had a few too many."

"So, you went hard last night, huh. You sound rough."

I rolled my eyes. "I definitely drank too much, and I'm not proud of it, so don't get giddy about it."

"Giddy... Dad, I don't think giddy is a term I'd use," he said laughing.

"Sorry, I'm not up with the lingo these days. What's up?"

"I just wanted you to know that I'm heading out with Emily for a few days. I've left Cory in charge. Things are pretty quiet here. How's it going for you other than tearing it up?"

I let his comment slide. "I've got one client to see today, and one tomorrow, that's it. The other two went fine. I'll be home tomorrow."

"Well, that sounds productive, but you don't have to rush back. Cory has it covered. Take a few more days for yourself, you deserve some time off."

"Yah, okay son, I'll think about it. Have fun with Emily and I'll see you mid-week."

"Sounds good. And get yourself a Bloody Mary, seriously, it will help. Maybe some eggs and toast too. Grab a shower and take care of yourself."

"Thanks son, talk soon."

~

I rolled over in bed, still feeling exhausted. It was 10 a.m. I had a 1 p.m. appointment so I had time to go for a walk and get the toxins out of my body. After that, maybe I'd take Justin's advice and grab a late breakfast. Funny, my kid giving me hangover advice. At least he gives a shit. Where would I be without my kids? Then it hit me. Shit: my car was still at the bar. I guess I'll need to get an Uber. At least I didn't drive last night.

When I walked to the bathroom, I noticed Julia's door was open. I walked into the room and took note that the bed was made. Did she get up early? I glanced around then saw something sparkly on the chair; it was a pink nightie. But it wasn't just any pink nightie, it was the one I gave her for Valentine's Day, all those years ago. I picked it up and brought it to my face, inhaling. It smelled of her perfume. Why would she bring it with her? I was shocked she hadn't thrown it away after the divorce. It made me wonder: did she still have feelings for me? After two years apart, was she having second thoughts? I know I was.

I put the nightie down and walked to the dresser. I ran my fingers gently over the sand dollar necklace I'd bought for her thirtieth birthday; she'd kept that too. But who was I kidding, its jewelry, women don't just chuck all their jewelry after a divorce. Other than her wedding and engagement rings, she probably still wore most of the jewelry I'd given her.

I walked to the door, then stopped abruptly. I was having a flashback from the night before or was it from years ago; I wasn't sure. Julia had locked herself in the bedroom. Was that last night?

I shook my head; get it together man. I walked into the bathroom and grabbed some aspirin. I looked rough. I walked to the kitchen, and that's where it all came back to me. Julia by the refrigerator, me trying to kiss her. Her slapping me. I know I must have said some shit for her to lock herself in her room. I felt anxious suddenly. I ran my hand over my head, then covered my mouth. Where the fuck is Julia? The last thing I remembered was her locking herself in the bedroom. And then I remembered Coop. "Was Coop at the door?" Suddenly, I could picture him, rain soaked, standing on the deck. I walked to the side door and opened it, like I was looking for a ghost.

"It wasn't a ghost," I said, the night's events now coming back to me. "Coop was here, he came to the door looking for Julia. Why was he looking for Julia? How the fuck did he even know Julia?"

Again, my memory was fuzzy, but it was all piecing its way back. He was the one on the date with Julia. It wasn't Sean, it was Coop.

"Fucking Coop!" my anger started to swell. "That fucking guy was out with my wife!" He's a player Julia, how can't you see that?"

Then I remembered him pushing his way into the cottage. I remembered him breaking into her room. I remembered she wasn't in there. He left to look for her and then came back and told me he'd found her, and he was taking her to his house. She wasn't here last night; how did I not remember that he'd taken her? How could I willingly let him take her?

I walked out onto the deck, still reeling from the Coop realization. I still loved Julia. I still wanted Julia. I knew last night wasn't the time to make advances on her because she was right—I remembered her telling me I was drunk.

"God damn it Jack… what the fuck is wrong with you! You think forcing yourself on her is going to help you win her back?" I was yelling at myself now. I didn't care if anyone heard me.

I just shook my pounding head, letting it drop into my hands. I walked back into the bedroom, grabbed my phone, and texted her.

~

Jack: "Julia, I'm worried about you. Are you okay? Please text me back. I'm sorry. I love you."

~

I dropped the phone on the bed. I needed to know if she was okay. All I could do now was wait. I blew it with her last night, but who was I kidding; I'd blown it with her years ago.

Chapter Thirty-Five
Julia

While Andrew was cleaning up the breakfast dishes, I walked out onto the deck. The sun felt warm on my face, and I just stood there, eyes closed, allowing myself to just be. Again, so much for being a pluviophile. Last night was awful, but today, after the conversation with Andrew, I felt revived. I could hear the birds singing, the squirrels scampering through the woods. It's crazy what you can hear when you close your eyes and just listen. It was peaceful.

Suddenly, I heard music coming from the outdoor speakers. I recognized the song immediately; Brother's Osbourne, "Stay A Little Longer," one of my favorite songs. I turned toward the house just as Andrew opened the door and walked toward me.

"How'd you know I love this song?" I said, looking dreamily into his eyes.

"I didn't," he said. "It's one of my favorites, and something just told me to play it."

I smiled at him as he took me in his arms. His hug was the same as the first night we met; gentle, slow, lingering, building in intensity. I felt like nothing could touch me, nothing could hurt me. He pulled back and took my face in his hands, then kissed me tenderly. I wrapped my arms around him, pulling him to me. When it ended, I was breathless, just like our goodbye kiss last night. At least that memory was clear. The heat between us was incredible. I relished every second.

He pulled away from me and reached into his pocket. He handed me my phone.

"Jack texted you... he's probably concerned. Not to tell you what to do, but you should probably tell him you're okay."

I stood there shocked that he would even tell me that, considering he was worried about what Jack would say to me about him.

"Thank you," I said, knowing that had to be hard for him. "I was wondering where this was." I took the phone and walked over to the railing, reading the text. My eyes welled up and I took a deep breath.

I stared out at the water. It didn't take me long to know what I had to do. I texted Jack back. When I turned around, Andrew hadn't moved. He was just standing there, watching me. I hesitated; I didn't want to say what I needed to say.

"I have to go back to the cottage Andrew. I have to see Jack and let him explain, apologize... whatever he needs to do."

He protested immediately. "Julia, he was pushing himself on you last night. How can I let you do that," his concern evident.

I had to compose myself. I knew he didn't mean it the way it sounded.

"Andrew, you, and I both know it's not up to you. I have a history with Jack, and that will never change. I respect how you feel, but Jack is clearly in trouble, and I feel compelled to help him. I have to give him a chance to find peace in his life. I mean, it may not even make a difference... I have no idea what frame of mind he's in, but I have to try," I said, staring back at him.

I could see the struggle on his face. I didn't want him to think I still had feelings for Jack, but I felt the need to make sure Jack was okay. I needed to reassure him that I wasn't putting us at risk.

"Julia," he said, lowering his head and crossing his arms across his chest, "I'm so uncomfortable with this for so many reasons. I'm trying to understand why you need to do this, but I know it's not my call." He hesitated for a moment then said, "Of course, I know you'll need me to drive you there, but I'd feel much better about the whole thing if I could stay within sight of you. I just need to be close by in case anything happens."

I lowered my head, then looked back up. I looked into those big brown eyes feeling so blessed to have this man in my life.

"Okay," I said, "I'll talk to him on the deck. You can park on the road where you can see us clearly. I'm good with that, are you?"

He shook his head in agreement, then he walked to me, pulling me close. This time his hug felt more desperate than comforting, but I understood why.

Chapter Thirty-Six
Julia

I texted Jack to tell him I'd be coming by. He told me he had a client to meet with, but he'd be back around 3 p.m. He also said he was looking forward to seeing me. I groaned with that last comment. The last thing I wanted was to give him false hope. This meeting would be difficult to say the least.

When I stepped into the shower, I had a flashback of the previous night. Andrew was in the shower with me. I remembered burying my face in his chest, but that's all I remember. I needed to let the memory fade before I freaked out. I didn't know what Andrew saw when he took my clothes off, and part of me didn't want to know. I felt self-conscious enough about my body, I really didn't need to picture him removing my bra and panties. I've lived in the shadows for a long time, literally. Maybe that's why I like rainy days; the shadows hide imperfections, and I am well aware of my imperfections.

Strangely enough, I trusted Andrew. We hadn't slept together yet, I mean we did just meet a few days ago, but again, the way we were acting, it was like we'd been in relationship for months, even years aside from not having sex. I was ready for the next step. At forty-five, and not having slept with anyone but Jack in well over two years, I was more than ready. I guess I just needed to find out Andrew's story, meaning, was he sexually active. The last thing I needed was to put myself at risk, physically, because the way I was thinking, the way I wanted things to go forward, didn't leave a lot of room for talking about sexual partners. What are the words I'm looking for: awkward, uncomfortable, embarrassing, but really important, and I knew that.

As I was walking into the bedroom Andrew yelled to me, "Your clothes are on the bed." I looked to my left, and there they were, folded, appearing to be clean. I smiled and got dressed wondering when he had time to do laundry with everything that had happened. Suddenly, I realized I had no makeup with me. Suddenly, I felt less than. These dramatic swings in my thought process were killing me. Just hours ago, I'd fully accepted the way I looked, but right now, not so much, which was so horribly typical for me. I didn't want to look so plain in front of Andrew. I wanted to look beautiful, and unfortunately for me, that meant applying just a small amount of makeup. Mascara would have sealed the deal. It was just another link in the chain of my issues.

He was standing by the front windows when I walked into the living room.

"Just so you know, I washed your clothes in cold water, and used the lowest heat setting in the dryer," he said, his back to me.

I just stared at him thinking, who the hell is this guy? Way too good to be true.

"I'm impressed... where'd you learn your laundering skills?"

He turned and smiled. "I can't take credit; my mother taught me well."

I smiled at this man I'd just met. This man who was protecting me, taking care of me, dare I say, loving me. It's been a long time since I felt so cared for.

"You ready to go?" he asked, with an air of trepidation.

"I'm ready," I said, knowing I really wasn't.

~

When we pulled up to the cottage, my stomach was doing flips. Even though I was the one who wanted to talk to Jack, I was nervous as hell. Even though I knew he was drunk last night, that whole scene terrified me, but I had to keep reminding myself that wasn't really him, it was the booze. There were only a few times in our marriage when liquor played a role in our fights. I would never say he was an alcoholic; if I did, I'd have to say I was one too. We both had used alcohol as an escape at times, from life, from ourselves, from each other. I knew it was wrong.

I was wringing my hands as Andrew pulled into the driveway. He put the car in Park and turned to me, placing his hand on mine, trying to squelch the fear.

"It's going to be fine," he said, then he leaned over and kissed the side of my head. "Just trust yourself. You're here to help him, not hurt him. I hope he realizes that."

I took a deep breath. "I know… I know," I said, trying to gather myself.

I blew out a few more breaths then exited the truck.

"I'll be fine," I said, reaching for his hand across the front seat. "He's not a bad man Andrew."

He nodded.

~

I walked up the stairs and saw Jack standing on the deck. Pensive people always stand with their hands on the deck railing, gripping tightly as if that's the only thing keeping them from falling over the edge—the edge of reality, or maybe the edge of sanity. He was staring out at the water when he heard me approach.

"Julia," he said, sounding relieved. I won't lie, I could sense something strange in his voice.

He walked toward me and hugged me immediately. I was surprised, but I wrapped my arms around him and held him tightly. I felt bad for him. I pulled back and looked into his eyes; he looked hopeful and sad all at the same time. I let him go and walked to the railing, gripping it tightly, proving my theory. He followed and started the conversation.

"Julia, I can't apologize enough for last night. I'm being honest with you when I say I don't remember it well; I didn't even realize you'd left the cottage, but I know I scared you and pushed you too far. I hope you can forgive me. I love you… still," his voice trailing off with a hint of desperation.

I took a deep breath. Choose your words Julia, don't give him false hope.

"I know Jack, I know. You were drunk and you weren't thinking straight and yes of course I forgive you… I've always forgiven you."

We both stared out at the ocean for a moment, neither of us wanting to speak. We were married for twenty-two years, we fought weekly for at least the last ten years. We knew how fights started, progressed, and ended. I could feel the fear emanating from both of us.

"Jack," I finally said, "I don't want to fight with you, and I'm saying that because I know you're not going to like what I'm about to say." I swallowed hard. "I'm concerned for you, for how you've been dealing with the divorce. I have no idea what's been going on in your life since we split, but the fact that something triggered you to get drunk and do what you did tells me that you need some help. Before you push back, just listen, please."

I turned to him, expecting to see the anger building in his face, but it wasn't, so I continued.

"I'm not sure if you know this, but I've been in therapy for the last two years."

He turned to look at me. He just stared at me questioningly.

I glanced back at the water. "I was having a hard time with our split, and I was falling back into old patterns of self-deprecation. Steph is the one who encouraged me to see a therapist. Of course, I fought it, vehemently, and I'm not sure what made me finally do it, but I did. It's been a lot of work, a lot of checks and balances, and a lot of being truthful. I can't lie… it has sucked, but in the end, at least I'm working toward a better me." Then I turned to face him again. "Do you understand what I'm saying?"

Jack lowered his head and sighed. It took him a solid minute to reply. When he looked at me, I knew something big was coming.

"I didn't want the divorce; you know that right?" He paused and then said exactly what I didn't want him to say. "Baby, it's terrible… I just can't stop loving you. I've never stopped loving you… never." Then he turned away and said, "I'm trying to hear you Julia, but all I hear is what you're not saying. You're not saying you still love me."

"Jack…" Now my voice was trailing off. My heart ached for him, and for me. I felt horrible now. I knew this would be tough. I didn't want to say the wrong thing here. Trust yourself Julia, just be honest.

I cleared my throat, still looking at him. "I will always love you, Jack. It's not easy to erase twenty-two years, but if I'm being truthful, the last ten years of our marriage, all we did was fight and that's no way to live a life. The one thing I've never said to you is that I'm sorry. I'm sorry for all the ways I've hurt you, and I'm sorry we couldn't figure things out. I would always say, after we'd made up, that love was never the issue, and it still isn't. We just don't seem to work together anymore. We both know that. It has nothing to do with love."

Jack shook his head and just stared at the water. I could tell he wasn't receiving any of this well. I hit him with some damaging blows; it's not what I wanted for him. I didn't want him to feel rejected. He placed his forearms on the railing, clasping his hands tightly. He seemed to be lost in the movement of the grass. And then he broke his silence.

"And you think Coop is the answer?" he said, then turned to look at me. "What do you even know about him Julia? I know him better than you. I'm sure he told you we were in college together, but I bet he didn't tell you what he was like then. The guy was a womanizer Julia, and the odds that he's changed are probably slim. He's never even been married... what does that say? I don't want you to be another notch in his belt." He looked away again. I felt his anger building.

There was the same old Jack I knew; jealous, insecure, and giving into ideas that he didn't need to. He didn't have all the answers. He was saying exactly what Andrew thought he would. I didn't hesitate to set him straight.

"People can change Jack. I realize I haven't known Andrew very long, but in the short amount of time that we've been together, he's been incredibly open with me. I'm quite sure I know more about him than you do. I'm a big girl Jack, and I'm no fool."

He shook his head. "I know Julia... I know, I just don't want you to get hurt, that's all."

"That's not all Jack," I said, now feeling my anger swell. "You're acting jealous, and you actually can choose not to. In case you forgot, we are divorced."

My words were sharp, and my frustration was beginning to overtake me, but then I remembered I didn't come here for a fight, and I tried to listen to Andrew's advice: "You're trying to help him, not hurt him."

I put my hand on his. "Jack, look at me." He raised his head; his eyes were welling with tears. "Jack, we both came into this marriage with a ton of baggage, and we tried like hell to fix each other. You were always there for me, and I tried to be there for you. The shit we've endured because of our upbringing, because of our choices, has been incredibly difficult. I'm trying to figure out a way to deal with my crap by going to therapy. I think you still have so much shit to sift through, from your childhood, and the divorce, that it's going to kill you if you don't get some help. Your insecurities and believing you don't measure up are the same as my anorexia and my struggles with needing to be more, needing to be perfect. They are no different; we are both left to deal with our perceived inadequacy. The only way our struggles are different is that we're alone in them." I knew he wasn't understanding me. "What I mean is, I can never truly know how you feel, and you can never truly understand how I feel. We have to walk alone on our paths to recovery, our paths to a better life, but that doesn't mean we can't seek out professional help to guide us there, and even though we're divorced, we can still support each other."

Jack turned to me and instinctively grabbed my hands. He rubbed his thumbs over mine, his eyes fixed on them. Then he pulled each of my hands to his mouth and kissed them one at a time. He looked up and stared into my eyes as if he were telling me he understood. I pulled him to me, wrapping my arms tightly around him. I felt a strange connection right then, hurdling over all the shit we let get in the way when we were married.

"It's okay Jack, we can both be okay now. We're all hiding from something, we just have to take the right steps, the steps that tell us we don't have to hide anymore."

I pulled back and looked at him, raising my hand to his cheek. "Love is not the issue Jack; it never was, and I love you too much to not be honest. I will support you through this, I will love you through this, but that's all I can offer right now. Getting back together won't fix you, and it won't fix me. I've moved on and I want the same for you. No more regrets."

Jack nodded hesitantly, then pulled me to him. We stood there for a bit, just holding one another. If only we could have found our way earlier; maybe we could have made it through the mine fields of our troubles. But we didn't. My path was different now, and although I held him in my arms, the intimacy of our embrace wasn't enough to change my course. Just because something is familiar doesn't mean it's safe—doesn't mean it's right. Andrew was in my life now, and I wanted him there. While we were embracing, I pictured Andrew watching us and I was praying he wasn't freaking out. Admittedly, it would be hard for me to be in his shoes.

"Can we actually be friends again?" Jack whispered in my ear.

"I'm willing if you are," I said.

He pulled back and kissed my forehead. I could give him that much, but that's all.

~

I walked into the cottage and packed a few things for the night. Jack was standing in the kitchen when I came out of the bedroom.

"You don't have to leave," he said, "I'm the one who crashed your getaway. I can find a room somewhere."

"Don't be silly Jack. Stay the night, it's okay."

He lowered his head, then chuckled lowly. "Well, Justin did encourage me to take some time off. I'll stay here tonight then find somewhere to stay if I decide to follow his advice."

"I think that's a good plan. When you get home, please text me so I know you made it back safely. I will contact my therapist for some recommendations. It's all going to be fine."

"Okay," he said, "Thank you Julia."

I smiled and walked out the door. Jack was a good man, just not the man for me, not anymore. I still felt strange, like I was abandoning him there. I felt sad. I felt bad. My emotions were all over the place. I teared up as I envisioned Jack standing alone in the cottage we once referred to as our honeymoon spot. I felt my chest tighten. I hated what I just did. But as soon as I turned the corner and saw Andrew's truck, all my thoughts did a one-eighty. I knew I did what I intrinsically needed to do for myself and for Jack, and maybe even for Andrew. I wiped away the tears, and walked toward the man who just might represent my future.

Chapter Thirty-Seven
Andrew

As soon as she got out of the truck, I regretted everything I'd said. What was I thinking? I'm letting her go to talk sense into her ex-husband who pushed himself on her last night. Who scared her enough that she locked herself in her bedroom, then bolted the first chance she had. She could have drowned in that storm.

I drove down the road to Sean's, turned around and parked in the road, far enough away to not be noticed, but close enough to see the deck. I watched as Jack walked to Julia and pulled her to him. Just the sight of that made my stomach turn. Right then was enough for me. I wanted to run over there and pull him away, but I could see she was hugging him back.

I had to turn away. This was a stupid idea. What made me think I could sit by and watch this potential love scene play out. I had no claim on Julia, which meant she had none on me. She could do whatever she wanted. For all I knew, he was telling her he still loved her, and she was reciprocating that love. I ran my hand through my hair and took a deep breath. Then turned back to see them talking. At least the hug had ended.

Suddenly, someone knocked on my window; it was Sean. He scared the shit out of me. I motioned for him to come around and get in the truck.

"Dude, what are you doing out here?" he said, as he climbed in.

I pointed to Julia's deck. He looked quickly to the right and saw Jack and Julia on the deck.

"What's going on," he said, confused by the scene playing out before him.

"Damn if I really know."

"Are they… are they…." Sean stopped mid-question and looked over at me.

"After we talked this morning, she came clean about a lot of stuff.

There's certainly more I could fill you in on. There's a lot going on in that little body. Man, I… I just don't know if I can handle all this."

"Okay," he said, rubbing his forehead. "Well, if they are talking things out, why are you here watching them? Does Julia know you're here watching?"

I sighed. "I dropped her off. The deal is that I stay just to make sure she's okay. I know I told you about him kissing her, but some other shit went down with him last night, and that's why she was out on the beach during the storm. Even so, she felt the need to talk to him today, and reluctantly, I agreed. I'm trying to be supportive," I said, rolling my eyes, because I knew how ludicrous it all sounded.

"Jesus… sounds like I am out of the loop. But it sounds like you are being supportive and for someone you literally just met, that's pretty impressive," he said, his eyes still fixed on the two of them.

I looked away from the deck and stared straight ahead.

"Christ, I don't know if I can do this. I have real feelings for her, and I don't know if I can take what may happen between them and the reality of what won't happen between us. I mean, they were married for a long time, how can I compete with that? They have history, they have kids, they know each other inside and out… the good and the bad. Sean," I said, lowering my head, "I just don't know if I'm up for this."

Sean put his hand on my shoulder.

"I get it. This is truly an unorthodox situation. When I introduced you two, I had no idea things could play out like this. I wanted it to be a fairytale, you know me, romanticizing everything. You obviously talked with her about this, you had a plan, right?"

"Yah, a plan of sorts. But you never know how things will play out, despite your best intentions. She could be falling for him all over again and I'm sitting here in my fucking truck watching it happen."

Sean paused, running his hand over his head. "Well, first of all, you don't know what's being said out there, and second, you seem to have deep feelings for her. Don't bolt yet man. Don't make assumptions. I've watched enough Hallmark movies to know that things aren't always what the seem." He raised his eyebrows at me.

We both started laughing, which was an awesome distraction. After a few minutes we watched them break from their conversation. We watched Jack take Julia's hands in his. We watched as he kissed her hands and then she pulled him to her. I had to look away at this point.

I hated myself for allowing her to break through my barriers. All these years I didn't realize I was living in protection mode, and then she comes along and suddenly I'm dropping the armor I didn't even know was there. And look where that's got me now.

"Crap, he's hugging her. He just kissed her on the forehead," Sean said, still intently watching the scene. "Wait, she's walking away," he said, with an uplifting tone. "She left him on the deck. She walked into the house."

We both watched Jack follow her. I slammed my fists down on the steering wheel.

"God damn it," I said, now in a full-on panic rage. "What the hell did I just do?"

"I'm telling you, just give her a minute," Sean said. "You don't know what that means. I couldn't see her face, but I highly doubt she was telling him to meet her in the bedroom."

I shook my head and turned to stare out the driver's side window.

"I'm getting out now Andrew. Don't leave yet. I know she's going to walk out the door to find you. I can feel it."

I looked at Sean and said, "I hope your right, you fucking romantic. Now get the fuck out of my truck."

I shoved his shoulder and he smiled. He got out of the truck without another word and walked back to his house. I sat there for another five minutes letting my mind go places it shouldn't.

I pictured the two of them passionately kissing. I pictured the two of them in the bedroom. I pictured the two of them pulling each other's clothes away. I pictured the two of them rekindling their romance. I hadn't even been with Julia yet; I hadn't been able to act on my feelings for her physically.

My mind wandered to this morning when I walked into the bedroom. I panicked at first, when I saw the bed was empty, and then I saw her standing in front of the glass doors, naked. She wasn't moving, she was just standing there, like it was completely normal. I couldn't take my eyes off her. Even in the dim light, I could see her bikini tan lines. She was fit for sure, I already knew that, but seeing her naked, even if it was from behind, was stunning. I grabbed the blanket from the bed, even though I would rather have walked up to her and just wrapped my arms around her naked body. I knew that wouldn't be right though, so instead, I wrapped her in the blanket, and pulled her to me. She leaned into me, and I felt like the moment was beyond perfect. How did things go from that incredible scene to this one?

All of this was making me sick. I was reaching my limit, but just as I thought it, just as I felt the urge to run, I saw her. She was walking toward me carrying a bag. She smiled at me, raising her hand, giving me a small wave.

I let my head fall to the steering wheel. "Thank you, God," I moaned. I'd never been so relieved to see anyone in my life.

I reached over and opened the door for her. She climbed in, letting her head fall back against the seat. She released a huge sigh. I put my hand on hers. She looked at me and smiled.

"Are you okay," I asked.

"I'm more than okay," she said calmly. "I feel relieved. I feel like I did the right thing for once."

I smiled, then let my inhibitions and my negative imagination go. I placed my hand on her cheek, and she leaned into my palm. I couldn't wait another second. I leaned in and kissed her. I had to let go of everything I'd just watched. I didn't really know what went down on that deck, but I also knew, as much as I wanted to know, it was none of my business. She would tell me when she wanted to if she wanted to. But there was one thing I knew for sure; she was right where I wanted her to be, sitting beside me, in my truck, and we were heading home.

Chapter Thirty-Eight
Julia

It felt like I'd been gone for more than a few hours. And strangely enough, I felt like I was coming home. I'd only stayed here one night, and although it was all new to me, it felt so natural to be here. The last few hours were intense, and I just needed to catch my breath.

Andrew unlocked the door and stepped to the side to let me go in first. I could still smell the bacon from breakfast, and the fireplace coals were still hot and fragrant. The day was flying by, but the light was still shining intensely through the front windows. The lake spoke to me, not like this morning, but more like it was welcoming me home. The sun had moved over the house now, but the way it caused the water to shimmer, it was like the two entities had forged together; they had bonded, forming one giant beacon of hope. They were calling out to me; "Have faith Julia."

I set my bag down in the entry and walked into the living room. I stood by the windows and just stared out at the lake. I wrapped myself in an embrace, just like this morning, but this time I didn't feel like I was going to fall apart; I felt whole. I heard Andrew walk up behind me. He wrapped his arms around me and nestled his face into my neck. I could feel his beard and his warm breath caressing my skin. I closed my eyes and leaned into him, clutching his arms. He felt warm against me. He felt muscular, sturdy, safe; I needed that. I needed to feel like he could hold me up, no matter what was to come.

"You hungry?" he whispered softly, pulling me closer.

"Not yet," I said, not wanting him to let me go.

"How 'bout I build a fire, warm us up," he offered.

"I'd love that," I whispered back, nuzzling into his beard.

He removed his arms and started to pull away, but I quickly turned, gently placing my hands on each side of his face. I let my fingers run through his hair. He stared down at me; he just kept staring at me. We stood there for a moment, just taking one another in. It was like I'd never looked at him before—like it was all new. I noticed a small scar above his left eyebrow. I moved my hand, deliberately, touching it delicately with the tips of my fingers.

"Battle scar," he said, still staring at me.

"One of many I bet," I said, smiling at him.

Then it was his turn. His fingers caressed my face, softly touching the scar just under my right eye.

"Battle scar?" he asked.

"Yes… a battle I've won so far."

He looked at me questioningly, so I offered what I could.

"The cosmetic surgeon did an excellent job stitching me up. I was lucky."

I knew he understood, and he knew why I didn't want to talk about it. I wanted to protect him. He didn't need old memories to resurface, not now. He kissed my scar tenderly.

I continued to let my fingers glide effortlessly down the side of his face, and then over his lips. They were soft to my touch. When I lowered my hands, I let them wander down his chest to his waist. I glanced up at him, he was still staring at me. He placed his hands on either side of my head, holding me gently, and brought his lips to mine. He released his grip just enough to let his fingers slide into my hair, gently massaging. His tongue met mine, and we let them dance together with little effort. He pulled back, looking at me again, then gave me a tender peck on the mouth. Then he closed his eyes and pulled me against him. His breaths were shallow and wanting.

"You are going to get me in trouble," he said, as his hands roamed over my back.

"Uh-huh," I said dreamily, acknowledging the struggle we both felt.

He kissed my forehead and released me. "I'm going to get the firewood," he said reluctantly, then he turned and walked toward the front door.

Neither of us wanted this to move too fast, and yet, we did. We wanted it to be slow and easy, but also fast and reckless. We never actually said that to one another, but from my standpoint, we were both thinking it.

While he made the fire, I grabbed my bag and headed to the bedroom. It was a spacious room; I didn't recall what it looked like from the night before. It was dark and cozy. Large wooden beams crossed the ceiling. The walls were a hunter green. The floors were wide planked pine. An upholstered red chair sat in the corner. The sturdily built king size log bed was decorated simply with a light sage green duvet. It took up a good portion of the room. A bohemian multi-colored rug peeked out from underneath the bed. For a single guy, he certainly had an eye for décor. A field stone fireplace stood majestically opposite the bed, just like the one in the living room. I placed my hand on the stone; it was cold and smooth, reminding me of the fireplace I grew up with at our camp in New Hampshire.

I took my necklace and earrings off, placing them on the dresser, next to his watch. There were two framed photos flanking the mirror. One was of an attractive woman with light brown hair sitting on the front steps of a farmer's porch; she was wearing overalls and a wide brimmed straw hat. She was holding a pair of gardening gloves. The other photo was the same woman, wrapping her arms around a young boy on the same steps. I could only guess that was Andrew and his mother. An old Bible lay directly between the photos, with a card protruding from the binding. A woman's name was engraved on the front: Lily Rose Monroe; it had to be his mother. I carefully opened the Bible to the page marked. The card simply said, "Andrew, I will always be watching over you; I will always love you," and the passage Ecclesiastes 3:1-8 was referenced. I recognized it from Andrew's tattoo. He had verses 1-4 tattooed on his arm. I read the passage; it was familiar to me. Of course I'd heard it before, but there was more to it than that, and I wasn't sure why.

~

There is a time for everything, and a season for every activity under the heavens:
    A time to be born and a time to die,
    A time to plant and a time to uproot
    A time to kill and a time to heal,
    A time to tear down and a time to build,
    A time to weep and a time to laugh,
    A time to mourn and a time to dance,
    A time to scatter stones and a time to gather them,
    A time to embrace and a time to refrain from embracing,
    A time to search and a time to give up,

A time to keep and a time to throw away,
A time to tear and a time to mend,
A time to be silent and a time to speak,
A time to love and a time to hate,
A time for war and a time for peace.

~

I couldn't stop them; the tears ran gently down my cheeks. I closed the Bible, placing my hand on her name and whispered, "Is this all part of some bigger plan? Have you brought us together? Is this our time?"

I pushed the Bible back into place, then turned to see Andrew's clothes lying on the chair in the corner. I walked over to the chair, placing my bag on the floor. I picked up one of his shirts and held it to my face, breathing in anything that was left of him. His smell was intoxicating. I proceeded to fold his clothes and set them on the left side of the chair, then retrieved my clothes and placed them on the right side. I just stood there and stared for a moment. It felt a bit strange to see the two sets of clothes, together, on the chair, but suddenly, I felt like it looked right. Nothing was out of place. Was this really happening? A few days ago, I was driving to the Cape to spend some much-needed time alone, and now I was placing my clothes next to a man's I hardly knew. I was letting my guard down. I was letting him in. I wondered briefly if it was all going too fast.

I walked to the bathroom and shut the door. I splashed cold water on my face to get rid of my fear. I instinctively grabbed my makeup bag, and then I stopped. Did I need it, after all the times he'd seen me without it? I could easily not put anything on, but I knew myself. It made me feel better about me, right or wrong. I've learned over the years that it's better to do the things you need to do to feel better about yourself than live in turmoil. In the end, I just feel more like myself with a little bit of makeup, just like I feel better about myself if I exercise and eat healthy.

"It's okay, do what you need to do," I whispered into the mirror.

I put some mascara on, and then I stared at her, the woman in the mirror. My thoughts were all consuming about what would happen next. "You told Sean you're not that kind of woman Julia," I said, whispering again. I'm pretty sure my reflection mouthed back, "Maybe you are tonight."

And then, just like that, I felt myself weaken. I wanted to question why Andrew would want to be with someone my age when he could clearly hook up with someone younger. Those thoughts were haunting and once again, I was in the position of fight or flight. I always thought the way I looked defined me, like it was the most valued part of me. On the other hand, I couldn't see what other people saw, but I wished I could. Kind of crazy to be pulled in two completely opposite directions. The inadequacy I felt was familiar. It could take me over in an instant, rendering me helpless to fight back. It's such a sad commentary on my life. I want it to stop. I want to understand why this has happened to me. When I'm weak, I let society's view of me reign supreme. Maybe Jack was right; maybe I am conceited, wanting men to look at me. But I know that's not really true; my need to be liked, even desired by others, is not what it seems. I'm realizing it's just what I think I need to be accepted by others, and to accept myself. It's all a bit off; why can't I get rid of this part of me?

When Jack and I were together, when we were young, I was so caught up in my feelings for him, and I believed him when he would give me a compliment. But after a while, I didn't take him seriously, and I didn't think about needing to impress him anymore. He'd seen me at my best and at my worst. He accepted me and my body for what it was; I was the problem. He hated it when I would pick on myself; when I would point out everything that wasn't perfect. Whether it was my boobs, my stomach, my ass; any little defect was so apparent to me. He would always tell me I was wrong, that I was focusing too much on what I perceived to be negative. I knew he was right, but he was my husband; I felt like he had to say those things to me.

I wished I could understand how I got caught in this web of conceit. Even defining it that way is wrong; I know that now, but it's so hard to stop doing something you've done most of your life. Obviously, I'm older now, and getting older with each passing minute. There's no competing with younger women anymore. Andrew seems to be attracted to me. Why can't I just believe that's true without scrutinizing everything.

I looked at myself in the mirror. I felt disgusted with this person looking back at me. Again, someone needed a peptalk.

"Stop it Julia… stop be so awful to yourself. There's a handsome man waiting for you in the next room. Why can't you believe he wants you? At that moment, I realized I simply needed to be me, and no one else. I needed to stop comparing myself to other women, or even comparing myself to the younger me. "He wants you Julia," I whispered, "stop making assumptions." I tried to smile. I tried to pull myself out of the negativity. I felt desperate for a moment, but what I really felt, what I really needed was to believe I was enough. I desperately needed to believe I was enough.

Chapter Thirty-Nine
Julia

When I opened the bathroom door, the fireplace was aglow in the bedroom. "You're so sneaky," I whispered, the smile spreading across my face. I could hear the record player in the living room. I walked out of the bedroom to find Andrew sitting on the floor, his back against the couch, with multiple pillows behind him and a blanket covering the rug. He raised a glass of red wine, trying to lure me in; it was working. I glanced at the album sitting next to the record player, The Best of Brett Young. One of my favorite songs was playing, "In case you didn't know."

Andrew looked at me then patted the blanket beside him encouraging me to take a seat. I smiled, then walked over. I motioned with my foot for him to move his legs apart so I could sit between them with my back to him; I wanted to feel his chest against me. Once I snuggled in, he wrapped his legs protectively around me, caressing my arms with his fingertips. I let my head fall back. I could feel him breathing me in. The fire was mesmerizing. I started to sing along to the song. After a few moments, I trailed off, and Andrew whispered in my ear.

"You have a beautiful voice."

I shrugged off the compliment, as usual.

"Julia..."

"Yes Andrew..."

"Julia... you are pure perfection," he said softly.

I couldn't help but cringe. He had no idea what that word did to me. I'd only corrected him once before.

"Andrew," I said hesitantly. "I... I don't want to explain right now, but could you choose any other word but that one? Please... it's just too much."

If I could have seen his face, I'm sure a look of confusion would have been there. But then he said, "Julia... Julia, you are completely captivating."

"Hmm, I like the sound of that," I said, more than satisfied by the word change. I didn't feel pressure. I felt desirable. It was nice.

We sat there silently, listening to one song after the other. The fire crackled; shouting at us at times. I could feel its heat, or was that just us?

He ran his beard down the side of my cheek, nestling his face into my neck. I squirmed playfully.

"That tickles," I said, my body twitching and pulling away slightly.

"I know," he said. "Do you want me to stop?"

I smiled, with my eyes closed, and leaned into him. "Don't stop," I said breathlessly as my hand reached up, pulling him back into me.

After a few minutes, I felt him pull away. "Your glass is empty," he whispered.

"I don't care," I said, pulling his face back to my neck again.

After a few more moments of glorious torture, he swiftly turned me around, now cradling me in his arms. I giggled like a teenager, shocked by the sudden change in position. He just smiled at me, brushing the hair from my face, and then he leaned in, kissing me softly. He pulled back for a moment, smiling back at me as he stroked my hair. Then he lifted my chin and kissed me again.

"Here Tonight," was playing now. Leave it to a country artist to make you feel like every emotion pulsing through you should be gathered up and shared with the entire world through a simple song. I quickly turned, got to my knees, and straddled him. The song and I were in sync. I just wanted time to stop. I wanted the outside world to stay out. I just wanted to stay right there, with him. I didn't want the moment to end. At least I didn't think I wanted it to.

I placed my hands on his face, forcing him to look at me. I let my fingers wander through his beard, then over his closed lips. For some reason, it was comforting to me. And then, I leaned in and kissed him. His hands were moving up and down my back. He pulled me flush to him. It was as if we were connected. The passion between us was palpable. I wanted to melt into him, become part of him. When we pulled away from each other we were breathless again. We sat for a moment, our foreheads touching; the only thing holding us upright.

"This floor is pretty hard," he said, under his breath.

"Is it? I hadn't noticed," I said, nuzzling my nose into his beard and across his lips.

He eased me back and off to the side. I had a moment of thinking it was over, he was rejecting me for some reason. I watched him stand, then he offered me his hand. My fears were immediately erased. Why do I do that?

He pulled me up and I followed him into the bedroom. The fire was burning fast now, lighting the room like hundreds of candles. He led me to stand beside the bed; my back was to the fire. He held my hands, dipping his forehead down to rest on mine.

"Is this too fast?" he whispered.

"No," I whispered back, "I don't want to stop but…" I trailed off. Somehow, I still had a rational thought in my head. I was hoping what I was about to say wouldn't ruin the moment.

I looked into his eyes, stroking his face. I could tell he had no idea what I was about to say.

"Before we go any further, I want you to know… I haven't been with anyone in over two years." I felt ridiculous saying that. I didn't know if he thought I was telling him I was out of practice or just uneasy, but as soon as he spoke, I knew we were on the same page.

He placed his hand tenderly on my cheek and said, "Julia, it's been a while for me too. I trust you, and I want you to trust me. I want you to know, I know for sure there's nothing for you to worry about. I wouldn't put you in a circumstance that would hurt you physically. Do you understand?"

Again, where in the hell did this guy come from. "I trust you," I said, lost in his eyes, "and I know for sure there's nothing for you to worry about either."

"I do have protection," he said. "I'm sure you don't want to get pregnant again."

I couldn't help but laugh. "You're right, I don't think my body could take it, but on that front, I've got it covered as well."

I had a thought flash through my mind right at that moment. I could almost hear my daughter trying to reason with me, telling me I'd only known this guy for a few days, and suddenly I'm trusting that he's not lying to me about being promiscuous. But I had to listen to my gut and not to the voices that would tell me he had a past. I decided right then to trust him, especially after everything we'd experienced together. Right or wrong, I felt like we were being honest with one another.

His hands lingered, running up and down my sides, then he delicately lifted the hem of my shirt, sliding his hands underneath. I felt the warmth of his palms as he reached around to my back, his hands investigating every part of me. I moaned at his touch. He pulled back for a moment and looked into my eyes. I could see the fire reflecting, dancing in his eyes as he took me in. He lowered his hands, then pulled my shirt over my head, tossing it to the floor. He looked me in the eyes again, then his glance cast downward. I closed my eyes and felt his fingers tracing the outline of my bra. I felt his hand at the button of my shorts. Soon I was stepping out of them. I stood there, trying not to question my worth at that moment. I pushed that part of me down and buried it beneath my passion.

His hands wandered over me; my hips, my back, my stomach, until they ended up in my hair again. He kissed my neck, and then leaned down and kissed the skin just above my breasts. I was tingling. I had goose bumps. I could barely stand there any longer. I quietly moaned again, giving into his touch.

He looked at me again, while my fingers wandered through his hair, swept across his cheeks, and made their way down to his waist. I pulled at the button on his jeans. He stepped back and pushed them down to the floor and off to the side. And then he removed what was left. It was hard not to look. I had twinges of embarrassment pulsing through me, but I didn't have long to think about it because before I knew it, he gracefully spun me around to face the fire. I could feel all of him pressed against me. I felt his hands wander down, gently teasing me. I raised my arms, placing them around his neck, pulling him closer. I couldn't help but push my pelvis forward, into his hands, wanting more. He swiftly pushed my panties down and then pulled back to undo my bra. As it fell to the floor, I closed my eyes, feeling his hands roam delicately over my breasts. I didn't want to feel self-conscious. I needed to just give in to the moment.

"Julia," he whispered, "open your eyes… look at us."

I opened my eyes and saw us standing there, naked. There was no hiding from the full-length mirror hanging next to the fireplace.

"Look how beautiful you are," he said, his hands sliding down the sides of my waist, and sweeping gently over my stomach.

I smiled. I didn't want him to be right. I wanted to give in to the negative voices, but I didn't because he was right, we looked good together. I looked good. I felt sexy. He made me feel sexy.

He turned me to him. Our lips met again, softly at first, then intensifying. It was as if we were searching for more, desperate to touch every bit of each other. His hands nestled into my hair, while my hands caressed his ass.

"Put your arms around my neck," he whispered, looking at me with purpose. I did, and then he swiftly scooped me up, leaning in for another kiss, as he moved toward the bed. Our lips never parted as he placed me on the mattress. Then he stood back, and I let his eyes take me in. I was totally vulnerable, but so was he. He slipped in next to me. I turned to my side. His hand caressed my waist and then slipped behind me until I felt his fingers moving back and forth over my ass. He gently pushed me to my back and climbed on top of me, kissing my neck. He pulled back and just stared down at me, his fingers loosely playing with my hair again. I had a few more twinges of embarrassment circle, but by this time, I was getting over it.

His fingers gently circled my breasts, then he held them, squeezing ever so slightly, eventually sliding his hands down to my belly button. He scooted backward, kissing my stomach. His lips lingered; his beard tickling me as he slowly moved his head back and forth. He didn't linger there for long though, he was making his way down. Before I knew it, I was arching my back, feeling the warmth of his breath on me. He was consuming me with every stroke of his tongue. His hands moved to my breasts again, engulfing them with his palms. I forcefully pushed my fingers through his hair, pulling at him. I didn't want him to stop. And just when I was almost at my breaking point, he slowly moved off me. I was inhaling and exhaling heavily at this point.

I watched as he leaned to the left and grabbed a condom from the nightstand drawer. I was surprised.

"I want you to feel safe," he said, "plus, I have other reasons why this will come in handy." He gave me a quick wink and put the condom on. He seemed to have a plan.

I pulled him to me. He was slow and methodical, kissing my breasts delicately. And then, in no time he was parting my legs; in no time he was slipping deep inside of me. He was breathing heavily; we were both moaning. I could barely breathe. I lifted my legs, pressing my feet into his hips, as if I could pull him deeper inside. I pushed my hands against his chest, again using my force to push him into me, but he didn't need my help; he was already there.

He looked down at me. I didn't take my eyes off him as we moved in unison. The music played softly in the background, but it all sounded muffled to me. All I could focus on was how good it felt, and how long it'd been. All my memories of Jack and me were there, it's all I knew, but I thought, in that split second, no Julia, he can't be part of this; he can't ruin this for you. You are here with Andrew. It's you and Andrew now.

"I feel all of you," I said breathlessly, "don't stop." We moved rhythmically, my hands exploring his chest, his shoulders, his hair. He lowered himself, his mouth wandering over my lips, and my neck. I grabbed his legs, pulling him into me. We were voracious at this point, neither of us wanting the passion to end. But eventually it was out of our control. Our bodies tensed and we both moaned, giving into the moment. And just like that, we were one. He pulled back, looking down at me; completely exhausted, completely satisfied. He placed his hand tenderly on my cheek. I turned into it, kissing his palm.

"Julia, you are so fucking beautiful… I can't get enough."

I smiled at him, still wanting more.

His head dropped next to mine. We were both breathing hard. I wrapped my arms and legs tightly around him. I could tell he didn't want to move; I didn't want him to move. We both wanted to stay connected for as long as we could.

"I don't want to move Julia," he said, "I just want to stay right here, with you."

"Me too," I said, my hands back in his hair again.

I nuzzled my face into his neck, breathing him in, relishing the fact that we had just shared the most intimate moment any couple could share. We lay there for a few minutes, quietly taking each other in, until he asked me a question that made me laugh.

"Am I crushing you?" he finally said, his breaths short and quick.

"Yes," I said stoically.

He pulled back, no doubt shocked by my response, but I was smiling at him, stroking the side of his face.

"You're funny," he said, then he ever so delicately kissed me. When the kiss was over, he brushed his closed lips gently over mine. Back and forth, back and forth, breathing me in. It was heavenly.

Eventually, he moved off me, lying on his back, his hand resting on his chest. I turned to my side, and he turned to face me, his fingers sweeping down the curve of my waist. I could see in his eyes that we weren't done. He rolled to his back again, pulling me on top of him. I laughed as I straddled his waist.

"Am I crushing you?" I said, smiling devilishly, as I ran my fingers over his chest.

"Yes," he said, then he abruptly grabbed my ass, pulling me up higher to straddle him. I braced myself against the headboard.

His tongue was warm, hitting parts of me I didn't even know existed. His hands cradled my ass. I let myself just feel; just feel every bit of his mouth. He was gentle, and God knows he was thorough. He was patient as well; dare I say, he was enjoying it as much as I was. I didn't think it would be possible, but just like that, I groaned and gave into him, my pleasure evident. My eyes were closed, but I swear I could see lights flashing. My body felt lifeless. I felt like I was going to pass out. I went to move off him, but he wouldn't let me; he wasn't done. He held me there, his hands forcefully holding me around the waist, relenting to let me go. I let him have me just a little bit longer, grasping for his arms to steady me as I pushed away from the headboard and leaned back. I let go of him, running my fingers through his hair, as I felt every stroke of his tongue. He in turn reached for my breasts, gently squeezing them, wanting more. I didn't want it to end but I needed to move; I couldn't hold myself up anymore. I pulled away a second time, and this time he let me go. I lay down on my back, breathless.

He looked at me, smiled, then got up, and went to the bathroom. I rolled over, clutching my breasts. That was intense. I could see the moon's glow coming through the French doors. I got up and walked over to take in the view. I smiled as I stood there in the same spot I'd stood in earlier, but this time my mind was clear. It seemed like the moon was smiling back at me. The sky was beaming. I was lost in the lake again. I suddenly felt him behind me; the wholeness of his body pressed against mine.

"Are you okay?" he asked, wrapping his arms around me. This was starting to be the place we stood together. This was the place where he accepted me for me. This was the place he made me feel whole again.

"Are you okay?" he whispered again, his grip tightening.

I started to shake.

I felt his hand at the side of my face. He was wiping away the tears.

"Julia," he said, "what's happening, are you okay?"

He started to pull away, but I reached my arm around, pulling him close. All I could do was nod that I was fine. My other hand gripped his arm tightly. I just wanted to feel him pressed firmly against me. I just wanted to be quiet for a few more seconds.

"I'm just overwhelmed I guess," I finally blurted out. "I feel so completely accepted by you. It's just… it's just nothing I expected and everything I've wanted."

I could almost feel him smile. He turned me around taking my face in his hands, wiping the tears away, and said, "Well, then, there's just one thing I need to know."

"What's that?" I said, wondering where this was going.

"Are you hungry now?" he said, straight faced with absolutely no emotion.

I lowered my head, letting it fall into his chest, trying to muffle my laughter. I looked up into his deep brown eyes while I forcefully placed both hands on his ass and squeezed. "After that, I don't know if I'm starving or completely satisfied."

He laughed and pulled me even closer. His face drifted into my neck, his breath warm and comforting. I felt myself melting into him again; exactly what I wanted, to be a part of him. I wanted to be absorbed by him. He kissed one cheek, then the other. I ran my hands along his back, pressing my fingers deeply into his muscles. Before I could catch my breath, he slid his arm under my legs and carried me to the bed. He placed me down gently, then slid in beside me. He lingered over my stomach again, covering it with tender kisses. He moaned, as my fingers roamed playfully through his hair. His lips seemed to have a mind of their own, roaming over me, caressing every inch of me. I could feel his warm breath; I was tingling again.

"You've got quite the ab muscles," he said, his mouth investigating each one.

"I try," I said, looking down at him, my hands sifting through his hair.

He groaned one last time then pulled away.

"If I don't walk away right now, I won't, and we may just starve to death, and I know we're going to need our strength for later." He had a devilish grin on his face.

"Later huh," I said, biting my lip, "can't wait." His grin widened.

"What do you have in the fridge?" I said, knowing neither of us wanted to cook.

"I have an idea," he said. "You get comfortable, I'll be right back."

I watched him stand, throw another log on the fire, and then walk out the bedroom door. He glanced back at me once, then a second time before he disappeared. I felt him taking me in and I liked it. I was taking him in as well. I shifted to my side, and just lay there uncovered picturing him as he walked away. He had the smallest amount of chest hair; just enough to play with. His pectoral muscles and abdomen were taut, and his ass, well, let's just say there wasn't any shaking going on there. And as for the rest of him, let's be honest, women are far superior to men when it comes to a beautiful physique, but let's just say, I had no complaints. Considering our ages, we seemed to be holding our own.

I turned onto my back, looking up at the ceiling fan. It whirred and spun, like it was out of control. I tried to slow it down with my mind, to see every blade as it moved, but that proved impossible. It was on high, just like us, and as much as we may have needed to slow down, we couldn't. I wanted time to stop, and yet, if it didn't proceed, we'd share nothing new together, and what fun would that be. Can't blame me for trying though.

He was carrying a wooden tray when he returned, containing the two glasses of wine, a bowl of strawberries, and two croissants, no doubt from the French Patisserie.

I sat up, fixing the pillows for both of us, and pulled the covers over me.

"Hey," he said, "that's not fair."

"Hey yourself," I said, "I can't eat naked." Then I laughed.

"Okay, I get it," he said, climbing into bed and pulling the covers over himself. My hand strayed for a moment. He looked at me, his eyebrows raised, and he said, "Now that is truly unfair Julia." I couldn't help but laugh.

He handed me a glass of wine, then placed a strawberry delicately into my mouth. I'm quite sure he didn't take his eyes off me while I closed my eyes and savored the berry. I grabbed a berry and teased him with it, drawing him closer to my mouth. I forced him to give me a kiss, then allowed him to eat.

We devoured the food quickly; I didn't even realize how hungry I was, and I didn't have one negative thought about eating a croissant. It felt good to be free. It reminded me of the day my Fitness tracker died; I was happy to not be a slave to it anymore. When we were done, Andrew placed the tray on the floor and pulled me to him. He wrapped one arm around me as I nestled into his chest. The fire was still crackling, casting the perfect flashes of light into the room. I ran my fingers through his chest hair, playfully stroking, sifting through them with my fingers. We were quiet for a while, until my hand traced over his tattoo.

"Julia," he said, his fingers gliding up and down my arm, "I need to tell you more... more about my father, and why I said I can't forgive him."

I moved my head off his chest, propping myself up to look at him.

"Are you sure," I asked, looking at him protectively.

He looked down at me briefly then he just stared ahead, losing himself in the fire's glow.

"I'm sure."

I ran my fingers over his tattoo as he spoke.

"My father was no role model. He was hard working, I'll give him that, but he was a... excuse my language, a fucking pig. My mother was a saint. She did everything for him, to a fault, but how could I fault her for loving her husband?"

He sighed deeply. "She was the best mom. She was always there for my brother and me, reading to us when we were young, taking us on adventures, teaching us the importance of being happy in a career... taking the time to listen. My father wasn't home much because of his work, but somehow, everything that he stood for seeped into my brother, and subsequently into me. I didn't appreciate women, like I said before. I had questioned whether my father was having affairs when I was a teenager, but I pushed the thought out of my mind... he wouldn't do that to my mother, or so I thought. I just accepted him flirting with the house staff as harmless. I certainly couldn't blame him for my choices, but I guess I could hold my brother partially responsible; watching him dodge meaningful relationships while still getting the girls, he was like a god to me. I idolized him. Believe me, I'm not making excuses for the man I was in college, the man Jack knew. It just took me a bit to see that the way I was leading my life was wrong."

I just kept running my hand over his tattoo as he talked, hoping to center his thoughts. His chest rose and fell.

"When I found out my mother was sick again, I made plans right then and there to leave school. It was the end of April, so I was able to finish the year without losing any credits. I stayed by my mother's side for the next two months. I watched her go from vivacious to withering. It was brutal. My father had moved into another bedroom, to give her the space she needed, or so I thought."

He paused, his fingers trickling up and down my arm.

"After a few weeks of being home, I saw the housekeeper leaving my father's room early one morning. She looked disheveled. I watched this happen, morning after morning, but couldn't bring myself to say anything. I needed to take care of my mother, not him. He was obviously taking care of himself. But I could feel the anger building in me, like, dare I say... like cancer. My mother was dying a few rooms down the hall, and he was fucking the god damn housekeeper," he said, his voice raising. "I couldn't believe he'd do that to my mother, not then, not when she was dying." He shook his head repeatedly, but the memory was fresh and not going anywhere.

Andrew's chest rose and fell again, and again. I could almost hear the tears forming in his eyes. I wrapped my arm around his waist, embracing him tightly.

"How could he do that to her?" he said, the pain seeping out through the memory like it'd just happened. "I just couldn't understand it. I'll never understand. When it came time for the funeral, after the service, he and I stood by the casket after everyone had left, including my brother. We just stood there, the two of us, in silence, and I was praying he wouldn't say anything, but he just couldn't help himself.

"She was a good woman, Andrew, one of a kind," he said, placing his hand on my shoulder. I remember seething inside. I didn't look at him, I just pulled myself away from his touch and responded without remorse saying, "It's too bad you didn't treat her with the respect she deserved, Dad." He looked at me incredulously. "And you're a saint?" he said, putting it back on me. "She was the saint Dad, not you, not me, not John. I'm choosing to change my ways. The one good thing you've given me is perspective. Thank you for being the role model I need right now; the kind no one should emulate."

Andrew took a deep breath. "I've never told that story to anyone," he said. "You're the only one I trust it with."

I turned to face him, kissing his chest repeatedly. I felt his pain, his sorrow, his anger. It was all there.

"I'm beyond sorry," I said. "No one should have to endure that. Sometimes parents really have no clue how much damage they do."

He sighed, rubbing my back, trying to ease his own pain. The fire crackled. We lay there quietly embracing one another for several minutes, until suddenly the silence was broken.

"Favorite ice cream?" he suddenly blurted out.

"What?" I was surprised by the sudden change in his demeanor, but then realized what he was doing.

"What's your favorite ice cream?" he asked again.

"Hmm… when I was a kid, it was black raspberry, but now, when I do partake, it's a soft serve twist."

"Guess mine," he said playfully.

I thought for a few seconds. "You seem like a pure vanilla kind of guy. Nothing fancy, just pure, natural, vanilla flavor."

"Interesting," he said. "You'd be right, but that would be more my taste in women; pure, natural, yet flavorful." He looked down at me and smiled. "If I had to choose one, it'd be fudge swirl, the best of both worlds, kind of like yours, I guess."

I laughed. "Well, that's fitting, considering your talents."

He grinned at me, pushing me playfully onto my back, hovering over me as he held my arms against the pillow. He just stared at me. I'd given him total control, and I liked the feeling. I was at his mercy. I watched his eyes move from my eyes to my lips, and then he leaned in and kissed me. When the kiss ended, his lips remained on mine. He was nibbling at them, pulling and caressing, causing us both to get lost in the moment. When he rolled to the side, I just lay there, amazed by the power of one kiss. It was quiet for a few minutes, until he turned to his side, so he was facing me. His fingers gently caressing my cheek. He looked serious. I knew a question was coming my way.

Chapter Forty
Julia

He was taking all of me in before he asked. His eyes followed his hand as it swept gracefully from my cheek, down the side of my breast to my waist, and over my hip. He looked back at me and said, "I don't want you to feel uncomfortable, but it's hard for me to understand. I don't see what you see, and I want to understand how you see yourself."

I knew where he was going. I knew it didn't make sense. Maybe it was time for me to truly come clean; to help him know me.

"Can you help me understand?" he asked, his eyes soft and caring. "Can you tell me why, why this happened to you... why anorexia?"

I could tell he wasn't trying to be intrusive. I could tell he just innocently wanted to know, to know my mindset. I couldn't help but feel tense immediately. Just hearing the word made me feel diseased, with no possibility of healing. I lost myself in his eyes for a moment, trying to gather my thoughts. I gently touched his cheek with my fingers; I knew he cared. I didn't want to face my fears while he was watching me, but he'd just given so much to me, I couldn't deny him. I knew he felt my body grow rigid.

"Too much too fast?" he asked. "I don't want to pressure you; you don't have to answer."

I cleared my throat, then pulled away from him. Fear was setting in. I sat up in bed, clutching the blanket to my chest. I just stared into the fire. It was crackling, flashing, almost telling me, "Now or never Julia." I felt his warm hand sliding soothingly up and down my back. He knew just how to calm me.

"Well," I said, trying to figure out how to start. "All bad things start somewhere, and if I had to say there was a particular starting point, it was when I was around eight years old."

I took a deep breath. His hand stopped and he just pressed it into my back as if to steady me. Everything I had told Suzanne was replaying in my head.

"My older brother was an idiot, like most brothers are," I said, rolling my eyes. "He loved to tease his sisters, making up stupid nicknames for us all. I feel so stupid telling you this," I said, giving him a quick glance. "My brother was relentless with "fat names" for me. Of course, I didn't like the nicknames, but I loved him... how does that make any sense? What was I going to do about it anyway? I didn't think those names really hurt me until I became a teenager, until I went to college, which is where I fell apart. I used that as a starting point... a starting point for my breaking point."

I paused again, trying to gather myself; his hand still steadying me.

"I was always an athlete, never fat, even when my brother gave me the nicknames, I truly wasn't fat. I was just a normal kid, and so was my brother. I don't hold any ill will toward him now, and I truly mean that, but I can't lie... I just don't understand why he singled me out. That's something I've been thinking about a lot lately. Anyway, it wouldn't be fair to just pin it all on him. When I was a teenager, he was no longer teasing me, but my older sister seemed to pick up where he left off. She was skinny and I was muscular. She never hesitated to remind me of that. What a "shit show. I would get so angry, but I never called her out. We weren't close at all. I'm not sure, but maybe I just believed her and that's why I took it.

I turned to look at him. Could he handle more? He smiled at me, encouraging me to go on. I looked back at the fire and kept going.

"Fast forward from the teasing years. I'm a teenage girl living in a world where stick-thin, super models were celebrated, desired, the norm. Not only was I an athlete but I wasn't that tall either, so I knew there was no stick-thin in my future, and I struggled with that. Looking back, I did have a stint in seventh grade when I tried to control my weight. My parents didn't seem to notice I was losing weight then, and the only reason I stopped was because I had no strength to run anymore. I successfully made the decision then to stop doing what I was doing so I could run. I regained my strength and became a competitive athlete. I still felt haunted by it all in high school, but somehow, the negative voices weren't as loud and I was able to enjoy my high school years, for the most part anyway."

"It seems like I've always wanted to not be me... even to this day, even at my age. It's like I see every flaw instead of seeing the positive things about myself. I wish I could stop doing that. I wish I wouldn't make food my enemy. We all need to eat to stay alive, but I've warped it so much now, it's like I'm on the battlefield every day and I never know if a bomb is coming my way. It's horrible to live with that kind of fear. It's horrible to feel the need to scrutinize every piece of food put in front of you. Should I eat the bread now? If I eat the bread now, then I can't have carbs later. If I eat cheese now, it will be on my hips tomorrow. If I go out to eat, will the restaurant have anything I can order without having a panic attack? We all need food to survive, and yet every fucking meal, every God damn time I have to make a decision about what I'm going to eat, it's like life or death. It is so painful, so tiring, and it makes me wonder if I can ever truly escape it." I sighed heavily. We sat there quietly for a minute. I'm sure it was a lot for him to process.

"So, there's that part of my life, cliff note version, always wanting not to be me, always comparing myself to other girls, always fighting the fight I truly didn't want to be in. But that's just the outcome. It may have started with my brother, but there is so much more behind it all. I needed desperately to believe I was enough, but I just couldn't."

I breathed in deeply, inhaling and exhaling, needing to breathe my way through the next admonition. Andrew started caressing my back again. "No rush," he said, "take as much time as you need."

I placed my hand on the blanket, finding his leg, and gently squeezed. I hated talking about this, but I needed to do it for me as much as I needed to do it for him.

"Much like your father, my dad was not home a lot. He was always away on business. I found out in later years that he wanted all of us to go to boarding school. My mother wouldn't hear of it. In the end she won; we went to the public school. She told me that she didn't have kids to ship them off and have someone else raise them."

"My father has a unique personality. We, meaning my siblings and I, dubbed him "the pusher." He wanted his kids to achieve more; plain and simple. He basically applied pressure to all of us to do more, be more, but it was disguised in so much positivity that we couldn't hold it against him. I mean, it's not like he told us we weren't doing enough, or that we were a disappointment to him. It was more like we could always achieve more, kind of sky's the limit, and we all should want to push that limit. It's hard to explain."

I could still feel Andrew's hand caressing my back, and I needed his reassurance that I wasn't telling lies; this was my truth.

"I think all of us felt it, but it morphed into different issues for each of us. I was the third child, the first to do well in school, in sports. I was the first to go away to college. When I left for school, I was lost, insecure, I was beyond homesick, maybe a little boyfriend sick too. I just couldn't handle the pressure, the need to do more, be more, to be the best, while I felt so alone. Emotionally, I was trashed. I started to act out, in my own way, trying to control my own destiny, or so I thought. I still had my work ethic, trying to do my best, to be the best when it came to school and competing on the track. I still wanted to do it for my father even though I felt so much pressure. The funny thing is, my father's positivity was actually debilitating, for me anyway." I had to stop talking for a few seconds; I needed to find the right words. "This is all so complicated to explain," I said, the frustration evident in my voice.

"It's okay Julia," Andrew said supportively. "I'm here, I'm listening."

I swallowed hard, trying to let him be supportive.

"So, why anorexia? I didn't intend it to happen. It just happened. I had gained some weight, the "freshman ten," and because of my past, I latched onto controlling something familiar to me. I mean, there wasn't anything wrong with getting in better shape, right? But the way I did it was extreme. I exercised like crazy. I scrutinized my food. My parents didn't understand. I know it was difficult for them, watching me wither away. I disregarded their concern because it wasn't part of my plan, and I was the one in control. I didn't care what anyone thought because when I looked at myself all I saw was a fat girl, and I just wanted to be thinner, like it was the answer to all my problems. I still was an over achiever but by becoming anorexic it was like I was slapping my father in the face, screaming at him through the weight loss to say you can't push me anymore, I'm in control now. You can't make me feel like I need to do more to be worthwhile. Of course, I truly didn't understand my control issues then or my father's place in any of it until I went to therapy. It took me years to stop trying to prove myself to him. I felt conflicted constantly. Suddenly, I was turning on my father, the man I'd put on a pedestal all my life. It was extremely hard to take him off, to admit he was human and not superhuman, but I finally did, many years later. Obviously, I still struggle, and I hate that I still want him to be proud of me… it's so warped."

I took a deep breath but continued.

"When all of this was going on, I wanted to rip things away from my father, things I knew he liked that I was doing. I couldn't handle his constant stories about the successes of my younger sister, whether in school or on the track. I couldn't reason my way out of feeling less than, of feeling abandoned. I needed to exert control in my life, and I did it by controlling my food. I did it by quitting track. I did it by losing my virginity, something I had fought to hold onto all my high school years. I was a mess. I was a fucking mess, but I didn't know it, or maybe I didn't want to admit it. By the time I finally realized I needed help, I weighed ninety pounds. Honestly, I couldn't compete anymore anyway… I had physically derailed myself to the point of exhaustion."

I heard Andrew sigh deeply. While he ran his hand over my back, all I could think was he was imagining me with twenty-five less pounds on me. Back then I would think that was a win; exactly what I wanted to look like, but even then, it wasn't enough. I was never enough.

"My father has never changed, to this day. He made it clear to me back then, that he was who he was, and he wasn't going to change. I remember having that conversation with him and my mother, telling them what I'd learned in therapy about the way his personality affected me. I remember it like it was yesterday when he admitted he wouldn't change." I stopped again, trying to breathe. "He couldn't even offer me an ounce of…of…"

I stopped. I started to shake. The tears were coming, and I couldn't fight them off. Andrew sat up and held me. "It's okay Julia, you're okay."

"I guess I wanted more from him than just a flat-out no. I wanted some emotion, dare I say some understanding. I was hurt, and I felt like he didn't care. I was left to work my way through it alone. It sounds harsh but I know he loved me then, still does, and I love him, but I had to figure out how to deal with his personality, and that hasn't been easy. When I met Jack, I was on the mend, so to speak. But all the damage was done. I struggled for years dodging anyone's expectations. I knew I was a great mom, but I was stuck in my own fears. I had pushed away attaining the important things, like having a career, pursuing my writing. Anytime anyone said I could do something, try to attain something, I shrunk, I hid, I doubted myself.

When they spoke, all I heard was my father, and the fear of achieving, then needing to achieve more, was just too much. I put myself in my own prison; I was unable to do anything. It was like I had a split personality; believing in myself fully until someone else did. Jack was always incredibly supportive of me; he knew my past struggles. We both had a lot of family issues to get through when we got married, but I don't think we knew the extent of them all."

I stopped to breathe; to gather myself. I didn't want to completely fall apart in front of Andrew, but I knew I probably would.

"I'm as tired of thinking about food decisions as I am about seeing my father raise that bar, not only for me, but anyone he encounters that is remotely trying to attain something worthwhile. He just can't help himself, and I hate it. Even at my age, I don't want what I know he thinks to influence my decisions anymore. I've had enough. Enough of the pride, enough of always having to climb higher because he puts it out there. I want to follow my own path, not his."

I took another deep breath after that rant. "My father is one thing," I said, wiping the tears away, "but I hate that I will struggle every day of my life with this disease. It will probably still be there, haunting me 'til the day I die. Back then it was like a cocktail gone wrong; all my ingredients and all my measurements were off, but I mixed them together anyway, and they almost killed me. Sometimes I wonder if I was trying to kill myself, slowly, painstakingly. That's a terrible admission. I'd like to think it wasn't my goal, but I'm not sure."

Andrew's grip tightened as he felt my body shake. I thought if he let me go right then, I might just break into a million pieces. "Don't let go," I said weakly, grasping for his arms. The tears were uncontrollable at this point. I don't think I'd ever come so clean about all of it to anyone before, not even Jack. "I'll never let go," he said, kissing the side of my head.

"I fight it every day," I said, through the sobs, "every fucking moment of my life. It's exhausting, feeling like you have to tear yourself apart, knowing that you'll just have to rebuild in order to do it all over again. Obviously, there's no competing with younger women anymore. I need to be me, not them. I need to stop comparing. I am extremely critical of myself and I'm trying my best to cope, which is why I finally decided to go back to therapy. I've grown tired of feeling trapped in my own body. I've grown tired of the dance."

He was quiet for a moment as he hugged me. I felt lucky he hadn't bolted already. With everything that had happened, I wondered why he wanted me, such damaged goods.

"Julia," he said softly, between the numerous kisses he planted on my shoulder, "I'm so sorry. I understand now."

"I'm sorry," I said crying, "the last thing you need is a headcase. I'm sure you just want a 'normal' woman, not a tortured woman. I wish I could be normal for you. I wish I could give you the undamaged Julia, but I don't think she ever existed. I wouldn't blame you for changing your mind about me. I'm not perfect Andrew, I never will be," I said, shaking my head.

"Julia," he said again, shaking me slightly, "did you hear me, I understand. I'm not looking for perfection, but I think I've been looking for you though. I've been looking for you my whole life."

I heard him this time; it had to be enough. He didn't say anything more. He held me tightly for a few minutes. The fire sparked. We didn't say a word.

"It's horrible to live with a disease like this. I hate calling it that. I feel like I'm not really suffering from a disease. I guess I feel responsible, like I chose it. I know I'll never be rid of it. It will always be there, looking for ways to trigger me, looking for the slightest opening to crawl into. That's what happened last night. It wants to take me over, and sometimes I'm just not strong enough to fight it. But I am better now," I said, shaking my head. "I'm better now." I paused then started laughing. "I just ate a chocolate croissant for God's sake, and I can see, I'm still alive despite it."

He didn't laugh. I heard him sigh. "One more thing," he said. I held my breath. "What made you go to therapy; in college I mean? What triggered you to do that?"

For some reason I looked over at the dresser where his mother's Bible stared back at me and suddenly, I remembered.

"I was sitting in the quad one day. I'd been crying, and this guy approached me riding a unicycle. I know… very weird. He probably could see I was upset. He sat down next to me and introduced himself. He wanted to make sure I was okay. He put his hand on my shoulder and said a prayer for me. I'd never had that happen before. Then he grabbed a notebook from his backpack, ripped a page from it and wrote something on it. He folded the paper and handed it to me." I turned to look at Andrew at this point. "I want you to know, I'm not making this up," I said, looking at him intently. "After he left, I opened the paper, and he'd written a Bible verse on it. It was Ecclesiastes 3: 1-8. When I got home, I looked it up. Those verses shook me. It was my wake-up call." I reached out, placing the palm of my hand on Andrew's cheek. I could see tears forming in his eyes. "I think your mother has been planning this all along," I said. "I looked at the Bible, what she wrote to you. She's still watching over you."

Andrew put his hand on mine, then pulled me backward to lie beside him. We cried together, our chests rising and falling in unison. I let my hand wander through his chest hair again, as he kissed my forehead. I wrapped my leg over his, nestling into his chest. I couldn't get close enough. I felt fully accepted; there were suddenly no open cracks in me; nowhere for the disease to attack. I had let all my ugly out, and he was still beside me.

We lay there silently for a bit longer, until the tears subsided, and then I needed an escape. I sat up, throwing my leg over his waist, straddling him. I grabbed his arms and pushed them into the pillow. He seemed shocked, not knowing what would happen next.

"Favorite pizza topping?" I blurted out. He just looked at me dumbfounded.

"What's your favorite pizza topping? But, before you answer," I said, gripping his arms tightly, "just know, if you put one anchovy on that pizza, I might have to leave right now." I didn't laugh, I didn't smile. This was a serious question. He just stared back at me.

"Pepperoni, mushroom, and pepper," he blurted out, like it was a life-or-death question.

I smiled. He smiled. I let his arms go and grabbed his face. I stared at him. He stared back. We were both begging to be kissed. The kiss was not sexual in any way; it felt like a combination of understanding and acceptance rolled into one. It was reassuring and affirming. It was necessary. When it was over, we lay quietly on the bed. His fingers trickled up and down my back. I could tell he was thinking.

"Julia," he said softly.

"Yes Andrew."

"Julia, you know you are completely captivating, right?"

I couldn't help but smile. He was trying. I loved that he was trying for me. Captivating: the word circled around me. No pressure, no expectations. I liked the sound of that, because little did he know, he was completely captivating as well. I felt like what was happening between us might never happen again for either one of us, and I didn't want to take that lightly. I was letting myself go, and I knew he was too. I think we both desperately wanted this, whatever it was, to represent a fresh start for us individually, and as a couple. A couple: just thinking that was a lot. But I felt like he knew me, and I knew him. What are the chances that you get to share your life completely with another human being for the second time in your life?

Chapter Forty-One
Jack

I watched her drive away in a Langdon Landscapes pick-up truck. My wife, I mean my ex-wife, just drove off with another man. And not just any man, a man I didn't trust. It was painful. I felt twinges, or more like a two by four upside my head, reminding me of what I'd let go. How could I have let her go?

I sat down in the Adirondack chair and just stared out at the ocean. I had to admit, I'd lost Julia long before Coop came along. She was right, we'd been divorced for years. But she said she still loved me, and I most definitely still loved her. Why are we not able to fix this, to fix each other? I didn't want to believe her; I didn't want to think I needed therapy. I didn't want to go down that road alone. I wanted her there, with me. I should have done it years ago. I wanted to forget all the bad truths about our marriage. I felt like I was mourning her all over again, but I guess I did that to myself.

I ran my hand over my head and sighed. I knew she was right; I knew I needed help. I was on a slippery slope as they say, and if I didn't do something, the avalanche would bury me. I never thought the way I grew up influenced everything I did, but it has. It's like this thing that's crept deep down inside of me and found a warm place to grow until it's set in motion by a trigger, and it doesn't seem to care whether the trigger is big or small. It still recognizes it and climbs out, making my life a living hell.

Just that call from my mother, her voicemail, was that a trigger? And then there's my reaction; guilt for not picking it up. Or was it seeing Sean and Julia sitting on the couch, huddled in deep conversation? I just didn't know. I felt like Julia, wondering if I'd ever be free from my own prison. And now, now it's Coop and Julia. It's like a never-ending stream of threats.

I got up and walked to the rail, gripping it tightly. I wanted to get Julia. I could still feel her in my arms. The smell of her lingered. I wanted to come face to face with her again and make her see that I was the one she should be with. My thoughts were racing. I could find out from Sean; I could get Coop's address from him. I could play it up that I was bringing her things over, being the bigger man. It's almost as if I wouldn't be satisfied until I faced Coop again, until I made him understand that he couldn't just play with her feelings.

"She's just confused right now," I said, convincing myself that I knew what was best for her.

I hung my head, feeling confused, feeling lost, feeling angry. And there it was, the anger pouring back in. I couldn't let it. It'd done me no good all my life. The only time it had a place was when I was playing football; I remember letting a lot of anger out on that field. I was angry with my parents then. Angry at my father for always making me feel less than, and angry at my mother for never being there for me, and for cheating on dad.

"Now what Jack?" I said into the air, as if the answers would come riding in on a breeze.

"Jack?"

I heard a male voice call to me from the driveway. I turned to see Sean standing there. He walked up the steps and joined me at the railing.

"Sean," I said, giving him a nod, then returned my gaze to the ocean.

"Jack, I just wanted to stop by and see how you're doing... how you're holding up?"

I looked at Sean and wondered, why is this guy concerned about me? He obviously knows about me and Julia, about everything that's been going on. I'm fairly sure he set Julia up with Coop. So, what does he want?

"I'm hangin' in there," I said. In some way, I felt like he was the enemy.

"I'm sorry for the way things have turned out," he said.

I could feel my anger swelling up until it hit the back of my throat. I tried to swallow it down. I turned away and couldn't help but laugh.

"Are you, Sean, are you sorry? Seems like things worked out just perfectly for you and your buddy."

Sean placed his arms on the railing and leaned forward, keeping his eyes focused on the water. He appeared to be calm.

"I want you to know that I had no idea about you and Julia. I set them up because Andrew is a great guy."

"Great guy," I laughed. "He's your boss Sean. Do you really know him because I do."

"Whatever you think you know, you're wrong, and you don't have to worry about Julia. I'm one hundred percent sure of that," he said, with conviction.

"Maybe I need to find out for myself," I said, knowing I really just wanted it to be true that he was still a womanizer. If he were, I could get my Julia back. I could show her the truth about him. Then she would come back to me.

"Jack, if you think that would help, maybe you should talk to Andrew. But know this, even if your theory is correct, Julia is going to do what she wants. It's her life Jack, just like it's yours. She's going to do what she wants regardless of what you find out."

I just stood there for a moment; I didn't want him to be right.

"You know Sean, you seem like a good guy. I don't hold anything against you. What can I say… I still love her. I want to protect her. I can't help it."

Sean nodded his head, not that he agreed, but more like an 'I understand how you feel' nod.

"Do what you need to do Jack, just don't make Julia collateral damage in the process. One thing your right about, she's one heck of a woman."

Sean pulled back from the railing, turned, and walked away.

What would my next move be? Should I just leave things alone or should I talk to Coop? I needed to think about this. The last thing I wanted was to push Julia away, but if I could get him alone, maybe I could convince him to let her go, convince him she was meant to be with me.

I needed to go for a walk. I didn't bother to change; I just walked down the path to the stairs, hoping to find the answers in the sand, in the surf. I needed clarity, but in the end, all I found was frustration.

When I got back, I grabbed a glass of wine and just sat on the deck, for hours, wondering how my life had gotten so fucked up. This was by far the loneliest vacation I'd ever taken. Finally, I gave up, went inside, locked the door, and went to my room. I glanced in at the master bedroom; most of Julia's things were still there. I knew she'd be coming back for them and her car at some point. I'd wait it out before I made any moves to find another place to stay.

Chapter Forty-Two
Andrew

Everything was making sense to me now, as I lay there rubbing Julia's back. What I considered normal behavior was an attempt to cope. Julia ate the sandwich at lunch, but she was trying to cope her way through. She was excited to hike more, obviously an attempt to make herself feel better about what she'd just eaten. And then the restaurant, that distant look in her eyes that I couldn't figure out; it was worry, pain, struggle. I could see it all so clearly now. I know I can't fix Julia. I can't erase her past, but I can affect her present. I just know she needs to feel accepted, fully accepted. What happened with her siblings, and her father was so unfortunate. My father was never supportive of me, of what I wanted. I never thought about having a parent who was overly positive, and that being a bad thing. Crazy; I think we are all damaged goods. I feel so bad for her. I just want her to see herself as I see her, but I know that's a lot to ask. I love the way she looks; I was attracted to her immediately, but I know that's not the entire reason I can't get enough of her. I almost feel ashamed that I was so into the fact that she didn't seem bothered by food like most women. I was putting her in a box, a box she'd felt trapped in her whole life, and it wasn't fair. She's not perfect; but to me, she's imperfectly perfect.

Julia's phone went off, a text message. She rolled over and reached for it on the nightstand. I couldn't help but move toward her, pulling myself against her. Our bodies just seemed to mold comfortably together. My head swayed back and forth, my lips softly rubbing against her back, while my hand gently squeezed her breasts.

"It's Jess," she said, leaning back against me. "We usually talk every few days, so she's probably wondering how things are going."

I moaned as I pulled her tighter. I felt her head fall backward as I reached lower. She started moving into me.

"You're driving me crazy," she said breathlessly, her hand finding mine.

"I'm pretty sure, you're the one driving me crazy," I said, planting kisses all over her shoulder. "You need to call Jess?" I asked, hoping the answer was no.

"I'm sorry. I'm afraid if I don't, she'll just keep texting. I'll just give her a quick call."

"It's okay," I said. "As much as I don't want to let you go, you need to call her." I released her unwillingly and sat up. "I'm still hungry, what about you?"

"A little," she said.

"I'll see what I can put together… we both probably need the fuel." She laughed and grabbed her phone.

I walked to the kitchen and found some more berries. I tried to think what would be healthy and pleasing for Julia without causing her to panic. Crackers and cheese? No; God no. Maybe some crackers and almond butter, and some nuts. That should do the trick. I could hear her talking to her daughter, her voice was light, unencumbered.

"I can't lie, it's been an interesting vacation so far… but don't worry honey, I feel good. I'm so happy right now. We have a lot to catch up on, but we'll save that for another call, okay?"

I was eaves dropping, but I didn't care. Julia just told her daughter everything I wanted to hear. I'd never felt as happy as I did right then. I heard her laughing; I loved to hear her laugh. I prepped the food and brought it over to the couch. I was awake enough to watch a show, so I sat down, grabbed a blanket for Julia, and waited for her to join me.

"Hey you," she said, emerging naked from the bedroom.

"Not fair," I said, eyeing her up and down. "Come sit with me, get some sustenance."

Julia walked to the couch and sat next to me, cuddling into me. I placed the blanket over her, even though I would rather just see her naked body. I put my arm around her and pulled her close.

"You up for a movie?" I asked. "The Proposal's on in five minutes."

"Yah," she said, "I think I can stay awake. That's one of my favorite movies, especially the shower scene."

We sat on the couch, eating, watching the movie, and laughing. After about an hour, I suddenly realized Julia was asleep.

"Time for bed baby," I whispered, then shut the television off. I stood up and removed the blanket. Once again, there she was, beautiful Julia. I gently placed one arm behind her back and the other under her legs, then carried her to the bedroom. I placed her gently on the bed; she rolled onto her side immediately, clutching the pillow. I just stood back and took her in. My eyes roamed over her naked body, starting with her gorgeous angelic face, sweeping down the curve of her waist, and ending at the tips of her toes. I wished she could see herself like I saw her. The fire's light was minimal, but just enough to outline her body with a warm glow. It was hard to stop looking. I walked to the other side of the bed, and climbed in, but before pulling up the blankets, I had to watch myself touch her one more time. My fingers followed the curves of her waist as it flowed into the slight swell of her hip. I was caught in a trance. I loved it that she slept naked. Yet another moment I didn't want to end.

Finally, I stopped and went to retrieve the blanket when she said, "Not so fast."

"I thought you were asleep," I whispered.

"Not a chance, not the way you're touching me," she said softly.

"You are hard to resist," I said, letting my fingers run down her curves again.

"Well," she said, "what are you going to do about it?"

I thought for a second. I knew what I wanted to do, but I also knew what she needed me to do.

"You're so sexy when you're bossy," I said laughing. "I'm going to let you sleep Julia. You're exhausted."

"You're no fun," she mumbled, then she was quiet.

I pulled the blanket over her and slid my body against hers. She moved slightly, pushing herself into me. I let my arm drape over her waist, then reached for her breast, so soft and warm in my hand. It was comforting, falling asleep with her in my arms. I hoped she felt the same.

Chapter Forty-Three
Julia

The sun was streaming in through the curtain panels on the French doors. I could hear Andrew purring ever so slightly; he was still asleep. We hadn't moved all night; he was still holding me snugly. The bed was warm and comfortable; I didn't want to move. I reached carefully for my phone to check the time—7 a.m. And then it suddenly hit me; it was Monday morning. I groaned at the thought.

Andrew stirred, his hand instinctively cupping my breast. I leaned back into him. He moaned. His hand wandered down and I felt a familiar tingle again. We started moving rhythmically, then he pushed me to my back, continuing to touch me, working his way down. There was no stopping this now.

When I succumbed to him, he crawled on top of me, kissing my stomach, working his way up to my breasts and neck. My hands roamed over his body, through his hair. He lay back on the bed and looked at me. He was so unselfish.

"Good morning," I said smiling.

"It is a good morning," he said, smiling back at me.

"It's Monday you know," I said, not wanting it to be true.

"I know," he said, turning to his side to face me.

"When do you have to go?" I questioned him sadly.

"I'm not going anywhere," he said, grinning at me. "No work today, no work tomorrow, no work for the rest of the week."

I turned to my side to face him. My fingers found their way into his hair, and I let them roam through it, doing what they needed to do.

"I called Sean yesterday, he's fully capable of handling the projects this week."

I thought for a second, realizing this man wanted to spend the entire week with me. For a split second I wondered if I could do that, and then I laughed to myself; of course I could do that. Nothing was tying me down. I had nowhere to be but here.

"When's the last time you took a vacation?" I asked.

"Not since before I started the company," he said, "has to be about fifteen years now."

"I think you're due then," I said, as I let my hand wander over his chest.

"Stay with me here Julia," he said, grabbing my hand and kissing it gently. "Stay with me for the week." His eyes were pleading, but little did he know, I'd already committed.

"I'm not sure," I teased, "what on earth will we do here all week, just the two of us?"

"We'll think of something," he said, still kissing my hand. I stretched across him, grabbing a condom from the nightstand drawer, but then I let it go. I wasn't afraid. I let my hand wander, kissing his abdomen, until he was ready. I climbed on top of him. His hands firmly grabbing my hips, pulling me, moving me in cadence with his movements. He never took his eyes off me. Enough said.

Once we pulled ourselves from the sheets, we stood in the shower, just letting the water wash over us. Kissing, caressing, exploring; we still weren't done. Water seemed to be a theme for us, whether it was trying to destroy us or revive us. I had no idea what the week would bring; maybe that's a good thing. I didn't want to worry, to over think, to not be present in every single moment. I was living in a dream and all I knew was that I didn't want it to end.

Chapter Forty-Four
Julia

While Andrew was in the kitchen making breakfast, I took a few moments to linger in the bedroom, looking out at the lake yet again. I knew I needed to get my car and the rest of my clothes from the cottage. I grabbed my phone; I needed to let Jack know I'd be coming by.

~

Julia: "I will be coming by later to get my car and the rest of my things. I'll be staying at Andrew's, which means you can stay at the cottage. It's probably better if you're not there when I come by. I'm sure you can understand. I'll text you when I'm on my way. I hope you are feeling better today."

Jack: "Okay."

~

Well, that was short and sweet. Something doesn't feel right, but I'm sure he's not happy about the circumstances. I got dressed and brushed off the feeling. Everything was fine, it was all going to work out.

I could smell breakfast aromas floating into the bedroom from the kitchen. I walked quietly down the hall, like a cat sneaking up on its prey, but he caught sight of me.

"Damn it, you spoiled it," I said laughing.

Andrew smiled at me. "Come here you," he said, as he put the plates on the counter.

I walked over and fell into his embrace. I couldn't help but feel like I'd lived here, in his arms, in his house, from the beginning. It all felt so right. I knew we just started this relationship, but it felt so natural to me. Even though there wasn't a trace of me here in the way of knickknacks, paintings, general décor, I felt as if I'd been a part of making this house a home.

"What do you think we should do today?" he asked, pulling back, his hands playfully sifting through my hair. "Wanna' go for a hike?"

I hesitated, not wanting to tell him I needed to go back to the cottage. I don't know why; I guess because it was like going back to the scene of the crime, meaning Jack. I wanted to put all of it behind me, behind us, but I needed to get my things. Part of me wished I had just done it the day before.

I looked up at him. He was full of hope for the day, and now I was going to ruin it.

"I would love to go on a hike with you. I just have one thing to do though," I hesitated, "I need to get my car and the rest of my things from the cottage. I texted Jack that I would be coming by at some point. Can we fit that in today?"

I could tell he was uneasy, but then his demeanor quickly changed.

"Of course, we can do that. We should do that. There's no reason for us not to get your things. You're staying here, with me," he said happily, as he pulled me in again.

His embrace was comforting. He wasn't fighting me on this, he was respecting me.

"Let's eat, go for a hike, and then stop by the cottage… sound good," he said, his hands caressing my back.

I pulled back and looked up at him, brushing my fingers through his hair.

"Thank you. I'll make sure we go when Jack isn't going to be there, okay?"

"Okay," he said, leaning down to give me a kiss.

He filled our plates with eggs and avocado toast, then we headed to the deck to eat. It was another warm day. The sun was shining again, that sliver of light streaming across the water, heading right for us. It gave me hope for some reason.

"You really love the lake, don't you?" he stated, as he caught me staring out at the water.

He'd already caught me numerous times either staring out the French doors in the bedroom, or the windows in the living room, or standing on the deck, simply lost in the tranquility.

"I grew up going to our camp in New Hampshire, right on the lake. It was always a special place for me. Swimming, tubbing, water skiing, hiking. It was nothing fancy, it even had an outhouse when we first started going, but it was homey. When it rained, we played board games or cards. We cooked marshmallows in the field stone fireplace… it wasn't as nice as this place, but it was still nice. The lake, the calmness of the water, it just speaks to me. I love it."

He looked out over the water. "I love it too," he said. "I grew up going to a lake as well. Those were good times. So, tell me about your childhood lake?"

Not all my childhood memories had to do with being teased. I did have some really great times with my siblings, whether it was at the Cape or at the Camp.

"The Camp, which is what we called it, was a great place for us to just be kids. It was very rustic, but we didn't care. We just wanted to spend our days outside, exploring or swimming in the lake." I had so many memories flying though my head. One in particular came to mind. "What?" he asked. "What's going on in that beautiful head of yours?" I smiled at him, the memory was fresh, like it just happened yesterday.

"My sister Jen was always getting into trouble," I said. "Something about her and water; like oil and water, they didn't mix. One time this huge black inner tube washed ashore, and we grabbed it. We'd sit on opposite sides, with our feet firmly tucked under it so we could rock back and forth. We spent days on that tube, laughing… it was so much fun… that is, until she fell off and thought she was drowning underneath it. I shouldn't laugh; she was scared to death. I pulled her to shore. It was just one of many lifesaving experiences I had with her and water."

"Sounds like you had some great times. Jen was lucky you were there to save her. I look forward to meeting her someday."

"Yah, she's pretty awesome; you're going to love her. Despite my struggles as a child, I guess I was pretty lucky."

Andrew sat back and looked out at the lake. He seemed contented.

"So, how 'bout we go to the Fort Hill Trail in Eastham today? It's a one-mile trail, so it's not like spending three hours at Great Island, but at least we'll be outside, getting some exercise," he said.

"That sounds like the ideal hike for today." I looked forward to incorporating some exercise into the day.

"Do you run?" I asked. He never told me if he exercised the way I did, or if that gorgeous body was just a freak of nature.

"I can run," he said smirking. "I usually go surfing to get exercise, but for you, I'd go for a run or maybe a brisk walk."

I laughed. "Maybe we can compromise. The beast in me says I'll need to do more than hike tomorrow."

He laughed and placed his hand on my leg. "As long as you don't get too exhausted."

"I'm not that old," I said amused. "I have pretty good stamina."

"I know," he said, grinning at me.

~

I texted Jack that I'd be coming to get my things around 2 p.m. He assured me he wouldn't be there, which was a good thing.

The Fort Hill hike was beautiful. Hiking is now my new favorite thing to do on the Cape. I had no idea there were so many trails. We finished after just thirty minutes, then headed to the cottage. I just wanted to get it over with, even though I knew Jack wouldn't be there. When we arrived, Jacks' car was gone, thank God. When we walked inside it was as if I had never been there before; it gave me a strange feeling. The kitchen was a mess, and when I walked down the short hallway, I glanced into the guest bedroom. Jack's bed wasn't made, and his clothes had taken up residence on the floor. Same old Jack.

As I walked into my bedroom, I noticed the door was in disrepair. Andrew said he broke into the room trying to get to me. Hopefully, Steph and Rob will understand. Andrew stayed in the living room while I packed. I knew he was in the cottage the other night, but it wasn't like he took a tour that wasn't fraught with panic. I figured he was taking it all in. When I returned, I found him standing in front of the fireplace, looking up at the watercolor. He heard me enter the room.

"Nice painting," he said. "I happen to know the artist well."

"Really. I love that painting, or should I say, I loved that painting. Jack bought it for me. I didn't want it in the divorce, so he took it. I guess he couldn't keep it either, and that's why he left it here, for Rob and Steph."

Andrew drew in a breath then turned toward me. "Well, you ready?" he asked. I could hear it in his voice; he needed to change the subject. I could only guess he didn't want to think about Jack and me having a past.

"I am, let's go," I said, extending my hand to him. We'd already been through enough. In no way did I want him to feel strange with me because of my past; because of Jack.

It wasn't hard to leave the cottage. The memories here were tainted for me. The refuge I wanted it to be had disintegrated over the past few days. I felt distanced from it, from this spot. I wanted to leave it behind, where it belonged. I didn't belong here anymore.

"See you at home," Andrew said, as he placed my bags in the back of the Explorer. I walked to him and hugged him tightly as if I couldn't possibly wait 'til we were back at his place.

"Home," I whispered, looking up at him, "I like the sound of that."

He gave me his signature peck on the forehead, then he pushed me toward my door, slapping my ass.

"Hey," I said surprised, but secretly loving it.

"You shouldn't be so sexy," he said grinning at me, "my hands seem to have a mind of their own."

Once we got back, I unpacked my things. Andrew had cleared a few drawers for me in the dresser. I tried not to junk up the counter space in the bathroom; I didn't want to be that woman. It was still his place, and I didn't want him to feel invaded. I mean, it wasn't like I'd brought throw pillows for the couch, but I wanted to respect his space.

He was on the phone when I walked into the kitchen with my computer. I signaled I'd be on the deck, writing. I suddenly had something to write about.

It was around 3 p.m. when I sat down. I had so many ideas. Writing an outline for a novel was daunting, but I was up for the challenge. I never heard the knock at the door.

Chapter Forty-Five
Andrew

"Perfect," I said, to the representative, "see you before five, thanks."

We had one hour before we needed to leave. I couldn't wait to surprise Julia. I saw her sitting on the deck, typing away, and was about to join her when I heard a knock at the door. Nobody ever knocks on my door. I can't lie, when I saw him standing there, I was pissed.

"Jack?" I said, taken aback by his presence at my house.

"Coop," he said, trying to get a look over my shoulder, I'm guessing for Julia. I didn't want her to see us standing there, so I stepped out, closing the door behind me.

"How'd you know where I lived Jack?" I asked, uncertain and a bit concerned as to how he found my house.

"Well, that's the beauty of following someone. I guess I should look into being a detective," he said, with a disturbing chuckle.

"You followed us? What do you want Jack?" My blood was starting to boil.

"Well Coop..."

I hated it when he called me Coop.

"I guess I'm not really satisfied with what's going on here. I don't think Julia is thinking clearly."

"Really… well that is a problem," I said sarcastically, crossing my arms across my chest. "Funny thing Jack, it's your problem not hers. She's perfectly content and safe here with me," I said, annunciating every word with an added touch of anger; the all too familiar anger that I'd felt for him the other night. I didn't want to lose my cool. Not now.

"C'mon man, you want me to think you've changed. You can't be serious," he said, with a sly smile.

"I am serious," I said, taking offense.

"Where is she," he demanded, invading my space. "I think the three of us should talk about your escapades."

I stood my ground. He had a few inches on me, but I knew if things escalated, I could hold my own.

"You're not going to drag her into this conversation Jack," I said adamantly.

He stepped back and grabbed his beard with his hand, looking frustrated. I took a deep breath. She wouldn't want me to hurt him, I didn't want to hurt him. So, I chose my words carefully.

"Listen Jack… I wasn't a good guy in college, we both know that. I disrespected women and I own that." I thought for a few seconds then decided to let him in. "Do you know why I left school Jack?" I said, looking him square in the eyes. It was time for some honesty, maybe that would make him stop.

He shook his head.

"I'm going to enlighten you then. My mother was dying of cancer and my father was cheating on her while the disease was eating her alive. I watched it all go down, and when she was gone, I decided to change my ways. Simple as that. That's the truth Jack, and you don't need to know any more than that."

He just stared back at me. I think I hit a nerve.

"I'm sorry… I didn't realize," he said stammering.

"I thought you and Julia figured things out yesterday, so why are you here Jack? Tell me why you're here?"

He turned away and took a step off the deck. "I uh, I uh…. it's fucking hard to know she's with you," he finally blurted out in frustration. He turned to face me. "Have you ever loved someone so much that it physically hurt to watch them leave, and not only that, but to watch them start a new life with someone else?"

I couldn't help but feel sorry for him, but I had to remind myself, she wasn't with him anymore, and for good reason. She was with me. That had to mean something.

"No Jack, I don't know what that feels like. I'm on the other side. I'm trying to live my life Jack, and as bad as I feel for you, I have to do me now. Julia has to do Julia. Do yourself a favor and take her advice; get some help. Live your life. You guys have been divorced for two years. What are you waiting for man? I just told you my truth; it's time for you to find yours. You owe it to Julia and the kids…

"Don't bring my kids into this," he said angrily.

"Fine. Let me rephrase. You owe it to yourself, to do you. I didn't start living until I made the changes in my life. I'm sure you'd like to start truly living again Jack, right?"

He just looked at me, like nothing I was saying made sense. I wanted it to make sense for him. I knew he wasn't a bad guy, just like Julia said, he was just struggling. He ran his hand through his hair, breathed in and out a few times, then turned to face me.

"I don't want you to be right, and I don't want your fucking pity. I think I need to go home… I just need to get out of here. I can't think straight here," he said, now backing away toward his car.

I walked over to him and placed my hand on his shoulder. "Remember when we played ball together Jack. You were a fullback, and I was a running back. You had my back on that field, even if you didn't like me then. I have your back now, along with Julia. We want you to figure things out. I will never stand in the way of your friendship with Julia, and I will never mistreat Julia."

He placed his hand on my shoulder, looked me in the eyes and nodded. And then he walked away.

As I watched him pull out of the driveway all I could think was, by the grace of God, that went far better than I thought it would. My thoughts circled around the events of the past few days; it was the craziest weekend of my life. I walked to the log pile and grabbed some wood for the fire. When I walked back into the house, she was standing near the hallway. I wondered if she knew Jack had been outside. Did she hear us?

"Hey," I said, shocked to see her there, "finish writing already," I asked as I walked to the fireplace, laying the wood down on the hearth.

She didn't say a word. She just walked to me, grabbing me around the waist, her head nestled into my chest. Her grip tightened. I could feel her body quivering. I grabbed her by the shoulders, pulling her back so I could see her face, then I wiped the tears away. Our eyes were locked. I kissed her, hoping to alleviate her fears, then pulled her back into me. I whispered in her ear, "You need to get ready, we have somewhere to be. Wear those sexy tight jeans and bring a jacket, we're going to 'P-town.'"

Chapter Forty-Six
Julia

My mind is fighting with itself. I think I'm really falling for this guy. No, nope; I actually know I've already fallen hard. We didn't talk much on the way to Provincetown, which was okay. I've never really had a problem with silence; it's introspective and necessary at times. When we pulled into the parking lot, it was 4:40 p.m. Andrew hopped out of the truck and rushed to my door; Mr. Chivalrous was still going strong. He offered me his hand and then led me to the dock. I was completely in the dark about what we were doing here.

The dock was quiet, except for one boat. The crew was milling about; it looked like they were prepping the schooner for a sail. We walked down the ramp and onto the boat.

"Just in time," the captain said to Andrew.

The two men shook hands. And suddenly it hit me, a sunset cruise. Andrew remembered.

"We have some cushions set up right over there for you. We'll be leaving port soon," the captain said.

I looked up at Andrew. "You are a sneak," I said, smiling at him. He just smiled, then led me to the bench.

We sat down and I could see him looking out over the dock, then he turned to me and said, "You don't know the half of it."

What a weird thing to say. What the hell did he mean by that? I looked around casually; no one else was on the pier. No one else was boarding.

"Where's is everyone?" I said confused, standing now to look down at the boardwalk.

Andrew grabbed my hand and pulled me to sit next to him. He placed his fingers gently under my chin, forcing me to look at him.

"It's just us baby," he said, and then he kissed me.

I pulled back, eyeing him hard. "You're going to spoil me you know. I'll be expecting this every time we go out," I said laughing.

"Every time?" he said, like he was savoring the words. "How many every times will there be Julia, because I have some savings, and business is good, so I'm planning on an infinite amount of every times."

I know I blushed, and I didn't care. "Me too," I said, threading my fingers through his hair. "It's all I want."

After ten minutes, the schooner pulled away from the dock and headed out of the marina. The wind had picked up, and my hair was flying, but I didn't care. When the sun finally set, the sky looked like a watercolor painting. It was as if all the blue had succumbed to the most magnificent tapestry of orange, pink, and purple hues. The water lapped on the sides of the boat peacefully, while we stood there, huddled together. It was perfect, yes perfect. But the truth is, I couldn't take my eyes off him. Even though I wouldn't let him say it to me, I could think it about him; he was perfect to me. It would be my little secret; he didn't need to know.

Suddenly, he turned toward me, wrapping his arms tightly around me. "I just have one question for you Julia," he said, very seriously, staring deep into my eyes. I felt a flash of panic; what could he possibly want to know?

"Red sox or Yankees?" he said, grinning at me.

I paused for dramatic effect. I already knew exactly what my response would be. With my best straight face, I looked seriously into his eyes and said, "Mets baby... Mets all the way."

He threw his head back as if I just plunged a sword through his heart. When he looked back down at me, he saw me smiling. He couldn't help but laugh. And then, I watched his face go from playful to serious.

"Julia," he said, brushing the hair from my eyes, "Julia, you are completely and utterly captivating." And then his lips met mine.

How many times does a man have to tell you you're completely captivating before you believe it?

Chapter Forty-Seven
Julia

I've been writing almost non-stop. With Andrew back at work, our fairytale time together has come to a halt. I miss him during the day, but I'm trying to make the most of my time by exercising, writing, and cooking. I've been able to continue my therapy via video call, something I know is important for my overall health. I've been thinking a lot lately about my childhood, about the things I told Andrew. I think divulging my secrets to him has awakened some sleeping beast in me, unfortunately or fortunately. I'm not sure which one it is, but I just feel like there's something I still have to face, something I'm blocking or something I'm just not putting together, and it scares the hell out of me.

I'm sitting on the deck right now, in my safe haven, looking out over the lake, computer on my lap. My writer's block has vanished. It's as if the elements have washed me clean of debris, kind of like the storm. I closed my eyes; I could hear the water delicately lapping the shore, like a lullaby whisking me off to a place of calm and focus.

When Andrew comes home at the end of the day, it's like the romance starts all over again. The passion is fresh each time. The sex had gone from passionate sex to passionate love making. We haven't uttered 'the words' yet, but I know how I feel.

I think Andrew is happy. I hope he's as happy as I am. I've stayed connected with Jess, told her about Andrew and me and she's been so supportive. She's probably happy I have someone in my life again, even though she wishes it was her father. Jack is another story, and when she and I talk, her concern for him is evident.

I've tried to do my due diligence with Jack by sending him therapist recommendations. I worry though, getting started is the hardest part and I don't know if he's done anything about it yet. I haven't texted him to see if he's following up, and God knows I'm not going to talk to Andrew about Jack right now. Things are going so well with us; I don't want to screw it up.

When I heard Andrew talking to him, over a week ago, I was so touched; he was being the bigger man. I can't lie, I thought I might hear a scuffle breakout, but thankfully they both stayed under control. Usually, Jack would have lost it.

My run this morning took me around the lake, ten miles in total, which was beyond what I'd normally do, but that runner's high kicked in at the five-mile mark and I just couldn't stop. The foliage is just starting to change, the air is brisk, and the weather is ideal for running. The woods are thick here; it's like nowhere I've ever been on the Cape. Andrew's house is like a hidden gem camouflaged in the forest; I can't believe how beautiful this spot is. I feel so at home, so much so that I don't even miss any of my things. It's crazy. I bet my plants have keeled over by now and I don't even care—my apologies plants.

Eventually, I know I'll have to go back. I can't lie, I'm getting sick of wearing the same clothes over and over, but I fight making the trip, probably because I'm so happy here. It's like I'm afraid if I leave, even for a few days, things won't be the same when I return. I simply don't want to go back.

I don't even mind the cold when I'm on the deck. Usually there's just enough sun to warm me, plus I usually grab one of Andrew's sweatshirts and breathe him in while I work. I finished my chapter book last week; my publisher seemed excited to finally receive it. I'm thinking about asking Sean to illustrate it; I think he'd be a perfect fit. I've decided to try my hand at the novel now, taking Sean's advice. I have the makings of a solid love story, but sometimes I doubt myself. Is it good enough, am I a good enough writer? And then I hear my college English professor telling me to stop trying to be someone I'm not; just be me. "Don't try to incorporate bigger words into your writing," she'd say, "just trust yourself." Those are difficult words for me to put into practice. I feel like I've been fighting my whole life just to be accepted by others, but in the end, I was the one who needed to accept myself. It's taken me awhile, but I think I'm there, or at least further down the path anyway.

I yawned. I needed coffee to wake me up. Andrew bought an espresso machine so I could get my daily jolt of caffeine, thank God! I went inside to grab a cup when my phone rang. It was Justin. My body stiffened; Justin only texts, he never calls. Something's up. Is there something wrong with Jack?

~

"Hey buddy, is everything okay, you don't usually call your mother," I said, with a tiny bit of sarcasm spilling out.

"Well, not really Mom." I could hear the concern in his voice. "It's Dad. Don't worry, he's fine, well sort of. He's acting weird. He refuses to come into the office. He won't see clients either. I think he's barricading himself in his apartment. He's been acting strangely since he got home."

Shit, this is what I was afraid of. "Strange how?"

"I haven't had many conversations with him, but he's talking a lot about his childhood, about you, about not wanting to get out of bed."

I shuddered. I had a feeling this would happen. I'd given him therapist names, we promised to support him, but obviously he didn't have the strength to look into it himself. If he's talking about his parents, about me, it's definitely not a good sign.

"What do you want me to do honey? Do you think I should come back?"

"At this point Mom, I don't see any other way to get to him. He always listens to you. He's not listening to me or Jess. She's concerned as well. We didn't want to put this on you, but we need your help."

God damn it! God damn it! I was pacing in the kitchen now. I don't want to leave, but I promised to be there for him. Figures, just when I find my happy place, Jack implodes, again. I feel guilty for thinking like that. I feel selfish and uncaring. What's wrong with me? I told him I'd support him, that I'd love him through his struggles. Now's a crucial time in his life and I can't deny him my support. This isn't about being husband and wife anymore; this is about being human.

"Okay Justin, okay… I'll come back, but I think we should get your brother and sister involved in this too."

"Get Jacob in on this? Are you saying we need to do an intervention? Mom… he's not an alcoholic or a drug addict… do you really think that's necessary?"

I knew exactly what I was inferring. This was serious. This was necessary.

"You said he's cutting himself off from the world. I think it's completely necessary. I'll leave later this afternoon. Call Jacob and Jess. Let's figure out how to do this as soon as possible. Tomorrow. Jacob could do a zoom call. I'll call you when I get back. Ask Jess if she can meet for dinner tonight so we can devise a plan."

"All right Mom," I could hear the hesitation in his voice, "and thank you. I know you've got a life too. I appreciate your help."

"Justin, I know it's hard to understand, because your father and I aren't together anymore, but I still love him... I still care about him. I won't turn my back on him, not now Justin, not ever."

~

My serene day imploded in a matter of seconds, like Jack's life. I had no other choice but to go back; right? Now wasn't the time to question myself. Jack needed me and the kids to help him through this. No matter what, we were still a family. I needed to pack some things and then distract myself until Andrew got home later this afternoon. I have to tell him face to face that I'm leaving. I'm not looking forward to telling him, and God knows I don't want to leave. He's got to understand though, at least I hope he will.

When I walked into the bedroom, I glanced at the Bible. "It's just another time," I murmured, looking to her for solace and strength. "It's just another time in this life and I swear, I swear I'm not going to screw this up. I have to help Jack, but please Lily, please prepare Andrew, because for some strange reason I'm preparing myself for the worst."

Chapter Forty-Eight
Julia

I was sitting in the bedroom, going through my emails when I heard Andrew walk through the door. Usually, I'd be in his arms immediately, but not today. Mistake on my part; I'd already made this awkward.

"Julia," he yelled, no doubt wondering why I wasn't right there.

I walked out of the bedroom and watched his eyes go from seeing the bags on the floor to looking at me.

"What's this?" he asked, nodding to the bags, the look on his face was telling.

I looked down for a moment, pensive, not wanting to tell him.

"I need to go back home," I said, wringing my hands. I looked up at him; confusion is what I saw, it's what I expected. "I got a call from Justin, and you know he never calls. He has deep concerns for Jack, he's become a recluse and is showing signs of depression. He needs my help Andrew… I'm sorry, but I need to go back."

Andrew looked at me with confusion. "Didn't you send him therapist names?" he said, desperately wanting that to be enough.

"I did, but just because he has them doesn't mean he'll do anything with them. He needs a push," I said, hoping he could detect the concern in my voice.

He put his head down, then shook it ever so slightly. "Why does that push need to come from you?" he said, his tone was changing. "Why can't Justin or Jess get involved?" He looked at me intensely, his words laced with sharpness.

"I can't put it all on them," I said, my voice becoming stronger. "They're still young Andrew. Jack needs me and the kids to intervene together." I looked down at my feet, avoiding his gaze. "I told Jack I'd be there to support him. I asked Justin to call Jess and Jacob so we can all talk to him together." I raised my head and looked him in the eyes. "I won't be alone in this." I was trying to reassure him everything would be fine, that he shouldn't feel threatened.

"Julia," he said, throwing his keys onto the side table, "he's manipulating you... can't you see that?" he said, with a tone I wasn't accustomed to.

"Andrew, even if he is, I still need to go. Plus, I haven't gone back in weeks, and I need to check on things, grab some more clothes. Please understand," I begged.

Andrew let his head drop. He put his hands on his hips and sighed deeply. I knew this was going to be tough, but I was wrong. This was excruciatingly tough.

"When are you going?" he asked, now seeming to give in to the idea.

"Now. I wanted to wait 'til you got home. I didn't want you to feel abandoned. I'm not trying to abandon you," I said, hoping he could read between the lines.

He rubbed his hand over his head, then looked at me piercingly. It was horrible. I was hurting him, and that's the last thing I wanted to do.

Then with the sharpest tone I'd ever heard him use with me he said, "Do what you need to do Julia," then he walked past me to the bedroom and shut the door.

I think my heart just broke. I felt like my heart just disintegrated into a million pieces. I took the hint. He wasn't going to touch me. He didn't want to talk anymore. Is it possible to be heartbroken and angry at the same time? I wiped my eyes, grabbed my bags, and walked out the door. I wanted to run back inside, say I'd stay, but I knew he'd had enough, and I just needed to go. This was now my worst nightmare. How many more would there be? Why does life always have to throw shit at you just when you've finally found happiness?

As I drove, I felt completely alone. I felt like I had ruined everything Andrew and I had shared over the past few weeks. Everything I'd felt earlier about leaving this place, him, was happening. To him, I was choosing Jack, and I was putting his feelings last. Was I? How does a mother tell her son, "Sorry your dad is falling apart, I'm not married to him anymore, so you'll just have to manage this on your own." It's not how I raised my kids, and as far as I was concerned, I was still a role model to them, no matter how old they were. Once a parent, always a parent.

But I couldn't get Andrew out of my head. I played back sweet scenarios of our time together. Waking in the morning with an uncontrollable desire to feel my body pressed against his. Not wanting to wake him, but needing to feel my breasts against his chest, needing to let my lips linger over his lips, his beard. Needing to feel his warm breath on my face. Needing to nuzzle his face with my nose. Needing to feel his caress. I can't control these sensual thoughts. I just want him to still want me, but does he? The intensity of sex has changed, becoming slower, rhythmic, more about the experience than the finish. It's about making love and not just having sex. The need to climax every time has given way to desperately wanting to be a part of the other person. I don't want that to end. I started to cry at the thought of losing him. I meant what I'd said weeks ago; it would crush me if he didn't want me anymore.

"Julia… STOP!" I hated that I had to talk to myself in order for me to listen, to tell the truth. "Refocus, Julia!" It's time to go forward, not backward. I focused on the road. I tried not to let my mind wander to the negative.

I hit traffic; a lot of traffic, but still made it back by 6 p.m. I walked through the door, into my sad little rental house. The place I used to call home, well, sort of, but now I felt like it was the saddest place in the world. I was right, the plants were dying. As I grabbed the watering can, I texted Justin and Jess, seeing if they still wanted to meet for dinner. They agreed. I never thought I'd have to do something like this with my kids. It's hard to fathom that Jack could be in such trouble.

Chapter Forty-Nine
Jack

I don't really know what's going on with me. Wait, yes, I do; I'm heartbroken. But why now? Julia and I have been divorced for years and suddenly she's on my mind, non-stop. She's always been there, popping up in different scenarios throughout my day, but this time, this time it's different. Why? Because she has a boyfriend, and I can't bear the thought of sharing her with anyone else?

"She's not your property Jack," I said, looking in the bathroom mirror. Suddenly, I noticed that my beard had grown in; it was out of control. I had bags under my eyes. I told Justin I felt hopeless. Way too much sharing on my part. What did I think he'd do? I guess, secretly, I wanted him to call Julia. I needed to see Julia; she's the only one that ever understood me, even if she hated me at times. I needed to feel like she was on my side again.

My phone buzzed. It was Julia. I felt a surge of hope. She was back in town and wanted to see me. Was I reading this correctly? Justin must have called her. She's worried about me. Should she be? Am I that bad off? I had to admit, I felt paralyzed to do anything. Picturing her with Andrew was killing me. I don't know how to get over her; over her with him.

I texted her back.

~

Jack: "I would love to see you. Should I come by your place?"
Julia: "Yes, that would work. How does around five sound?"
Jack: "That works. I'm looking forward to it."

~

My heart was racing, while my thoughts roamed. Maybe she was done with him. Maybe she realized that we were meant to be together. This could be my last chance to win her over. I had to be careful. I didn't want to come off weak, but being too strong could possibly drive her away. I had to play my cards right. I couldn't risk losing her again.

The entire day was in front of me. Suddenly, I felt trapped in the apartment. I needed to get out, clear my head of any negativity. I threw on some sweatpants and my sneakers and walked out the door with purpose. It was the first time I'd been outside in over a week. I jumped in my car and headed to the ocean; I suddenly felt the energy to go for a walk.

When I walked onto the beach, the water was gently lapping the shore. All was calm; it was exactly the scene I needed. I felt hopeful as I walked. Julia had reached out to me; she wanted to see me. This had to be a good thing. I'd convinced myself it was a good thing. So what if we'd been apart for two years; couples get back together all the time. We were good once, and I knew we could be good again. And the kids—this would make them so happy. I wouldn't take her for granted this time. I'd make the necessary changes to ensure we would stay together. My entire mindset was changing, changing because of Julia.

When I got home, I cleaned the apartment. I'd really let everything go. There were dirty clothes and dirty dishes everywhere. Julia used to hate it when I didn't pick up after myself. I laughed at the thought. When I jumped in the shower, the water seemed to rinse away the worst of me. I trimmed my beard, put some cologne on, and found a shirt in the closet she'd given me. I stood in front of the mirror; the tattoo on my shoulder stared back at me. The phoenix rising; it still meant something to me, maybe even more now than before. Rising from adversity; emerging stronger, more resilient, and more successful than before. I'd forgotten the message over the years. Everything was riding on this one meeting with Julia. I needed to rise above all the shit; I wasn't going to fuck this up.

"Flowers… Julia loves flowers," I said, as I got dressed. I'll stop at the florist on my way to her place. I'll do whatever is necessary to get her back. I've never stopped loving Julia, and all I've wanted is for her to love me again; love me like when we reconnected at that college party. I wanted her to want me as much as I wanted her.

Chapter Fifty
Julia

I paced the floor, wringing my hands in usual freaked out form. Deep breathes Julia, just take deep breaths.

"Mom, please stop pacing, you're making me nervous," Jess said sharply.

I looked up, shocked by her response to my coping methods. "I'm sorry honey, I just can't settle down. This has to go well."

"Mom, we have a plan, Jacob will join shortly. It's going to be what it's going to be. We can only do so much," she said.

At least she knew her boundaries, something I'd always struggled with. It was 5 p.m. on the dot when we heard the knock at the door. I looked at Jess and Justin, then walked to the door, my hands pressed together as if I were praying. I should be praying knowing how this could go. I opened the door and Jack was standing there with flowers.

"Julia," he said, his expression hopeful as he handed me the flowers.

"Jack, you didn't have to buy me flowers." I took them and gave him a hug. Again, the hug felt familiar, but I could sense that it meant something different to both of us. He pulled me close, like he didn't want to let go. I released him and turned to walk into the living room. He followed but stopped suddenly. He saw Jess and Justin. They stood quickly. Their expressions told their truth; they were worried about their father.

"Dad," Justin said, acknowledging him.

"Hey Dad," Jess said, in her usual upbeat tone.

"What's this?" Jack said, looking at them, then back at me. "What's going on... is it Jacob... is he okay?"

I walked to the kitchen to put the flowers in water, while Jess and Justin explained that Jacob was fine.

"If he's fine, what's this about," Jack asked, now clearly confused.

"Take a seat Dad," Justin motioned to the couch, "Jacob will be joining us in a few minutes," he said, gesturing to the computer.

Jack looked confused. I felt like I'd tricked him, which I guess I did. Once again, I gave him false hope. It's not what I wanted to happen, but he wouldn't have come if Jess or Justin had asked.

Jack reluctantly sat down on the couch, staring me down.

"Is this an intervention?" he asked angrily, looking straight at me. "Is this a fucking intervention Julia?" What have you been saying to the kids?"

God that tone. I thought, "Don't make me feel like I used to feel Jack; don't take us backwards. Don't put this on me."

"Dad," Justin said instantly, trying to get his father's attention off me. "This isn't about what Mom… you have to understand things from our perspective. You haven't' been to the office, you haven't been seeing clients, you told me you felt hopeless. That's more than enough reason for all of us to gather so we can talk this through with you. We care Dad… call it what you want, but we think you need to know how much we love you, care for you, and want you to feel good about yourself again."

Jack stared blankly at all of us.

Suddenly, I heard Jacob's voice interject from the computer. "Dad, I'm here for you as well. Please listen to what we have to say."

"We just want to help," Jess pleaded.

I walked into the room and knelt down in front of Jack, placing my hands on his legs. I looked into his eyes. "Jack, I told you I'd help you, that I'd support you in getting the help you needed. Remember I told you about me going to therapy. I didn't share that because it's an easy thing to do. Admittedly, it's been exceedingly difficult for me. I just wanted you to see that seeking out a therapist is nothing to be ashamed of. It's helped me so much. I want you to get on the road to recovery. You understand that right?"

Jack looked right at me, his eyes full of confusion and sadness. He placed his hand on my cheek. I could see this was killing him. He's not the kind of guy that wants to look weak in front of his kids. I watched him look at the kids, then he sat back, leaning his head against the couch cushion, staring up at the ceiling. He ran his hands over his head. I could see the struggle. No one wants to be told they're in trouble. No one wants to admit that. I didn't want to admit it. It took me a long time to get help for feeling inadequate, but when I finally did, it was like a weight was lifted.

"Jack, we have some ideas to get you started. Jacob has an idea."

"Dad, I want you to come out here. Come out to Utah. There's a Dude Ranch that offers therapy. It's a six-week program. You and I can spend some time together as well. It would be a win-win." He paused then said, "Dad, look at it like a renewal of sorts… a vacation or even a retreat. We all agree it's a great place to start. You deserve this, you really do." I could hear Jacob's voice trembling a bit, even though he was trying to be strong.

Jack looked at all of us. The tears were welling up, and he was far from being in fight or flight mode. He seemed to be listening to us. Please God let him listen. He stood up and paced the floor. I could tell the voices in his head were badgering him. Please God, please let him hear us and not the negative voices.

I walked toward him. "Jack, please consider this. We can't force you to go, but we can tell you how much we care. We all love you. We all think you have so many wonderful things ahead, you just have to let them in, believe they're possible, believe you deserve them. But we can't make you see that… that's up to you. We care Jack, we just want you to get to a place where you care about yourself."

Jack had his back to us, his hands on his hips. He was processing. Then suddenly, I watched his head fall forward. I could see his body shake. We all looked at one another. Jacob lowered his head. I quickly rushed to him, hugging him tightly. Jess and Justin followed, wrapping their arms around him from behind. We just stood there quietly holding him, consoling him, helping him to stand upright. We felt him giving into his tears, and we responded by hugging him even tighter. Then he pulled away, wiping the tears away. We were all crying at this point.

"I'm so sorry," he said. "I've just been struggling so much, and I thought I could beat it, you know, be a man and get over it. I can still hear my father telling me to stop being a baby… real men don't cry, but I don't think I can beat this on my own. I just can't do it and it makes me feel like… like such a failure."

It crushed me to see him suffering so much. I placed my hand on his cheek.

"Jack, that's what therapy is for… to help you know your truths. To help you move on, away from the demons that want to trick you into believing that you're no good." I gently wiped the tears from his eyes; they were flowing abundantly now. "You are good Jack… you are a good man. You deserve to put yourself first. Your father may have beat it into you that you needed to be a strong man, a man whose feelings should be hidden, but you have nothing to prove to him or anyone else. Being courageous doesn't mean you're not afraid Jack; courage is knowing you're afraid and facing your fears anyway. You are courageous. We're here for you Jack, but we can't fix you. I can't fix you… you have to want it for yourself. We want you to want it, but we can't force you. The decision is yours."

He took a deep breath, hugged us again, and said, "Okay."

I think we all breathed a collective sigh of relief. Thank you, God, was all I could think. Thank you, God!

Chapter Fifty-One
Julia

My phone rang. It wasn't Andrew.

"Hi honey. What's up?" I said, praying she wasn't calling to question me about returning to the Cape.

"Mom, are you still here... are you still at your house?" Jess asked. It'd been almost a week since I'd left the Cape.

"Yes," I said hesitantly. "Why?"

"Don't do that, you know why I'm asking. Why haven't you gone back to the Cape? Did you and Andrew have a fight? Have you even been talking with Andrew?"

I shuddered at the thought. After the way I left, after the way he walked away, I felt like it was over, and I was scared to call or text. He hadn't reached out to me either. I was paralyzed. I was listening to the negative voices, exactly what I told Jack not to do. It was wrong, and I knew it, but I was giving in.

"I don't think Andrew wants to see me," I said, "not after the way I left. He was pretty pissed, and no doubt hurt."

Then she asked again, "Have you texted or called him?"

I hesitated. "No," I said, glancing out the window, trying to distract myself from the truth.

"Well, Mom, you have no idea what he's thinking then. Don't you think you owe it to him, and to yourself, to find out if there's something still there? You gave dad that whole speech about being courageous, which was spot on, so when are you going to take your own advice?"

I sat there dumbfounded by this young woman's hutzpah. She's the one who was spot on, and I couldn't deny it. I'd been hiding for days. Hiding like it was my only choice, like something will hurt me if I come out of hiding. I'm doing what Jack did. Admittedly, I'm afraid Andrew won't want me back. After everything we'd been through, I knew I should trust him, but the fucking fear was eating me alive.

"I hear you Jess," I said, fumbling with the tassels on the throw pillow. "I'm… I'm scared. So much time has passed. I'm scared he'll reject me."

"Mom… Mom, I hear you too. But please don't give up on something that's just barely started. Please give him a chance. I know you might walk into a shit show, but you always taught us to try, to give whatever we were doing our best. You owe that to yourself, don't you think? Find the fighter in you and go get what you want. I know you're scared, but if you don't take the chance, how will you know for certain."

Damn these kids of mine. She's right. She's usually right. Now I was the one who needed to listen. The tides have turned; these kids of ours, how'd they get so fucking smart? As much as I think I have to take care of them, they're the ones taking care of me and Jack now. We need them just as much, maybe even more, than they need us.

I swallowed hard, trying to find my determined self. Finally, I gave in. "You're right Jess," I said, feeling a surge of positivity. "I'm going to fight for him, for us. I'm going to go back. I'm going to go back today."

I could hear her sigh from the other end of the phone.

"I love you Mom, you got this."

"I love you too honey and thank you… thank you for pushing me."

I didn't wait; I ran to the bedroom and started packing. Soon, all the good memories replaced the fear and I felt invincible for a moment. I felt like I had to go back, to find out if he still wanted me. She was right; I had nothing to lose and everything to gain. One of these damn days I wouldn't give in to my fears. One of these fucking, God damn days I would be secure in who I was; I just didn't want it to take too long. Time is so precious and here I am, just letting it go by like I don't care. But it was more than that. I was letting it go by like I deserved to feel horrible. I desperately needed to stop doing that. I desperately needed to go home.

Chapter Fifty-Two
Julia

I pulled into the driveway around 6 p.m. Andrew's truck was there. We hadn't spoken since I left. I never told him I was coming back today. What was I walking into?

The light was fading. The house seemed eerily quiet. My heart was racing, my breaths short and quick. I was afraid. I walked to the door, grabbed the key from under the stone, and unlocked it.

The living room was dark except for the glow of the fire; I'd missed that. I'd missed the smell. I'd missed us sitting in front of it, huddled together, sharing our day while we caressed one another. I walked in, peeking around the corner, Andrew wasn't in the kitchen, and he wasn't in the living room. The house was so quiet, it was as if he wasn't home. I felt a bit like an intruder. I'd been away too long, and I knew it.

I walked into the living room, peering out the windows to see if he was on the deck, but then my eye caught sight of two wine glasses on the coffee table. I walked over to them, the fire crackling and hissing at me while I just stared in disbelief. Two glasses? I hadn't been at the house for a week. We hadn't talked for a week. I placed my hand over my mouth. I felt like I could crumble on the spot. I felt weak, I needed to sit down for a second. The tears were coming, and I couldn't stop them. I'd left this house without a hug, without support from him, without knowing how he felt about me, and now, it was all right there, right in front of me; two glasses of red wine. Two glasses—our nightly cocktail. My glass of wine, waiting for someone else's lips to take it in. He'd already replaced me. I waited too long. All the should 'haves' filled my mind: I should have called, I should have texted, I should have come back right away. I shouldn't have left in the first place. Maybe I should have asked him to come with me. I'd never thought of that. I'd never thought to ask him to go. Maybe that was the reason he shut down so quickly that night.

Suddenly, I could hear the faint sound of a country ballad coming from the bedroom. My mind raced uncontrollably. Jesus, he had someone in there. He had someone else in our bed. Someone else's clothes were on the floor. Someone else was running their fingers through his hair. He was holding someone else while I stood out here, like a fucking idiot. My head was spinning. How could I be out here knowing this? Then my mind went back in time, back to The Watering Hole. It was her; it was that fucking bitch Erica. Suddenly, I felt like a stranger in this house. I wanted to vomit. The tears were coming in bursts, like a stream rolling down my cheeks. I had to question whether Jack had been right all along? The music seemed to be moving, getting closer, if that's possible. I felt glued to the couch, but I had to get out of there. I forced myself to stand up, wiping the tears from my face, and then, there he was, standing in the living room, just staring at me. His shirt was partially unbuttoned. I swallowed hard. I couldn't breathe.

His beard looked scraggly. He looked disheveled. I could hear the music even louder. He grabbed his phone from his pocket and shut it off. I knew he was shocked to see me standing there. The fire crackled; I was center stage. I just stared at him not knowing what to say. I've missed you; I want you; I love you; those phrases raced around in my brain, never making their way out of my mouth. How could I offer those now? It didn't matter anymore what I thought, he was going down a different path. And then in the matter of seconds it took for me to reason my way out, he broke the silence.

"You came back," he said quietly, the surprise evident in his voice.

I couldn't read him; his emotions were tightly contained behind those deep brown eyes. I just stared at him. I wanted to bear my soul to him, tell him how I felt about him, but then fear and anger filled my cracks. I wanted to know how he could have moved on so quickly after just a week, but then, I didn't want that either. Make up your mind Julia, what the fuck do you want? The negative voices in my head were screaming. I didn't know what to say. I brushed the tears away and bit the side of my lip. And then I just spit it out.

"I… I'm sorry… I didn't know," I said, looking back at the wine glasses.

He looked at me with confusion. "What's there to be confused about Andrew, it's right there," I thought. His eyes looked past me, focusing on the wine glasses. He shook his head no. No what? No there aren't two glasses there waiting for you and Erica. No, you just got caught. No, I'm too late.

"I should go," I said. "You've moved on, and I need to go." I felt flustered, hurt, and embarrassed.

He said nothing, but he looked like I'd just broken his heart, when I'm quite sure it was the other way around.

"It's okay," I said, waving my hand, "I get it. I left when you didn't want me to. I didn't contact you while I was gone, and I stayed for an entire week. I get it. It's too much. It wasn't fair to you. How could I expect you to wait, especially when she wants you so badly. I can't deal with this... I'm going to leave."

I knew I had to walk past him to get out. I just wanted out of this. I walked toward him, but I didn't want to be close to him. I felt like I was stuck, and he didn't care. He wouldn't move, he wasn't saying anything. I decided to just go, to swallow my feelings, my fears, and just get by him, but then he shifted to his right, blocking me completely.

I stopped, shocked by his movement. I steadied myself on the back of the chair. I didn't shout, I pleaded, my voice trembling. "Please Andrew, please let me go. I don't want to see her," casting my eyes to the bedroom.

And then his sad voice softly said, "Who Julia, there's no one in there."

I couldn't help but fire back. "That's not true," I said, my voice still trembling. "It's all right there Andrew! The wine glasses, the music, your disheveled look... what else am I supposed to think. It's Erica, isn't it? You're with her now."

And then I noticed a duffle bag sitting on the hall floor behind him. It was like it was screaming out to me, "You're too late Julia. You waited way too long." He was going away with her. My mind was like a runaway train now, and I couldn't stop it.

"And what about the bag behind you, were you planning on going somewhere, somewhere with her?"

He moved toward me, and I put my hand up. "Please don't," I said, "I don't know why I'm asking... I don't want to know. I need to get out of here. I need to leave it all behind me and just get the hell out of here." And then I just stood there, frozen in place, my eyes trained on my feet, as if staring at them would make them move. I didn't really want to go. I felt the slightest thread holding us together and as much as I wanted to leave, I wanted that thread to become a rope; a strong, unyielding, binding rope. A rope that would tether us together.

"Julia... Julia," he pleaded, his voice low, yet strong, "listen to me, she's not here, no one is here but us. I've been here alone, all week, just me."

I couldn't look at him. I wanted to believe him, but the voices were swirling.

"Please Julia, what happened to you trusting me. Don't do this... I don't want her. I'm begging you to trust me, to have faith in me."

My tears had gone from a stream to a river. His words fell away as well. I wanted to believe him, but he seemed so distant. None of it made sense. I finally made eye contact with him. The tears in his eyes melted me.

"Julia," he said, looking intently at me, his voice quivering. "I've made a fire every night since you left. I've filled two wine glasses every night since you left, because... because it was my way of willing you to come back to me. I waited for your call, your text, any sign that you still cared for me. I was hoping you'd come back, hoping you'd come back to me." He sniffled, the tears falling down his cheeks. "Today I packed a bag, not to go somewhere with someone else, but to find you. I couldn't wait anymore. If you weren't coming back to me, I was going to take you back myself, even if I had to drag you back here."

I just stared at him. I covered my mouth, never taking my eyes off his. I felt confused and responsible for creating this ridiculous scene. If you could put every emotion, every thought you'd ever felt into one person's head at one time, that's how I felt right then: overloaded. My grip on the chair tightened. I tried to steady myself, but I crumbled anyway, my knees hit the floor. I tried to muffle my sobs; I tried to push them down, back down my throat. I wanted to disappear. I felt like I was in the storm all over again. Andrew rushed to me, and just like that stormy night, I felt him reach for me. He pulled me to my feet and held me tightly. He placed his forehead against mine. He was breathing heavily.

My voice trembled; I was completely overtaken by emotion. "You don't deserve any of this crazy Andrew... you deserve someone who isn't running off to help their ex-husband, someone who isn't going to be triggered into self-esteem melt downs. You deserve more, you deserve better... you deserve normal."

I could feel his head shaking. "No Julia, you're wrong. I was wrong. I should have been more supportive of you going. I said I would support Jack, which means I would support you being in his life. I just felt like he was playing you, using your son to get to you. Maybe… maybe I was surprised, even hurt, that you didn't ask me to go. No… I know I was hurt. I felt left out; I felt like you were choosing him over me. When you met with him at the cottage, watching you hug him, watching him grab your hands and kiss them, watching you embrace him in the end… I'd lost faith then; I didn't expect you to leave him. I was afraid to lose you then, and I'm still afraid… I'm still afraid to lose you now. I convinced myself you'd never come back, especially after the way I acted. I knew I blew it. I can't even tell you how much I missed you, all of you, even what you say is crazy. You are my normal Julia, there's nothing I would change about you."

"Julia," he said, brushing the hair from my face, "please look at me."

I looked up. We hadn't been this close in over a week. It felt right, but I was fighting it, not because of him, but because of me, for how horrible I was to leave the way I did, for how horrible I'd just been, assuming he'd found someone so quickly to replace me.

He took a tissue from his pocket, tenderly wiping the tears from my cheeks. "I'm so sorry for what you thought this was… I can't apologize enough. I would never, ever do that to you."

I looked up at him, his beautiful dark eyes full of painful tears. Did I do this to him? I stroked his cheek and let my fingers roam over his beard. I started to let go, to let him in, to let us in. "I'm sorry," I said, gasping for breath, "I'm so sorry for all of this." My head fell into his chest. He wrapped his arms around me. It was as if he couldn't get close enough.

He held onto me, consoling me while I cried, and I in turn held him tightly while he cried. We both felt the surge; we both needed to get everything that made us question one another out. I gasped for breath like I couldn't get enough air into my lungs, shuddering with every tear that fell. Would this river ever end? I needed to make it stop. I don't want to stay in this place for too long. The only thing remotely wonderful about this moment is being in his arms again. Once I stopped, once he pulled away from me, he held my face tenderly in his hands.

"Julia… I love you. Do you understand what I'm saying to you? I love you, Julia. I don't… I can't be without you." Then he pulled me to him again and begged, "Please, please don't ever leave me again." I could feel his hands trembling as he told me his truth.

I pushed myself away from him, just enough to look in his eyes. All I could do was shake my head. I was so overtaken by his words that I couldn't find my own. I just kept shaking my head, shaking it to assure him I wouldn't leave again. Shaking it in agreement; I loved him too. We stared into each other's eyes, wiping the tears away. And then he looked at my lips; I felt consumed by his stare. His lips slowly descended on mine. We were both lost in each other, lost in the moment.

He deliberately held my face, tenderly kissing my forehead and then both cheeks. I wasn't fighting anymore; I was letting him in, letting him try to restore our faith in one another. He was all I wanted and everything I needed.

"Julia," he said quietly, forcing me to look at him. "You are so completely captivating," he said, stroking my hair. "You may not see what I see, and you may not feel what I feel, but you are complete in my eyes. I lost my heart to you the first day I saw you in that parking lot. That was it for me. I love you Julia, more than I ever thought possible… please stay here with me, for all the days we have left in this life. I want to share every one of them with you, every single millisecond of it. I don't want you to have a home somewhere else. Move in here, with me, and make this your home… our home. Please Julia, please."

I heard everything he was saying. Despite all the tears, all the wasted thoughts, all the making up, I wasn't really surprised by his request because I'd been wanting, waiting for him to say those words to me. Words that took this from a fairytale romance to real. But I couldn't just make assumptions. This was his home and I needed him to ask.

"Andrew," I said, touching his cheek softly, my voice still trembling, "it's all I've wanted. I let the voices take me over, and I'm so sorry. It's not right," I said, lowering my eyes. And then he did what he always does, he placed his fingers purposely under my chin and made me look at him. He made me see the want in his eyes, and the look that told me to let it go.

I sighed in his arms. "I don't ever want to leave you. You've never made me feel like this wasn't my home too. I felt a part of this place, even when I didn't know where I was on that first night. You invited me in and made me feel like I belonged. My home is here now, here with you."

I placed my hand on his cheek, then lifted my lips to his, giving him the tenderest kiss I could. The kind of kiss that should say it all. But then, I had one more thing to make clear.

I pulled back and said, "I love you Andrew, with everything good that's in me, I love you, I love you completely."

His eyes teared as he stared at me. They were big and telling. He pulled me close; it was the most intense hug I'd ever felt. It wasn't his usual slow building hug. It was forceful and strong. It almost depleted my breath. It was like that hug put all our fears to rest. I reciprocated sinking my fingers into his back. He needed to know how desperately I wanted him. All our hopes and intentions for a future together were all right there in that hug. It was all there. There'd be no more hiding.

And then, things swiftly seemed to calm. He released me, and unzipped my coat, pushing it off my shoulders, letting it drop to the floor. He looked at me, those brown eyes now clearly telling me what he wanted. He took my hand in his, and tenderly kissed my palm. I knew where this was headed. I decided it was my turn to lead him to the bedroom, so I did. We stood by the bed, looking intently at one another, using only our eyes to communicate how badly we missed each other and how much we wanted each other right then. We weren't in a rush. His fingertips glided intimately up and down my sides, then he pulled me in, wrapping his arms tightly around me. I felt him pressing into me. Did I say we weren't in a rush, because suddenly I couldn't breathe. I wanted him right then. I pulled back and let my hands roam over his chest, then I unbuttoned his shirt pushing it over his shoulders and down to the floor. We stood by the bed, are hands roaming over each other, then he leaned in whispering softly, breathlessly into my ear, "I've missed this."

I could smell his cologne. I was losing myself in him.

"Remind me again what you've missed," I said, running my fingertips playfully through his hair, while he nestled his mouth into my neck.

He didn't wait long to take me up on my banter. His hands wandered down to the tie of my wrap dress. He loosened it, exposing my stomach, then slipped his hands under it, caressing my waist and hips. When it fell to the floor, he knelt down to unzip my boots, never losing eye contact with me. He worked his way back up, releasing me from the prison of my bra and panties.

His pants were next on the list, and so forth.

I wrapped my arms around his neck. He swiftly placed one arm around my back, and the other arm under my legs. He picked me up, then just stood there for a moment, kissing me, holding me. It was like he wasn't in a rush. He was just breathing me in, reacquainting himself with my body. He was savoring every bit of me through his warm touch; his tongue moving deliberately, searching for mine. My heart was beating rapidly; I felt like it was the first time all over again. When he was satisfied, he placed me gently on the bed; again, his eyes still focused on me. He climbed on top of me, placing his hand on my cheek, stroking my face tenderly. I stroked his hair, taking in those brown eyes; it was like I'd never really looked at him before. We melded together instantly. The room was aglow with the fire. I could hear it crackling, snapping, burning. I could hear each breath we took. I could clearly hear his moans, and my whimpers, and just before it was over, just before everything came to a sudden crescendo, I pushed my hands forcefully into his chest, like I was trying to push him away, and I exhaled in ecstasy. The pleasure I felt in that moment was like nothing I'd ever felt before. I was uninhibited, carefree, in the moment.

We just lay there, after, caressing one another, trying to make up for the week we'd missed. The most intense and crazy few weeks of our lives were in the past. I wanted to forget them, but I didn't as well. I needed to be in this moment though, not jumping back, not moving too far forward. I didn't need to derail myself again. I needed to live right now, more fully than I ever thought possible. That book I'd placed on the shelf, the one with chapters full of negativity and past mistakes; I didn't just need to leave it on the shelf—I needed to take it down and burn it.

~

It shouldn't have been a surprise to me. We'd just rekindled our romance, but there was more to our relationship than that. As I lay contentedly on top of him, I felt his chest rise and fall, which could only mean one thing: a question was coming my way.

"Julia," he said, running his hand up and down my back, "I just have one question."

I smiled, knowing this game. "What is it? What is it that you want?"

"I have a craving."

"What kind of craving," I said smiling, thinking it had to do with what just happened between us.

"Well, I was just wondering if you had time this week... time to make me that chocolate cake?"

I couldn't help but laugh. He always knew how to make me laugh. I thought for a second and said, "That depends on what I get in return."

He laughed and said, "What is it that you want from me Julia?"

I rolled on top of him, pinning his arms back, and smiled. By the look in those gorgeous, perfect, yes perfect brown eyes, I knew he had no idea what I was going to say.

"Andrew, I have one simple request..." I paused for effect, "I want smore's by the fire, with you."

He grinned at me, then pulled me to him.

"Considering I'm not much of a baker, I think I can handle that," he said with a chuckle.

"Lucky for you I am, and I promise, you'll never go hungry while I'm here."

"That's good to know," he said, "I'm going to hold you to that, especially in the bedroom."

I looked up at him and smirked. Again, there he was, making me laugh.

"You are a silly, greedy man Andrew Langdon," I said, gazing into his eyes.

"I know," he said. "When it comes to you, I'm always going to be greedy."

We lay there a bit longer, until his curiosity got the best of him. He asked me about Jack—he asked me what happened.

~

"It was extremely emotional," I said, "but he listened to us, and he seemed to understand the trouble he was in. He's going to Utah to spend time at a rehab facility. He's going to spend time with Jacob. We're hoping that six weeks away from everything will start him on a new path... a path to recovery."

"Well, it sounds like he's on the right road. I am glad for him... for all of you. I mean it Julia," he said, glancing down at me.

"I know you do. I know you care. And…" I paused, raising myself up to look at him, "I know you're probably relieved. None of this has been easy… not for me and the kids, not for Jack, and especially not for you."

"No, it hasn't," he replied, "but all of it was necessary for us to be where we are now, and I wouldn't trade that for anything."

Just knowing he understood, just hearing him say that he cared meant so much to me. He was who I thought he was. He was a caring, loving, protective man, and I needed to not question that anymore. It was time to move forward, and I needed to let the excitement of a future with him take over. I was ready. I was ready to be loved and to love again. I was ready to pursue a real career and not let the voices tell me I had to do it to be more. I needed to want it for myself, and not for anyone else. I had to shake off the past and walk bravely in the present. I'd found myself again, or just maybe, I'd stumbled upon a me that I didn't know existed. Maybe, after everything that had happened, I'd actually found a piece of the untouched, undamaged Julia. God, I wanted that to be true.

Chapter Fifty-Three
Jack

Six weeks in Utah. Six weeks of intense therapy. Six weeks of hiking, biking, and spending time with my son. I never thought I could feel this good again, this good without her.

I put the car in Drive and headed to the office. My mind wandered.

I hadn't talked to Julia since I left. I was working on me. She had sent me references for therapists, but I decided to go with one from the clinic. Everything today is done online anyway, so it was my best option. I talk with the therapist twice a week. We've quickly outlined my issues growing up, but I have a feeling, we're nowhere near done. I have a long road ahead of me, but the difference is, now I'm ready to be on that road.

I missed Julia terribly, especially when I was gone. That hadn't changed, but now I knew that despite loving her, I was desperately hoping she could fix me, and I could fix her. That's how we lived our entire life together; always trying to help each other, to fix each other. When we got divorced, all that went away for me. The constant need to fix was gone. She seemed okay with it, but I never got accustomed to manning the boat myself. What I have learned so far is that both Julia and I have experienced significant trauma growing up, and not many couples can get through it and come out the other side intact. We may not be together, but at least we still love each other, despite everything.

The kids have told me she's doing well, and although it was hard to hear, she's living with Andrew. As much as the mere mention of his name can send my jealousy into a tailspin, I can't let it control me. Julia has to live her own life and so do I. It's time to keep putting one foot in front of the other. Someone once told me that we're all standing in the middle of a staircase, and it's up to us to ascend or descend. I was descending at a rapid pace before, but no more. It's time to ascend, even though it's hard.

I pulled over and grabbed a coffee before I went to the office. As I took the cash from my wallet, a business card fell onto the seat. It was Denise's card. I hadn't thought about her until now. With everything that had happened, I wasn't exactly in dating mode. But maybe it wasn't too late to act on it. I smiled, grabbed my coffee, and thought, possibilities, so many possibilities were in front of me now.

When I pulled into the parking lot, I could see Justin's car. I'm not gonna' lie, I felt nervous to see my boy. I didn't want him to look at me like I was weak.

~

"Dad," he said, quickly getting up from his chair and grabbing me tightly. "I've missed you, we've all missed our captain here," he said, with a huge grin. "How you doin'?"

That hug was exactly what I needed right then. I held him tightly, then pulled back. "I'm good Justin, I'm really doin' good." I smiled reassuringly at him. The last thing I wanted to ever do again was upset my kids.

"You ready to dive back in?" he asked. "Big property coming our way in Plymouth."

"You bet," I said. "Let me see the specs."

We talked about everything I'd missed. We talked about the status of the properties on the Cape. It was like going back to a time that I didn't want to revisit, but it also made me feel like I was missing something in my life, and it wasn't Julia.

"What's the status on Sean's cottage, any bites?"

Justin brought up the listing and we both could see there had been a few interested parties but nothing of substance, which surprised me. It was such a desirable location.

I stood there for a moment, staring at the cottage. The thoughts I had were ridiculous, at least that's what I told myself. I wasn't even sure if my therapist would agree to what I was thinking.

Chapter Fifty-Four
Andrew

It's been almost two months to the day since I met Julia. Two months of attraction, lust, love. Two months of disaster, healing, peace. Two months I could have never predicted in my life, but worth every damn second.

Most days I wake up before her. The light is just starting to peek through the curtains. She's lying on her side with her back to me. I see her tattoo, trace her curves with my eyes. I want to touch her so badly and yet I don't want to wake her. Sexually, it's like we've both gone from nothing to all the time; now we were in it, all, or nothing.

When the weekends come, we lie in bed for as long as we can. Sometimes she stirs first, turning toward me, her breasts firmly pressed against my back. I wait for a few seconds until I feel her leg swing over my hip, then I reach down and grab it while she slips her arm underneath mine. She pulls herself as close to me as she can; our bodies tightly knit together. I feel her lips roam over my back.

Eventually she rolls on her back, then it's my turn. I roll toward her and pull her close. Her breasts are on my chest now, and my hands roam through her hair, over her back, and down, until they find their way to the sexist part of her. I can't help but breathe her in. She pulls back, her fingers roaming over my beard and lips; she doesn't open her eyes. She's just feeling me. I pull her to me; her lips to mine; we let them linger, our mouths closed, rubbing back and forth. The only reason I'm eager to let her get out of bed is because I want to watch her walk over to open the curtains. I want to linger over her naked body while she stands there, looking out over the lake. And when she's finally done teasing me, she turns sideways and smiles. She knows I love to watch her. Just that turn, her sun kissed profile; it kills me every time.

She's invaded every crevice that was void in me; she's like a good disease, filling me, making me whole. Just two months has made all the difference in my life; two months of Julia. I'm not sure what it is, and I don't really need to know, but it's different with her and I can't explain it; I don't want to try. Maybe it's love. I guess I've never been in love before. She's my first, and she'll be my last.

I don't want to get up this morning. It's the same every day. I just want to lose myself in her. I don't want to leave the comfort of the bed; I don't want to leave her. When I have to go to work, I can't wait to come home. Sometimes, I find her sitting on the deck, her wavy auburn hair swirled up loosely in a bun, a few strands hanging down by her cheeks. Sometimes, I walk through the door to find her in the kitchen, making dinner, listening to music. I love to sneak up on her, slowly, and dip my head into her neck, so I can breathe her in. She's so fucking sexy, no matter what she's doing. And the nights of lovemaking, why does that ever need to end? I don't want them to, but I know we need endings to have new beginnings, and I want more beginnings with her.

This morning I'm waiting; waiting for her to wake up; waiting for her to nestle into me. But I don't have to wait long; I feel her stirring. She moves toward me, her hand gently caressing my beard. I love it when she invades my space, like she just can't get close enough. She's kissing me with her mouth closed and I'm kissing her back in the same way. Morning sex; it's easy and effortless. We're still a bit groggy, but we go through all the motions like we're living in a dream; we just let it happen. When it's over, we fight the need to get up. This morning is no different.

~

"I don't want to move," she said, kissing my chest repeatedly.

"Then stay… don't go yet. We can be lazy this morning."

She doesn't move. She dips in and out of sleep as I caress her back.

After a few minutes, she rolls away from me. I can tell she's fighting the urge to get out of bed. I turn to my side, just taking her in, but I can't help but tease her.

"You ready to do some work?" I asked, knowing what her answer would be.

"I thought we just did."

She's a master at making me laugh—always quick with that dry sense of humor.

"That's what I mean… you ready for round two?"

She doesn't miss a beat. Suddenly, it's like she's full of energy. She sits up and leans over me, poking me in the chest.

"You wanna' go?"

"You know I do." I can't fight the grin spreading across my face.

I lunge for her, swiftly wrapping my arm around her waist, pushing her backward onto the mattress. I know what she wants. I lower my mouth to her stomach, sweeping my beard slowly over her abs. She reaches for my hand, and I let her guide me; I just want to please her. I can't resist her, and I'm quite sure she can't resist me. We have time this morning—but who am I kidding—we always have time for that; for more of that.

~

Today is the day I've been waiting for; she's finally moving in. She broke her lease and left the South Shore for good. We rented a small U-Haul and filled it with her stuff yesterday. She said she didn't need much, my house had everything. She was cutting ties with the past, most of it anyway. She seemed happy to call this house her home.

I couldn't help but take her in as she stood by the truck, laughing with Sean and Chad. Just hearing her laugh, seeing her face light up—it made me so happy. I just stood there, frozen in the doorway, watching her from a distance. I felt like I couldn't move; I was caught up in her, in all of her. Yet another moment I didn't want to end.

As I stood there, I couldn't help but think how much she'd opened up over the last month. She's been writing almost non-stop, and she hasn't been as critical of herself, her body, what she eats. It's like she's found freedom; she's found herself again.

Watching her when she doesn't know I'm looking has become my new favorite pastime. When she's cooking, listening to Pink, she acts like a little kid, so unincumbered, dancing her way around the kitchen. Conversely, she's introspective and calm when a Brett Young song is playing. Like most people, her moods are affected greatly by music, or maybe it's the other way around? I recalled one time when we were in the grocery store, and she recognized an old song they were playing. She instantly cut loose in the aisle. She once told me that grocery stores had the best playlists, and she was right. She didn't seem to care if anyone was watching. She didn't seem to care how she sounded or what she looked like. She was living in the moment, and I loved every second of it.

Suddenly, she spotted me watching her. She's smiling, but I have a feeling she's got something to say.

"What are you doing over here? Are you trying to get out of helping?"

"I just can't stop looking at you baby… can you blame me?"

She smirked at me as she walked by carrying a box into the living room.

"They can't do dinner tonight," she said. "They said Thursday would work. Let's make a reservation at Glenn's… sound good?"

"Sounds great," I said, "I'll call tomorrow." To be honest, I was relieved. I wanted her to myself tonight.

I watched her as she set the box promptly on the floor; the lake caught her eye. She stood there quietly, enveloping herself in her own arms, just staring out at the water. It was a familiar scene; one I'd grown to love. I couldn't take my eyes off her. Then she turned to me, catching me in my silent adoration of her.

"What are you looking at?" she said, turning at the waist, and brushing her hand against her backside. "Is there something on my butt?"

Now I was laughing. "Not yet," I said, smiling at her.

She smirked at me again.

"Get over here," I said, "I need a hug."

She walked slowly toward me, like a cat eyeing its prey. She pressed her body into mine, hugging me around the waist. I grabbed her ass and smiled at her. She smiled back, and then she leaned to the side, peeking around me, looking at Sean and Chad in the distance. She pulled back; I felt her hand slide down the front of my jeans.

"Hey, not fair," I whispered. Then with my hands still firmly on her ass, I pulled her even closer.

She groaned softly. I pushed back, then kissed her, my hands roaming over her back. I wanted her right then, right there, but I had to settle for just breathing her in.

"Hey, you two, enough already. There's a bunch of boxes in the truck with your names on them," Sean yelled. The moment was suddenly over, and I couldn't wait for the next one.

We worked through the afternoon carrying box after box into the house. She gave most of her furniture to Jess and Justin; all she wanted to keep was one dresser, and the desk and chair her grandmother had given her. I can't lie, I've never shared a space with a woman before; she had a lot of clothes, and even more shoes.

Once Sean and Chad left, it was just us. Julia was in the bedroom, hanging up the last of her clothes while I stayed in the kitchen, cooking dinner. I could hear her singing. I walked to the bedroom and peeked in. "Raise your glass," by Pink was playing and she was totally in another world. I watched her dance, her arms flying, her feet pounding the wood floor, her body turning round and round. She looked so free. How the hell does she have so much energy? I couldn't help but chuckle, as I slipped away, back to the living room.

I started a fire and grabbed two glasses of red wine while the chicken simmered. I don't think I even knew I could cook like this. Maybe she was the reason I was taking the time to do the things I never thought I could, like running. She actually had me running, but I got her to surf, so all in all, we were both trying new things, and it felt good.

I stood by the fire, lost in the flames when she walked into the room. She came up behind me, wrapping her arms around me. Usually that was my move.

"S'mores I see," she said softly, glancing down at the coffee table. "You remembered... took you long enough."

I turned to her and smiled, still loving the way she teased me.

"How could I forget?" I said, stroking her hair. "Glass of wine?"

"Definitely," she said, giving me a peck on the lips.

We sat on the couch; she snuggled into me. We sipped the wine, both exhausted from the day. And when the time was right, I put my wine glass down and stood up; I was on a mission.

"Where are you going?" she asked, totally puzzled by my sudden departure.

"None of your business my dear," I said, sneaking off to the storage closet.

When I reappeared, I was holding a large, thin cardboard box. I placed it carefully in front of her.

"What's this?" she said, with childlike wonder. "It's not my birthday. It's not Christmas. Please don't tell me you're one of those people who count the days to our monthly anniversary."

I looked down at her with disgust. "Really Julia, you think I'm that kind of guy?"

"Thank God," she said, laughing it off.

"Well, open it," I said, barely able to wait another second.

She pulled the box open from the top, and looked up at me, her eyes wide. She grabbed the contents and slowly, carefully, lifted it from the box. She stood it up against the coffee table and then pulled the brown paper away. Her hand immediately went to her mouth.

"Oh my God!" she gasped. And there it was, the reaction I was looking for.

"This is so beautiful," she said, clearly stunned by the painting.

"Do you recognize the scene?" I asked.

"It's Great Island… it's the spot we picnicked in. The marsh, the trees, the ocean. It's our spot."

It wasn't long before she engulfed me. That hug ranked right up there; actually, it was the most satisfying hug I'd ever received. I pulled her back.

"Did you notice the artist?"

She released me and leaned down. "Sean Morse." Her hand instantly covered her mouth again. "Sean did this? Oh… my… God! When did he start this?"

"The day after we went to the cottage to get your things. You told me about the watercolor, how much you loved it at one time. I wanted us to have something, something that meant something to both of us. Something we could call our own."

"Andrew, this is so… so incredible! I love it, I absolutely love it! Where should we hang it?" she said excitedly.

"I have a spot in mind." I turned and walked to the fireplace, removing the framed artwork I had there. I picked up the watercolor and placed it on the mantel. I stood back to take it all in. Julia walked over to me, mesmerized by it as well. I put my arm around her, and we just stood there for a few moments recognizing this was our beginning.

I turned to her, just taking her in while my fingers wandered through her thick auburn hair. I was lost in her eyes; lost in her natural beauty. The fire sparked and flickered; her eyes reflecting each flame.

"Julia, you are so beautiful… so completely captivating."

She smiled at me, placing her hand on my cheek.

"I wish I could say it… what I really want to say," I said, almost begging her to give me permission.

She put her head down, burying it into my chest. I felt her sigh. Then she looked back up at me.

"You can say it," she said. "Say what it is you need to say Andrew."

I gently took her delicate hands in mine, caressing them mindlessly over and over. I needed this to come out right.

"Julia, what I need to say is that you are perfect, perfect to me… but because I know you don't really want to hear that, because it puts too much pressure on you, I've come up with another way to tell you."

She just stared at me perplexed, probably wondering what the hell I was going to say.

"Julia, you are… you are imperfectly perfect to me, and I love you and all your perfect imperfections."

She was still staring, but I could see the corners of her mouth turn upward. She lifted her hands, cradling my face, and then she stood as tall as she could, and kissed me softly, tenderly, and without a trace of worry.

"That is truly perfect," she said in a whisper. "It's the truth… and I can't deny it. I love you Andrew, you and all your perfect imperfections as well."

~

The fire crackled and sputtered while we just stood there, holding one another. So imperfectly perfect; the two of us. I made myself a promise, right then and there, to never forget this moment. To never forget the honesty and respect necessary to bind two people together. This moment was destined to become a cherished memory, one I would gladly relive over and over again.

I desperately wanted to build a life with this imperfectly perfect woman. This woman who danced shamelessly down grocery store aisles, teased me unapologetically with her dry sense of humor, and entrusted me with her darkest secrets. I wanted to laugh and cry and thrive with her, every day, for all the years we would share together. I'd spent forty-six years of my life alone, never thinking I was looking for anyone, never realizing that I needed someone to complete me. And now, I'm standing here, holding her, and it all makes sense.

She completes me. I've finally found the piece I never knew I was missing, and I'm not about to let her go. I'll never let her go.

The End

About the Author

KG Milewski is a new author desiring to connect with her readers through honest and transparent prose. Her attention to 'real life' scenarios draws the reader in, giving them an undeniably honest connection to the characters. This is her first novel. Her previous writing endeavors have primarily focused on children's books, newspaper and magazine articles, and personal essays written on her blog, prettymamacares.com. She lives in Massachusetts with her husband.

Printed in the USA
CPSIA information can be obtained
at www.ICGtesting.com
CBHW031607150824
13252CB00010B/158